"Pat Bradley's *Justice Buried* takes readers on a wild ride with twists and turns. The heroine, Kelsey, is a character we can relate to and root for. If you love a gripping romantic suspense, this is one not to miss."

—**Robin Caroll**, bestselling author of the Bayou series and the Evil series

Praise for *Justice Delayed*

"Bradley's new Memphis Cold Case series offers readers uniquely flawed protagonists, which is a refreshing and relatable shift from the often-seen perfect heroes."

—*Booklist*

"Bradley's action-packed, dialogue-heavy police procedural is a quick and tense story, enthralling readers with its thrilling, high-octane plot."

—*Library Journal*

"With the perfect mixture of intrigue and nail-biting suspense, award-winning author Patricia Bradley invites her readers to crack the case—if they can—alongside the best Memphis has to offer."

—*Fresh Fiction*

"*Justice Delayed* turns out to be a great thriller. It's a suspense that has time literally running out with each page."

—*Suspense Magazine*

"I loved every page of *Justice Delayed*, and I'm giving it 4½ stars."

—*TWJ* magazine

Other Books by Patricia Bradley

JUSTICE BURIED

PATRICIA BRADLEY

Revell

a division of Baker Publishing Group
Grand Rapids, Michigan

Published by Revell
a division of Baker Publishing Group
P.O. Box 6287, Grand Rapids, MI 49516-6287
www.revellbooks.com

Printed in the United States of America

Library of Congress Cataloging-in-Publication Data
Names: Bradley, Patricia (Educator), author.
Title: Justice buried / Patricia Bradley.
Description: Grand Rapids, MI : Revell, a division of Baker Publishing Group,
   [2017]
Identifiers: LCCN 2017017124| ISBN 9780800727123 (pbk.) | ISBN 9780800729738
   (print on demand)
Subjects: | GSAFD: Christian fiction. | Mystery fiction.
Classification: LCC PS3602.R34275 J86 2017 | DDC 813/.6—dc23
LC record available at https://lccn.loc.gov/2017017124

This book is a work of fiction. Names, characters, places, and incidents are the product of the author's imagination or are used fictitiously.

17 18 19 20 21 22 23   7 6 5 4 3 2 1

To our heroes in blue
who put their lives on the line 24/7
to keep us safe
and to their families.

ACKNOWLEDGMENTS

As always, to God, who gives me the words.

To my family and friends, who believe in me.

To my editors at Revell, Lonnie Hull DuPont and Kristin Kornoelje, thank you for making my stories so much better. To the art, editorial, marketing, and sales team at Revell, thank you for your hard work. You are the best!

To Julie Gwinn, thank you for being not only my agent but my friend as well.

To Sgt. Joe Stark, MPD, thank you for always answering my questions. I apologize for not getting it right sometimes, because what you said and what I heard may not always be the same thing.

Thanks to the wonderful women (Louella Weaver, Jestein Gibson, Laurel Albrecht, and Tammy Braithwaite) at the Pink Palace Museum who took me from the dark basement to the attic on the third floor in search of a place to hide a body.

And last but not least, to my awesome readers, thank you for loving my stories.

1

It wasn't too hot for 10:00 p.m. in the middle of May unless you were about to climb over the ledge of a fourteen-story building in downtown Memphis. Kelsey Allen peered over the edge of the building, the distance to the street dizzying.

She ignored the tantalizing aroma that floated up from Tom Lee Park, where ninety contestants were grilling all night for the World Championship Barbecue Contest. Instead, she turned and concentrated on securing a small, motorized winch to the edge of the roof.

Once it was anchored, she attached the cable to her harness and then paused to take a deep breath. Slowly she released it, but her heart still thumped in her ears. She was about to break in to the building next to her stepfather's company. If Sam found out . . . She didn't want to go there.

Time to refocus, to calm her nerves. Kelsey glanced toward the lighted bridge over the Mississippi River and the double arc reflected in the water below. Overhead, the quarter moon vied with stars that glittered against the night sky. She closed her eyes and concentrated on her breathing. *I can do this.*

Her cell phone vibrated in her backpack, and she jerked it out. Sabra.

"I'm kind of busy."

"I know. Just checking on you. Where are you in the scheme of things?"

"About to go down."

"You don't have to do it, you know."

She never should have told her sister what she was into. A siren raked Kelsey's ears, sending her heart into double overdrive.

"What's that?" Sabra asked.

"A patrol car." Her heart slowed as the flashing lights sped toward the park. "Looks like a problem at the cook-off."

"I *told* you there'd be more security. That barbecue contest draws a lot of people. Just turn around and leave. Now."

Kelsey grunted, and her gaze swept the hordes of people below her as she took her tablet from her backpack. "It's one of the reasons I chose tonight. There's a wall of people from Beale Street to the river. It ought to keep the police busy, so don't worry about me."

"But I do. We might not be blood sisters, but you're the only sister I have."

"Thank you, but I'm telling you, I'll be fine." She'd never thought of Sabra as anything other than a sister either, especially since Sam and her mother never made any difference between the two of them.

There was a sigh on the other end. "Have you hacked into the security system?"

"I'm doing it now." Kelsey tapped the tablet, and with a few clicks, she was into the security company's control panel. "That's funny."

"What do you mean?"

"The security cameras are off, but they were on earlier when I checked."

"That's a sign you should call it off."

"No. I have to do this." Sabra didn't understand because *her* father had never done anything wrong. And she wasn't the one trying to get her security business off the ground.

Sabra was silent a few seconds and then said, "Is anything else off?"

Kelsey checked the infrared grid for the eighth floor. "No," she said and inserted code to turn off the grid on that floor. The grid had to be returned to normal as quickly as possible. "Gotta go. I only have an hour before the next security check."

"You sound nervous."

"I don't like heights."

"Then you picked the wrong field for that." Sabra chuckled. "No, for you it's all about seeing how close you can get to the fire without getting burned."

"Not true." Kelsey set her jaw. It wasn't about the danger or the adrenaline racing through her body. It was about redeeming her family name and being able to get a job in her chosen field.

"You can't undo what your dad did."

It was like Sabra had read her mind. "You're right, and that's why I'm testing security systems—to protect businesses against thieves like him. It's not like I'm breaking and entering, since Mr. Rutherford hired me to check the building's security."

"Then why doesn't he correct the newspaper reports that make you sound like some kind of thief?"

"He will." She just didn't know when. "Talk to you later."

Kelsey slid the phone into her backpack and pulled on a

black beanie cap, tucking her short hair inside it, then felt to make sure none of her curls had escaped. Should have bought a tan one to match her ash-blonde hair. She felt fairly confident that if anyone saw her, they would assume she was male.

She tested the cable one last time before climbing over the side of the building. This was the part she really didn't like—dangling fourteen floors above the street with only a cable attached to the electric winch to keep her from plunging to the alley below. At least it wasn't forty floors, like the last time.

The news reports stated she had nerves of steel, but if those same reporters could hear the drumbeat of her heart pounding against her chest, they would know better. But if she passed this test and Rutherford hired her for his other buildings, more jobs would roll in. She forced the air out of her lungs and breathed in again.

Don't look down.

No worry there. She was too busy keeping her body from bumping against the side of the wall as she lowered herself to the corner window she'd discovered unlocked two days ago. The building had been built in the 1930s and still had functioning windows.

Her cover as a temporary secretary got her into the buildings Rutherford had been hired to keep secure, this time giving her access to Turner Accounting. After poking around for a couple of days, she penetrated their firewall and then found the window.

The window rose easily. She slid inside and slipped out of the harness, letting it fall to the floor. The winch weighed fifteen pounds, enough to keep it from going anywhere while she left her calling card. There were four desks in the room, one that had been hers in her temporary employment.

The camera in the corner of the ceiling drew her attention even though she knew the guards only saw a video of an empty room. Habit made her hug the wall as she crept to the door that opened into the hallway, then walked to the CEO's office. She pulled a small black case from the backpack and chose a pick. It took her fifteen seconds to unlock the door.

Once inside the office, she padded across the thick carpet to the desk. Walnut. Expensive. Nice computer too. Kelsey placed a business card on the keyboard and then retraced her steps. In the beginning, the cards were for publicity, but now they were her trademark. She didn't want Rutherford to have any doubts about who breached the security.

Back at the window, Kelsey slipped into the harness and climbed through the casement. As she dangled above the street, she pressed the red button on the winch and shifted the gear to ascend.

Three floors up, she bumped against a window and stopped the winch. Suddenly the whop-whop-whop of a helicopter threw her body into panic mode. She looked up and saw strobe lights streaking the sky.

Kelsey gripped the cable. What if they saw her? Images of handcuffs and the back seat of a patrol car hit her at warp speed. Seconds later the chopper swung toward the river, and she breathed again. Probably a news helicopter taking video of the festivities, but she needed to get on the roof and inside the building before it returned.

Kelsey adjusted the harness and glanced into the office. The skin on the back of her neck prickled. She didn't remember a light in any of the rooms, but right here, right now, she was staring at a dimly lit room.

Movement caught her attention. A man? Could it get any worse? Her blood pulsing in her ears muffled all other sounds, and she barely heard the chopper as it made another sweep of the area.

She narrowed her eyes at the silhouette of a large man in front of the light source. *What if he sees me?* No sooner had the thought taken root than he turned and faced the window. The backlighting made it impossible to distinguish his features, but the tilt of his head made her feel as though his eyes were boring into hers.

Then for a second, light flashed in the room, illuminating him. She blinked, and the room darkened once more. Had the light even happened?

The silhouette moved. Coming to the window. She punched the button on the winch, and like a snail, it inched upward. Kelsey unhooked from her harness and grabbed the cable. Using her rock-climbing skills, she half pulled and half walked up the side of the building. One misstep . . .

Just as she swung over the ledge, she heard a muffled pop, and a bullet whizzed past her ear. A chip from the concrete grazed her cheek. He was shooting at her? *Go!*

Kelsey scrambled to get the winch loose from the ledge, but it wouldn't budge. She kicked the hook and finally it released, and she crammed the winch into her backpack. How much time had passed? He'd been three stories below her. *If* he was familiar with the building and knew how to reach the roof, any second now he'd burst through the door on this side of the roof. The one between Kelsey and her escape route.

It looked like a mile to the door she'd left propped open. She scanned the roof. There were several heating and cooling units large enough to hide behind, and she darted behind the nearest one just as the door to the roof opened and a light flicked past the unit.

Kelsey had counted on the darkness hiding her, never considered that he might have a flashlight. She flattened against the metal wall as the beam swept past the air-conditioning unit again. *God, if you'll get me out of this, I'll never do it again.* When the light disappeared and his steps tapped away, she breathed a thank-you.

Seconds later, she inched from behind the unit and checked his location. He was bent over, examining the ledge. His back was to her, and she dashed to the next unit, her sneakers barely making a sound. Two more and she could make a break for the door.

Silently she inched along the wall and almost lost her balance when her foot hit something solid. Unable to see in the shadows, she knelt, and her fingers closed over a brick. The light flashed in front of the air-conditioning unit where she'd hidden, then flicked behind her. His footsteps neared. She tossed the brick, and it landed with a thud on the other side of the building. The light swung away, and the sound of him running across the roof was music to her ears.

Kelsey raced for the door and jerked it open, dislodging the block of wood she'd wedged under it to keep the door ajar. She yanked it shut and lowered the security bar that would keep it from being opened from the outside. Then she leaned her head against the metal.

Fists pounding on the door made her jump back, and she froze at three sharp pings. Was he crazy? Bullets would never move the bar. She turned and flew down the steps. At the first landing she halted, aware of an eerie silence.

He's left.

Probably planned to catch her when she went out the alley door. Wouldn't he be surprised when she didn't exit? She'd left her car on the fourth level of the parking garage and walked up to the roof. The adrenaline that had flowed through her veins dropped, leaving her legs shaky, and she held on to the steel rail as she sank to the bottom step. Home free.

Or she would be as soon she reversed the changes to the security system. Kelsey's wrist shook as she checked her watch. Still ten minutes before the next check. She slid her tablet from the backpack and flexed her fingers, then opened the program and quickly restored the system. Her cell phone buzzed, and she retrieved it from the backpack, glancing at the name on the ID. "I'm out."

"Good," Sabra said. "What took so long?"

"You won't believe me." Quickly Kelsey filled her sister in on what had happened. "I'm on the way to my car."

"I told you not to break into that office!"

"It's what I was hired to do." Kelsey didn't have time for this. "I'll call you once I get out of the parking garage."

"You can't do that! You'll be a sitting duck if he's waiting for you."

Kelsey should have thought of that. The guy had rattled her more than she'd thought.

"You need to call the police."

"And say what? Someone shot at me as I made my getaway after breaking into the building? They would arrest me first and ask questions later. And probably not even look for him—great way to get my business off the ground."

"Would Mr. Rutherford vouch for you?"

"Yeah, but the bad publicity might cost me the job. He wants to find the weak spots in the security and fix them, not tell the world they're there."

"But what if the man killed someone?"

"I never heard any gunshots except the ones aimed at me,

so he probably thought I was a criminal." She relived the muted pops, the bullet whizzing by her ear. "Oh my goodness. He was using a silencer. Why would he be in that building with—"

"I'm coming after you. You can get your car tomorrow. I'll pick you up at the front door in five minutes."

But would Sabra be safe? Kelsey tried to think. The shipping crew should be changing shifts now. Hopefully, whoever had shot at her would think Kelsey was leaving work, and more than likely thought she was a man as well. He wouldn't be looking for a woman to come out the front door. "Okay. Call me when you turn on Front Street."

Grabbing the backpack, Kelsey hurried down the steps, shedding the black sweater and ski cap, and ran her fingers through her short hair to lift the flat curls. All the guards knew her, and once she reached the lobby, she would chat up whoever was on duty, tell him she'd come from the barbecue festivities through the shipping room to use the facilities.

Weak. But it'd have to do.

2

SATURDAY MORNING AT THE ROCK-CLIMBING GYM Kelsey stepped into the harness Sabra handed her. How in the world did her sister manage to look so put together this early in the morning without makeup? Her straight copper hair was pulled into a ponytail, making her look about eighteen instead of her actual thirty-three.

"Thanks for getting up so early to belay for me." Kelsey attached the rope to the harness and then adjusted the hair band that kept her unruly blonde curls out of her face. It was strange how something as dangerous as rock climbing helped settle her nerves. Maybe it was the total concentration.

After two nightmarish nights with someone chasing her through her dreams, she had to refocus. Put the sound of those bullets chipping the concrete two inches from her head out of her mind. She'd been in the shadows of the building, and he couldn't have seen her face. And if she wanted to be in the security business, she had to keep in mind that danger was always a possibility.

"You owe me one for getting up at eight o'clock so I can

throw the brake when you fall." Sabra slipped into her own harness and attached the Grigri. "White chocolate mocha and an apple scone when we're done here."

"You got it," Kelsey said with a grin. "And I'm not falling this time."

"Says you. You get in too big of a hurry at the overhang."

Of all the people who belayed for her, Sabra was the best. Kelsey could depend on her to be ready to throw the lever on the Grigri whenever she made a misstep, halting her fall. And her sister was right about going too fast.

Kelsey took a small bottle of chalk from the pack around her waist and squirted a few drops on her fingers before she approached the wall. "Climbing?" she said.

Sabra took the slack out of the rope before replying. "Climb on."

Kelsey began her ascent, using her legs to push up from the knobs rather than pulling her body up with her arms. Everything faded from her mind except working out the path to the top. She inched her way up the wall, shifting her body at times to keep her center of gravity over her legs.

At the overhang, she slowed her pace, determined to make it over and all the way to the top. Carefully placing her foot at strategic holds, she managed to pull herself over the ledge and was soon at the top. Exhilarated, she gave Sabra a thumbs-up before her sister lowered her to the floor.

"Good job!" Sabra said.

"Thanks. Want to go up?"

She shook her head. "Not on your life. What I want is that mocha."

An hour later they were sitting in a nearby Starbucks. "I'm still amazed that you do that," Sabra said.

"I'm amazed myself sometimes."

19

Sabra stirred her mocha. "Whatever happened to that guy in Jackson who got you into rock-climbing?"

"Joey DeMarzo?" Kelsey noticed some chalk on her fingertips and used a napkin to wipe it off. "He found a cute little brunette that suited him better."

"That was a blessing." Sabra broke a piece of the scone off and popped it into her mouth.

While Kelsey could look back now and see the breakup in a different light, she hadn't thought it was a blessing at the time. She'd really thought Joey was the one. That's how smart she was about men. But now, she realized she'd been more in love with the idea of marriage and having a family than she had been with Joey.

"What made you keep on with the rock-climbing after you two broke up?"

She thought a minute, trying to find the words to explain the way she felt when she pitted herself against a cliff or an indoor rock wall. "I love the personal challenge—me against the rock. And the satisfaction of conquering the vertical face of a cliff or a ledge like today—it's a high like no other. Don't you feel that way when you boulder?"

Her sister shrugged. "Not really. The way I boulder is safe—even Lily can do it. But if you want my opinion, it's the danger that you're attracted to. Some of those cliffs I've seen you climb are scary."

Sabra was right that she hadn't progressed in climbing boulders, and in fact, her daughter, Lily, was at a higher skill level than Sabra was. "Try the wall just one time," Kelsey said.

"I'm leaving that to you and Lily. Someone has to stay on the ground and keep you safe," she said. "And speaking of safe, I hope you're not breaking into any more buildings. What if that man had shot you Thursday night?"

"But he didn't." She fought the vise that suddenly gripped her stomach. "Come on, we've been over this already. I'm meeting Mr. Rutherford later to go over what happened and find out when he's going to release the news that the Phantom Hawk is actually working for him."

"Did you tell him about the shooter?"

"I briefed him on it, and he's checking it out."

"Where are you meeting him?"

She stared into the bottom of her cup. "Sam's office."

"What? Why Dad's office?"

"Mr. Rutherford handles Sam's security, and I found another bug on his computer system. Rutherford wants me to explain it to him."

"So you're going to tell him you're the Phantom Hawk?"

"I don't know about *that*, but I hope when he finds out I'm working for Rutherford Security, he'll quit bugging me to get a 'real' job instead of the temp work I've been doing."

"He won't be satisfied until you're working as a conservator in a museum again."

"Then he might be dissatisfied for a very long time."

3

Two HOURS LATER Kelsey squared her shoulders and marched through the doors of her stepfather's spacious office. The river view from the fourteenth floor of the Allen Auto Parts building was gorgeous, but she wasn't there for the view.

Sam looked up from whatever he was reading and raised his eyebrows. "I wasn't expecting you. I have another appointment, but while you're here I have a couple of things I want to discuss with you." Sam Allen leaned back in his leather chair and stretched his long legs. The enigmatic smile he gave Kelsey set off red flags.

"Discuss what with me?"

"First I want you to watch this." He nodded toward the TV screen on the wall. "Let me connect my computer to the TV."

Kelsey perched on the edge of a rounded club chair to keep it from hemming her in, feeling like a teenager waiting for the boom to lower instead of the thirty-five-year-old woman she was. But her stepfather could have that effect on her, especially when she had something to hide.

Seconds later, news reporter Andi Hollister appeared on the screen in what appeared to be last night's ten o'clock news. Evidently Sam had recorded the program. He tapped the play button, and her heart dipped when the background sharpened and the building next door came into focus. Her break-in *had* hit the news.

"Police have no leads on the cat burglar and hacker who has breached yet another security system in Memphis last night. For the fourth week in a row, a business has reported that their security systems were bypassed by someone calling themselves the Phantom Hawk. As before, nothing was taken. The only evidence of the break-in was the calling card left on the CEO's desk at Turner Accounting."

The reporter paused, and then she smiled. "It looks as though Memphis has its own Good Samaritan break-in artist. This is Andi Hollister in downtown Memphis reporting for WLTZ."

"This ran Friday morning," Sam said and closed the site before turning to face her. "Practically in my own building, Kelsey?"

Mr. Rutherford was supposed to inform Turner Accounting's office manager that he was behind the break-in. This was not good. Her stepfather suspected her of being the Phantom Hawk. He would not be happy when he found out she was, and even more unhappy to discover she was working with Rutherford Security.

And her mother. Kelsey didn't even want to think about that. They couldn't see her as anything except a museum conservator. Had encouraged her toward that career as far back as she could remember. Which wasn't surprising, given their love for antiquities. And she had loved working in the museum until budget cuts eliminated her job. Almost as much as she loved what she was doing now.

She swallowed down the lump wedged in her throat. "What do you mean?"

"Phantom Hawk? Come on—that was your code name when you were thirteen and hacking into Nintendo." He leveled his brown eyes at her and waited. With his premature white hair and square jaw, her stepfather could be an imposing figure.

Buy time and maybe Mr. Rutherford would arrive and save her.

"Blame that on the computer you gave me." Learning code had been as natural as breathing. Sam and her mom should have known better than to put a computer in the hands of a bored ten-year-old.

When he didn't seem convinced, she added, "Phantom Hawk is a pretty common hacker name. You can check it out if you don't believe me. Besides, it looks to me like someone did these companies a favor, pointing out their weak spots." Too bad she couldn't cash in on her publicity. But so far, no one had come after her, and she wanted to keep it that way.

"So you're saying that you didn't break into these buildings?" Sam raised his eyebrows, still seeming to wait for her to confess.

He could wait until the cows came home. "I did not break into even one of those buildings." But even if she had, she'd been hired to check the security. "What else did you want to discuss?"

"Your mother and Sabra—" His phone rang, and he picked up the receiver. "Yes?" He listened briefly and then said, "Send him in."

She relaxed as Walter Rutherford entered the room.

"I see you're already here," he said.

"Yep."

24

"You knew she'd be here?" Sam asked.

"Oh yes," Walter said. "I hired her after we met here the last time." He turned to Kelsey. "Sorry about the newscast Friday morning. Didn't dream the CEO would go into the office at six o'clock Friday morning. He called the police instead of me, and the reporter was Johnny-on-the-spot."

Sam blinked and slowly turned to look at Kelsey, then back at Walter. "What are you talking about? Kelsey is a museum conservator."

"*Was* a conservator," Kelsey said. "After the job at the Jackson museum fell through, I haven't been able to get another one as a conservator, at least not in Memphis. And I don't want to relocate again."

Three conservator jobs since college, and each ended when lack of funds mandated personnel cuts. When Mr. Rutherford had offered her a job, she jumped at it. Sam had actually been the one to introduce her to the head of the security company after she pointed out serious holes in the internet firewall at Allen Brothers.

Sam eyed her. "I offered to put in a word at the Pink Palace Museum."

"And they already have a conservator. Besides, I want to be hired on my own merits." Not because her mother was married to a trustee of the Pink Palace Museum. Besides that, when her job was cut at the last museum and the director moved her to security, she discovered she loved the security work. Not only had she found her niche, but she was also able to learn every aspect of the security field. It was now or never to start her own security consulting business.

She sighed. "Besides, I don't think the museum would hire me after what my father did there, not even with you putting in a good word."

"You don't have to prove yourself as a conservator, Kelsey. Your work in Jackson and the other museums speaks for itself. But you have to let go of the past and what your father did. And it's okay to accept a little help."

"You don't understand. I'm not sure I even want to be a conservator." Why was it so hard for her to tell him? Even now she hedged with vague words. But the fact was—plain and simple—a month ago, she'd actually started her own security firm with licenses and everything. *Wait.* She'd missed something Sam had said. "What did you say?"

He leaned forward. "I said, so instead you break into businesses and hack their computer systems as the Phantom Hawk. You could be hauled off to jail." Sam folded his arms across his chest.

Just like my father if they could find him. Sam would never say that, but she couldn't help but think it. Taunts echoed from her childhood. *You stole my lunch money. You're a thief, just like your daddy.*

Walter Rutherford cleared his throat. "Kelsey has done nothing illegal. I hired her to test the security of the buildings after she found the bugs in your system—she's found another one I want her to discuss with you. And the reason I asked her to meet me here was to discuss a security matter at the Pink Palace Museum, since you're the chairman of the board."

Sam turned and stared at him. "She *is* the Phantom Hawk, then? And you hired her to break in?"

"Nothing illegal about that since I'm in charge of security." The older man turned to Kelsey, tilting his head. "Are you interested?"

"Exactly what would I be doing?" She kept her tone neutral. This was the first she'd heard about testing the security at the Pink Palace.

Rutherford's smile spread across his face, exposing even white teeth. "Using your master's degree in historic preservation."

"I've already been turned down by the Pink Palace, and they already have a conservator."

Rutherford waved his hand, dismissing her words. "She's taking a maternity leave at the end of the month. You'll take her place temporarily, but that's only a cover for your real job—that of finding holes in the security. Artifacts have been disappearing from the museum for a number of years—a piece here and there—nothing particularly valuable other than each piece was unique. I want you to find who's doing it." He nodded toward her stepfather. "That is, if Sam approves. I don't want to lose his account."

Kelsey turned to him. He looked as though he'd been ambushed.

"You'll have to give me a minute to absorb everything you've said." Sam leaned back and rubbed his jaw with his thumb. After a minute he looked up at Rutherford. "If it's been going on for years, why now?"

"In two weeks, a priceless Egyptian death mask will arrive, and because it is one of a kind, I'm afraid whoever is taking the other pieces may go after it." He turned to Kelsey. "I want you to find out how someone has been gaining access to the rooms where the artifacts are stored. What do you think? Can you do it?"

A shiver of excitement shot through her body. It would be like a dream come true. She sat taller and straightened her shoulders. "I'll do it, but not as your employee."

He frowned. "What do you mean?"

"You can hire me as a consultant, like now, but for more money."

Rutherford pursed his lips and then nodded. "Can you start now?"

"I'll take a look at the museum internet security system this afternoon." She kept her voice calm, but on the inside she happy-danced around the room.

"I'll give you the passwords." Rutherford took out a black notebook.

"No, I want to see how secure it is first. If I can't hack into your system, I'll get them Monday." She didn't respond to his look of skepticism. "About my fee . . ."

Rutherford named a figure higher than she'd dreamed. "And if you can get past the firewall, I'll double it—once you explain how you did it."

"Deal."

He nodded his agreement and then said, "Tonight there's a fundraiser at the museum in the ballroom. You need to be there since all the players should be there."

"Players?" she asked.

"Whoever is stealing the artifacts has to have access, and several of the people attending are ones with access, including some of the employees."

Sam cleared his throat. "This must be meant to be. That was the other thing I wanted to talk to you about. I was supposed to call you this morning and twist your arm to come to the gala tonight."

"I . . . don't know," she said.

"You can accompany your mother and me. Sabra and Mason and Lily are going as well. It'll be a family outing."

"And it'll give you a chance to get a feel for the building," Rutherford said.

Memories of walking the halls of the Pink Palace with her dad before he took off washed over her. He'd held her hand and shown her all the exhibits, instilling in Kelsey a love for all things old. Years later when she'd applied for a job at the museum as conservator and was turned down, she suspected it was because of her father. But now she was going back to that very job, and tonight she would probably mix and mingle with some of the ones who didn't approve her. "I'll be there."

"I look forward to working with you." Rutherford tipped his head to the side. "I've only had a chance to skim your report, but I'm impressed at how easily you breached the security at Turner Accounting. How did you do it?"

Because she'd inherited her father's "thief gene." She shook the thought away—there was no such thing as a thief gene. And she wasn't a thief—her life's goal was to live her life honestly. She was doing a favor to the places she broke into by pointing out their weaknesses. *But you love the challenge.* Kelsey ignored the voice in her head. "Someone left a window unlocked—it was unlocked the two days I worked there and still unlocked Thursday night."

He set his jaw, and she figured someone would be appointed to check all the windows.

"How did you get past the firewall?"

"That was a little harder—you have an almost impenetrable system. It took me a couple of days to find a back door that allowed me to make a code change." Since she was a temporary employee, she was afraid someone might recognize her voice if she tried the same technique she had at Allen Brothers Auto Parts to get the passwords. That time, she'd used her status as Sam's daughter when she made a few calls to key personnel and had been given the passwords she'd needed.

"I closed the back door, by the way, and removed the code

I inserted to gain access." She wished she could have seen the face of the IT specialist who created the entry point when her message popped up.

"Do you know who was responsible?"

She shook her head, not about to get a fellow programmer into trouble. "It would be a mistake to replace the IT guy. I doubt he'll be that careless again, whereas someone new might be."

"I had planned to announce that you were the Phantom Hawk and had been working for me," Rutherford said, "but now it would blow your cover at the museum. So we need to keep it quiet until we discover who's been stealing the artifacts."

"I agree." Not to mention she didn't want the man who fired at her Thursday night to know her identity. While he may have seen her, she doubted he would be able to recognize her again. It had happened so quickly, and with the cap covering her hair and the dark clothes disguising her body, she was banking that he would assume it'd been a man. As long as he didn't discover Kelsey Allen was the Phantom Hawk, she should be safe.

That settled, her mind jumped to another problem. She didn't have anything to wear to the gala, and she hated shopping. "I'll call Mom and ask about what to wear tonight."

"No need. She and Sabra are picking out an outfit for you to wear."

"Sabra didn't say a word about the gala when I saw her earlier," Kelsey said.

"I don't think your mom called her until ten thirty this morning to go shopping."

"And they didn't trust me to pick out something, huh?" Unlike Kelsey, Sabra and her mom had a natural flair for fashion. They would know what went with her porcelain skin and ash-blonde hair. When she was shopping on her own, it was hit and miss.

She glanced down at the jeans and cobalt-blue sweater she'd pulled on, pleased that today was a hit. Tomorrow might be a miss.

"No, it wasn't that," Sam said and checked his watch. "But you do have an appointment with Sabra's hairdresser in two hours."

"And you're just now telling me?" She wondered what Sabra had to pay for that. What if she'd said no to attending the fundraiser?

"That's what I was starting to tell you when Walter arrived."

"You were that sure I would go?"

"Sabra figured she could talk you into it."

Suddenly, terror struck her heart. Everyone else was a couple . . . "She didn't set me up with a blind date—" The twinkle in Sam's eyes chopped the question off. "Who?"

"Brad Hollister."

She narrowed her eyes. "Sabra set me up with Brad?"

"No. Your mother."

4

"MOM DID WHAT?" Brad Hollister dropped the sponge in the bucket and stared at his sister. His half Labrador, half something else dropped to the ground and whimpered. He massaged the dog's neck. "I'm sorry, Tripod. I'm not upset with you." He narrowed his eyes at Andi. "I'm waiting."

Her lips curled into a smug grin. "You heard me right the first time, and Mom didn't, I did. I was at the house when Cynthia Allen dropped by for coffee with Mom and asked if there was any possibility that you might accompany Kelsey tonight. I don't remember it, but from what Mrs. Allen said, Kelsey had a crush on you in high school. Mom hedged and Mrs. Allen looked so down, I told her you would be happy to accompany her daughter to the Pink Palace fundraiser tonight."

Andi pushed a strand of hair from her face. "I knew when I did it you wouldn't be happy about it, but it was an emergency. Mom was on the hook."

It'd been a month since he'd had a weekend off, and the temptation to spray Andi with the water hose almost overcame his better judgment.

"What if I'd had a previous engagement? Like a Saturday night date," Brad said, his stomach curdling at the thought of wearing a tux and mingling with people he didn't know. He blasted the red 1968 Mustang with water, and the three-legged dog thumped his tail, waiting for Brad to start their game.

"You never have a date. You're too busy working on a homicide case or you're down at the youth center with those boys. You really need to socialize more, and not all women are like Elle." She smiled sweetly at him and grabbed a chamois to help wipe down the car. "Come on, it's for a good cause, and it repays a social obligation for Mom. Besides, you remember Kelsey from high school. She was so cool."

"She almost blew up the chemistry lab. That's what I remember." That, and her disdain of him. He never knew if it was because she didn't like him or she'd heard him ask for a different partner the first day of class. So her mom was totally wrong about the crush thing.

"Well, what I remember about her was how kind she was," Andi said. "She mentored me the year after Steph . . . Anyway, I was a seventh grader and she was a senior and she didn't have to be so nice."

"Does she know that her mother set us up?" Because he couldn't believe she'd agree to a date with him. Fundraiser or not.

"Uhh . . ." Andi rubbed a spot on the fender. "I'm not sure. You're supposed to meet them in front of the Pink Palace at seven."

Joy. "Them?"

"Yeah. She'll be with her parents."

They must be afraid she'll bolt. "Are you and Will going?"

"Nope. This is a blue chip affair—only the elite of Memphis are invited. Will and I are taking his mom out to eat."

More joy. He wrung water from the chamois. "That means a tuxedo."

"No, just business casual." Andi offered an encouraging smile.

He glared at her. Business casual didn't change the fact that he'd probably be rubbing elbows with the mayor and people way out of his league. For that matter, Kelsey Allen was out of his league, something she never let him forget in high school.

While not old money in Memphis, neither were the Allen brothers nouveaux riche. Sam and his brother, Grant, had taken the small automotive parts business that their grandfather had started and turned it into a franchise. They had their fingers in lots of pots in Memphis, Sam especially. Brad frowned. Kelsey was thirty-five, a year younger than he was. She must not have changed one bit if her mother had to bribe someone to take her out.

He jutted his jaw. "You owe me. Big-time."

"No, I figure we're even. I ran into Elle yesterday. She seemed very interested in what was going on with you, especially after I told her you were transferring to the Cold Case Unit."

Words escaped him. He'd been engaged to Elle for a year before she suddenly decided she didn't want to marry a cop and broke it off. "That's interesting." Tripod nudged him, and Brad looked down. "Sorry, big boy, but your aunt here has given me an assignment."

"It's only three—you have plenty of time to exercise him," she said and grabbed the water hose. "And you don't fool me about Elle. You're still interested. Give her a call."

He didn't know if his heart could take a conversation with his former fiancée.

But it was impossible to stay mad at Andi for long, and he laughed as she arced the water over the yard and the dog chased it. Tripod could outmaneuver Brad. His thoughts returned to the date. Unless Kelsey Allen *had* changed, she probably wouldn't want to stay at the fundraiser long. He could hope, at least. Because tonight was it, as far as he and Kelsey Allen were concerned.

And he certainly wasn't calling Elle.

◆

At seven o'clock, Brad parked the Mustang in the crowded parking lot and pocketed his keys. The angled sun glinted on the mansion's pink Georgian facade, the reason for the Pink Palace name. He stopped to let a cleaning van drive by, then as he approached the entrance, he sensed someone watching him and scanned the area. The ten or so people ahead of him were intent on getting inside, and his gaze slid past the petite blonde with short, spiked hair to a couple walking from the parking lot.

He stopped and looked at the blonde again. There was something familiar . . . or maybe it was just the way the simple black dress hugged her willowy body. Recognition dawned, rocking him back on his heels. This . . . couldn't be Kelsey.

"Brad?"

The question on her lips turned into an amused grin, and he swallowed hard. "Kelsey?"

Tonight might not be as bad as he'd thought.

"What? People grow up, you know. Even nerdy teenage girls with thick glasses." She folded her arms across her chest. "And just so you know—our . . . *date* . . . wasn't my idea."

So much for thinking it might not be so bad. She was as

35

sarcastic as she was in school. And he would never understand how she managed to look down her nose at him when he towered above her. He forced a smile. "Never thought it was. And for the record, I never thought of you as nerdy even if you did have a crush on me."

"No, just inept, bungling, klutzy. Wait! What do you mean, crush?" She narrowed her green eyes.

"That's what your mom told my mom." He gave her a "so there" look.

"I hate to disappoint you, but I did not have a crush on you," she said. "And while we're clearing the record, that explosion in the chemistry lab back in high school wasn't my fault. The picric acid was out of date, but I don't suppose Mr. Crenshaw told you that when you were asking for a new partner."

Heat crawled up his neck. He'd always suspected she heard his rant to their chemistry teacher when he'd assigned them as partners. Brad owed her a long overdue apology. "Like you said, people do grow up. And no, he didn't tell me about the picric acid."

He glanced down at his spit-'n-polished shoes, glad he'd taken the time to shine them. When he looked up, those green eyes were guarded. "Ended up, you were a pretty good lab partner."

She held his gaze. "I suppose that's the best you can do for an apology." Then she crooked her arm. "Why don't we get this over with, and then you can leave—you don't have to babysit me all night."

That was another thing that hadn't changed. Her attitude could change in an instant. And he was relieved he didn't have to hang around once they made an appearance. "Yes, ma'am."

As they walked through the door, she said, "So, what are you doing now?"

"I'm a cop. Homicide tonight, but starting Monday, I'm switching over to the Cold Case Unit."

The arm that was looped through his twitched. "Really? Maybe you can discover what happened to my father."

"Your father? I thought Sam Allen was your dad."

"He's my stepfather. He and my mom married after my real dad, Paul Carter, stole artifacts from this very museum and skipped the country. Sam wanted to adopt me," she said. "Partly so Sabra and I wouldn't have different last names, and partly because I had to change schools after I was teased unmercifully about my real dad being branded a thief. Mom decided a new school warranted a new last name, and because my real father wasn't around to say no—voilà."

He could understand that. "Was there a trial?"

"No, they never tracked him down."

He didn't remember anything about her father from school and glanced at her. For an instant, Kelsey's hard veneer cracked, exposing pain. So all was not perfect in the rich girl's life. His attitude toward her softened. "So you have no idea where he went?"

"Nope. No one has heard from him since. He's probably in Argentina, enjoying his spoils," she said, her mask back in place.

"Maybe he's afraid he would be arrested if he came back."

"That's the thing, the statute of limitations on his crimes has run out—he could come back if he wanted to."

The yearning in her voice scraped his heart. "The unit focuses mostly on murders, but I haven't been assigned a case. If you'd like, I'll find the file and look it over."

Her eyes widened. "You'd do that?"

What was he thinking? Opening the case would put him in constant contact with this prickly woman from his past. But all his life he'd been a rescuer of animals and people. Looking into her face, which held a glimmer of hope and an emotion he couldn't identify, stirred that need to make things right.

"Why not." Brad gave her a reassuring smile. "Not sure how long it'll take to find the file, but I'll keep you posted."

5

KELSEY DIDN'T KNOW if she was more surprised at Brad's offer to help or that she'd blurted out about her dad. He wasn't a subject she usually shared with anyone. She had such mixed feelings about him. But one thing was for sure—he'd taught her that men couldn't be trusted, especially the ones she loved.

She studied Brad out of the corner of her eye as they walked through the crowd moving toward the ballroom, trying to figure him out. She hadn't expected the apology *or* that he would remember he'd asked the chemistry teacher to give him a new partner.

But then, Brad seemed to have changed into a softer person, and he looked nothing like the teenager Kelsey remembered. He'd aged nicely . . . not that thirty-six was old, but the skinny senior had filled out since high school. She'd bet those broad shoulders under his jacket were well toned. Mentally, she brought herself up short. She didn't have the time or inclination to think about Brad Hollister's muscles.

"Stairs or take the escalator?" Brad asked, glancing down at her stiletto heels.

"Stairs. I'm always afraid I'll get something caught in those things." She did take his arm as they climbed the steps to the second floor.

"I'm impressed—you're not winded," Brad said at the top.

Kelsey grinned at him. "What kind of wimps do you date?" She held up her hand. "Oh wait, I know. A macho guy like you likes his women soft and clingy, not someone who runs five miles a day."

"Do you have to turn everything into an issue?" Without waiting for an answer, he glanced up at the dome ceiling. "I haven't been here in years and had forgotten how beautiful it is. Do you come often?"

"I haven't been here in years, either," she said, gazing at the rich colors. So he didn't like talking about the women he dated. Something to remember. "I didn't realize so many people would be here . . . or kids," she said as they stopped to let a family walk ahead of them. "I suppose we should try and find the rest of my bunch."

"So they won't think I ditched you?"

"No, that I ditched you," she said. "They're probably in the ballroom."

They walked across the marble floor to an arched doorway. She searched the room for her parents, spying them on the other side of the room. "I start work here Monday."

"You're kidding," Brad replied. "Doing what?"

"Temporary conservator." She decided not to tell him about the security angle even though he was a cop.

"Really? I meant to ask earlier what career path you took. Never would have figured you for that."

"What did you figure me for?" She didn't understand his surprise. But then, he'd never really known her.

"Maybe something in science . . . a doctor . . ."

He thought she could be a doctor? Her heart swelled with unexpected pleasure. Maybe she'd pegged him all wrong back then. "I love art, and I love history." Not to mention breaking into computers and buildings.

"So why only temporary?"

"Let's just say I have something else on the back burner." A cop totally would not understand about the Phantom Hawk. "With the economy like it is, there's not much money for museums. I lost my last job in Jackson, Mississippi, because of funding cuts, and when the current conservator returns from maternity leave, I'll lose this one." She nodded toward her parents. "Let's say hello to Mom and Sam, and then you can cut out of here, if you'd like."

"I'm in no hurry to leave. We're here and might as well stay for the meal."

She suppressed a groan. What if she couldn't get rid of him? She was planning to test a theory about how the thief was getting inside the museum as soon as it became dark. The backpack with the grappling hook and work clothes was in the car, and her plan was to walk out with Brad when he left so everyone would assume she'd left with him.

"Aunt Kelsey!"

She looked around as her six-year-old niece barreled toward her, blonde curls flying. Kelsey caught her when Lily threw herself into Kelsey's arms. "What's the matter?"

"Billy says I run like a girl and girls can't run." Huge tears brimmed in her eyes. "Come make him stop saying that."

"We will later." Kelsey hugged her niece and set her down. "And you'll just have to teach him that girls can run as good as boys. Let's go see what your mom is doing."

"But you have to tell him *now*."

She sighed. Lily would not let up until she talked to the boy. "Where is this Billy?"

Lily pointed toward a carrot-haired boy standing near a display of Native American art. Beside him was the museum director, Robert Tomlinson. His father? More likely the balding, midfifties director was the boy's grandfather, and they could be more protective than fathers. "Excuse me a minute," she said to Brad.

"Don't you think you should let her fight her own battles?" he asked softly.

"I plan to. But I need to speak to his grandfather, anyway."

She took Lily's hand, and the two of them approached Mr. Tomlinson and the chubby boy by his side. She certainly didn't want to ruffle Mr. Tomlinson's or Billy's feathers, but from the belligerent look in the boy's eyes, his feathers were not only already ruffled but plucked out. What in the world had her niece said to him?

She'd barely nodded at the director when Lily said, "My aunt said we'd show you girls can run better than boys."

"They can not!" Billy retorted.

"Lily! That's not what I said." She wanted to drop through the floor. She turned to Robert Tomlinson and held out her hand. "I'm Kelsey Allen."

"Ah, Ms. Allen, our temporary conservator. I'm looking forward to your joining our little family here at the mansion."

Lily tugged on her hand. "Tell him, Aunt Kelsey."

Heat rose in her cheeks. Expectation in Lily's face squeezed her heart. "Maybe Billy would like a play date soon. We could go to the park and you could show him how you can climb the monkey bars."

The girl tilted her head up at Kelsey. "And how to run. I don't think he runs much."

Let it go, kiddo. She smiled brightly at Tomlinson. "We'd love it if Billy could come to the park with us sometime."

"I'll speak to my daughter and tell her to expect a call from you." He eyed his grandson. "He doesn't get much socialization, so interaction with your niece would be excellent."

Whatever happened to just letting kids play?

"I'll see you Monday." Kelsey pulled a reluctant Lily away.

Lily pouted. "But I thought you were going—"

She swooped the child up in her arms. "We don't want to hurt his feelings, right?"

"Why are you whispering?" Lily's plaintive voice carried over the buzz of the crowd.

"Shh. I'll explain in a minute, okay?" She hurried toward where Brad was standing.

"Are you sure she's not yours?" he asked.

She ignored his remark and made a beeline to a side room. "Come meet my parents and sister. And my uncle," she said over her shoulder. As they entered the room, her stepfather, Sam, turned from talking to his brother, and her mother and sister waved them over. She didn't see her brother-in-law.

"Sabra, did you lose someone?" Kelsey asked. Sam met Brad with an outstretched hand.

"Lily!" her sister said. "I thought you were with your dad."

"Daddy had a phone call, and he told me to talk to Billy until he finished. Billy's in my kindergarten class."

"That was nice that your friend is here. And thanks for corralling her," Sabra said to Kelsey. Then under her breath, she said, "I'm going to ring Mason's neck for not watching her better."

"No, Billy's not nice!" Lily folded her arms. "He's mean."

Kelsey smoothed her niece's curls back. "He wasn't being mean. He was just being a boy. We have to overlook things like that until we can show them differently. Okay?"

The glower slowly faded, and Lily nodded. "I guess." Then her face brightened. "Tomorrow is church day, and Mama said I could sit in big church. You coming?"

"Yes, ma'am," she replied.

"Good. You can sit with me." Then she wiggled out of Kelsey's arms. "Aunt Kelsey asked if Billy could come for a play date at the park," she said to her mom. "Can we do it tomorrow after church?"

"We'll see," Sabra said.

Satisfied, Lily skipped over to the polar bear display, and Sabra eyed Kelsey. "Play date, huh? Was she about to beat him up?"

"Something like that. His grandfather thought it'd be great for Billy to *socialize*. I'll iron out the details with Billy's mom, unless you want to. She'll be expecting a call." When Sabra continued to frown, Kelsey said, "Lily was definitely ready to pound the kid, and I thought it'd be a way to smooth things over."

"I think I have her number." Her sister shook her head. "I swear, sometimes I think Lily is mine in name only. She got all of your genes even if we're not blood kin."

Kelsey laughed. "It's my revenge for you being so ladylike." And the pretty one in the family. She pulled Brad forward. "Have you met my date? Mom and Sam already know him." At least she figured they did since they set the date up.

"I was wondering—"

"Then wonder no more. Brad Hollister, my sister Sabra O'Donnell."

Interest flicked across her sister's face and Kelsey could

44

see the wheels turning in Sabra's brain. Before the night was over, Kelsey and Brad would be an item.

"It's so nice to meet you, Brad." Then she turned to Kelsey. "That dress is drop-dead gorgeous on you."

It felt more like putting lipstick on a mop head. Although she'd have to admit, while she didn't feel gorgeous, tonight she did feel elegant in pearls and the form-fitting sheath Sabra and her mother had bought. Getting used to the blonde spikes would take time.

"Nice to meet you," Brad said. "But I don't remember you from high school."

"You and Kelsey were ahead of me," Sabra said. "You do know our parents, right?"

"Your dad, yes," he said. He turned to her mother, who had been standing quietly in the background. "Mrs. Allen, I believe you know my mom."

"Barbara is one of the most genuine people I know, not to mention the sweetest," Cynthia Allen said. "I hope you don't mind that you were volunteered for tonight. We had an extra ticket, and it is for a good cause." Her face colored. "The fundraiser, you know."

Kelsey pretended she was on a beach thousands of miles from Memphis. She could not believe her mother had just said that.

Brad squeezed her hand. "I'm actually glad I was volunteered. I'm really enjoying myself."

Sam Allen cleared his throat. "Brad, I'd like you to meet my brother, Grant. He's a trustee here at the Pink Palace Museum too."

"Where have you been keeping yourself?" Kelsey asked her uncle. She shot her stepfather a question with her eyes. Did Grant know she was working with security?

"Here and there," Grant said, wrapping her in a hug. "I understand you're finally coming to work at the museum. Conservator, right?"

"Yep. I'm looking forward to it." She disentangled herself from the embrace and kissed him on the cheek. Grant had always taken an interest in her, often slipping her spending money during her studies abroad when she was younger. In his early sixties, he stood a head taller than Sam. "Thank you if you had anything to do with the museum hiring me."

Grant grinned at her. "Nope. Didn't know about it until Sam told me half an hour ago." He glanced toward the banquet room. "I believe the caterers have everything set up. What do you say we grab a plate?"

A few minutes later, Kelsey balanced a plate of barbecue and coleslaw as she looked for a table. "How's this?" she asked, nodding toward one in the corner.

"Fine by me," Brad said. "You have an interesting family. I heard you tell Lily you'd go to church with her. Which church?"

"The Orchard."

His eyes widened. "You're kidding. I don't remember seeing any of you there."

"It's a big church. Not sure why you haven't seen Sabra and Lily, but I usually get there late, so I sit in the back." So she could be the first one out the door. But not tomorrow. Sabra liked to sit up front. She set her plate on the table. "Would you like me to get you a glass of tea when I get mine?"

"You're my date, remember? I'll get them both." He smiled at her. "Sweet or unsweet?"

"Sweet, and lemon, please." While he walked toward the beverage bar, she scanned the room. Mr. Rutherford had said all the players would be here tonight, and she looked for anyone suspicious. A sea of Ralph Lauren and Armani sport coats filled her line of vision.

And then there was Brad, who was walking toward the table with their tea. He carried himself with the same confidence as the other men in the room—the movers and shakers of Memphis. He'd shed his navy sport coat when he set his plate down, and he looked eye-catching with his white dress shirt unbuttoned at the neck and tie loosened.

"I never thought of you as nerdy even if you did have a crush on me." The memory of how he'd looked at her outside the museum earlier hitched her heart. It almost erased the memory of his expression when he climbed out of the Mustang, looking as though he'd rather be getting a root canal than escorting her to the fundraiser.

Maybe he'd even thought she was pretty when he first saw her. Kelsey brushed the thought away. Men always let her down. Even if he was right that she'd had a crush on him in her senior year. Which he pretty well destroyed when he rejected her as a lab partner.

She smiled as he handed her a glass. "Thank you."

Music played in the background for the next half hour as they made small talk about high school and ate the barbecue. When they finished, he looked over the dessert list.

"That was so good, I'm not sure I have room for dessert," he said.

"I'm pretty sure Corky's catered it," she said. Finally she couldn't stand it any longer. "Why did you agree to come tonight?"

His mouth twitched. "Honestly? I didn't see any way out of it without embarrassing someone. But it hasn't been bad at all. The food was good."

But not her company. "We can leave any time now—you don't have to stay for the pitch."

"Pitch?"

"For money." *He couldn't stay.* She had work to do, and she couldn't do it with him here. "Everyone here is expected to cough up at least a grand after dinner."

He paled. "Everyone?"

"Well, not you. Or me. Sam will, and most of the businesspeople."

"Oh. Won't it seem rude for me to eat and run?"

"Not if I leave with you." She smiled. "And frankly, it'll be a relief to get out of this dress and these shoes."

Brad laid the dessert list down. "You really do look very beautiful tonight."

Her heart skipped a beat, and she shifted her gaze away from him, waiting for him to crack a joke. Laser surgery may have fixed the glasses she'd worn as a teenager and scissors tamed the mop of hair, and once she'd quit running track she'd filled out, but in her mind's eye, she hadn't changed— she was still that nerdy girl who kept everyone at bay to keep from being hurt.

She turned and caught him staring at her. The man was serious. She'd forgotten how his hazel eyes had flecks of blue and green in them. Her fingers trembled as she reached for her glass. "Thank you. You look pretty good yourself."

"It's hard for you to accept a compliment."

"I wouldn't know—I haven't had that many."

"I don't believe that."

She frowned, and for the first time all day realized a man like Brad probably had plans for tonight. "You didn't break a date to come here, did you?"

"I . . . don't know what you're talking about."

He had. Now she felt horrible. "It just dawned on me that it's Saturday night, and you probably already had a date that you must have broken. I'm sorry that you were put in a difficult position."

"Oh."

He seemed about to say more when the toastmaster stood. Kelsey grabbed his hand. "Let's split before we get trapped. Maybe you can still salvage that date."

6

THE HUMID NIGHT AIR enveloped them as they stepped through the doors and out onto the portico. Kelsey fanned herself with the program she'd picked up. It wouldn't be long before the summer heat would be the main topic of conversation everywhere.

"Are you leaving as well?" Brad asked.

How easily a lie would have rolled off her tongue six months ago, and she was tempted even now since she was leaving the fundraiser but not the grounds. "I'll probably hang around a little longer after I walk with you to your car," she said and looked up at him. Even with her strappy three-inch heels, he towered over her, and whatever she'd intended to say was suddenly gone. "How tall are you, anyway?"

"What?"

"I don't recall you being so tall." Or handsome. The years had been good to him, allowing his square jaw to catch up with the narrow face that had filled out, adding laughter lines around his eyes.

"I've been six-three forever. You don't remember me playing center in basketball?"

"I don't ever recall going to a basketball game in high school."

He laughed. "Oh, that's right. You were too busy making valedictorian."

"Is that an insult?"

"Never. I thought it was quite an accomplishment for you to finish high school in three years. And for the record, by the end of the year, I realized having you for a lab partner probably kept me from failing chemistry."

She studied him, looking for any hint of sarcasm. "You could have told me."

"You're kidding. I wasn't about to admit anything to you. Not after the way you looked down at me with that snooty nose of yours."

"I never . . ." The look on his face stopped her. Maybe she had, but not because she thought she was better than he was. Kelsey had been aware that her classmates thought she was high and mighty because of Sam's wealth, and she never did anything to correct their impression. In high school it hadn't taken her long to figure out most kids wanted to be around her because they thought she was rich. Staying aloof kept her from being hurt. "Sorry if I came off that way. It was a coping mechanism."

She felt for the strand of hair she usually twisted, forgetting for a second that Sabra's hairdresser had cut her hair really short. "Anyway, thanks for showing up. And apologize for me to whoever you had a date with."

"There's no one to apologize to," he said softly. "Hasn't been for a while now."

If it weren't for the hurt that darkened his eyes, she wouldn't have believed him. "Any time you want to hang out, give me a call."

"Really?"

"Yeah, I'm free most weekends."

He gave her a lopsided grin as he tossed his keys in the air and caught them. "I might just do that," he said and unlocked the door to his car.

Whatever possessed her to tell him that? They were so mismatched it was beyond the pale of possibility. And if he discovered she was the Phantom Hawk, he'd probably arrest her until Mr. Rutherford could explain.

She turned and hurried to her Jeep Wrangler that she'd parked in a dark, out-of-the-way space near the back of the building. Perfect for changing clothes. A few minutes later, she'd shed the stilettos and skinny black dress for sneakers and dark green climbing clothes. Once dressed, she fastened a pack around her waist that contained picks and other tools she might need. Then she slipped a coiled rope with a collapsible grappling hook at one end around her shoulder.

Adrenaline surged through her. Doing this tonight, when so many people were around, upped the stakes. And security would be focused on the front area of the museum and not the back where she would be.

Preliminary work this afternoon on the electronic security system had shown that the only outside security cameras in operation were the ones that monitored the entrances and exits. She hadn't been able to hack into the system, but sometimes that took days. Tomorrow she planned to see if she could access the software that operated the cameras.

At this point, she believed she was dealing with someone who worked for the museum. An employee with access to the building and artifacts, but she needed to rule out an outside hacker and burglar, confirming what she *wasn't* working with.

The stored artifacts were in a caged area on the second floor but were normally accessed through the first floor. Kelsey wanted to see if the storage area could be reached from the roof. She'd studied the layout of the Palace and decided her best option was to scale the back wall, using the drainpipe, if it would hold her weight.

Normally there was time to test that sort of thing out, but not this time—she wanted to have something to tell Mr. Rutherford Monday morning. She also didn't like the lighted windows that were adjacent to the pipe, but it was the best way up.

She took her liquid chalk from the pack she wore around her waist. After squirting a few drops on her palm, she rubbed her hands together, making sure her fingertips were well covered. Then she took out the green beanie she'd bought that afternoon and pulled it low over her head, leaving it just high enough to see. If it hadn't been May and already in the nineties, she would have bought a ski mask. The humidity was already making her forehead itch.

The pipe was sturdy enough for her weight, and it was secured to the pink Georgian marble with brackets that made resting places for her feet. As she started up, she hoped no one passing by the windows decided to look out, but no one should be in this wing of the building, anyway. With the brackets to start her off, she automatically changed to finding finger holds in the granite.

Rock-climbing was a lot like her life. Just as she'd rehearsed techniques until she overlearned them and they became automatic, she'd rehearsed ways to keep people like Brad at bay. It wasn't that he didn't attract her—he did—and she no longer feared people liked her because of Sam's money, but it was hard to unlearn something she'd practiced so long. She wasn't sure she knew how to let anyone other than family into her life.

Before she realized it, she'd reached the flat roof on the second floor of the building. After uncoiling the rope around her shoulder, she expanded the grappling hook on the end and tossed it underhand like a softball to the top of the next roof.

It landed with a soft thud, and she pulled on it, testing to see if it had caught. It had, and she tested it again, making sure it would hold her weight. Laughter floated up from the parking lot below as a few guests departed. She waited until their taillights disappeared out of sight—no need to take a chance on them seeing her. Not that they probably would. There were no floodlights shining against the building on the back, a flaw she needed to point out to Rutherford.

Once she made it to the next roof, she walked the steep incline to the dormer window and tested to see if it would rise. Stuck fast. She scrambled across to the next gable and tried that window. Silently, it slid up. *Victory!*

Blood raced through her body, electrifying every nerve ending. The exhilaration from breaking into a building because she could almost scared her. Had her father felt this way when he'd stolen artifacts from the museum? Maybe there *was* such a thing as a thief gene.

Kelsey shook her thoughts away and climbed through the window. She was doing nothing illegal. A flashlight helped her navigate past the boxes stored in the alcove, and then she crept down the darkened stairs that led to the artifact room. The itching on her forehead had intensified, and she pushed the cap back on her head.

At the first landing, the stairs turned, revealing light in the room. She stopped midstep. It was Saturday night, so why were the lights on? The cleaning crew. She'd seen them in the drive earlier, but what if they were working this area? She eased further down until she could scan the floor, listening for anything that announced someone's presence. All quiet.

She'd proven someone could access the building from the roof, so why not just leave? She would, but first she wanted to leave her card as proof to Mr. Rutherford that she'd been there. It wouldn't take long.

Everything seemed clear, and she crept down the metal steps to the first floor and the desk by the door. She placed the card in the middle of the desk, where it couldn't be missed. With her job done, she returned the way she'd come.

Halfway up the steps, a sound stopped her, sending an icy shiver down her spine. She cocked her head, listening.

Music filtered through the walls, and she relaxed. It was only the band starting up again. Shaking her head, she hurried up the steps and ignored the feeling in her gut that all was not well.

Once Kelsey climbed out the dormer window and down the rope, she inched across the roof to the drainpipe and swung her body over the side, her hands gripping the steel pipe that ran along the gutter. Good thing she'd used the chalk, making her grip more secure. Crossing hand over hand, she worked her way to the drainpipe. Shouldn't take a minute to descend the pipe, and then she was home free. She'd almost reached the ground when a cold chill shivered down her back like a bad omen.

"Need some help there?"

She froze and looked over her shoulder. Brad Hollister. And he looked as though he was in full police mode. Kelsey released her hold on the pipe and jumped, landing softly on the ground. She dusted her hands. "Nope. I don't need any help."

"Kelsey?" His voice cracked. "What are you doing?"

"A better question might be what are *you* doing here?" She cocked her head and looked up at him, the soft glow from a nearby window offering barely enough light to see the glint in his eyes. "I thought I saw you drive away."

"I see you did," he said. "I realized I hadn't thanked your parents for inviting me to the benefit or said good night. When I circled the lot looking for a parking space, I saw someone running across the roof. So I investigated. And now if you don't mind, what are you doing out here?"

Kelsey opened her mouth to explain, and a blood-curdling scream came from inside the mansion.

◆

Brad jerked his head toward the sound. "Stay put," he ordered, then jogged toward the entrance. Why was Kelsey breaking into the museum? It didn't make sense.

Inside, he found a distraught member of the cleaning crew rattling off a string of Spanish to the museum director. Even though Brad had a rudimentary knowledge of the language, she spoke too fast for him to follow. Except he caught something about a body. "I'm Sergeant Brad Hollister with the Memphis Police Department," he said to the director. "What is she saying?"

"Thank goodness you're here. I'm Robert Tomlinson, the—"

"Director of the museum. I know. What happened?"

"She says there's a man on the first floor. She thinks he may be dead."

"Has anyone called 911?" Brad asked.

"Yes," Tomlinson said. "A dispatcher said officers would arrive soon."

Brad turned to the cleaning lady. "Can you show me where the body is?"

Her eyes widened and she stepped back, shaking her head. "No, no, no!"

Robert Tomlinson spoke to her in Spanish, and she nodded slowly. "There," she said in Spanish, pointing toward a door down the hallway. "He is there. Blood is"—she waved her hands—"everywhere!"

This time Brad had no trouble understanding her.

"I'll show you where she's talking about," the director said. He turned and spoke to her again in Spanish and frowned when she answered him. "She says the door to the registrar's office is opened, and she doesn't think the man is alive."

Brad followed him to a locked door. "Does the cleaning crew have access to all the rooms?"

"No. Only to the general offices. Certainly not to the registrar's office where the safe is located." He took out his phone and dialed a number. "That's odd. Rutherford isn't answering."

"Rutherford?"

"He's in charge of security. He would have let the cleaning crew into this area."

Brad heard footsteps behind him and looked over his shoulder. Kelsey. She had pulled off the beanie, leaving her hair flat against her head. She looked like a pixie . . . or Peter Pan, with the green tights and pullover. "What happened?" Kelsey asked as Tomlinson keyed in a number on the door lock.

"I told you to stay put."

"I didn't think you meant it literally, just to not leave."

"The vault is this way," Tomlinson said and opened the door.

Brad looked from the director back to Kelsey. The man didn't seem at all disturbed that she was here. Brad held his questions until he had a better idea of the crime. Then Ms. Allen had a few answers to come up with.

They hurried down one hallway to another and finally through another door to a room with stairs to an overhead caged room on one side and a walk-in vault on the other. He followed Tomlinson into the vault, where a body lay on the floor in a puddle of blood.

"Oh no," Tomlinson said softly as Kelsey gasped.

"Do you know him?" Brad felt for a pulse even though experience taught him he was looking at a corpse.

"It's Walter Rutherford," she said.

That Rutherford. Brad looked closer. "You're talking about Rutherford Security?"

"Yes," Tomlinson said. "But how did he end up here?"

"I don't know, but it got him shot. Call and have your security team secure the area until my people get here." He took out his phone as he stood. "We need to back out of here. And don't touch anything."

Once they were out of the vault, he dialed his friend Reggie Lane. "Are you on call this weekend?" he asked when Reggie answered with sleep in his voice.

"Yeah."

"There's a homicide at the Pink Palace."

"Already got it," Reggie said. "I'm on my way."

"Call the Crime Scene Unit too." From the corner of his eye, he could see Kelsey leaning over the desk by the door.

"Looking for something?" he asked after he hung up. Either it was the fluorescent lighting or she was about to pass out. "You okay?"

"Just a little woozy."

He understood that. It was probably her first murder scene to witness, and violent death was never pretty. For that matter, Mr. Tomlinson looked a little green as well. "Let's get to the ballroom, where you two can sit down and get a glass of water."

Kelsey swayed.

"Are you all right?" Brad asked.

"I—" Kelsey crumpled to the floor.

7

HER BUSINESS CARD HADN'T BEEN ON THE DESK, and Kelsey had only a few seconds to search the floor after her faint, which was closer to being real than pretend. *Mr. Rutherford is dead?* The shock of seeing his body hadn't worn off.

She pushed aside her emotions and looked for anything white. The desk and the area around it was paper free. What happened to the Phantom Hawk card she'd left less than half an hour ago?

Suddenly, she felt herself being gently lifted from the floor and cradled in Brad's arms. *What is he doing?* "I can walk, so put me down," she said.

He looked down at her. "Are you sure?"

No, she wasn't. She felt safe, protected in his arms. Until he found that card. "Yes," she said, and he set her feet on the floor. "I don't know what happened to me."

"Don't feel bad," Tomlinson said. "I thought I was going to keel over too."

Wrapping her mind around the death of a good man who only wanted to help people was almost impossible. Who could have killed him? Had he already been dead when she was in the storage area? If she'd been there earlier, maybe she could have prevented his murder.

She caught her breath. If Brad discovered she was the Phantom Hawk, she'd be his number one suspect. Might be anyway, given the circumstances. But at least Mr. Rutherford seemed to have informed Tomlinson that she was working with security since he didn't seem at all surprised to see her.

Kelsey had to find that card, but where could it be? Or who could have taken it? Mentally she clicked through the possibilities and came up with four. The cleaning woman found it and threw it away. That one she dismissed. Cleaning personnel never touched anything on a desk. Or it could have been knocked to the floor, but if that were true, it would still be there.

That left only two possibilities.

Rutherford found it . . . or the man who killed him had seen her leave it and took it. She hoped it was Mr. Rutherford.

If it was the murderer, he now knew it was the Phantom Hawk who had broken into the museum tonight and had been there about the time he killed Rutherford. Maybe he even thought she'd seen him. If it became public knowledge that Kelsey and the Phantom Hawk were the same person . . . The newscast flashed in her mind. Andi Hollister had reported the Phantom Hawk had broken into the Turner Accounting building. The person who'd fired at her Thursday night would know she was the one climbing the wall. It would be easy enough to track her down. She swayed as her knees buckled.

Brad caught her before she fell. "That does it. I'm carrying you out."

Kelsey didn't protest. She couldn't make it under her own steam this time. Tomlinson held the door open, and Brad strode to the banquet room and settled her in a chair.

"Be right back."

In less than a minute, he was back with a glass of water. "Drink this, and then we need to talk."

Her hand shook as she took the glass. She didn't want to talk to him, not until she knew how much Rutherford had told Tomlinson. Her head swam. "Do you think you could find a Coke or something? I need a pick-me-up."

Sirens wailed in the distance. Maybe by the time he returned, the mansion would be full of police officers and he'd be otherwise engaged.

"Do you have diabetes?"

"It's nothing like that, I'm just shaky. Please find something."

He pinned her with a stern look. "Don't go anywhere."

Seriously? Did he think she'd run away? "Don't worry, I'll be here when you get back."

As soon as he was out of hearing range, she turned to the museum director. "What did Mr. Rutherford tell you about me?"

Tomlinson rubbed his forehead. "I can't believe he's dead."

Neither could Kelsey, but she needed his answer before Brad returned. "Did he tell you I was working for him?"

"He did and that the conservator job would be a cover. Your résumé is impressive."

If Rutherford had told the museum director she was the Phantom Hawk, it didn't seem to matter. "Thank you," she said to his reference to her résumé. "I noticed the cameras are newer ones. When were they installed?"

"Just last week, and you've changed clothes since I last saw you in the ballroom," Tomlinson said as a man in a navy sport coat approached them.

"I was checking out the security system. I had intended to tell Rutherford the weaknesses I found on Monday."

The man who joined them directed his gaze at the director. "Do you know how the murderer accessed the inner offices?"

Tomlinson turned to Kelsey. "This is my brother Mark. He's the building manager and was working with Mr. Rutherford on some issues we've had with security. Mark, Kelsey Allen. Rutherford hired her this morning to investigate the missing artifacts."

Mark Tomlinson looked to be older than his brother Robert, probably in his late fifties or early sixties. She didn't know if the scowl on his face was a permanent fixture or because he wasn't pleased that she'd been hired.

"Why didn't anyone tell me?"

Uh-oh. Appeared Mr. Mark Tomlinson might be a control freak.

The museum director sighed. "I only found out late this afternoon. I'll brief you tomorrow. Right now we have Rutherford's death to deal with." He turned to Kelsey and repeated his brother's question about how the murderer accessed the rooms.

"If Rutherford was already inside, the person could have simply walked in."

"You believe an employee killed him?"

"I didn't say that, but wouldn't it take someone with knowledge of the codes to get into the rooms?" From the corner of her eye she caught sight of Brad returning. "Can we meet tomorrow afternoon and discuss this?"

Tomlinson nodded.

"I hope this makes you feel better," Brad said as he handed her a soda.

"Thanks." She pulled the tab back and took a long sip of the drink. She hadn't been lying about needing something to boost her. After a few sips, she began to feel better.

"You really ought to get that checked out," Brad said. "You were very pale earlier."

"It's not often I see someone I know murdered. But thank you." She looked past him as a man who could easily play tackle on an NFL team approached them. The gun and badge on his belt told her he was a cop. "I believe the cavalry has arrived. You better steer them in the right direction."

He glanced over his shoulder, then back at her. "Hang around until I can get back here. All of you."

◈

Brad dodged people as he trotted toward Reggie, who was standing in the arched doorway, scanning the room. "Over here," Brad called, and the lieutenant turned toward him.

"What do you have?" Reggie asked, his face pinched in a frown.

"Walter Rutherford. Dead in the vault." Brad checked his watch. Ten minutes. "How did you get here so fast? You sounded like you were asleep when I called."

"No, just tired. I live a few blocks away, and I had stopped by home to grab a bite to eat. The security guy is the one killed?"

Brad nodded and led the way to the crime scene. "No one knows what he was doing in the vault. The director said he was supposed to be home. His crew is making sure no one leaves."

"Good." Reggie tilted his head. "Looks like there are quite a few people here. I could use your help getting statements once we're done here."

"Sure." Reggie had been a year ahead of him at the academy and had just made lieutenant. It wouldn't surprise Brad if the detective didn't end up being director one day. "I'm not an official Cold Case investigator until Monday, anyway."

Reggie eyed him dryly. "I wish David Raines would keep his hands off Homicide. Every time he gets a little money, he steals one of our guys. First Will Kincade and now you."

"Maybe it'll be you next time."

"Nah. I like my cases hot. Don't have the patience to go digging in the past. Show me the body."

They wound around to the vault and, after slipping on booties at the door, entered the office with the vault.

"Whose office is this?" Reggie asked.

"The registrar's. She's been called and is on her way to identify any missing artifacts." Brad stood back as Reggie stepped into the vault and stared at the body on the floor. They'd both dealt with Rutherford during different investigations and respected the man's integrity.

He shook his head. "Poor guy, just trying to do his job and this happens."

Brad nodded. While Rutherford wasn't a cop, he was well respected among police officers. His murder drove home how dangerous protecting people and even property could be.

Reggie took out his phone and snapped photos of the body and surrounding area. The CSI team would take plenty of pictures, but Reggie would want his own. Brad turned as the outside door opened, and the medical examiner stepped into the room with the forensic team filing in behind him.

"Close quarters . . . and dim," the ME said, nodding to the two detectives. "Let's get some lights rigged up."

"We'll be downstairs taking statements if you need us," Reggie said.

The ME glanced at Rutherford then back at Reggie. "I'm sure the first thing you'll want to know is when he died. I should be able to give you an approximate time directly. I'll have a firm time after the autopsy."

Brad didn't believe Kelsey had anything to do with Rutherford's death, but if the man had been killed a couple of hours ago, it'd keep her out of the loop of suspicion altogether.

Rutherford's security team had settled the fundraiser guests in the banquet room where Brad and Kelsey had eaten less than two hours ago. He stepped into the room and looked for Tomlinson and Kelsey. She was sitting at a table surrounded by her family, but he didn't see the director. Sam Allen broke away from the others and approached them.

"Kelsey said Walter has been killed. What can you tell me?"

"Afraid nothing at this point." He turned to Reggie and made the introductions. "Mr. Allen is a trustee for the museum."

The two men shook hands, and Reggie took out a notepad. He handed it to Brad. "Why don't you take statements from people on this side of the room, and I'll cover the other."

Brad agreed and took the pad and pen, then turned to Sam. "What can you tell me about Walter Rutherford?"

"We were together just this morning with Kelsey," Sam said.

"Did he hire her for something in particular?" If Rutherford had, it would explain a lot, like the clothes she had changed into. He glanced toward the table where Kelsey was studying him like he was a specimen under a microscope. Then Lily crawled up in her lap, and she focused on the child.

Sam had turned to look at Kelsey as well. "Yes. Lately the museum has experienced the loss of a few artifacts, and Walter wanted to take advantage of my daughter's . . . uh . . . talents."

He had Brad's attention now. "What talents?"

"Kelsey has a master's degree in historic preservation. Walter wanted her to assume the temporary position of conservator of the museum while the current conservator is out on maternity leave."

"Why would the head of security hire her for that position?"

Sam hesitated. "She also has a phenomenal ability with computers, and when funding dried up for her job at the museum in Jackson, she worked for the security division until there were more cutbacks."

"So the conservator position is a cover?"

"Yes, although she is quite qualified to fill the position. Walter wanted her to attempt a breach of the museum security."

Which was what she'd done tonight. "Does anyone else know what her real job is?"

"The director, Robert Tomlinson, but I don't know who he's told."

"Thank you. Do you know where he is now?"

"He said something about calling the museum's lawyer, who left just before all this happened."

Brad nodded. "Let me get a statement from your wife, and you'll be free to leave." Then he would talk to Kelsey.

The statement from Cynthia Allen didn't take long, and he walked to the table where Kelsey was holding her sleeping niece in her lap as she talked with her sister. A man he hadn't met earlier was at the table as well. Before he could say anything, Kelsey nodded toward Sabra.

"Why don't you take Sabra and her husband's statement so they can take Lily home."

Sabra's statement was brief. Her husband, it turned out, had been outside on his cell phone most of the evening and had seen nothing. Once they left, Brad sat in the chair Kelsey's sister had vacated. "Why didn't you tell me you were working with Rutherford?"

"You didn't ask."

She wasn't going to make the night get any shorter. "Did you or did you not breach the security tonight?"

A struggle showed in her eyes.

"Come on, your dad just confirmed that Rutherford hired you earlier today. Is that why you were coming down the side of the building?"

"I'll answer your questions on one condition. Whatever I tell you is confidential."

He looked toward the ceiling, then dropped his glance back to Kelsey. "I'm not your psychiatrist or your lawyer."

"Do I need a lawyer?"

"I don't know, do you?"

She folded her arms and leaned back in the chair, her lips pressed together.

"Okay." He gritted his teeth. "For now I'll keep it confidential."

"Not good enough. If you talked to Sam or Robert Tomlinson, you know I'm working undercover. I don't want that blown."

"Could you just trust me, Kelsey?" Her expression didn't change. "How about I share on a need-to-know basis. Right now, that will only be Lieutenant Lane. And we'll start with you giving me your cell phone number."

She recited the number, and he put it in his cell phone and waited while she sat, tense as a wound spring, and then suddenly her shoulders relaxed.

"Okay," Kelsey said. "Mr. Rutherford hired me to help catch the person stealing artifacts, and the first thing I needed to know was whether anyone could break into the museum from the outside."

"And?"

"It's possible—I did, but I don't believe that's the way the murderer got into the vault tonight."

"Why not?"

"I didn't see any evidence that anyone had climbed in the window I went through, and it would have been the most logical entry point other than walking through the doors. I planned to check the other windows Monday with Mr. Rutherford. Do you have any idea when he was murdered?"

"Not yet. The ME promised to give me an approximate time before he leaves. You're pretty good at climbing. Where did you learn?"

She shrugged. "In Jackson. I could do what I did tonight in my sleep." When he questioned her with his eyes, she said, "Sorry. I climb rocks and do 5.10 climbs all the time, which only dedicated climbers attempt. This would be no more than a 3 or 4. I just wish now I'd gone into the room with the vault."

"You didn't?"

"No. I'd found out that it was possible for someone to get into the museum from the roof." She dropped her head. "I just keep thinking he may have still been alive, and I could have saved him."

"Well, at least your fingerprints won't be in the vault."

Her head jerked up. "Did you think I killed him?"

8

KELSEY'S HEART BEAT LIKE A JACKHAMMER on steroids as she ignored the people staring at them.

"Of course I don't think you killed Rutherford." Brad flipped his notebook to a new page. "You're not a murderer, or even a burglar, in spite of the fact that you obviously broke into the building tonight. Legally, of course, since Rutherford hired you to do that." He tapped his pen. "Doesn't change the fact that it would be hard to explain if your fingerprints were found near the body."

An invisible band squeezed Kelsey's lungs, cutting off her breath. The only reason he didn't consider her a suspect was because she was part of the museum's security team. If Brad discovered she was the Phantom Hawk . . . well, it was something she'd rather keep to herself. She glanced down at her fingers, where traces of liquid chalk remained. Either Brad hadn't noticed her hands, or he didn't know the magnesium carbonate that rock-climbers used to ensure a better grip also filled in the ridges on their fingers, masking fingerprints.

Other thoughts struck her. What if Rutherford was killed just before she broke in? What if the killer wore gloves? And there was the missing card and whether or not the murderer might have seen her. Even if he had, with the cap and dark clothes, she doubted anyone would recognize her. She needed to focus on the job Rutherford hired her for.

"It's really important that no one knows I'm part of security or that I broke into the museum tonight."

"Why is that so important?" he asked.

"That should be obvious. My cover will be blown, and Mr. Rutherford's death doesn't change the fact that I've been hired to find out who's stealing."

"No!"

"What do you mean, no?"

"A man's been killed. It's too dangerous for you to be nosing around. This is a police matter now."

Brad could not keep her from doing this job.

"Excuse me?" She stood and fisted her hands on her hips. "You didn't hire me, and you can't fire me. And if you think about it, the safest place I probably can be is working here with security guards all around."

"What's going on? I heard you two arguing across the room."

They both turned as Reggie asked the question.

Kelsey shot a covert glance around the room. More people were staring their way. "He doesn't want me to do my job," she said, keeping her voice low.

"What job?" Reggie's face registered confusion. "And who exactly are you?"

She lifted her chin. "I'm Kelsey Allen, and like I've already said, he doesn't want me to do my job."

Reggie's gaze shifted to Brad. "Can we start at the beginning?"

"I'm not sure where the beginning is," Brad replied. "And

for the record, this is Lieutenant Reggie Lane. He's in charge of this case."

"Good," Kelsey said and turned to Reggie, lowering her voice. "Mr. Rutherford hired me today as a consultant to help investigate the thefts occurring here at the museum." She jerked her head toward Brad. "He wants to blow my cover, and he doesn't want me investigating."

"Your cover? I still don't understand what you're talking about."

She rolled her lips in, pressing her teeth against them. There had to be a way to explain this without revealing her extracurricular activities. "Not long ago I discovered . . . flaws . . . in the security system at the Allen Brothers building. I pointed them out to Dad and he happened to mention it to Mr. Rutherford."

"How did you discover these flaws?" Reggie asked.

"I'm good with computers, and I found a way around the firewall and was able to access the company's financial files." She hoped he would let it go at that, as she did not want to reveal her trade secrets.

Reggie's eyes widened. "You're a hacker?"

"A white-hat hacker. There's a difference—I only hack to help people."

"She's good at climbing buildings too."

Kelsey narrowed her eyes at Brad. She could do without his cheeky attitude. "I happen to be an expert-level rock-climber, and the last time I checked, there wasn't a law against it."

"Climbing up the side of the museum and entering the building isn't rock-climbing. And that is against the law," Brad said.

"Was she breaking and entering?" the lieutenant asked.

Brad's lips turned down. "No. The victim had hired her to test the security at the museum."

Reggie raised his hand and eyed Brad. "You can't stop her from doing what she was hired to do. And arguing isn't getting people interviewed. Can you two finish this later?"

"I believe we're done," Kelsey said.

"Good." Reggie shifted his attention to Brad. "It's getting late and these people want to go home."

Brad's eye twitched, then he turned and jerked his head toward a table where a couple was seated. "I'll start with them," he said.

Before he stood, he shot Kelsey a look she had no trouble reading.

"What?"

"I'm not finished with your statement."

"Then find me Monday. I'll be here, in the conservator's office." She turned to Reggie. "Am I free to leave?"

"As far as I'm concerned. I assume Brad has your contact information?"

"He does, but starting Monday, you can find me here at the museum, filling in until the conservator returns from her maternity leave."

He handed her his card. "And if you discover anything I need to know, contact me at the number on the card."

Instead of leaving after Reggie walked back across the room, Kelsey wandered around, remembering what Mr. Rutherford had said about the thief probably being there tonight. Did one of the guests kill him? She wished she'd mingled more before eating when everyone was still there.

"Aren't you Sam Allen's daughter?"

Kelsey turned at the question. She'd seen the man in deep conversation with Robert Tomlinson while she'd waited for Brad to return. He appeared to have at least ten years on her. "His stepdaughter, actually. And you are . . . ?"

"Jackson King. Would you like to sit here at the table for a minute?"

The name rang a bell. Her eyes widened as she took a chair across from him. "You're this year's Cotton Carnival King."

She'd heard her mother and sister talking about it earlier today and thought it unusual that the king was a King. Kelsey had no idea why her mind stored such useless trivia.

"The term is actually Carnival King. The cotton part was dropped years ago when the powers-that-be decided to honor different businesses in the industry. But regardless what it's called, it's going to be fun." Then he turned serious. "I'm also Walter Rutherford's partner. Not that he always confided in me. I had to learn from Robert that he'd hired you to check into the thefts going on here."

She stared at him. This was the first she'd heard of Rutherford having a partner. "Why didn't Mr. Rutherford tell me about you?"

"I was more of a silent partner. He ran into financial difficulty a few years ago and I invested in the company. You'll be reporting to me now," he said. "I saw you talking to the two detectives. Tell me what happened tonight."

The memory of the security chief's body on the vault floor was lodged in her brain. She refocused. "There's not much to tell." She went over what she'd already told Brad. "Once I accomplished my mission, I left."

"You didn't see or hear anything?"

"I thought I heard a door creak, but it was probably the band starting up." She tilted her head. "Why aren't you helping the police with the investigation?"

"I was, but once they arrived, I let them take over." Jackson glanced past her and nodded. Kelsey turned, and a brunette about his age approached their table. A brunette who seemed

74

to be trying to appear younger with her short skirt and off-the-shoulder top.

"Do you mind if I join you two?" she asked.

"Of course not. Kelsey Allen, Helen Peterson," he said.

"Nice to meet you," Helen said, speaking first. "I heard you were coming to work here. I work as Robert, ah, Mr. Tomlinson's assistant."

"Nice to meet you," Kelsey murmured. She glanced back at Jackson. She'd seen him somewhere before tonight. "You seem familiar. Have we met before?"

"We have," he said with a smile.

Kelsey studied him. Casually dressed in a dark silk sport coat and with a deep tan that emphasized his silver hair—she couldn't imagine forgetting anyone as distinguished-looking as the man who waited expectantly, but apparently she had. "We have?"

His face fell. "Ouch," he said. "And it was only this week that we met. Turner Accounting?"

"Oh!" The pieces fell into place. "Yes. You brought papers to the office . . . but you wore a cap that made you look quite different."

"I'll throw that cap away as soon as I get home."

Helen laughed politely, but Kelsey sensed she wasn't enthusiastic about Jackson's interest in her.

The woman glanced around and then pinned Jackson with a frank stare. "Who was murdered?"

Jackson hesitated. "Walter Rutherford."

"Are you serious? What—"

"You know I can't tell you anything more."

Helen appeared put out, then she shook her head. "Who would have thought something like that would happen here

75

tonight." She shifted her gaze to Kelsey. "Weren't you wearing a different outfit earlier?"

She glanced down at her sweater and tights. "I, uh, changed after we ate. I start work as interim conservator on Monday, and I wanted to set up my office."

"So you're the one taking Erin's place during her leave," Helen said.

"Yes." She saw Brad stop to speak to Mr. Tomlinson. "I think I'll leave before the detective wants to talk to me again. It's been a pleasure meeting you two." She nodded to Jackson. "And I'll remember you the next time."

Brad's back was to her and she tried to slip past him.

"Kelsey," he called after her.

Grimacing, she stopped and turned around. "Yes?"

"I want to talk to you before you leave."

"Sorry, but I'm beat, and I'm going home. Besides, I think we finished our discussion earlier. If you have any additional questions, I'll be here Monday." Kelsey shivered as he leveled an icy stare at her.

"Nine o'clock?"

"Nine will be fine." She'd walked into that one. But there was nothing he could say that would deter her from finishing the job she'd been hired to do.

9

SUNDAY MORNING, Kelsey closed the kitchen door to the small apartment over her sister's garage and hurried down the steps and through the garage. Lily had called and asked her to ride to church with them, and she could see Sabra checking her watch now. Sometimes she regretted not getting a place of her own when she returned to Memphis. But living in her sister's backyard had its perks. Like seeing Lily every day.

The back door opened before Kelsey reached it, and her niece grabbed her by the hand. Her heart warmed as Lily pulled her inside the kitchen. Once it'd been her dream to have a daughter like Lily or a son like . . . whoever. It was the *whoever* that was the problem. She was thirty-five, and no husband in sight.

"C'mon, Mom's waiting."

"Good morning to you too," Kelsey said. "You look very pretty in your white dress and with ribbons in your hair. Did your mom do the smocking?"

"Yes." Lily looked over her shoulder and rolled her eyes. "I wanted to wear my new shorts."

Kelsey hid a smile. No need to encourage her niece, but

77

she understood. Girly clothes and ribbons had never been on her agenda, either.

"Car's out front. If we hurry, we'll make it on time," Sabra called from the living room.

"Where's Mason?" Kelsey asked.

"At the office. That phone call he had last night was another fire he had to put out this morning."

Inwardly, Kelsey winced at her sister's sharp tone. Her brother-in-law spent more time at the office than he did at home. His excuse was always that, since he was fifteen years older than Sabra, he needed to make sure she and Lily were well provided for in the event of his death. Kelsey wished he could see that some things were more important than money.

In spite of her sister's best intentions, they were late due to a road detour, and the front pews were filled. Kelsey guided them to her normal spot on the back row.

"I don't know how you hear from back here," Sabra said.

"Sorry." Actually she wasn't. She heard quite well from the back row, actually better than anywhere else in the sanctuary. It was as though her mind recognized this spot and tuned in to what the pastor was saying, and after praise and worship, Kelsey settled in to listen to him. As usual, his words were uplifting, and before she knew it, they were standing to leave.

"You really do sit in the back row."

Kelsey froze, recognizing Brad's smooth baritone. She looked around. He was holding up the line of people behind him to let them out of the row. "Thank you." She stepped out and then let Sabra and Lily go ahead of her.

"Why were you looking for me?" she asked, glancing at him. The navy polo shirt he was wearing brought out the blue in his eyes, disturbing the rhythm of her heart.

"Who said I was?"

"I've been going to this church for six months and have never seen you here. Let's just say I don't believe in coincidences."

"That makes two of us."

She followed Sabra and Lily out the side door. Lily's eyes widened when she turned and spied the detective. "Mr. Brad! Do you go to church here?"

"Yes, ma'am. I've been coming here a long time," he said.

"Why haven't I ever seen you?"

"It's a big church." He knelt beside Lily. "But now that I know who you are, I'll look for you."

She beamed a smile up at him. "You want to come eat lunch with us?"

"Lily!" Kelsey said.

"It's okay. I have plenty—Mason won't be joining us," Sabra said, turning to Brad. "It's only sandwiches, but you're welcome to come."

"I'd love to, but I promised a friend I'd help him with a job." He turned to Kelsey. "And you were right, I *was* looking for you. Do you have time to talk a minute about last night?"

"Now?"

"It won't take five minutes," he said.

"But I missed breakfast and I'm hungry. And I have questions I want answered before I say anything more. You said you'd see me tomorrow at the museum, so let's leave it at that."

His lips pressed into a thin line, and for a second, she wondered if he might haul her downtown to the Criminal Justice Center to get her statement.

"Okay. Have it your way. Tomorrow at nine?"

She smiled sweetly. "How about eleven? It's my first day

79

on a new job, and I'm not sure it'd look good to start it off being grilled by the police."

He gave her a curt nod. "Eleven it is, then, but please be ready to finish giving me your statement."

As he walked away, Sabra nudged her. "He's cute. You really should be nicer to him. It wouldn't have hurt you to answer his questions. Or does it have something to do with why you changed clothes last night?"

"I'll explain later," Kelsey said.

After lunch her sister set Lily up with her crayons and coloring book in her room. "Are you ready to explain what's going on?" she asked as they settled on the sofa in Sabra's den. "Or why you were back at the museum in tights and a sweater last night after you supposedly left with Brad?"

Kelsey stared at a spot on the carpet. For the hundreth time, she wished she hadn't confided in her sister about her secret life. "I'm working undercover for Mr. Rutherford—at least I was until he was murdered. Not sure if I still am, but last night I was testing the security at the museum."

"I thought you were taking a job with the museum as conservator and that I could finally relax." Sabra pinched the bridge of her nose. "Why do you take these risks? Breaking into buildings . . . getting shot at? And now you're involved in a murder? I just don't understand."

"You're right, you don't understand." Kelsey stood and paced the floor. "You don't know what it's like to have a father who left a legacy of thievery and deception. It's . . . like I have to make amends. I have to prove I didn't inherit his gene for stealing."

"Stop pacing! You're making me dizzy. And you didn't inherit any stealing gene—there's no such thing."

Kelsey stopped in front of her sister. "Okay! I'll admit

it—it's more than that. When I'm breaking into a computer or scaling a building or coming down in a winch, I get this . . . this feeling of being invincible."

Sabra took her hand and pulled Kelsey next to her on the sofa. "That I understand. It's because you crave the excitement. You like living on the edge, always have, even when we were kids and you were jumping out of barns with an umbrella."

"You'll never let me live that down, will you?"

"You were lucky you didn't break your neck," she said, giving Kelsey a warm smile. "Growing up was never boring with you around, but let's get back to this job with Mr. Rutherford. I thought you wanted to start your own business."

"That's just it—I'm working as a consultant, not an employee. If I do a good job, my business will take off." She chewed the inside of her cheek. "As for the Phantom Hawk, I think she pulled her last job last night."

"Good. I've been worried to death since someone shot at you. Did you tell your policeman about the man who fired at you?"

"No, and he's not *my* policeman. I am a little worried about something, though. I left one of the Phantom Hawk cards outside the murder scene."

"Does that mean Brad and that other officer know who your alter ego is?"

Kelsey lifted one shoulder in a shrug. "I don't think so, but they may start wondering. Brad caught me coming down the pipe, and I had to explain that Mr. Rutherford hired me. I hope he doesn't look any deeper."

"But what happened to the card?"

"I don't know. After we found Mr. Rutherford's body, I went to retrieve it, but it was gone."

"Do you think the murderer found it?"

"I don't think the cleaning lady took it. I'm meeting Mr. Tomlinson at the museum in a couple of hours, and while I'm there, I'll double-check to see if it could have fallen behind something." She licked her dry lips. "But if the murderer took it, and he saw my face when I put the card on the desk, he knows who the Phantom Hawk is."

10

BRAD OPENED HIS BACK DOOR and let Tripod in when he arrived home from church. The dog's toes clicked on the tile floor as he followed every step Brad made. "Lonesome?" he asked.

A whine and Tripod's tail thumped for an answer, and Brad knelt and scratched behind the dog's ears. The thumping became louder. "I don't know about you, but I'm hungry," he said and opened the refrigerator door. Pickings were slim. He should have taken Sabra O'Donnell up on her offer for lunch. Probably would have if Kelsey hadn't looked so stricken. He didn't think last night went that bad. At least not personally.

He took out a package of ham for himself and an opened can of dog food for Tripod. "Here you go," he said and emptied what was left in the dog's bowl. "Don't eat so fast," he said to the dog as his cell phone rang. He glanced at the caller ID. Elle? His heart dropped to the soles of his shoes.

Answer it or let it ring? His curiosity about what she wanted won. "Hello?"

"Brad, it's me, Elle."

He steeled himself against her silvery voice. "Yeah, I saw that on the ID."

She chuckled. "I'm surprised you answered, considering how rude I was the last time we spoke. I've been meaning to call and apologize for that."

"You weren't rude, just brutally honest." *"I can't marry you. Every day I would wonder if you were coming home to me, or if I'd have to plan a funeral."*

"Then I'll apologize for that. Have you eaten?"

"What?"

"I'm on your street and I have your favorite sandwich in a bag beside me. I really would like to apologize in person."

She was on his street? "You want to come here?"

"Yes." She drew the word out as only she could. "But only if you're interested in accepting my mea culpa."

Was she saying what he thought? His heart thudded in his chest. Eighteen months ago, he would have jumped at the chance to see her, but now he wasn't sure he wanted to risk his heart again. "Sure, come on by."

Evidently his mouth had a mind of its own. But then, it'd be interesting to discover why she wanted to apologize.

Brad snatched up the Sunday paper scattered across his den and checked the sink for dirty dishes. By the time his doorbell rang, he had folded the paper neatly and stuffed his breakfast dishes in the dishwasher. He opened the front door, and Elle stood on the other side, as beautiful as ever. "Come in."

"Thanks."

She handed him the white paper bag and then swept past him, her rose-scented perfume triggering memories of their five years together. Good memories mostly, he'd have to admit. He followed her to the den area and held up the sack that didn't smell even remotely like barbecue. "What did you bring?"

"Your favorite. Chicken salad wrap."

"I believe that was *your* favorite."

She tilted her head to the side, placing her finger against her cheek. "You know, I believe you're right." Then she gave a low chuckle. "But I think I remember that you liked it too."

Her blue eyes held such hope that he couldn't tell her it was probably his least favorite sandwich. But it was two o'clock and he was starved. "Yeah. Coke?"

"Absolutely. You get the soda, and I'll put ice in the glasses." She walked to the cabinet and took down two goblets. "I love this kitchen." She looked over her shoulder. "You know, you did a really good job when you found this place."

Did Elle think she could come in and act as though nothing had happened eighteen months ago? The question must have shown on his face.

She set the goblets down and faced him. "Oh, Brad. Breaking up with you was the worst mistake I ever made. Can you ever forgive me? I was so foolish."

"I forgave you a long time ago." And he had. But if she wanted to pick up where they left off, that was another matter.

A sigh whooshed from her lips. "Thank you. I . . . I know you don't feel the same way you did, but would you . . ." She bit her lip and looked away, composing herself. She took a breath and turned back to him. "You're not making this easy."

Elle was beautiful, her long auburn hair framing her delicate features, and she was standing in the kitchen just the way he'd imagined when he bought the house.

"I, uh, don't know what to say." His palms were sweating. How many times had he dreamed this very scene in the months after Elle had given him his ring back? "What changed your mind?"

She came around the island and took his hands. "I missed you more than I ever dreamed I would. I don't feel complete without you."

"But I'm still a cop."

"Yes, but Andi said when I ran into her the other day that you're working in the Cold Case Unit now. I figure the bad guys won't be shooting at you."

"There's no guarantee that won't happen."

"But you'll be working on cold cases, not hot ones with people with guns."

She had no idea what he did.

Elle touched his cheek. "I've missed you so much."

Her blue eyes held him captive, and he gave up all pretense that her nearness didn't confuse him. Everything in him wanted to take her in his arms and kiss her. But she'd broken his heart before, and he wasn't about to let her do it again. He stepped back. "I've missed you too, but I can't just forget what happened."

Disappointment filled her eyes, and she took a shaky breath. "I understand. I'm not saying we should pick up where we left off, but could we start over? Maybe dinner at my place Saturday night . . . or I could come and make something here?"

Brad's heart hammered his ribs. He wanted his cool, rational brain back, but Elle had turned him upside down. He heard himself say, "That sounds wonderful." And wondered if he'd lost his mind.

But seeing her here, in the house he'd bought for them to live in, reminded him they'd had something good once. Maybe it wasn't too late for them.

11

KELSEY LOOKED AWAY from the computer screen and rubbed the back of her neck. She'd been at the computer for two hours now, and the walls in the small bedroom she called her office were closing in. However, she had managed to get past the firewall on the museum's computers, but there was another layer of security that asked for passwords to the employee records she was trying to hack. Besides testing the system, she'd wanted to see if her name had been added to the list of employees. Not that she expected it to be.

Anyone without an employee badge wouldn't be admitted to the inner sanctum of the museum through the employee entrance. But she'd noticed last night that getting to other parts of the building was as simple as going through a door marked "Employees Only." While that door wouldn't give her access to the conservator's office, she planned to see this afternoon what it did give her access to. Of course, she could go in like she had last night. But she doubted the window was still unlocked.

There was one more thing she wanted to check before she left. Kelsey launched a program that soon gave her the

IP address of the museum's closed-circuit TV. She'd noticed cameras in the hallway of the museum, and since the murderer hadn't entered the storage room from above, how had he gotten past the cameras mounted in the hallways?

That was what she wanted to check—the camera feed from last night. Tomlinson had said the cameras were installed last week. Perhaps they hadn't changed the default passwords yet. After a few clicks, she was at the login site for the closed-circuit camera. After copying the camera company's name, she opened another site and pasted in the name and then added default passwords into the Google search engine.

In her experience even companies with good security systems often failed to change those settings. Time to see if Rutherford had on the new system. Once she located the information that was free for the taking, she returned to the camera site and typed in *admin* for the user name and *12345* for the password.

When the site came up, Kelsey released the breath she'd been holding. There were five cameras in operation. Now to download the program that would allow her to watch the videos. Once she had the program running on her computer, she clicked *Camera 1*, and the live feed opened up, showing people milling about in the ballroom. Good. At the top of the screen was the playback button.

After a few false starts, she found the camera for the hallway that led to the storage room and started the recording at 6:00 p.m. Saturday night. Looked good. Kelsey moved the button, fast-forwarding the feed, and then suddenly stopped when the screen went to snow. "Uh-oh," she murmured and checked her watch. Uh-oh again. Her appointment with Tomlinson was in ten minutes. Time disappeared when she was hacking into systems.

But at least now she knew something about the killer—he knew how to turn the cameras off and on. She would check to make sure, but she didn't believe for one second the camera had failed. Either the killer was computer savvy or worked for the security firm and had access to the cameras. She wished she'd gotten a list of the missing artifacts. She would ask Mr. Tomlinson for one during the meeting.

Before she shut her computer down, she checked her email, scrolling through the inbox. When a contact form from her website popped up, she caught her breath. *Yes!* It was a company interested in her security services. She clicked on the attachment and scanned the specs. Oh, wow. They needed everything from network security and cameras to an alarm system. She filled out the form and sent it back. A return email said they would contact her in a day or two for an appointment.

Kelsey shut down her computer and slipped it into its case to take with her. Her career as a security specialist was looking up. She checked her watch. Filling out the form had taken longer than she'd thought, so she hurried to her car.

The Sunday afternoon traffic was light. Living within a few miles of the museum was a plus, she decided as she pulled into the Pink Palace drive. Sitting back off the road, the mansion was quite an eyeful. She'd read somewhere that people back in the 1920s took Sunday drives out in the country just to see the thirty-six-thousand-square-foot mansion that Clarence Saunders was building. They soon dubbed it the Pink Palace because of the pink marble covering it. Too bad the founder of the modern-day grocery store never lived in it, having lost all of his money in the stock market before it could be completed. Maybe he would be proud to know it was a world-famous museum.

It looked as though there was a good crowd touring the exhibits today, but she'd seen that on the live feed. Kelsey dialed Mr. Tomlinson's number, and when he answered, she said, "I'm here at the front entrance."

"Come around to the employee entrance, and I'll meet you."

Tomlinson met her at the sign-in station. "Once you fill out your paperwork tomorrow, you'll be given a badge," he said as they walked to his office.

Kelsey shifted the laptop she'd brought to her left hand. "So, I'm keeping my job?"

"As far as I'm concerned. I especially need you now since the present conservator may have to take an early maternity leave."

"I was actually referring to the security part of the job. Do you still want me to investigate the thefts?"

"That will depend on Jackson King, the new security director."

"I talked with him last night, and he didn't say anything about me not continuing."

"I'm surprised you want to continue after what happened to Rutherford."

"I was hired to find out how the thefts happened, and I had barely started." It was important that she finish the job he'd given her.

"I just figured the police would handle all of that," he said as he stopped in front of a closed door and keyed in a code.

She followed him into a spacious office. "They'll be focusing on his killer, not necessarily how the past robberies occurred. If a breach in security happened once, it could happen again."

Tomlinson rubbed his jaw with his thumb. "I don't want you putting yourself at risk."

"Don't worry." She was already at risk. Her best defense was to find the person responsible. And besides, while working as a security analyst wasn't as dangerous as being a cop, she accepted that it held a certain amount of risk. "I'm not looking for a person, per se—that's the job of the police. I'm searching for a process—how the thief found a way around the security the museum has in place. Who has keys to the entire building?"

"Three people—Rutherford, me, and I keep my set in the vault, and my brother Mark. But I know he's not the thief."

"I wasn't thinking that." Although she wasn't ruling him out, either. He was the only person who would have access to every room in the complex. "Why is your set of keys in the vault?"

"I don't like carrying them around and there are too many people in and out of my office..If I ever need them, I can ask the registrar to let me into the vault."

She nodded. "Do you have a list of the stolen items? And who do I talk to about the security cameras? The one for the hallway was off last night, but it's back on today."

"What?" Tomlinson said. "How do you know that?"

"I tapped into the closed-circuit TV."

He sat on the edge of his desk. "How? Never mind. Save it for Jackson. He'll be here in a few minutes. While we're waiting, I'll find that list of stolen artifacts. I need to send a copy to Sergeant Hollister as well." While he looked for the list, she sat in the leather Queen Anne chair across from his desk.

"The registrar discovered a mint Penny Black stamp missing from the vault and added it to the list last night," he said as he handed her a sheet of paper. "It was donated only a little over a month ago."

"What's it worth?"

"Only about twenty thousand."

"Only?"

"A Penny Red went for almost a million dollars last year."

"Who knew it had been donated?"

"The *Commercial Appeal* ran an article about it along with a photo of the gentleman donating it, so almost everyone who keeps up with that sort of thing."

Kelsey had missed the article. Someone rapped sharply at the door.

"That's probably Jackson," Tomlinson said. He opened the door. "Come in and have a seat. I'm afraid Ms. Allen has a bit of bad news for you."

"More bad news? Walter's death was enough for a lifetime," Jackson King said as he acknowledged Kelsey with a slight bow. He took the chair opposite her. "So what's this bad news?"

"It's something we can fix. You want to tell him about it, Kelsey?" Tomlinson said.

Both men fixed their attention on her, and she sat up straighter. "It's about the closed-circuit TV. I accessed it earlier this afternoon to play back—"

"What?" Jackson shot forward. "How did you get into the feed?"

"Any amateur hacker can access your IP address and detect your cameras. Why haven't you changed your username and password from the default?"

"I don't know, but I'll be finding out."

"Good. Because if I can google the serial model of the camera and find the default username and password, anyone can."

Jackson sat back in his chair.

"That may not be the worst part," she said.

"There's more?"

"Maybe. I haven't had time to check, but either the camera in the hallway leading to the vault malfunctioned or someone turned it off. I didn't take time to see how long it was off, but the timing corresponds to Mr. Rutherford's murder."

Jackson took out his phone and dialed a number. "Were there any malfunctions with any camera Saturday night?" He listened and grimaced. "Why was I not told?"

A minute later he ended the call. "Show me how you hacked into my cameras, and then let's change that password."

As Kelsey booted up her laptop she'd brought with her, she said, "Was there a malfunction?"

"The screen went blank, but the security officer monitoring the feed couldn't find a cause. Unfortunately, he didn't notice when the screen first went blank—evidently it happened when he took his dinner break at seven thirty and didn't have anyone cover for him. It was when he returned that he noticed the blank screen and was in the process of determining why when the feed mysteriously came back on at nine forty-five."

"And by then Mr. Rutherford's body had been found." Could Jackson's employee be involved? "Why didn't he mention this Saturday night?"

"In the excitement, it slipped his mind. He did say that they'd had trouble with this particular camera since it was installed and the company was sending an IT specialist this week."

"Do you know if that happens with any of the other cameras?"

"When we finish here, we'll interview the security officer and find out," Jackson said.

"So, you want me to stay on?"

"Definitely."

"Still using the conservator job as a cover?"

Jackson glanced at Tomlinson. "What do you think?"

"I need a conservator, and Kelsey might get more information from the employees if they don't know she's working with security."

"Then I wouldn't want anyone to see me with you when you talk to your security officer," Kelsey said. "But ask him to pull the records from the old cameras as well as the new ones. We'll check the dates of any malfunctions against the thefts."

"Done," Jackson said. He raked his fingers through his silver hair and then studied her for a minute. "Are you certain you want to continue on in this job? It could be dangerous."

Quitting wasn't an option with her. "Mr. Tomlinson and I have already discussed this. Any security job can be dangerous. Knew that when I applied for my license. That's why I'm an expert shot with a gun and know enough self-defense moves to protect myself."

It was hard to explain, but discovering the camera had possibly been tampered with whet her appetite for the investigation. The adrenaline pumping through her veins was the same high she got scaling a building. "Someone is stealing artifacts from the museum, and I intend to figure out how."

"All right—as long as you work with the police on this, we'll continue with the contract you had with Walter. And by the way, I only learned this morning when I went over the contract that you are actually the one testing our security systems as the Phantom Hawk."

She nodded, acknowledging his statement. It was a relief to know it was in writing somewhere.

"That's quite an accomplishment, but I don't want you going after Mr. Rutherford's murderer."

"Don't worry, I'll leave that up to the detective." Thank goodness that meant working with Reggie, not Brad.

12

Monday morning, Brad transitioned from Homicide to the Cold Case Unit in less than half an hour. He cleaned out his desk and threw out a few things. Everything else he arranged in the desk in his new office, then hung the photo of Tripod catching a Frisbee on the wall and walked across the hall to the conference room for orientation. That wouldn't take long, either. His lieutenant, David Raines, was a man of brief words unless there was a need for more.

He leaned back in his chair. It was good to sit at the conference table sharing stories and drinking strong coffee with Raines and Will Kincade, another cold case detective.

"I hear you had a rather interesting weekend," Lieutenant Raines said.

"You could say that. I was just telling Will earlier that between us, Reggie and I combed through 146 statements."

It hadn't been how he wanted to spend his Sunday afternoon and evening, especially after Elle showed up on his doorstep, but he hated to bail on Reggie. At least this time, she hadn't gotten upset with him because of his job. In the past, choosing to work over spending time with her was a bad move. Maybe she had changed her attitude about his job.

"Think you'll miss Homicide?" Will asked.

He took a sip of lukewarm coffee and set the cup down. "Sure, but I'm looking forward to investigating cold cases. There's something about being able to finally give families closure that appeals to me."

"I know what you mean," his friend replied.

Brad looked forward to working with Will again. They'd been friends since they were kids and had worked together in Homicide until David recruited his friend for the Cold Case Unit. They'd even worked together on Will's first cold case, which involved the death of Brad's sister.

"You both better be glad you're not in Burglary. Did you hear about their problem?" David asked.

Brad shot his boss a quizzical glance. "No. What?"

Will laughed. "I heard they're chasing a ghost who breaks into security systems."

"What are you talking about?" Brad hadn't heard anything about a hacker, which he assumed Will meant.

David leaned forward. "There's a cat burglar breaking into businesses and leaving his calling card. Something about being breached by the Phantom Hawk."

"You're kidding." He swallowed. The image of Kelsey climbing down the side of the Pink Palace popped into his mind. It wasn't possible . . . "You say it's a man?"

Will nodded. "Burglary is assuming it is. Outside of the movies, a female cat burglar is rare. Besides, I don't see a woman rappelling from the roof of a 400-foot building to get into an office on the thirty-fifth floor—that was the first break-in. Thursday night's was only a 160-foot building."

His friend hadn't seen Kelsey climbing down the drainpipe with the ease of an acrobat.

"I understand he's also hacking into the company's computers," Will said.

Tension increased in Brad's shoulders. Kelsey was into history and art *and* computers. But surely she wasn't this Phantom Hawk. He checked his watch and remembered he was supposed to see her at eleven this morning, and it was almost that time. He'd better call. Before he could excuse himself, there was a knock at the door, and Reggie entered.

"Don't mean to interrupt you, but I need to ask Brad a question," he said.

"Privately?" Brad asked. Reggie looked as though he'd never gone to bed last night.

"No, I just need to know if you have the interview with Kelsey Allen. I'm handing the case off to Rachel Sloan, and I need to include it with the others."

"It's not complete, but I'm leaving shortly to go by the Pink Palace and talk with her again," he said. "Why are you giving Rachel the case?"

Reggie blew out a tired breath. "The inspector moved me to a new murder. At one this morning, a man's body washed up at McKellar Lake. Finally got an ID on him two hours ago. Troy Hendrix. He worked in that building the Phantom Hawk broke into after hacking their security system and turning off the cameras."

"You're kidding," David said.

"Nope." Reggie shook his head. "And the odd thing is, his email had an automatic response saying he'd be out of town a few days, but nobody knew anything about him taking off. When I talked to his secretary, she said he missed an important meeting Friday."

Brad rubbed his jaw. "So the killer left the automatic response? He would have to know Hendrix's email password . . . or he hacked into it."

"Yep. Hacker plus burglar—if we can come up with the identity of the Phantom Hawk, I think we'll have our murderer." He turned to Brad. "Would you mind contacting Rachel? I have to get back to work."

"Sure thing. I'll even wrap up the interview for her."

After Reggie left, David gathered his papers. "You seem interested in this case."

Will laughed. "I don't think it's the case. According to Andi, he had a date with Kelsey Allen on Saturday night."

"Can't you and my sister find anything better to do than discuss my social life? I don't suppose she told you she helped set it up?" When Will shook his head, Brad said, "I didn't think so."

"Thing is, I don't get why you're jumping mad at a little teasing," Will said. "Maybe if you dated more, it wouldn't be such a big deal. And I sure don't understand why a looker like Kelsey Allen—"

"I'm not interested in Ms. Allen." Brad narrowed his eyes. He wasn't about to tell his friend he'd talked to Elle—it would go straight back to his sister, and he wasn't ready to answer her questions.

Brushing the thoughts away, he turned to David. "Is there any particular cold case you want me to start with?"

The lieutenant nodded toward the inside door. "You can have your choice of cases. I think there are over a thousand files in the storage room."

"Alphabetical order?" He'd promised Kelsey he'd look into her father's case, and if he could tell her he'd pulled the file, she might be more willing to work with him.

"I wish. They're arranged according to the year the crime occurred. Do you have a particular case in mind?"

"A man disappeared twenty-eight years ago, and I halfway promised the family I'd look into it." But first he needed to call Kelsey and tell her it would be closer to noon before he got to the museum.

Thirty minutes later, he decided Paul Carter's case was not in the cold case files. He'd found the year the file should be in, but so far, nothing. Then he spied a box without a date and pulled it down from the shelf. At least it was the right year, and he thumbed through the files. Nothing under Cs. Brad kept looking and found it under the Ps and slid it out.

He set an alarm on his watch for fifteen minutes, then took the thin folder to the conference room and pulled up a chair for a quick look before he drove to the museum. First he checked to see who investigated the crime, recognizing the name of a retired sergeant with a reputation for being thorough. Good. That would save time.

Sergeant Warren's report was concise, painting a circumstantial case for Paul Carter stealing artifacts from the museum and attempting to sell them to the highest bidder and then hightailing it out of town before the thefts were discovered.

Brad scanned the names of people interviewed for the report and wondered how many of them were still living. Maybe Kelsey knew some of them. He recognized a few—many of them he'd seen Saturday night. Like Sam and Cynthia and Grant Allen. Sam and Grant would have been in their late twenties or early thirties. A note in parentheses stated Sam and Cynthia married six months after Carter skipped town. Another note on the next page indicated Sam was on the museum's board of trustees. That was odd. Board members usually rotated off after a few years. Maybe he'd rotated off and then came back on.

Jackson King was on the list. He leaned back in the chair. Twenty-eight years ago, he would have only been eighteen or nineteen. Why was he interviewed in the first place? A quick scan down the page revealed another note on him—he had worked as a summer intern at Coon Creek in McNairy County, but the year Carter disappeared, he'd worked at the museum in the Pink Palace. The alarm he'd set on his phone buzzed, and he closed the file and hurried to the elevator. This looked to be an intriguing case.

Brad exited the parking garage on Washington Avenue and wove his way through Midtown to Central Avenue. Midtown was his favorite section of Memphis, with its grand old homes and businesses that had been around since the early 1900s. But none of the homes rivaled his destination. When he turned into the drive leading to the museum, he admired what undoubtedly would have been the largest residential home in Memphis at the time if Clarence Saunders hadn't lost it in a financial crisis. But Saunders's loss had been the city's gain.

He parked in the employee lot and walked to the back entrance. Judging by the three school buses parked next to the curb, someone was having a field day, and he bet it wasn't the teachers. At the sign-in window, Detective Rachel Sloan stood talking to one of the security officers, and she motioned that she wanted to see him.

After he signed in, he texted Kelsey that he was in the building, and she replied that she would be in the sandwich shop on the first floor.

Rachel stepped out into the hallway, and he put his phone away. The detective had recently been transferred to Homicide from Burglary, and Brad admired her investigative skills.

"What are you doing here? This is my investigation."

He didn't admire the chip on her shoulder, but he understood it. With some members of the Homicide team, female detectives constantly had to prove themselves. This was particularly true of Rachel since she hadn't made sergeant yet. Brad thought she knew he wasn't one of them. "Finishing up what I started Saturday night."

"Which is?"

"Getting Kelsey Allen's statement."

"Give me what you have, and I'll take care of it."

"Do you mind if I do it?" He kept his voice neutral.

"Why?"

"Kelsey doesn't warm up to people very quickly. And I have a history with her."

Rachel looked down at her notes, then back up at him. "According to Reggie's notes, your history may be why you didn't get her statement Saturday night."

Heat burned his neck. "I need to see Kelsey about something else as well."

"Why don't we go together? I'll get her statement, then you can discuss the something else."

Brad swallowed his objection. It was Rachel's case, after all. "She's in the sandwich shop."

13

THE BELLA CAFFE SURPRISED KELSEY. She'd had no idea the museum even had a coffee and sandwich shop when the very pregnant conservator offered to buy her lunch after a busy morning. And she'd been quite glad when Brad texted that he would be late.

"You didn't have to do this," Kelsey said.

"It's the least I can do, leaving you high and dry like this," Erin Dolan said.

"Don't worry about it. If the doctor says you have to be off your feet for the next six weeks, then that's what you have to do."

"He didn't even want me to come back to the museum today. I had to promise him and my husband, who will be picking me up shortly, that I wouldn't lift so much as a pencil. But I just couldn't leave without showing you a few more things."

"No worries," Kelsey said. "I worked as a conservator for years, so I know what to do."

Erin was about to say more when the waitress brought their lunches, and they concentrated on eating the tangy chicken salad. When she finished, the conservator brushed some crumbs from her chin and leaned back in her chair. "I had so hoped to work on the circus with you."

"There will be plenty for you to work on after the baby is born," Kelsey said. The restoration of Clyde Parke's replica of a big top circus would take a few years to finish. "Did you ever see it in action?"

"No. Did you?"

"When I was a little girl." It was one of the attractions Kelsey had been fascinated with as a child. The circus was animated by a series of pulleys and belts, and if she closed her eyes, she could still see the horse-drawn wagons and the bareback rider balancing on a dapple horse that circled around and around.

Erin's face brightened. "Maybe I can work on some of the pieces at home. Help pass the time."

Kelsey nodded. "I can box up a few pieces and bring them by your house."

"I don't know where Mr. Tomlinson found you," the conservator said, "but you are a godsend."

Kelsey waved her off. "Tell me something. Someone said that a rare stamp was stolen Saturday night when Mr. Rutherford was killed. Do you know if any other things are missing?"

Erin sipped her water. "You've heard about that already?"

She nodded, hoping she hadn't pushed for information too quickly. "Can't remember exactly who said anything, but I think it was at the fundraiser after his body was found."

Prodding her newfound friend to gossip made her feel guilty, but today was her only chance to ask Erin about the thefts. It was too bad she wasn't keeping this job. She would enjoy having the chance to know Erin better . . . but she wasn't. This was the first of what Kelsey hoped would be many security jobs.

"Oh yes, I can see how his murder might make people's tongues looser. The thing is, a few artifacts have gone missing over a period of time, but I figured they were simply misplaced." She studied her fingernails. "That was before Saturday night. That stamp wasn't misplaced. And poor Mr. Rutherford must have caught the person in the act."

Kelsey glanced toward the doorway. "The way security is around here, I don't see how anyone could even get into the vault. You have to have a key and a code."

"I've wondered if it's someone in security," Erin said. "There are three keys that fit all the locks. Mr. Rutherford had one and so does Mark Tomlinson, but he never lets his out of his sight. He never even lets anyone in his office. Oh, and Robert Tomlinson has one. But as far as I know, he's never used his key—he always relies on his brother." She leaned forward. "Mark seems like a grouch, but I think it's because he has so much responsibility on his shoulders. There are seven brothers in that family, and Mark is the oldest and takes care of their frail mother. Robert is the youngest, and Mark even helped to put him through college. He's always looking out for him."

Her phone beeped with a text, and Erin glanced at it. "My husband is here. Thanks again so much."

Erin was full of information, and not just about the museum. Kelsey leaned back in the chair and sipped her peach tea. The chicken salad had been delicious, and she certainly hadn't expected to find peach tea. Both had refreshed her after an overwhelming morning with Erin showing Kelsey around before and after her doctor's appointment, and the collections director filling in while she was gone. Right now, it seemed the restoration of the circus was the primary focus, and it was a huge undertaking.

She was prepared for the task, though. The three years she'd spent restoring Native American artifacts at her last job would come in handy here. Her cell phone rang, and Erin's number showed on her caller ID.

"Did you forget something?" she asked just as Brad and a woman she didn't recognize entered the sandwich shop. A cop, judging by her serious face and the gun attached to her side.

"Yes. I don't know where my mind is. While you were filling out your paperwork, the shipping department brought up a crate from Coon Creek."

"Coon Creek . . . what is that?"

"The science center—you haven't heard of it? It's this big, important fossil site."

Kelsey laughed. "I restore art, not fossils."

"Well, you'll be dealing with a few fossils too. The archaeological site is connected to the museum, and they send important finds from time to time that you'll have to catalog. I wasn't expecting anything and have no idea what they've sent."

"Got it," she said as Brad and the woman approached. "Uh, Erin, can I get back with you? I have visitors." She disconnected and nodded to Brad, then to the woman.

"Good morning," he said.

"Afternoon."

Brad looked good in his white shirt and navy pants. The woman detective had opted for a red blouse and khakis and was all business.

He checked his watch. "Give or take thirty minutes." He gave her a small smile before he nodded to the other cop.

"Kelsey Allen, Detective Rachel Sloan. She's investigating the Rutherford murder."

"Why don't you sit down?" Kelsey said, indicating the two empty chairs at the table.

Once they were seated, Detective Sloan took out a notebook and pen. "I'd like to get your statement," she said.

"What happened to the other detective?" Kelsey had liked him. This one looked like a hard case.

"He's investigating another case, one involving a break-in at a building next to your stepfather's auto parts company."

Even before Sloan shot Brad a questioning glare for answering, Kelsey felt her face go icy cold. Did they know she was the Phantom? When she could finally talk, she kept her voice low and said, "I hadn't heard of a murder there, just a break-in."

Maybe she should tell Brad what happened Thursday night. Her stomach roiled. Maybe she should have told him Saturday night. If she admitted it now—

"What made you say *murder*?" Sloan asked.

Still looking at Brad, Kelsey lifted a shoulder. "Lieutenant Lane is a homicide detective. Who was murdered?"

"Troy Hendrix," Brad said. "He had an office on the eleventh floor."

Brad clearly expected something from her, but only one thing ran through her mind. If anyone discovered she was the Phantom Hawk, she'd be connected to not one murder but two. She furrowed her brow, Thursday night's activities flashing through her mind. She looked up and saw he was still waiting. "Don't know him."

Detective Sloan opened her notebook. "Then let's get to my murder case. The notes indicate Rutherford hired you to investigate thefts occurring at the museum. Is that correct?"

Kelsey glanced around, hoping no one could overhear Sloan's questions. The nearest person was two tables away. "I'm working undercover," she said, keeping her voice low, "and I'd appreciate it if you wouldn't give me away."

"Why did he hire you?"

"He wanted me to test the security system at the museum." It seemed she was repeating that sentence every time she turned around, but at least Sloan had lowered her voice. When she appeared to be waiting for more, Kelsey continued. "Someone is stealing artifacts from the museum's storage area, and with the arrival of an Egyptian death mask soon, Mr. Rutherford feared the mask might be too great a temptation for the thief to pass up. He thought someone undercover might discover his identity."

"That still doesn't tell me why he hired *you*. You're a conservator for a museum."

How was she going to explain without inviting more questions? "During my last job, I worked with a security specialist who set up the Jackson museum's new security system, and I seem to have an aptitude for it. When I returned home, I checked out the security system at my stepfather's business and discovered it wasn't very secure. He told Mr. Rutherford what I'd found, and he hired me."

"How exactly did you hack into their system?"

Kelsey didn't like what she heard in Brad's voice. Suspicion. And it looked as though she wouldn't get out of revealing her trade secrets. "I didn't have to. I made a few calls, asked a few questions, and got the information I needed to get into the system." She eyed him coolly. "Needless to say, since then, the employees have been properly trained not to give out that type of information again."

Kelsey glanced at Brad, and he seemed to be struggling

with something. Probably trying to decide whether to tell Detective Sloan he'd caught Kelsey climbing down the side of the museum.

"Did you test the security system Saturday night?" Sloan asked.

"Yes. After Brad left, I changed clothes and explored the area where the artifacts are stored."

Sloan lifted her pen from the notebook. "Why did you change clothes?"

"Kind of hard to climb a wall in stilettos and a dress."

Understanding flashed across the detective's face. "That's right, you climbed the side of the building to get in. I understand you were there just before the body was discovered. Did you hear or see anything?"

So that wasn't what was bothering Brad. She focused on the question. "The music from the ballroom was too loud."

Sloan put away her pen and notebook and handed Kelsey a card. "I may check back with you after I view the murder scene, but if you think of anything you'd like to add, call me."

Brad stood as well. "I'm going to grab a sandwich. Can I get you one?"

Sloan shook her head. "I'm not hungry."

Kelsey had hoped Brad would accompany the detective. Something seemed to be eating at him, and she figured it wouldn't be long before she discovered what as he marched back to the table after placing his order, his jaw set and shoulders square.

"I assume my statement is finished since you don't work in Homicide any longer," she said.

"Not quite. I have a few questions of my own."

She concentrated on her almost-empty glass of tea, trying to prepare herself for his questions.

"Are you the Phantom Hawk?"

For the second time today, he'd stunned her into silence. She forced the muscles in her face to relax. Widening her eyes, she said, "What are you talking about?"

"Don't play coy with me." He held up a hand. "I caught you coming down the side of the building like it's something you do every day, and you hack into computer systems. I—"

"Your order is coming," she said.

He clamped his mouth shut until the waitress left. "I want an answer."

She looked past him. "You may have to wait. Detective Sloan is back, and she doesn't look too happy."

The detective stopped in front of Kelsey, her hand resting on the gun at her side.

"Ms. Allen, I'd like you to come down to the CJC and answer a few questions."

14

Brad stared at the detective. What had happened in the last ten minutes? He glanced at Kelsey. Her green eyes had darkened almost to black. "What's going on?" he asked.

"Answer questions about what?" Kelsey said.

Rachel Sloan ignored Brad, keeping her focus on Kelsey. "Something has come to light that I'd prefer to discuss downtown."

Kelsey's only reaction was a slight flinch, and then she lifted her chin. "Am I under arrest?"

"No." Rachel's stance relaxed slightly, but her voice held a *not yet* in it.

"Then I can drive my own car to the Criminal Justice Center? And I can leave at any time?"

Rachel hesitated and then nodded. "Would you mind coming right now?"

"Let me tell someone I have to go out for an hour." She stood. "It won't take over an hour, will it?"

"Shouldn't. I'll wait and you can follow me."

He rose as Kelsey walked out of the coffee shop with her

shoulders straight, and then he wheeled on Rachel. "What's going on?"

"Reggie called. An anonymous tip came in saying Kelsey Allen is the Phantom Hawk."

Anonymous tips usually didn't get this type of response. Unless there was something to back them up. "Proof?"

She nodded. "A photo that may or may not be Ms. Allen."

No. He clenched his jaw. If she was the cat burglar . . . just when he thought Kelsey was different, it turned out she was just like Elle, knowing all that time she hated his being a cop. Both were deceptive.

Rachel hesitated. "You seem more than a little defensive of her. It's my turn to ask what's going on."

He skittered his gaze past her. Rachel was a lot like him, seeing most things as black or white with very little gray area. "We went to high school together, and I just don't see her doing something like this."

"That was a lot of years ago," Rachel said. "People change."

"But why would she? Not for the money—you know who her dad is, right?"

"I know who her stepdad is—Sam Allen." She placed her hand on his arm. "Look, she didn't deny it."

"She was in shock." He didn't quite understand why he was defending Kelsey. Except he'd seen a vulnerable side to her Saturday night, one that told him she would never hurt anyone. But if she was this burglar, she'd probably conned him.

"I'm ready," Kelsey said from the doorway.

Brad hadn't heard her return. He searched her face, looking for signs of fear, and he hated to admit, guilt. He saw neither. What he saw was a spunky blonde with spiked hair ready to take on the world.

"I told my supervisor I'd be back in an hour. I also called my stepfather. He's meeting us downtown."

"That's fine. Thank you for telling me," Rachel said.

Brad followed them out of the building and waited by his car while Kelsey walked past the three school buses to where her car was parked near the street. As he unlocked his car, what sounded like a handclap froze his hand on the key fob. He instantly knew the *thwack* wasn't a handclap. *Who's firing a gun with a silencer?*

He pulled his automatic while scanning the parking lot for Kelsey and Rachel.

Rachel crouched beside her car with her gun in one hand and her phone in the other. Calling for backup, he imagined. *Where is Kelsey?* He scanned past the yellow buses to where he'd last seen her. There she was, behind an oak tree.

Another *thwack*, and bark splintered off the tree Kelsey was huddled behind. He looked to his left, the direction the bullets came from, but he couldn't pinpoint the shooter's location. He crept back to his car trunk to get his body armor. By the time he had it on, sirens were blaring on the next block.

"I think he's gone," Rachel yelled.

He scanned the area, seeing no evidence of anyone. Still he waited. Then tires squealed on the street behind the parking lot. He glanced at Rachel. She'd heard it as well and was talking on the phone again.

Still holding his gun, Brad eased around the car as two patrol units barreled into the parking lot. He hurried to help Kelsey. Color had drained from her face. "You okay?" He helped her to stand.

"No, I'm not okay—someone just tried to kill me!" Her voice quaked and she hugged her arms to her body as she scanned the area.

Rachel ran to them. "Why would anyone shoot at you?"

"I don't know," Kelsey said as security personnel came toward them. "Maybe it's whoever killed Rutherford and he thinks I saw him Saturday night. Or saw something that might identify him."

He followed her gaze to the school buses, and her breath hitched.

"What if the children had been out here?" she whispered.

"Seems convenient that this happened just as we're leaving for the CJC," Rachel said. "You called your stepfather. Did you call anyone else?"

Beside him, Kelsey stiffened. "Of course I didn't."

Rachel grunted and nodded to Brad. "See to it that she gets downtown. I'll be there as soon as I can."

"Wait," Kelsey said as the detective turned to leave. "You make it sound like I'm under arrest."

Rachel studied her. "Well, you're not."

"What if I don't want to go downtown now?"

The detective shrugged and glanced toward the people standing in the doorway. "We'll take your statement here with all your colleagues watching."

Kelsey shifted her gaze toward the employee entrance. She seemed to fold in on herself, probably because the adrenaline rush had faded. Brad itched to put his arm around her shoulders. Instead, he said, "Why don't you ride downtown with me. I'll bring you back here afterward."

She nodded her consent. "Should I say anything to the security people?"

He looked over at Rachel, who had walked toward the employee entrance. "Let Detective Sloan handle that right now."

"I'd rather she didn't tell anyone the shots were fired at me."

He gave her a reassuring smile. "She won't. That's 'I'll

tell you when you need to know' information, and I'm pretty sure she doesn't think they need to know."

His wordplay brought a tiny smile to Kelsey's face.

"Thanks," she said.

He opened the passenger door for her and waited until she fastened her seat belt before he hurried around to the driver's side.

She glanced at Rachel as they drove away. "Why did she imply I called someone other than my stepdad?"

"It's the way cops think." Why wasn't Kelsey asking the more obvious question—why did Rachel think she was the Phantom Hawk? "She's fair, though, and she's not the kind to railroad you."

"I'm not sure I agree. Do you think I set it up?"

He didn't want to believe that. "I—"

"Never mind," she snapped. "It's obvious you do."

"Kelsey—"

"Do you mind if we don't talk? I'd like to get my brain settled before I'm *interrogated*."

15

Kelsey practiced yoga breathing as they walked from the parking garage, past the round brick structure with "Shelby County Justice Center" on it to the tan building. *Breathe in through the nose, out through the nose.* Didn't help.

The numbing iciness around her lips stayed even as her heart concentrated on getting blood to her legs so she could walk. Kelsey paused at the entrance, and the austere CJC loomed above her. What if Sloan didn't believe her? She squared her shoulders. She'd done nothing wrong. But what would happen if she had to tell them she was the Phantom Hawk? So far she'd danced around answering the question. Maybe it was time to tell them. And that would blow her cover.

She jumped when Brad put his hand just above her elbow as they entered the building and he guided her past the security at the door.

"I'm not going to run away," she said.

"Didn't think you were," he said as he showed the guard his badge. "I'll sign us in."

After they signed in, she pinned her visitor badge on before they walked to the elevator. Several people crowded in with them, and Brad punched the button for the eleventh floor. Normally elevators didn't bother her, but today her senses were on high alert. She took a step back to get away from the overpowering perfume of the woman in front of her and bumped against the wall. No more yoga breathing as her head thumped with the beginnings of a headache.

When they stepped out of the elevator, she sucked in a deep breath of perfume-free air.

"Rachel's desk is in here," he said and took her arm again.

His touch, like his voice, was gentler this time and warmed her heart, then she caught herself and steeled against the reaction. Brad was a cop, just like Rachel Sloan. And he had practically admitted on the drive downtown that he believed she was a criminal.

Kelsey caught her breath. Why had she told him about her dad? That was the reason for the suspicion in Brad's eyes. Had he found her father's file and assumed she was a thief just like he was? They rounded the corner, and her legs faltered when she saw *Homicide* over the archway. She searched for Sam. Where was he? A woman in a business suit glanced at them and stood.

"Kelsey," she called. "Sam sent me to meet you."

Tension released from her body as she recognized Madeline Starr. "Maggie?"

Sam had come through for her by sending the best defense attorney in Memphis. She scanned the room again. "Where's Sam?"

"He can't make it, so he sent me." Maggie glanced past her and smiled. "Good to see you again, Brad."

"You too, Maggie."

Kelsey shifted her gaze from one to the other. Was it a

good thing for her defense attorney to be on a first-name basis with someone who might want to arrest her? "You two know each other?"

"He helped save my life earlier this year," Maggie said. "Now, who wants to tell me what this is all about?"

A shadow crossed Brad's face, and he cleared his throat. "Detective Rachel Sloan has a few questions she'd like to ask Kelsey and thought the CJC would be more appropriate than the Pink Palace. Sloan was delayed, but she should be here soon."

Maggie raised her eyebrows. "Then I would like to confer with my client before the detective arrives."

"Let me see if I can find an empty conference room."

As Brad walked away, Maggie turned to her.

"Let me do the talking when Detective Sloan arrives. Don't volunteer anything, and if she asks a question, let me decide if you need to answer. Afterwards we'll go to my office and discuss your situation in detail."

"Gladly, but I have to get back to the museum—it's my first day, and I told my supervisor I'd be back in an hour."

"How did you get here?"

"Brad drove me."

"I'll take you back and we'll talk on the way."

"This way, ladies," Brad said, motioning them to a side room. "I'll let you know when the detective arrives."

Maggie shut the door behind him and sat opposite Kelsey. "The only thing Sam told me when he called was that you were being brought to the CJC, so tell me what's going on."

She didn't know where to start or how much she wanted to tell the lawyer. But lawyers had to keep what their clients told them confidential . . . right? But was she really Madeline Starr's client? "Are you my lawyer?"

She nodded. "Unless you prefer someone else."

"No! I just wanted to make that clear."

"Good. Sam said he'd take care of any other details."

Meaning financial. "Don't bother him. I have money saved. I don't want what we discuss relayed to my stepfather, either."

"He's not my client, you are, and I only discuss details with whomever you approve," she said. "And we'll talk about money later. Like I said before, we don't have much time. Tell me what to expect from the detective."

Kelsey tried to arrange the events in her mind and decided to start at the end and work backward. "She believes I called and had someone fire at us as we were leaving the museum. And she hasn't said it, but she thinks I killed Mr. Rutherford and maybe that Hendrix guy they found in McKellar Lake this morning."

"Whoa!" Maggie shook her head as if to clear it, then she pressed her lips together. "Did she read you your rights?"

"No."

"Good. At this point, you're not really a suspect."

Kelsey grunted. She'd hate to see how suspects were treated. Quickly, she filled Maggie in on what happened Saturday night. "I'm not sure why she wanted me to come downtown, unless it has to do with what happened at the Pink Palace this weekend."

She turned her head at a knock on the door.

"Come in," Maggie said.

The door opened, and Brad and Detective Sloan entered the room. Sloan didn't look too happy. "Ms. Allen doesn't need legal services," she said.

"Sam Allen phoned me when his daughter called, upset that she was being required to come to the CJC." Maggie moved to the same side of the table next to Kelsey.

"I'm sorry if I gave her that impression. I have some questions that need answers and thought here would be better than her place of employment." Sloan sat opposite them and placed an electronic tablet on the table before she glanced up at Brad. "Did you intend to stay?"

"If you don't mind." When she nodded, he took a seat at the end of the table.

Kelsey leaned forward. Best way to face something was head-on. "Before we get started, may I ask something first?"

Sloan shifted in her chair. "I'm the only one asking questions here."

"Then you won't get any answers from me today." She looked at Maggie and scooted her chair back. "I think it's time to leave."

It only took the detective a second to realize her interview was over before it had started.

Sloan raised her hand. "Hold up. What do you want to know?"

"Do you think I had someone shoot at us?"

"No." The detective said. "And if it sounded like I was implying that, I apologize. I was upset with myself that you were almost killed, and I'm by nature a suspicious person."

Maggie folded her arms. "So you no longer believe Ms. Allen is responsible for the shooting."

"Let's just say I'm reserving judgment." She turned to Kelsey. "Can you tell me where you were Thursday night?"

Kelsey stilled, her mind too stunned to come up with an answer.

"Thursday night?" Maggie said. "I thought she was here to give a statement about what she may have seen Saturday night."

Detective Sloan tapped on her tablet. "I have reason to believe your client is the Phantom Hawk. While this photo isn't sharp, there's enough detail to make out Ms. Allen's face."

Kelsey let Maggie take the tablet from Sloan so no one could see how badly her fingers were shaking. Brad stood and walked to where he could see it as well. When Kelsey saw the photo, her heart almost stopped. It was a photo of her scaling a building, and judging from the Allen Brothers sign in the background, it was the building she'd broken into Thursday night.

"The photo is so grainy, it's difficult to accurately identify the person," Maggie said. "Where did it come from?"

"In an email from an anonymous source," Sloan said. "And before you ask, we couldn't trace where it originated."

Kelsey leaned over her lawyer's arm and studied the photo. Something about it was wrong . . . Then she saw it. The coiled rope on her shoulder that was barely visible. She had not used the rope Thursday. She'd used the winch. Kelsey went over the photo again. The beanie cap—she'd bought it Saturday afternoon when she couldn't find the one she'd worn earlier in the week.

The photo hadn't been taken Thursday. Somehow that didn't make her feel any better. Only two people could have taken a picture of her Saturday night. Brad, except the angle was wrong for him, and Rutherford's murderer.

But how?

The noise she'd heard on the steps . . . Her stomach plummeted. He'd been in the vault . . . and somehow managed to get a photo of her climbing down the pipe. There'd only been one spot with enough light to capture a photo—by the lighted window. But did he have enough time to walk from the vault to the window in the hallway while she was escaping through the roof?

Kelsey looked up. "I admit it's me, but it's been photo-shopped."

Sloan grabbed the tablet. "What are you talking about?"

"The cap." She looked up at Brad. "You saw it Saturday night. I had only bought it that afternoon. Hold on a minute," she said and rummaged through her purse until she found the receipt.

"Here," she said and handed the thin slip of paper to the detective.

"I'd like a copy of that," Maggie said. "And of the photo."

"I bet if you have an expert examine the photo," Kelsey said, "you'll discover I've been cut and pasted into this photo. Might even find a touch of the Pink Palace's Georgian pink marble that he probably missed. This was taken Saturday night when I was testing the security at the museum."

"Are you saying the two murders are linked?" Rachel asked.

"I don't know about that. All I know is this photo was taken Saturday night, not Thursday night."

"Why would someone try to set you up as the Phantom Hawk?" Brad asked.

Maggie stood. "I need to confer with my client before this goes any further, and she needs to go back to work. How about we continue this in my office tomorrow morning at nine?"

Kelsey had almost blurted out the truth—that Hendrix's murderer feared she'd seen him. A man had died, and she couldn't keep silent any longer. But Maggie was right. Her attorney needed to know the whole story, and then whatever she advised, Kelsey would do.

◆

Brad was disappointed when Kelsey left with Maggie to return to the museum. He'd wanted a chance to talk to her.

He picked up Rachel's tablet and studied the photo again. The cap in the photo looked like the same one he'd seen Saturday night.

"Do you think the two murders are linked?" Rachel asked.

"If this photo is to be believed, they must be. And either Kelsey killed both men or the true murderer is trying to make it look as though she's the Phantom Hawk and pin the murders on her."

"There's no doubt in my mind that Kelsey Allen is hiding something," Rachel said, taking the tablet he handed her. She stared at the photo a second, then pinned him with a frown. "Either she knows who the cat burglar is or Kelsey Allen *is* the Phantom Hawk. I'm inclined to believe the latter."

"I don't know." Except, he'd seen the fear in Kelsey's eyes when she saw the photo. "I don't think I've ever run into a female cat burglar. Or even heard of one outside of books and films. Most women aren't strong enough."

"Your notes said she was a rock-climber," Rachel said. "That would account for upper body strength."

"Maybe." Kelsey had said she loved rock-climbing, and she'd come down the side of the Pink Palace like it was something she did all the time.

"If she is the Phantom Hawk, it doesn't necessarily follow that she killed the two men," Rachel said. "But she may have seen something."

"Assuming she's the cat burglar, could be that the murderer saw her."

She nodded. "And saw her again Saturday night, but he could only know she was the cat burglar if he was present both nights."

Brad drummed the table, thinking. And he didn't like what came to mind. "Or Hendrix's killer saw the Phantom Hawk

Thursday night or read about the cat burglar and decided to pin the murder on him—or her. But to get this photo, he had to be at the museum Saturday night . . ."

"If he was there Saturday night, it was to steal the stamp," Rachel said.

"And Rutherford got in the way." He groaned.

"What?"

"If Kelsey is this Phantom Hawk, and the killer saw her Thursday night, it would explain the shooting when she left the museum with us."

She nodded. "He may be afraid she can identify him, so he's not trying to pin the murders on her. But how did he know that she was leaving? Unless he overheard her tell someone."

16

THIS TIME IT WAS THE ODOR of lemon cleaning solution that stung Kelsey's nose as the elevator doors closed. She kept her gaze pointed at her shoes on the ride to the first floor.

"I'm parked in the garage on Washington," Maggie said as they exited the elevator.

Kelsey nodded. She knew better than to discuss the case until they were out of the CJC. Once they turned in their badges and signed out, she breathed a little easier.

Maggie held the door open for her. "Are you all right?"

"I've been better." Kelsey couldn't believe she was actually looking forward to telling Maggie everything, but the attorney would know what to do.

In Maggie's car, Kelsey fastened her seat belt. "I didn't kill either of those men."

"I didn't think you did. Why don't you start at the beginning and tell me everything that's happened since Saturday night?"

"I'm afraid I need to start with Thursday night." She looked to see Maggie's reaction. Evidently nothing fazed the attorney.

"Go ahead, I'm listening."

As they drove to the museum, Kelsey fingered the smooth nylon seat belt as she told Maggie the whole story, going back to when she climbed down the first building and entered through an unlocked window.

Maggie was quiet for a minute as she navigated traffic. "How many people know you're the Phantom Hawk?" she asked, turning onto Central.

She didn't want to bring Sabra and Sam into this mess, but it was unavoidable. "My sister, Sabra. Robert Tomlinson and Jackson King. And Sam knows."

"Anyone else?"

She needed to be honest with her attorney. "Only a few friends in a chat room, but I don't know their names."

"Do you use the Phantom Hawk as your identity?"

"Yeah. But no one knows my real name. None of them live here, and the Phantom Hawk hasn't made national headlines."

"Okay." Maggie turned into the long drive and circled around to the employee entrance to the Pink Palace. "Stay out of the chat room until this is over."

That wouldn't be a problem. "Any other concerns?"

Maggie didn't answer right away as she put the car in park. She turned to her. "You have bigger problems than informing the authorities that you're the Phantom Hawk. From what you've said, it appears the same person committed the two murders. Since he saw you Thursday night, he figures you saw him as well and can identify him."

"But I couldn't. He was nothing but a silhouette."

"He doesn't know that. That's why he fired at you today. If you're dead, you can't defend yourself against the evidence he's planting. Did you leave your calling card Saturday night?"

Kelsey gasped. "I forgot to tell you about that. I did leave a card on the desk. After we found Mr. Rutherford's body, I looked for it, but it was gone." Her heart thudded against her chest. "The murderer was still in the vault, and he found the card after I left. When he took my photo . . ." she said, her voice cracking.

Maggie finished for her. "He must have recognized you—or at least recognized that you were the same person climbing the building Thursday night."

The shots this afternoon had definitely been aimed at her, and not at Brad or Sloan. But even worse, it was someone who knew her well enough to know she'd be at the museum today . . . and what time she'd be leaving. She jerked her head toward the line of trees where he'd fired from earlier, searching for any sign of another attack.

"I'm going to talk to Sam about hiring a bodyguard for you."

Kelsey nodded. "I'm almost afraid to ask what else you're worried about."

"That he's trying to frame the Phantom Hawk—you—for the two murders."

She glanced toward the door. "I need time to process all of this. Can we continue this discussion in your office this afternoon? I think I can sign out at four without raising eyebrows."

"Sure. See you around four thirty, but in the meantime, don't discuss this with anyone."

◆

Brad scanned the list of missing artifacts that Robert Tomlinson had faxed over. The most unique one was the shrunken head. He laid the paper on his desk. He just couldn't get Kelsey off his mind.

No one had to tell him that she was in danger, and she didn't trust him. Investigating her father's disappearance might be the key to getting her trust. He settled in behind his desk and ran a computer search for Carter's social security number. He came up empty, which didn't surprise him. Carter would have obtained a new social security number. He opened the file again and skimmed through each page, stopping when he came to Sergeant Warren's background notes.

Paul Carter had earned his PhD in Egyptology at the University of Pennsylvania and taught archaeology at what was then Memphis State University. It was there that he met and married Kelsey's mother, Cynthia. After that, they both worked at the Giza Pyramid Plateau in Egypt in late 1979 and early 1980.

According to the notes, Cynthia returned to the States when she became pregnant, and a year after Kelsey was born, Carter returned to take over as director of the Pink Palace Museum. It looked like they divorced when Kelsey was three, and she was seven when her mother remarried shortly after Carter disappeared.

"What if he didn't steal the artifacts?" Brad said softly. He flipped back to the investigation notes to see if Warren had checked Sam Allen's alibi. He frowned. No mention of even asking. Once the thefts came to light, either Warren totally bought the supposition that Carter had stolen the artifacts and fled, or he'd asked and Allen's alibi had been strong and Warren hadn't recorded it.

Brad picked up his phone and dialed Human Resources for Warren's contact information. While he waited for the clerk to return his call with the information, he made copies of the file to take with him. A few minutes after he finished, the call came in. Sergeant Harvey Warren had a broken leg and was currently a temporary resident at the Country Manor Nursing Home.

Country Manor was in East Memphis. He checked his watch: one thirty. If the interview with Warren took an hour, which he doubted it would, he could swing by the Pink Palace and talk to Kelsey on his way back to the office. The backflip his heart did when he thought about seeing Kelsey startled him, and he quickly dismissed it.

She was a person of interest in two murders and the Phantom Hawk cases. Not that he believed for one second that she'd committed either of the murders, but as for the other, if she was the cat burglar, she was playing a game of deception and all the more reason to guard his heart.

She hadn't stolen anything. Immaterial. Elle had been less than honest with him, and he wasn't going that route again. Or was he? Maybe Elle wasn't the person to compare Kelsey with since she'd admitted she was wrong. His cell rang and he glanced at the ID. *Elle?* "Hello?" he said.

"Good. You're not tied up."

"I'm on my way across town to interview someone."

"This won't take a second. I thought I'd make dinner for us tomorrow night."

She was wasting no time. "I don't know. Can't tell you what time I'll finish up tomorrow."

"But aren't you working on old cases now? I thought that was a nine-to-five job."

"It is still an investigation, and things come up."

"Of course." Silence stretched between them. "Instead of my place, why don't I make dinner at your house? I have work I can do on my computer until you get home."

Elle was trying, he'd have to give her that. "That sounds good," he said.

"Is your key still where it was before?"

She remembered. "Yes. On a nail in the garage."

"Good. Tomorrow night, I'll just let myself in and have dinner ready for you when you get home."

Brad disconnected. Elle making dinner for him should have him over the moon. He tapped the steering wheel. It was worrying about this case—that was the problem. And when it was over, he could focus on their relationship.

That settled, he turned his attention to the interview with Sergeant Warren, and twenty minutes later he turned into the nursing home drive. An aide helped him find the right room, telling him that Harvey Warren's roommate had been transported to the hospital for tests. The sergeant was sitting up in bed and hadn't changed much in his retirement—still had a full head of white hair and appeared to be trim. Brad showed his gold badge and said, "Sergeant Warren, you probably don't remember me, but I'm Brad Hollister."

Creases formed above his blue eyes, and then recognition smoothed his brow. "I do remember you. Have a seat and tell me what a homicide detective wants with an old coot like me."

The sergeant hadn't lost his sense of humor. "Actually, I've transferred to the Cold Case Unit, and I'd like to ask a few questions about one of your cases."

Interest lit his face. "Which one?"

"The Paul Carter case." When he didn't seem to recognize the name, Brad added, "After his disappearance twenty-eight years ago, artifacts were discovered missing from the Pink Palace."

"That *is* a cold case. Carter . . . Pink Palace . . ." He rubbed his neck. "I transferred from Robbery about that time . . ." He looked up. "Do you have the file?"

Brad had hoped he might remember it without the file, that for some reason it had stood out in his mind. He handed him the folder and sat in the chair by the bed while Warren read the first page.

Nodding, he turned to the second page. "I remember this now. Seemed like it was pretty straightforward. I was investigating Carter's disappearance when missing artifacts came to light. The man just dropped out of sight. I concluded that he stole the artifacts and then relocated."

"I saw that, but can you remember any details that might not be in your report?"

Warren popped a toothpick into the corner of his mouth and flipped through the rest of the file, quickly scanning each page, and then he went back to the beginning and flipped through the pages again. "I thought I referenced an audit at the museum, but I don't see it here."

"An audit?" He'd like to see if the audit was different from the list Tomlinson had sent him.

"Yeah. As I recall, the president of the museum's board of trustees requested an audit . . . at least I think it was him. It's been so long ago, and my memory isn't what it used to be."

"So when you first investigated his disappearance, you didn't know anything was missing?"

"You're right. Originally I did think there might be foul play involved, and then someone told me there had been rumors floating around before he left that someone was stealing the artifacts. After that came to light, I concluded he'd hightailed it out of town with the pieces."

It still looked like that was what had happened. "Do you remember who the president was?" Brad could get the name, but it'd be quicker if Warren remembered.

He chewed the toothpick. "King, I believe. Or Allen . . ."

He shook his head. "No, I remember Sam Allen telling me it was his first year on the board. Don't know why that stuck in my mind, and I can't remember who the president was, but you ought to be able to find the information on the museum's website."

Couldn't be Jackson King, who was at the benefit Saturday night, so it must be his father. "Do you know if this person is still alive?"

"If it's the King fella, he is. King had a son working at the museum. As for Allen . . . I don't remember much about him other than he seemed like a nice guy."

"Do you remember if he had an alibi when Carter went missing?"

"Alibi?" Warren frowned. "Once the thefts were confirmed, I never went in the direction of asking anyone for an alibi." He pinned him with pale blue eyes. "Are you thinking he might have been murdered?"

"I'm not sure what I'm thinking, but there are a few things that don't add up." He took a card from his wallet and handed it to Warren. "If you remember anything else, give me a call."

"I will, and come back any time. Days get awful long here."

"What happened to get you here, anyway?"

"Fell off a ladder."

From his tone of voice, the retired sergeant was thoroughly disgusted with himself.

"Hey, anybody can do that," Brad said.

"I never did before. Now my girls think I'm too old to be painting or doing anything else that involves climbing." He turned to gaze out the window. "Thinking about selling out and moving to Florida, or maybe Alaska. Then they won't know what I do."

It sounded as though Harvey Warren needed something

useful to do. "Look, when you get out of here and your leg is healed, we could use some help at the youth center near the University of Memphis."

He looked at Brad's business card and then cocked his head. "I might just do that. Always liked working with kids."

17

AFTER KELSEY SIGNED IN AT THE MUSEUM, she went looking for her supervisor to put out at least one fire. She knocked on her door and was invited in.

"Ms. Webb, I wanted to let you know I was back, and to apologize for having to leave," Kelsey said as she shut the door behind her. Helen Peterson sat in a wingback chair. "I'm sorry. I didn't know someone was with you."

"I told you to call me Julie, and it was no problem. Do you know Helen?"

"Yes, we met Saturday night." Today the brunette was dressed conservatively in a patterned midi skirt and a blue silk blouse.

"Did your meeting with the police have to do with poor Mr. Rutherford's death?" Helen asked, tucking a stray lock of hair into the clip holding her ponytail.

"Yes." The meeting with Detective Sloan included the murder, so she didn't feel as though she were lying.

Julie picked up a stack of files and placed them on top of the cabinet. "Did you find out what the shooting this afternoon was all about?"

She shrugged. "Not really."

"Probably someone on drugs or who knows what," Helen said, shuddering.

"Whatever the reason, we've beefed up security." Julie shook her head. "For the foreseeable future, everyone will be escorted to and from their cars."

Kelsey massaged her temples. "As late as it is, I think I'll start work on the circus in the morning. Is there anything in particular that needs to be done today?"

"Why don't we open the box from the Coon Creek Science Center," Julie said, "and you can catalog whatever they've sent."

"And I need to get back to work myself," Helen said.

Julie and Kelsey walked to Erin's office, now temporarily hers. A wooden crate sat on the workstation, and Kelsey walked to it. "Erin seemed surprised to get this."

"They do usually call or email that they're sending something." Julie turned and scanned the office. "Where would Erin store a pry bar?"

Kelsey surveyed the room and found a short steel bar on the bookcase. "Is this what you're looking for?"

"That's it."

Her supervisor slid the lever between the nails and pried the box open, then removed packing to reach a heavy-duty black garbage bag. She picked up a pair of scissors and cut the bag open. "More plastic," Julie said. "I've never known them to double wrap anything. There should be a carpet knife in Erin's desk."

Kelsey rummaged in the top drawer and handed Julie the knife. Seconds later, she slashed through the white plastic. "Oh!" Julie stepped back.

Kelsey wrinkled her nose at the earthy scent coming from

the bag. She peered into the box. "That's a skeleton, not fossils."

A skeleton that was nothing more than a skull and a pile of bones.

"I see that. Maybe they found an Indian burial ground." The collections manager took out her cell phone, and when someone answered her call, she said, "May I speak to Luther McCoy?" While she waited, she put her hand over the speaker. "He'll know what's going on."

Today was full of surprises. Kelsey pulled on a pair of latex gloves from a box on the desk, half listening to Julie as she peeled back the plastic.

"Luther," Julie said as she walked toward the door. "Why did you send a box of bones to the museum?"

Kelsey gently opened the bag wider, revealing more of the skull. She swallowed the unease that pushed up from her stomach. She hadn't signed on for this. *Get a grip.*

A somber mood enveloped her. The bones were once a living, breathing person, and no one's remains should be dumped into a box like this. "Who are you?" she murmured. "And where did you come from?"

Not that she expected an answer. She bent closer to examine the ancient skull.

Why was there a gold cap on one of the teeth?

"Julie!" Kelsey carefully picked up the skull.

Her supervisor stepped back into the room, the cell phone still stuck to her ear. "Yes?"

"There's a gold crown here." She pointed toward the jawbone.

"Oh my—let me call you back, Luther." Julie continued to hold the phone as she walked to the worktable. "Then it can't be an ancient skeleton."

"My thoughts exactly."

"I better call 911."

Kelsey thought of the card Detective Sloan had given her. "Wait—why not call the detective who was here earlier?"

"Good thought. She'll be familiar with all of us."

Maybe too familiar. She found the card and handed it to Julie, and then she turned back to the skeleton, curious about why it would be mailed to the museum. Using a pencil, she opened the plastic wider, and a nick in the sternum caught her attention. She picked it up and examined it. Caused by a bullet, maybe . . . or knife?

"Don't touch anything!"

Kelsey dropped the necktie-shaped bone like it was a hot piece of charcoal.

"I'm sorry I startled you," Julie said, "but Detective Sloan is on the way, and she said not to touch anything. She's bringing a medical examiner with her."

"I'm sorry, I should have known better," Kelsey said. She wanted to get another look at the sternum, but Julie might come unhinged.

"What did you find?"

"The sternum looks like it might have a nick or chipped place in it."

Interest lit Julie's eyes, but then she shook her head. "Better leave that for the detective. Why don't we wait for her in my office."

It wasn't a question, and Kelsey removed her gloves and followed the collections manager down the hall. At least this time when the police cruisers arrived, it was without the sirens. Detective Sloan wasted little time when she arrived with another man wearing a badge on his belt next to his gun. Not the medical examiner, since detective was written all over him, and Sloan confirmed it.

"This is Lieutenant Boone Callahan," she said, nodding toward him.

Her superior, and from the hard edge to her voice, Sloan was not happy about him being along. Authority oozed from the lieutenant, from the way he stood to the way he took everything in with his serious brown eyes.

"Show me what you called about."

"Where's the medical examiner?" Kelsey asked. Evidently the lieutenant was letting Sloan take charge.

"Not coming." Her tone indicated it was none of Kelsey's business where the ME was, and then Sloan glanced at Julie, who had not moved. "You were showing me . . . ?"

"Oh, I'm sorry. It's this way."

Kelsey followed the three down the hallway to her office, half expecting the detective to dismiss her.

Sloan peered into the box. "You say the crate arrived this morning?"

Julie shot a questioning glance at Kelsey.

"Yes. The conservator I'm temporarily replacing said it was brought up from the shipping department," she said. "It has a Coon Creek shipping label on it."

"That's our fossil site in McNairy County," Julie said.

Sloan nodded. "Where is this conservator and what's her name?"

"Erin Dolan. Kelsey is taking her place temporarily while she's on maternity leave."

"So these bones are from an archaeological dig?"

"I doubt it," Kelsey said. "I mean, they may be, but they aren't ancient."

"And you know this how?"

She would not match Sloan's patronizing tone. She would not. "There's a gold crown on one of the teeth." She did.

The lieutenant looked away, but it was evident he was trying not to smile. The red flush that crept up his detective's neck made Kelsey regret her tone. But it wasn't her fault. Rachel Sloan needed to learn she'd get more by being nice than nasty.

Still, it had to be hard with her superior looking over her shoulder. It occurred to Kelsey that Rachel Sloan might think being hard-nosed was the only way she could survive in what had long been considered a man's job.

"But you couldn't have known that," Kelsey said, gentling her voice.

Sloan snapped a look at Kelsey that said *Don't do me any favors.* "Anything else I should know?"

Kelsey clamped her mouth shut. Pigs would fly before she told her about the sternum.

"You found something else," Julie said, turning to her. "Didn't you say the sternum looked as though it had a chip in it?"

Everyone's attention focused on her, except Sloan's, and she was staring in the crate.

"Yes," Kelsey said. "But I didn't have time to examine it in detail."

"It would have been better left alone since this is a possible homicide. You could have contaminated the evidence," Callahan said. He eyed the detective. "I expect we're done here for now. Do you need me to help take the crate to your car?"

"I've got it," Sloan said. "You go ahead. I have a couple more things to do around here before I leave."

Kelsey wasn't sure, but she thought the detective muttered something about not needing him in the first place as the lieutenant left. Then she pulled on a pair of latex gloves and pinned her gaze on Kelsey. "I'd like to take a look at that chipped sternum."

"It's right there on top."

"Thanks." Sloan leaned over the crate. "Smells like the bones have been in the ground, probably in the white polyethylene. They say that stuff will last five hundred years, so no telling how long it's been there."

Julie cleared her throat. "Not that long, I dare say, since that type of plastic only became available to the general population in the sixties and factories a short time before that."

Sloan looked over her shoulder. "You know that for fact?"

"The history of plastic was a featured exhibit until recently," Julie replied with a smile, "and that looks like the early greenhouse polyethylene they had on display. I believe the museum began using it in the mid-eighties—and that was in the historical notes. I didn't start work here until the late eighties."

"So that means the body could have been buried since the sixties." Rachel made notes in her tablet. "How was the box delivered?"

"I have no idea," Kelsey said, and they both looked at Julie.

"Don't look at me. I didn't know it was here until Erin told me." She tapped her foot. "But I can check with shipping. They're the ones who deliver items to our offices. I'll go around the corner and talk to the supervisor."

Once Julie had clattered down the hallway, Rachel lifted the sternum and examined it. "You're right, it does look as though a bullet could have done this. What else can you tell me?"

"Or it could have been caused by a knife." Kelsey slipped her hands into gloves and took the bone. "If it is a bullet, it entered here," she said, pointing out the notch, "and judging by the angle, it traveled through the body in a downward slant. I'd say the killer was taller than the victim or the victim was sitting down. And, if the bullet didn't exit the body, you may find it or at least fragments among the remains or loose in the plastic."

"Is there anything that you don't know about?" Rachel Sloan asked.

At least the detective had lost her sarcasm, and Kelsey offered a tentative smile. "I didn't know about the plastic."

Rachel's surprise gave way to a chuckle. "No, you didn't, did you."

Maybe they could have a truce. Kelsey certainly wouldn't object to one. "How soon do you think the bones will be examined?"

The detective took out her phone. "I'll see." She speed-dialed a number, and when someone answered, she said, "Dr. Caldwell, please." After a short wait, she said, "Dr. Caldwell, I have a possible homicide that I need your help with. A box of bones was delivered to the Pink Palace Museum, and the sternum appears to have a nick in it. I was wondering how soon you could autopsy the bones." Rachel nodded. "Great. I'll deliver the remains to your office this afternoon."

She slipped the phone onto her belt and took a deep breath as she turned to Kelsey. "He'll start on it ASAP."

"As soon as possible" could mean days, and an urgency inside her wanted to push for quicker. "Do you think I could sit in on the autopsy?"

Rachel startled. "Why would you want to do that?"

Kelsey didn't have an answer for the detective since she had no idea why she'd asked that question. But there was something about the bones that drew her, and she had worked with skeletons before—in college and then on an archaeological dig in Arizona. "Maybe finishing something I started," she said, pointing to the sternum.

"I'll ask Dr. Caldwell when I deliver the box. He allows medical students to sit in. Who knows, he may allow you to as well."

"Then it would be okay for me to touch base with the office and see when?"

"Sure. Maybe a citizen wanting answers will move the autopsy up."

18

AT THREE FIFTEEN, Brad pulled into the museum drive and met Boone Callahan going in the opposite direction.

Before he could wonder why Callahan was there, he spied Rachel Sloan's car. What were two homicide detectives doing here? What if Kelsey had been shot? It took him a minute to swallow down the lump that leaped into his throat. But he didn't see an ambulance, unless it had come and gone. He voice-dialed Rachel Sloan's number.

"What's going on at the museum? Did someone take more shots at Kelsey?"

"No," Rachel said. "I'm here about bones. Where are you?"

"In the parking lot."

"What are *you* doing here?"

"Just, uh, touching base with Kelsey. Wanted to make sure she was okay after what happened earlier."

"I see. Just professional courtesy. We're in her office, although I'm about to leave."

He ignored her sarcasm and disconnected. After signing in, he asked for directions to the conservator's office. When Brad stepped through the door, Kelsey and Rachel were standing by a worktable that held a wooden crate. "What's going on?"

They turned toward him. "We're resealing this box with bones in it," Rachel said.

Bones? He stepped closer, noticing the Coon Creek Science Center shipping label on the side of the box. "Don't tell me they found a dinosaur at the dig. I've never seen anything there but fossils."

"Dinosaur?" Rachel said.

"You know where it is?" Kelsey said.

They both spoke at the same time, and he answered Kelsey's question first. "Yep. It's a little over a hundred miles east of Memphis. Found a shark's tooth there one time when I was a kid. I got to write my name in the official fossil-finding book and the museum got to keep the tooth," he said and nodded toward the crate. "If you ever visit the site, look for my name. There've only been nine shark's teeth found since the dig started."

"Wow. I'm duly impressed," Rachel said. "But this is not dinosaur bones."

"No," Kelsey said. "It's human bones."

Brad rocked back on his heels. "Then why are they in a crate from the science center?"

"That is the million dollar question. Right?" Rachel said. She shot Kelsey a look, and Kelsey nodded.

Something was different about the two women. They almost seemed to share a . . . camaraderie. He felt a presence and looked around, recognizing the collections manager in the doorway.

Julie acknowledged him and then said, "Sorry it took me so long, but I had to track down the shipping department supervisor. He said the crate was sitting beside another shipment that came in Saturday. He assumed it came in then. No one saw either delivery."

"I'm still in the dark about what's going on," he said. "Is it unusual for the museum to get shipments from Coon Creek?"

"No," Julie said. "But we've never received bones from them. When I contacted the director in McNairy County, he said they hadn't sent any."

"And there's a nick in the sternum that could be from a bullet," Rachel said, "and the gold crown in the skull indicates it's not old."

Finally, his mind clued in to what they were talking about. Someone, they didn't know who, had sent a crate of bones with a Coon Creek label on the box to the museum. Intriguing. And more than likely a homicide, and maybe even a cold case.

"Have you sealed the box?" he asked. "I'd like to see this sternum you're talking about."

"Sure," Rachel said and pried the lid up.

Kelsey slipped on fresh gloves and removed the sternum. Brad reached for it, and she drew her hand back.

"Gloves, please."

Brad pulled on the pair of gloves she handed him and took the flat bone from her. He examined it, then ran his finger around the nick before shifting his gaze back to the women. "This black on the inside of the circle may be traces of gunpowder."

"Why do you think the sender used the Coon Creek label?" Kelsey asked.

"I don't know . . ." Rachel turned to Julie. "What's the process for shipments when they arrive?"

"Unless it's addressed to a particular person, security opens it first." Julie glanced at the crate. "But one like this, addressed

145

to the conservator, would be delivered to her office. No one would question it if it had the Coon Creek label."

Why would anyone send skeletal remains to the Pink Palace? Brad examined the label. "Evidently, whoever sent this has access to the science center's shipping labels."

"Or they created their own," Kelsey said. "Anyone knowledgeable with computers could print a label like this." She stared at the box again. "But they'd also need a working knowledge of how the museum handles shipments."

"All good points that I will follow up on, but for now, I need to get the crate to Dr. Caldwell to see if it's even a homicide," Rachel said.

She fastened the lid in place, and Brad shifted the box to a cart.

"You want me to put it in your car?" he asked.

"I can handle it." She pushed the cart toward the door and then stopped. "I almost forgot to tell you—I dug a bullet out of the tree earlier and sent it to ballistics. That should tell us if the gun used today has been used in other crimes. And Kelsey, you were right about the photo being altered. Got the report back right before Julie's call came in. Meant to say something when I first arrived, but seems like other things got in the way."

Brad could imagine, with Boone Callahan in the mix. He liked the lieutenant, but he could be something of a micromanager. "I saw Boone as I drove in. Why was he here? Doesn't he have enough to do without your cases?"

She shrugged. "You'd think. We were in a meeting together when the call came in, and he offered to help. Actually, he insisted."

Yeah, Boone pushed the detectives under him to be the best they could be, and if that took "helping" them, he didn't hesitate to jump in. And Rachel *was* new to Homicide. After Julie and Rachel left, he turned to Kelsey. "When I saw the two detectives' cars, I was afraid something had happened to you again."

She hugged her arms to her chest. "So far, nothing else has happened. But why were you coming to see me, anyway?"

"I found your dad's file."

"Really?" Her face lost some of its color.

"You okay?"

She took a deep breath. "Yeah. I just didn't expect you to find it so quickly."

Their eyes locked, and he couldn't look away from eyes the color of a lush meadow on a summer day. He swallowed and jerked his gaze away from hers, breaking the electricity that crackled between them. "Umm, do you think the coffee shop is still open?"

"I don't know. It's my first day here, remember?"

They both laughed, and just like that, everything returned to normal. "Let's go see."

He held out his arm, and she looped hers through it, sending electric tingles up his arm. Maybe not quite back to normal. He didn't know what was going on. Women usually didn't get past his defenses, not since Elle. *Elle.* For half a minute, he'd forgotten she was back in his life.

When they stepped into the café area, it was closed, but he spied a worker in the kitchen. "You sit here, and I'm going to see if they have something to drink back there."

He walked over to the counter and tapped on it, and a woman looked his way.

"We're closed," she called.

"Any chance of getting coffee or tea?" he asked.

She glanced away from him and then back. "I haven't poured the coffee out. Would you like a cup?"

"Make it two." When she brought the cups out, she wouldn't take any money. "Okay, how about a two-dollar tip?" he said and laid the bills on the counter. "And thanks."

Brad walked over to Kelsey and handed her one of the cups. "I noticed creamer on the sideboard if you'd like some."

"No, black is good."

He sat across from her and sipped his coffee. Strong but not bitter.

"I'm sorry about almost passing out on you again."

"I should be the one apologizing," he said. "You've had a hard day, and I should have found a better way of unloading that information."

"Thanks. I never expected hearing you'd found my father's file to throw me. What was in it?"

After her earlier reaction, he wasn't sure today was the day to discuss what he'd learned. "Nothing you wouldn't expect in a case like his."

She laughed. "That bad, huh?"

"Why do you say that?"

"I've learned over the years that when someone starts using language like you just used, it's always bad news, or it's something they don't want to talk about."

"Let's just say that I'd like to investigate the case a little more. There are a few details that raised questions, and I'd like to have those questions answered first."

"I guess I'll have to trust you on that."

"Yeah, I guess you will." He couldn't keep from grinning, at least on the inside. Her trust was something he had not expected.

19

At four thirty Kelsey shut down her computer and texted Maggie that she was on her way. It would be a relief to get this whole thing behind her. If she was arrested . . . she'd deal with that when it happened.

The attorney texted back. *Twelfth floor. Be careful.*

"Don't worry," she muttered under her breath. She'd know if a leaf moved when she stepped outside the building. Still thinking about her father's file as she stepped out of her office, she almost ran into Jackson King.

"Excuse me. I—"

"Sorry, didn't mean—" He reached to steady her. "Kelsey? I was looking for you. Didn't mean to run over you, though. Are you okay? I just got back from Nashville and heard about the shooting."

The adrenaline rush left her knees weak. She couldn't jump every time someone startled her. "I'm okay. Not used to being shot at, I guess." Kelsey checked her watch. "Did you need anything else?"

"No, I was also coming to tell you the camera malfunctions did correspond within the time frame of the thefts. I say time frame since it might have been days before the thefts were discovered."

"That answers one question. Our thief is very familiar with the security system here. Have you reviewed your employees' records?" she asked.

"We're in the process." He ran his hand over his silver hair. "And what's this I hear about the science center shipping some bones here? Is it true?"

"The part about the bones is true, but no one knows how they got here," she said and explained what she knew. "Detective Sloan took the remains to the Forensic Center for autopsy."

"I'll look at the playback on the shipping dock camera," Jackson said. "We'll get together in the morning."

"Thank you. I would suggest now, but I have an appointment . . ."

"No problem," he said. "Let me walk out with you."

After this morning, she was glad to have his company. As they approached the sign-out station, Jackson's phone rang, and when it sounded as though the conversation would be a long one, she motioned that she was going on.

"Hold on a minute," he said into the phone and turned to the security officer on duty. "Raymond, would you walk out with Ms. Allen?"

"Yes, sir."

He was the same security officer Kelsey had signed in with—Raymond Ray. She bet the grandkids she saw in the photos on his desk called him Ray-Ray. She would hate for anything to happen to him.

"I hope your second day will be smoother," he said. "Don't believe we've ever had a shooting here before, but these days, you never know what some crazy fool is going to do."

"Don't suppose you've heard if the police have caught the shooter?" It was possible the police had shared more with the security officer than her.

"Nope. We figure he came under the fence on Lafayette Street and hid behind the school buses. Can't figure out how he did it without the camera catching him. Just glad the children were still inside."

"How do they know he didn't go into the museum?"

"Because of the kids, Mr. King had guards stationed at every door. They were in the IMAX theater when it all happened, and we were prepared to keep them there," he said. "But the police concluded the shooter was no longer a threat and were through with their investigation before the movie ended. The kids never even knew anything happened."

She shuddered. *What if Lily had been here?* If a child had been injured because of her . . . it would be impossible to live with.

"If you're ready, Ms. Allen."

Part of her wanted to say no, that she didn't want to endanger anyone else, but the look on his face said that wasn't an acceptable answer. "Thank you."

"We're doing it for all the employees." He half turned to another security officer standing nearby. "Knight, cover the desk for me."

"I still hate for you to have to do this," she said as they exited the building. Her muscles tensed as she scanned the parking lot, and she noticed Ray did as well. When it seemed clear, she pointed out her Wrangler.

"I hate that we didn't do our job today," he said as they approached the car. "Just can't figure out why the cameras didn't see him, unless they malfunctioned. Seems like they're doing that a lot lately—thought the new ones would fix that."

Kelsey had an idea how the video missed it. "Did you notice a blip on any of the screens around the time the shooting occurred?"

He glanced sharply at her. "How did you know?"

"Just a guess." Something else to discuss with Jackson in the morning. He would not be happy when she told him that the shooter had more than likely gained access to the security system again and inserted an old video of the gate in place of live streaming.

"Thank you," she said and slid under the steering wheel. "See you tomorrow."

"Yes, ma'am. And there'll be security officers patrolling in the morning."

Even though traffic was light going downtown to Maggie's Front Street office, her muscles stayed on high alert. Rather than driving straight to the office, Kelsey took a roundabout way, turning right off Central and then left onto Poplar. She kept an eye on the traffic behind her and right away noticed a motorcycle made the same turn.

Kelsey quickly made another left, and her heart leaped into her throat when the motorcycle did as well. Then it pulled beside her at the red light, and she relaxed. MPD motorcycle unit. When the light changed, he fell in behind, and she breathed easier until her phone rang. Her mom. She went on high alert again. "Hello?"

"Are you all right?"

"Sure, why wouldn't I be?" Surely she didn't know about the shooting yet.

"The early news reported shots were fired near the Pink Palace today. They were asking for anyone with information about the shooter to come forward."

She'd forgotten her mom listened to all the news broadcasts. "I don't think it's anything to worry about. How are you feeling?"

"Tired. I've been cleaning the house on Snowden. Do you mind stopping by here on your way home?"

The renters must have moved again. "I'm on my way to a meeting. How about around six or six thirty?"

"Perfect. I'll tell Dru you'll be here for dinner. By the way, you haven't told me what you think of Brad Hollister."

She gripped the steering wheel. Now she had the real reason why her mom wanted her to come by. Kelsey wished she would quit trying to set her up with dates. "He's nice. Traffic is getting heavy. I'll see you later."

On Front Street, she glanced up at the building she'd scaled Thursday night. At first she hadn't understood why the man had been determined to kill her. She hadn't seen his face, only his outline. But as Brad pointed out, the man hadn't known that, like she hadn't known he'd killed someone. Kelsey had read once that most murders were solved because of witnesses being where they shouldn't be—like her Thursday night.

There were several parking spaces in the lot adjacent to Maggie's building, and she checked her mirror before she pulled in. Her motor escort was still behind her. Brad's or Rachel Sloan's work? Either way, she was thankful. The motorcycle pulled in and waited for her to park, then the cyclist nodded as she climbed out of her car. Once she was at the front entrance, he waved and roared off.

Her heart lighter, Kelsey walked across the marble floor to the elevator and punched the up button. She would have to find out whose idea the escort was and thank them for covering her.

The receptionist looked up from her computer when Kelsey approached her desk.

"May I help you?" she asked in a soft voice.

"I'm supposed to see Maggie Starr." She glanced at the nameplate on the desk. Shawna Patterson.

Her face crinkled in a smile. "You must be Kelsey Allen. I'll let Ms. Starr know you're here."

"Thank you, Shawna." While Kelsey waited, she glanced around the penthouse office. Even though they had lunch together sometimes, she'd never been to Maggie's office. A few expensive drawings hung over the custom-made furniture. The effect was an understated yet elegant feel to the room that reflected Maggie's high standing as a defense attorney.

Kelsey's mom had been friends with Maggie first, after meeting her at a Keep Memphis Beautiful meeting, then Sam became a friend and eventually Kelsey. Over the years she'd pieced together the story of how the attorney's brother had been wrongly convicted of a crime and had died in prison. It was why Maggie chose law as her career. Kelsey turned as muted footsteps neared and then Maggie appeared at the door.

"Kelsey, come on back to my office." She led the way to another room just as tastefully decorated as the reception area with a beautiful oak desk in the center. After they were both seated, Maggie said, "I hope the rest of your day went better than the first half."

"It was certainly interesting." She explained about the remains that had been delivered to the museum and the time spent with Detective Rachel Sloan. Kelsey couldn't believe what a turnaround that had been. Of course, it could change if real evidence surfaced pointing toward Kelsey. "I don't believe Rachel considers me a suspect."

Maggie raised her eyebrows. "So it's Rachel now?"

Kelsey hadn't noticed how easily her mind had gone from

Detective Sloan to Rachel. "I think we both have a better understanding of where we're coming from."

"And where is that?"

"She feels she always has to prove herself, and I know how she feels. One of the reasons I didn't pursue a career in computer programming was the resistance I met in college. It was a male-dominated field, and I got tired of trying to prove I belonged there."

"Maybe that's why you became the Phantom Hawk," Maggie said.

"I don't know what you mean."

"Come on, you describe yourself as a white-hat hacker. It's a way to thumb your nose at the community that put you down, but in a way that benefits someone else."

She'd never thought of herself that way. It had always been about the challenge, but she couldn't say she didn't enjoy besting the people she hacked. Who, as she thought about it, had all been male. Kelsey crossed her arms. "How much longer did it take you to get to where you are than your male counterparts?"

Maggie's answer was a shrug. "I don't waste my energy railing against the system. I'd rather change it by being the best I can be, and because I'm good, the women studying law now will have an easier walk."

She placed a notepad on her desk. "You said resistance was one of the reasons you didn't pursue programming. What are the others? Why did you become a conservator? It's the polar opposite from computer technology."

It was odd even to Kelsey that she was drawn to such diverse fields. "I do love preserving art and other antiquities, and it was what my parents wanted me to do. They've always been into archaeology, and in fact that's how they met,"

155

she said. "Art won out when I received a scholarship to the Conservation Center at New York University."

"Your mom told me about that when it happened."

"Funny thing, though. It was there that I became interested in white-hat hackers, and the seed of starting my own security company was planted."

"And here you are."

"Yes, here I am." Kelsey stood and walked to the window and looked out over the powerful Mississippi River. Red channel markers bobbed against the current, and a tugboat chugged upstream.

"If I'd gone to the police Thursday night, Mr. Rutherford might not be dead," she said softly and turned around. "I want to tell Rachel what happened. Can we move tomorrow morning's meeting to now?"

"We can, but let's go over a few things first." Maggie made notes in the tablet and then leaned back. "You didn't really see anything other than the person was a man. You can't identify him, so your information will not help to arrest him."

"But it'll give the police a timeline."

She made a few more notes. "There is that. Do you know who's handling the Hendrix case? We probably need to include that person as well."

"The detective who first covered Mr. Rutherford's death. Reggie Lane."

Maggie leaned forward and scrolled through her contacts. "I have his cell," she said and tapped on the number. When he answered, she identified herself and asked if he could drop by her office. "I have information on the Hendrix murder that might help you." Then she disconnected and made the same call to Rachel Sloan. After she disconnected, she turned to Kelsey. "They'll be here in ten minutes."

20

In his office, Brad glanced at the photo of Tripod catching a Frisbee that hung on the wall opposite his desk. He really needed to get home early and exercise the dog.

A text dinged and he checked it. Eddie from the motorcycle division. Kelsey had made it to Maggie Starr's office. He thanked him and glanced at the photo again. If Sam Allen didn't arrange for a bodyguard for Kelsey, he might have to apologize to his dog. He couldn't let her drive home without some sort of protection.

Brad picked up the list of artifacts that were missing after Paul Carter disappeared. He'd checked with an antique collector about the artifacts and learned that while each one was unique, the items were not worth hundreds of thousands of dollars, as he had supposed. They were priceless because they were not for sale and therefore couldn't be bought.

He propped his feet on his desk and leaned back in his chair, his tented fingers against his pursed lips. The way he saw it, each item was stolen because Carter couldn't buy it and one like it wasn't for sale, actually couldn't be for sale. Like the shrunken head—even if there was one for sale somewhere, it wouldn't be the one from the Pink Palace.

That's it! Carter wanted something no one else had. And that was what had made the artifacts valuable to him. He put his feet on the floor and sat up straight. But why would Carter steal them? He had access to them every day. And if Carter stole them, why did artifacts still go missing after he left? Unless he had returned to Memphis. Things about this case did not add up.

He looked up as Reggie stuck his head in the door. "What's up?"

"Remember Maggie Starr?" Reggie asked.

"Yeah. I was with her earlier today. What about her?"

"She has information about the Hendrix murder. I'm on my way over there now, but I thought I'd see what you could tell me about her. Only time I ever met the lady, she grilled me pretty good."

"Yeah, she's a bulldog in the courtroom, not so much out of it, though. Just play it straight with her and you won't have any problems." Brad glanced at his cleared desk and back at Reggie. "I'm done here for the day. Why don't I tag along?"

"It's always good to have backup when you go into the lion's den."

Brad grabbed his laptop. "I'll follow you. Should be plenty of parking spaces in their lot by now."

◈

As they rode the elevator to the twelfth floor in Maggie's building, Brad said, "How's it going with Treece?"

A broad grin spread across Reggie's face. "Great, now that your sister has calmed down a little. We don't argue nearly as much."

"Will has been a good influence on Andi."

"Have they set a date?"

"No. I think they're taking it slow. Andi is still dealing with the aftereffects of taking the pain medication for her back. How about you? I saw that ring you gave Treece. Nice."

"We're working on it. Can't get her to set a date, though. We still argue over her quitting the job at WLTZ, or at least moving into something besides investigative reporting. Some of the stuff she sees really gets to her."

"I know. Some of it rivals what we see. Just don't give her an ultimatum." The elevator opened and they stepped into the hallway. "It's this way," Brad said.

The receptionist showed them to Maggie's office and opened the door. Brad followed Reggie and stopped short when he saw Kelsey. She seemed surprised to see him.

"I didn't know you were coming," she said.

"Gentlemen, have a seat," Maggie said, nodding to the two wingback chairs across from her desk. "Kelsey, do you have any objections to Brad being here?"

For a second she looked as though she might, then she shook her head. "It's probably better this way."

Brad took the seat closest to Kelsey as another soft knock sounded at the door and Rachel Sloan entered the office. What did Kelsey mean by it being better this way? What was going on?

Rachel took a seat, and Maggie leaned forward. "Kelsey reported something to me that we feel you all should know regarding the Hendrix murder. I want you to know she did not have to come forward with this information, but she felt justice would be better served if she did."

"I'm listening," Rachel said and Reggie nodded.

Brad wasn't certain he wanted to hear what Kelsey had to say.

Maggie turned to Kelsey. "Why don't you tell them what happened Thursday night?"

She lifted her chin and slipped him a guarded look before she turned to focus on Rachel. "Last Thursday night I lowered myself down the side of the building where Turner Accounting has offices and entered through an unlocked window. After I left my card, I climbed out the window and returned the same way I came down—by way of an electric winch—which by the way, is why I knew that photo had been doctored. On the eleventh floor, I noticed a lamp on in an office. It hadn't been on when I went down. I saw a man's silhouette, and evidently he saw me."

Winch? Was she admitting she was a cat burglar? The Phantom Hawk?

"How do you know he saw you?" Reggie said.

"He raised the window and fired several shots. He—"

"And no one heard and reported the gunfire?" Rachel's voice was skeptical.

"He used a silencer. Just like today." Color rose in Kelsey's cheeks, and she crossed her arms over her chest. "And even though a silencer doesn't completely muffle the sound of gunfire, no one would have heard the shots coming from the eleventh floor. One of the bullets should be embedded in the concrete, or there should at least be a chip."

Rachel sat forward. "And you didn't see the man's face?"

"No."

"How did you get to the roof?" Brad asked. Even to his own ears, he sounded harsh. But she'd lied to him . . . or at least hadn't told him the truth, and he'd given her plenty of opportunity.

"I don't get it. Three hours ago you were accusing me of being the Phantom Hawk, and now you don't believe me. Why don't I just show you . . . people?"

He figured she was about to call them something unflattering, like *bozos*, when she caught herself. Instead she turned to Maggie.

"Would that be all right?" she asked. "Can we take a trip to the building in question?"

"It might settle things quicker, and I'd like to see how you accomplished it myself," her attorney replied, then addressed the three detectives. "What do you think?"

"I'm game," Rachel said, and Reggie echoed her sentiment as everyone stood.

Brad was ready as well. It was one thing to think this slender, five-five woman with the spiked hair was a cat burglar, and another to hear her admit it.

Kelsey grabbed the backpack from her car, and they all walked to the Allen Auto Parts building. In the elevator, she punched the button for the thirteenth floor. "We have to walk up one flight."

Once they exited through the service door on the roof, they followed her to the adjoining building, where she took a small, motorized winch with a hook on the end from the backpack and walked to the edge of the roof. "This is where I attached the winch," she said, pointing to a metal pipe anchored a foot from the ledge.

Rays from the afternoon sun popped sweat across Brad's forehead. Fresh markings that matched the size of the hook verified her words. Whether he wanted to believe it or not, she was indeed the cat burglar.

"After I secured the winch I went over the side and down to the eighth floor. It was when I came up that I noticed a light was on in an office that hadn't been on when I went down."

The three detectives knelt at the edge of the roof. Again there were markings on the concrete.

"That's where the cable rubbed. And right there is where the bullet ricocheted," she said, pointing at a gouge in the concrete. Vindication echoed in her voice.

After Rachel took photos of the edge of the building, Reggie and Brad took a couple. "Did the Crime Scene Unit process the roof?" he asked.

"No. Didn't know they needed to." Reggie peered over the side of the building and shuddered. "She has more guts than I do."

Visualizing Kelsey dangling fourteen stories above the street was hard to imagine, but if it were true, and it seemed to be, she'd outsmarted some of the best security specialists in Memphis.

She was also on the wrong side of the law.

21

Kelsey's steps were troubled as they walked back to Maggie's office. While she'd stood at the edge of the building looking down, she remembered seeing a white flash before the man fired at her. Only today, it was more than a flash . . . more like a face. But the image didn't hang around long enough for her to make out any features—if it was real. She still wasn't sure.

Once they were settled in Maggie's office again, Reggie took out a notepad. "So you say this happened around ten thirty?"

Kelsey nodded. This was the second time he'd asked a variation of this question. She still had no indication of whether either of them would arrest her or not. "I remember checking my watch before I went down, and it was ten. When I came out the front door of Allen Auto Parts, the barbecue cook-off hadn't shut down yet, and they close at eleven."

"Can you describe the man you saw?" Brad asked.

"There was a light right behind him, and I only saw his silhouette." She hesitated, not sure if she wanted to mention the image. "Except maybe for half a second. There was a flash of light, but it was gone so quickly, I'm not even sure it was real." She shook her head. "No, the light was real, but it lasted such a brief time, I'm not sure what I saw."

"You don't remember his face at all?" Rachel asked.

She closed her eyes and pressed her fingers against them. "No. I'm sure I saw it, but when I try to bring it up, all I see is his silhouette."

Reggie looked up from his notes. "Did you hear any gunshots before he fired at you? Or see anyone else?"

The questions were coming faster than she could answer. "No," she said sharply, "and I didn't see Mr. Hendrix, if that's what you're thinking. I figure the murderer had already killed him and disposed of the body, or he would have run instead of taking shots at me."

"I think that's enough for now," Maggie said. "Except, I don't think she's mentioned this, but Walter Rutherford hired her to test the security in all his buildings, not just the Pink Palace, so Kelsey was doing nothing illegal."

"Why didn't you say so before?" Reggie said.

"I thought I did," Kelsey said.

Brad shook his head. "Why didn't you reveal what you've told us Saturday night?"

"Partly because I was in shock. And I wanted to do the job Mr. Rutherford hired me to do, so I didn't want to compromise my cover. I would appreciate it if this wasn't made public." Kelsey stood and walked to the window. It was hard to explain her state of mind then. She squared her shoulders and turned around. "But the main reason I didn't was that I had no idea if he had told anyone else he'd hired me for the jobs I did as the Phantom Hawk. Jackson wasn't aware of it. I . . . I was afraid you wouldn't believe me."

She said this last to Brad. She couldn't understand why it was so important that he believed her now.

"I can understand that," he said. "But it would have made everything much simpler if you had just told the truth."

She snorted. "You would have believed me?"

He pinned her with a solemn stare. "We'll never know now."

Fine. If he wanted to be that way, there was nothing she could do about it. Kelsey turned to Rachel. "Did you get the bones to Dr. Caldwell?"

"Yes, and he said you were welcome to sit in." Rachel stood and moved toward the door. "Do you know who's taking over for Mr. Rutherford?"

"Jackson King. He was his partner."

"Thanks," the detective said. "I'll touch base with him tomorrow."

"Rachel, wait and I'll walk out with you," Reggie said and stood. "I wish we could provide security for you, Kelsey, but we don't have the manpower."

"Her father is providing a bodyguard as soon as he can arrange it," Maggie said.

Reggie turned to Brad. "You going with us?"

"No, I need to ask Kelsey a couple of questions."

"I'll see you tomorrow then."

As soon as Reggie and Rachel left, she realized she'd never thanked Brad for the motorcycle officer who had shadowed her. "By the way, thanks for the escort."

"I wish I could do more," he said.

At least he didn't still sound angry. "I hate that I have to have a bodyguard."

"If it were me," Maggie said, "I'd feel better knowing someone had my back."

"Why don't you want someone protecting you?"

Brad looked truly puzzled, and she tried to find an answer he would accept. "Don't get me wrong. I'm glad for the protection. But I don't want to put someone else in danger." She thought of her tiny apartment. "And, the thought of being under someone's eye all the time makes me antsy, and I don't know where I'd put them."

"Let them worry about that," he said. "Are you going home from here?"

She picked up her purse. "No. My mom called and wants me to come by the house."

Brad stood as well. "I'm on my way there, so I'll have your back for now."

Surely he wasn't applying for the job as her bodyguard, but before she could protest, Maggie spoke up.

"Good," she said. "Maybe Sam will have the security detail in place when you get there."

Maggie's phone buzzed, and she answered it. "If you two will excuse me a minute, I have to see Shawna before she leaves."

"We'll walk out with you," Brad said.

In the elevator Kelsey asked, "Why are you going to my parents' house?"

"I want to ask your mom a few questions about your dad."

"Sam?" What kind of questions could he have about her stepfather?

"No, Paul Carter. Do you think she'll mind?"

She hadn't expected that, and all argument left her as she realized her father's investigation would involve the rest of her family. Like so many other things in her life, she hadn't thought this through. "I-I don't know."

"Do you talk to your mom about him often?"

"How about never? I was so young when they divorced.

After he left when I was seven, I just wanted to forget about him, especially after a classmate accused me of being a thief when his lunch money came up missing," She shrugged. "I never stole the kid's lunch money, but I was still ashamed. What kind of questions are you going to ask her?"

"Just a couple of general questions. Once I have the facts I need, I'll share what I've learned."

She started to quiz him again, but the set of his jaw told her it'd do no good.

Traffic had thinned on Poplar, and soon Kelsey turned into her parents' drive, with Brad right behind her. As far as she could tell, no one had followed them. She keyed the code in for the automatic gate and stared through the ornate bars while she waited for it to open. Her mother and Sam's house sat at the end of a circle drive, and she wondered what Brad thought about the antebellum house she'd grown up in.

A cross between the Federal and Greek Revival styles, it had top and bottom porches that wrapped three quarters of the way around the house. When the gate opened, she pulled through and parked in the circle near the front door. Brad parked next to her.

"This is nice," he said as he climbed out of his car. "Almost homey for something so grand."

"I guess." She scanned the house and yard, trying to see it through Brad's eyes. The house did have an inviting appeal, maybe because it looked as though someone actually lived in it and sat in the swing and rocking chairs on the front porch. "Mom and Sam enjoy sitting out here in the evening."

"Who tends the roses?" Brad bent over to sniff the flowers.

"Mom. The azaleas too." No gardener for her. The fresh scent of mowed grass tickled Kelsey's nose. "She mows too, all two acres." A picture of her mother flying around the yard in her zero-turn mower made Kelsey smile as she climbed the steps to the wraparound porch. "Come on in."

Behind her, Brad whistled as they stepped into the marble entry hall. "So this is how the other half lives."

Once again, she tried to see through his eyes, and realized just how much she took Sam's wealth for granted. Crystal chandeliers hung in all the downstairs rooms, and expensive antiques in keeping with the style of the house filled every room. How did she explain that she and Sabra were raised to do chores, some they were paid for and some were just-because chores? And they were expected to save part of their small allowance. Not only that, but as teens, they'd been expected to find a place to volunteer every summer. From as far back as she could remember, her parents' mantra had been "with wealth comes responsibility."

"Kelsey, I didn't know you were here," her mother said as she came from the back of the house. "And you brought a friend?"

"You remember Brad," she said. Her mother should after setting them up Saturday night.

"Of course. I just couldn't tell who it was with the light behind him." She extended her hand. "Welcome to our home."

"Thank you, Mrs. Allen."

"Please, call me Cynthia."

"He's actually here on police business and wants to talk to you. Is Sam home?"

"Business?" Cynthia tilted her head, confusion crossing her brown eyes.

"Yes, ma'am." He glanced at Kelsey. "Do you mind if I talk with your mother privately?"

Privately? Why didn't he want her in the room with them? She searched his face for answers and decided he'd make a good poker player. "Uh, sure. I'll go hang out with Sam."

22

THE SCENT OF BASIL AND OREGANO in the entryway followed Brad as Mrs. Allen led the way to a small study off the hall.

"How is this?" she asked.

"Good." Like the rest of the house, the study was magazine-worthy. His shoes squeaked as he crossed the hardwood floors to the gold-and-white-striped sofa. He sat down and took out a notepad and pen while she pulled out the desk chair from the antique secretary and sat opposite him with her hands in her lap.

"What do you want to speak to me about? Does it have anything to do with the murder Saturday night at the museum?"

He'd been looking for a way to explain his questions without involving Kelsey. "It may. But first, could I get your cell phone number in case I have more questions down the road?"

"Certainly."

"Thank you." He entered the number she gave him to his phone contacts and then looked up at her. "The reason I'm here is to find out a little about your first husband, Paul Carter."

"Paul?" A faint flush colored her cheeks. "Why?"

"After the murder Saturday night, we're looking at anything that involved previous crimes committed at the museum."

"I see." She rested her fingertips on the side of her face. "How could Paul's case be related to the murder?"

"That's what I'm trying to determine—if it even is."

"What exactly do you want to know?" she asked.

"Do you remember if your husband was acting strangely just before he disappeared?"

"Ex-husband," she said. "And yes, he did seem troubled, and after he left, I regretted not asking if anything was wrong," she said. "But you have to understand that Sam and I were talking about getting married, and I was paying attention to him, not to what Paul was doing. The day before he left, Kelsey spent the day with him at the Pink Palace. The next day she had a soccer game, and when he didn't show up, I knew something was terribly wrong. He never missed one of her games."

"Do you have any idea what he was troubled about?"

She clasped her hands together and stared at the floor. After a minute, she took a handkerchief from her pocket and dabbed her eyes. "He never talked business with me, not when we were married and certainly not after we divorced."

Brad made a few notes. He hadn't meant to distress her. He paused his writing and looked up. "I noticed his full name was not in any of the records."

"Paul was his middle name. John Paul Carter. His father went by John, so my ex-husband was called Paul all his life." She looked away. "Of course, I have no idea what he's going by now."

Brad nodded. "And he obtained his doctorate from the University of Pennsylvania?"

"Yes, but what does that have to do—"

"I'm just double-checking what's in the records. Can you tell me if he collected anything?"

She looked at him strangely. "Indeed he did—he had a whole museum of things he'd collected."

"I meant a personal collection."

"Oh, good grief, no. Everything he owned is locked up in a shed on Snowden Avenue. He took nothing with him except the clothes on his back."

"I see." He tried to think of a way to ask the next question and finally decided straight out was the best way. "Do you believe he stole the artifacts he's been accused of taking?"

She didn't hesitate. "At first I didn't, but nothing else explains him just walking away from Kelsey and his job. He loved both of them."

"Did he have any enemies?"

Her brow furrowed. "Why would you ask that?"

Brad softened his voice as he said, "Just trying to get a feel for his life."

"Do you think something might have happened to him?" Cynthia twisted the handkerchief. "I never even considered that . . ." She looked at him, her eyes wide. "But that would mean someone . . ."

"I know." He tapped the pen on his leg. "I noticed in the report you and Sam married not long after Paul left."

"Yes. Paul and I were divorced almost four years when my friendship with Sam blossomed into something deeper." She smoothed the fabric of her skirt. "I divorced Paul because he was married to his fieldwork. Sure, he came home because I insisted, but he resented it. We argued all the time, and when he informed me he'd put in for a six-month sabbatical so he could go on a dig back in Egypt, I'd had it. I filed for divorce."

171

"But he didn't go," Brad said. "Or at least, I haven't found any record of him leaving after he became director of the museum."

"He didn't. When he saw how serious I was about it, he canceled the trip, thinking I would cancel the divorce." She looked down at her hands, where she'd twisted the fabric into a knot. "But I knew nothing had changed. His first love was still working the digs in Egypt. When he took the museum directorship, it was with the condition that he have the option of a sabbatical every two years. Paul would have come to despise me in the end for making him give it up. I imagine that's where he is now. Off somewhere digging for relics."

"How was your relationship after the divorce?"

"Better than it ever had been." She smiled. "Paul always lived in his own little world, and the responsibilities of marriage were too much for him. He never should have married in the first place. But he really loved Kelsey."

It would seem there were no real villains in the divorce. "And then you married Sam."

"Yes. About a year before Paul left town, my friendship with Sam turned into romantic love. We were seeing each other, and he wanted me to marry him. But . . . I wasn't ready. Then when Paul left and it came out that he'd been stealing artifacts, Sam was so wonderful, not only to me but to Kelsey as well. We married soon afterward . . . and here we are."

"Yes." Brad put his pad away. "Thank you. I have a better picture of your ex-husband now." He stood. "I guess I'd better find Kelsey and say my good-byes. Thanks for seeing me."

"She's probably in the den with Sam. I'll show you the way." She stopped at the door. "Would you like to join us for dinner? We're having spaghetti."

So that was what that tantalizing aroma was. He hoped

she hadn't heard his stomach growl. "No, I won't bother you any further."

"No bother at all. I'll tell Dru to set another plate." She pointed down the hall. "And you should find Kelsey in that room."

He walked to the room she pointed out. Kelsey and her stepfather appeared to be in a heavy discussion, and he backpedaled out of the room until she looked his way.

Kelsey motioned him in. "The bodyguard question is all settled."

"Bodyguard? Whatever for?" Cynthia said behind him.

Kelsey flinched. Evidently she hadn't seen her mother behind him. "It's nothing," she said, her eyes imploring him to back her up.

So a bodyguard was what they were discussing. As headstrong as Kelsey was, he pitied the poor soul who got that job. Just then a soft gong sounded and was followed by a very British voice at the door. Brad turned as a tiny woman in a black uniform informed them dinner was ready.

"Thank you, Dru. We'll be there shortly," Cynthia said and turned to Kelsey. "I want to know more about this business of you needing a bodyguard."

Kelsey clasped her hands together. "And be late for dinner? It's not worth Dru's wrath."

"Honey, it can wait until after dinner," Sam said.

Dru must be formidable in spite of her size.

Cynthia Allen looked from her husband to her daughter and sighed. "Very well."

Brad followed the others to the dining room, where true to Sam's words, the subject of a bodyguard didn't come up until they had finished a wonderful meal of spaghetti and rolls that melted in his mouth.

Cynthia placed her napkin on her plate. "Now can we discuss the matter at hand?"

"Mom, it's nothing," Kelsey said.

"It is something," Sam said. "Someone fired shots at her today when she came out of the museum."

Her mother gasped and turned to Kelsey. "That person was shooting at *you*?"

"We don't know, and that's why she is going to have a security detail." He turned to Brad. "Any chance of you taking it on until I can get someone in place?"

23

THE DINING ROOM BECAME EERILY QUIET, and Kelsey stared at her stepfather. Surely Sam wasn't serious. From the stunned look on Brad's face, he agreed with her.

"No!" Kelsey said to Sam. "He has a full-time job."

"That's the only reason I'm not offering him the job permanently. I'm only talking about for tonight until you get home. Rutherford Security will have a man at your apartment by nine." Sam turned to Brad. "How about it?"

"I can manage tonight, but I won't accept pay."

Sam chuckled and slapped him on the back. "Can't say as I blame you, and I doubt I have that much money anyway."

She swore she heard a "You don't" in Brad's return chuckle. "He can escort me home and then leave. I'm not going anywhere the rest of the night."

"Good," Cynthia said. "By the way, I hope you can go by the house on Snowden and go through the boxes in the shed sometime this week."

Her Grandmother Carter's house, where they'd lived before her parents' divorce. She hadn't been there in years. She turned to her mother. "Why?"

"I'm selling the house and the shed has to be emptied. Sam said a couple of his employees can deliver what you want and take everything else to the dump."

"You sold the house? I thought it belonged to my father."

"Your grandmother had planned to leave it to him, but Paul didn't want the responsibility of keeping it up, so at his suggestion, she left it to me. Of course, he lived there until . . ." She raised her eyebrows. "I have an appointment to show it Friday. The shed needs to be emptied before then."

Did everything in her life have to upend at the same time? Her dad had stayed on in the house after the divorce because the house belonged to his mother, and going there on weekends had been like going home. One of her favorite rooms was the bright yellow kitchen.

"Kelsey, watch me double-flip your flapjack." He'd double-flipped it all right, right onto the black-and-white tile floor, where her puppy gobbled it down. He'd grinned and called for a do-over. The puppy had a good breakfast that morning.

It was the last weekend she'd spent with her dad.

Her mom leaned toward her. "I never thought to ask if you wanted it . . ."

The distress on her face prompted Kelsey to assure her she didn't. "It's too big for me," she said, remembering the ugly brown brick house. "But what's in the shed?"

"Your dad's papers are there, and I saw a box labeled 'museum papers'—"

Sam leaned forward. "He had files from the museum at the house?"

"I suppose, but I'm not sure what's in them," her mother said and turned her attention back to Kelsey. "There's a desk that I thought you might like, and a few boxes with mementos of our years there, and a few other things. I

176

have what I want to keep, and whatever you don't want, I'll discard."

"I'll go by there tonight and see what needs to be done."

"Great. I'll get the key."

Kelsey pushed her chair back and glanced toward Brad. "I should have asked if you have time."

"I have nothing planned. But if you're coming back this way, we could go in my car and pick yours up later."

"Sure. Sabra's house is around the corner." When he looked puzzled, she said, "I live in her backyard in the garage apartment."

They drove to the house on Snowden in comfortable silence with the GPS giving directions. "I'm sorry that Sam wrangled you into this."

"No problem. I enjoyed dinner. And I like your folks."

"Me too." She smiled. "Sam has been good to me. Treats me like his own."

"How about your biological dad? What do you remember about him?"

"I have a few good memories. I was three when he and Mom divorced, and he was so busy we didn't spend a lot of time together—he was often tied up on the weekends I was supposed to be with him. But when I did get to spend time with him, he treated me like a princess."

She gazed out the passenger window at the tree-lined sidewalks. At the light, a father lifted his son onto his shoulders. "I think that made it harder for me to understand why he left. But then, if I think about it much, it's hard to understand now, so why would I expect a seven-year-old to? How about you and your parents?"

He cocked his head toward her. "I didn't know how lucky I was until I started school and found out most of the kids lived in blended or single-parent families. Not that we didn't have problems. I don't know if you remember my older sister, Stephanie?"

"No, but Andi talked a lot about her sister in our mentoring sessions during my senior year," she said and glanced up at him. "I assume Andi is doing well from what I see on television."

"She's doing great. Maybe a little too reckless sometimes, and she says I'm too hard on her." He turned left as the GPS directed. "She and Will Kincade are seeing each other."

"I don't believe I know Will."

"You'll probably get to know him—he's in the Cold Case Unit with me." He turned again onto Snowden. "Do you and your sister get along?"

"The house is on the next block," she said. "Yes, Sabra is only two years younger than I am and my best friend. Her mother died when she was four, and Sam and Mom married a little over a year later."

"Was it hard growing up in a blended family?"

"Not really. There was never any partiality shown by Sam or my mom. Which was surprising, since Sabra was a near-perfect child. Me, I always stayed in trouble," she said, chuckling. "It's the next house on the right."

"Why does that not surprise me?" He slowed and turned into the drive.

She warmed under his grin. When Brad wasn't being bossy, he was almost appealing.

"Wow," he said softly. "I wish I'd known this was for sale. What era was this house built in?"

"I think 1920s." Kelsey followed his gaze. The attractive bungalow was not the house she remembered; she tried to recall the last time she was here. It must have been at least ten years ago, and even then she had not gone inside. When had her mom painted the brick that sage green color? And who put flower boxes under the living room windows? Seeing it in this light—

"You wouldn't rather live here than in a garage apartment?" he asked.

"It never looked like this before. Ten years ago, it was a plain brown brick house jammed up under the houses on either side." While the closeness hadn't changed, a privacy fence had fixed the problem. The place stirred emotions that left her yearning for something she couldn't quite put her finger on. "If this sale doesn't go through, I think I'll talk to my mom about moving in here."

"I don't blame you. This is a homey place."

Homey. That was the yearning that settled in her heart. She could see herself living there.

"The shed is in the back." She broke off a piece of honeysuckle climbing the wooden fence as they walked the concrete drive to the backyard. Honeysuckle had grown wild in the backyard when she was a child, and making necklaces with the fragrant vine tickled her memory.

Kelsey unlocked the double doors on the shed and swung them open to give them some light. Boxes were neatly stacked against the wall, and a rolltop desk covered with clear plastic sat to their left. She scanned the labels on the boxes. One was marked "Paul's Files." Another was marked "Museum Files."

"You may want to look at these," she said, pointing the boxes out.

"Good idea. Are you taking anything home tonight?"

"No. This has been one of the hardest days I can remember, and I don't want to deal with anything else."

"How about meeting me here tomorrow evening, and I'll help you load whatever you want to take?"

His offer touched her. "Five thirty?"

He nodded, and she removed the plastic that covered the desk and rubbed her hand over the oak slats, then rolled the top back. "Daddy used to sit at this desk and work on the weekends I spent with him," she said, surprised at the recollection. "And when he finished, we would go for ice cream."

"Sounds like you have a few good memories. What's this?" he asked and lifted a wooden box.

"I don't know." She looked on as he opened the lid. "Oh my goodness. A croquet set." Tears suddenly sprang to her eyes. "He taught me how to play."

"Our family used to play." He picked up a mallet. "I was pretty good. Want to play? You need to wind down, and this game is perfect for relaxing."

It was still light enough, but did she even remember how the game went? She glanced at Brad, and her heart did a flutter dance when he winked at her.

"Unless, of course, you're afraid I'll beat you."

"You're on, buster." She grabbed the mallet he was holding.

In a matter of minutes, Brad had the wickets and stakes in place, and they agreed on the sidewalk and a row of tulips as the boundaries. "Who's going first?"

"When *we* played, ladies always went first," Kelsey said.

"Well, go ahead if you think you need the advantage."

If he thought she'd take the bait and let him go first, he was dead wrong. "Don't need it, but I'm taking it."

She chose the blue ball and knocked it through the first two wickets, which gave her two attempts at the next wire. On the second shot, the ball went out of bounds, and she groaned. She was rusty.

Brad chortled. "You're dead in the water now."

He knocked his ball through the first wires but rolled past the next wicket on his second shot. He was rusty as well, but when her ball stopped short on the next shot, he took aim and knocked it out of the way as his sailed through the wire. He made two more wickets before he missed and it was her turn again. She lined up her mallet and ball, intending to knock his out of the way.

"You're using the wrong stance, and you're pushing the ball instead of hitting it," he said.

"You're crazy."

"I'm getting the balls through the wicket," he said. "And you're not."

She watched as he made an imaginary shot. His shots *were* different. Maybe it was worth a try. She tried to imitate his stance.

"No, not like that. Let me show you."

The next thing she knew, Brad was behind her and turning her to face the wicket.

"Now, turn the mallet so it hits the ball on the flat side."

She tried to do as he instructed.

"No, not like that," he said. "Like this."

He put his arms around her and his hands over hers and swung the mallet. The woodsy scent of his aftershave reminded her of the last time she'd hiked the Appalachian Trail. She could almost hear the sound of a brook rushing down the mountainside. With a start, she realized the sound was her heartbeat pulsing in her ears.

"Now you try it." Brad released her and returned the ball to where she stood.

She stared at the ball, unable to ignore the way she'd felt with his arms around her. Safe . . . and in a way she didn't want to consider. Kelsey repositioned her hands that still tingled where he'd held them and whacked the ball, sending it through the wicket and bouncing off his ball.

"Way to go!" He high-fived her, and their gazes locked.

Electricity filled the short space between them. Her lips softened.

No, she wasn't going there. She jerked her hand back. "I . . . uh, think I get another shot now."

24

WARMTH RUSHED THROUGH BRAD'S VEINS. What was happening here? A minute ago, he'd lost himself in Kelsey's enormous green eyes, his thoughts carrying him places he didn't want to go. He could no longer deny the attraction. Would he have broken the connection between the two of them if she hadn't stepped back?

"You know, it's getting late," he said. "Maybe we better put the set away until another day."

"Yeah. That's probably a good idea."

She didn't sound convinced.

"I won, though."

"I don't think so," Kelsey shot back, sounding more like herself. "No way you can beat me at croquet."

Looked like that had gotten their relationship back on track. He tossed the red ball in his hand. "Rematch?"

"You're on. Just name the day." Then she glanced toward the shed. "I really should look through more of the boxes."

"I thought you'd decided to wait until tomorrow. And I'll help you."

"Oh, you don't have to. Sam's bodyguard can come with me."

"But he won't play croquet with you." It surprised him that he wasn't ready to relinquish her safety to someone else. If he had vacation time, he might take it and accept Sam's job offer. Except he'd just started a new job.

And Elle had just stepped back into his life. Elle. Why hadn't he ever played croquet with her? He shook his head, dismissing the thought. "Where do you want to put this?" he asked, nodding at the wooden box.

"Just set it on top of the desk. That way it'll be handy when we play again"—her eyes gleamed as she gave him a wicked grin—"and I beat you."

"I can see why you're not married—too competitive." He had not meant to say that.

"Probably. What's your excuse?"

He swallowed hard and speared the ground with his gaze. Her hand on his arm sent his heart rate even higher, something that shouldn't happen if he wanted to get back with Elle. But did he? His life had become complicated, and he wasn't used to complicated, at least not with his personal affairs.

"I-I'm sorry. That's none of my business."

"No need to apologize," he said, reining in his emotions. "I kind of walked into that one, anyway. But since you asked so nicely, my fiancée broke our engagement because she decided she didn't want to marry a cop."

"How long did you date?"

"Five years, engaged one." And right up until she gave his ring back, he'd thought they had a relationship that would last.

Kelsey shook her head. "After dating a cop for so long,

she should have known how she felt about the risks before accepting your ring."

"You'd think." He shifted the wooden box he was still holding.

"Not all her fault, though," she said and took the croquet set from him and set it on top of the desk.

"What?" It *was* her fault. He'd always been honest with her about his job and how much he loved it.

"In five years you didn't pick up on her fear?"

He pressed his teeth against his top lip. He had known, but he thought she would get used to the danger he faced. He had—he didn't even think about it anymore. "Okay, maybe I did."

"So why didn't you two hash it out?" Her green eyes held warmth and concern.

He tilted his head. Maybe it was time to acknowledge he'd had a few doubts about their relationship himself. That he'd wondered if Elle wasn't the one. "I don't know. She was very definite when she finally told me. Except . . . it's weird. Just yesterday she told me she made a mistake."

Briefly, the light in Kelsey's eyes dimmed, and then she raised her eyebrows. "So, what's the big deal? You two can still get married."

He shook his head. "Not that easy. Who's to say she won't change her mind again?"

"I think . . ." She looked away. "Never mind."

"No, I want to hear what you have to say."

Kelsey lifted her hand. "It's just that I've noticed you always have to be in charge, you know, be the boss."

"What are you talking about?" He did not have to always be in charge. If anyone was bossy, it was Kelsey.

She raised her eyebrows. "So, whatever you're involved in, you *don't* have to be in control?"

"No. It didn't work out with Elle because she hated my job." He was tired of this conversation. "So, why aren't you married?" he asked and was rewarded with a blush filling her face.

"Because I choose not to be." She closed the double doors and snapped the lock together. "Are you ready to take me home?"

"Yes, but there's usually a reason behind choosing not to." He lifted an eyebrow.

"My life has been just fine and dandy without a man in it."

He folded his arms across his chest. "Still doesn't tell me why you choose not to."

"You're not going to let this go, are you?" She lifted her chin. "Because most men I've met are like you," she said. "Control freaks. Or they don't stick around. Satisfied?"

He saluted. "Yes, ma'am."

What in the world was wrong with him? Why was he baiting her? It was like when he had a sore tooth and kept pressing against it, making it hurt. Not because she was getting under his skin. No. He might be dense in the area of love, but he had enough sense to know it was because she threatened the fortress he'd built around his heart. The heart that was already in a tangled mess with Elle's confession yesterday.

He opened the car door for her, and she held his gaze just before she slid into the passenger seat, her eyes a dark jade.

They don't stick around. Just like him, she was hurting, but he could not afford to let his heart get involved with Kelsey. He never knew what she would do next. Everything about her screamed "seat of the pants," and his life was structured and orderly. And she had no problem disregarding rules—look at the way she bent the rules to justify breaking into buildings. No, wait. He had that wrong—Rutherford had hired her to test his security.

It didn't matter either way. He shut her door and walked to the driver's side. If he was going to let someone into his heart again, Elle was much better suited for him.

◆

Brad was quiet as they drove across town to her parents' house to pick up her car. She'd pushed him too far trying to find out why he didn't have a girlfriend. Not that Kelsey cared one way or the other. She was just trying to find out why a good-looking catch like Brad hadn't been caught. So why had she been disappointed when he said he'd seen his ex?

"Look, I'm sorry if I crossed a line or something about your fiancée," she said. "It must have hurt to give her your heart and have her trample all over it."

He shrugged. "No big deal. I'm a big boy, and I got over it."

She didn't believe that for a second. "Are you thinking about giving this Elle another chance? I mean, you're still a cop. How will she deal with that?"

"We're just talking right now. How about you? Who broke your heart?"

"No one."

"Are you saying that never happened to you?"

"Yep. I never gave any guy the opportunity to break my heart." Actually, she never gave anyone the chance to get close enough.

"Why not? Haven't you heard that 'tis better to have loved and lost than never to have loved at all?"

She thought about the relationships she'd been in. Did any of them qualify as love? One man in particular surfaced.

187

Joey DeMarzo. Laughing blue eyes, more muscles than brains . . . They'd wanted different things out of the relationship. "I might have loved someone once, but it wasn't enough to keep him around."

"Your dad? That had nothing to do with you."

"My dad?" She shot him a quick glance. "No. I mean, yeah, he took off, but it was because he didn't want to get caught stealing. It had nothing to do with me. I've had a really good male role model in Sam, anyway. The guy I referred to was someone I met in Jackson."

"What happened?"

"I don't know. Like all my relationships, it started out well. We were having fun, no arguments, lots of common interests—I do play a good game in the beginning. But that's as far as it went. Once he got to know me, the relationship was toast . . . again." She turned to him and grinned. "But at least my heart's never been broken, not even by him."

He caught her eyes and held them. "Maybe because your heart was never involved."

"Involving one's heart is highly overrated," she said and turned to look out the window at the empty storefronts they were passing. "Sabra says I pick men who have no staying power. And she says I do it on purpose."

"Is she right?"

"Maybe it's me who doesn't have the staying power." Not in men, not in jobs, not in anything.

They stopped for a red light, and Kelsey shifted her gaze to him. His dark brown hair curled on his neck, like he was a week past a haircut. And the resolute cut of his square jaw reminded her of how he didn't back down when she challenged him. Brad was the kind of man who had staying power. Suddenly the reasons she could so easily tick off to her sister for not getting involved romantically evaded her.

He let the subject rest as they drove down Poplar, still busy even though rush hour was long past and darkness encroached. Brad turned onto her parents' street and a few minutes later turned into their drive and keyed in the code she gave him.

Once he parked beside her car, he said, "And maybe you haven't met someone you can trust enough to give your heart to."

She'd hoped they were done with her love life or the lack of it. She turned to tell him to bug off. Their gazes collided, and in the dim light of the console, his blue-green eyes turned her muscles to liquid. For the second time that day, she wondered what it would be like to kiss him. She broke the gaze first.

"Thank you for protecting me today." Why did her voice sound breathy?

With a slow smile, he tipped his head. "Just doing my job, ma'am."

"Then it can end here. You don't have to follow me home," she said.

"But I do. Otherwise I don't get paid." Grinning, he hopped out and came around to her side of the car to open the door.

"You know, I could get used to this," she said, accepting the hand he held out.

"Proof you've been associating with the wrong men, as they obviously don't get your door. Or do you get out before they have the chance?"

She grinned and cocked her finger at him. "Bingo."

"Figures," he muttered. "What's your address, in case you run off and leave me?"

"Don't worry. I won't." She gave it to him and then climbed into her car. "See you in a minute."

Kelsey really did appreciate his concern, even if it was hard to get used to. Almost as hard as getting used to a man trying to kill her. She'd heard soldiers in battle often became hardened to the danger, and that's what she was experiencing. She should be afraid, but it was as though her mind blocked the worst of the fear.

Kelsey waited until he was past the gate before she pulled into traffic. On the next block, she took a left and wound her way around the neighborhood to Sabra's drive. Looked like her sister and Lily were gone. Brother-in-law too. She'd bet they weren't together.

Sabra's marriage was another reason she was in no hurry to tie the knot with anyone. Marriage was about spending time together and developing a deeper relationship. She did not see that with Sabra and Mason. What she saw was two people doing their own thing. Mason was too wrapped up in his work, and Sabra was too focused on Lily. Her sister would be lost when Lily went off to college. But hey! At least she had Lily, which was more than Kelsey could say for herself.

She drove behind Sabra's house and parked in front of the garage apartment, getting out as Brad pulled in behind her. "Where's the bodyguard Sam was sending over?" he asked as he climbed out of his car. "And did you leave your front door open?"

"What?" She jerked her head up toward the front door. It stood wide open. Adrenaline pumped through her veins. "N-no."

He walked to the back of his car and popped the trunk. "Stay here. I'm going to check it out."

"Sorry, but I'm coming with you. Whoever left the door open may be waiting for you to leave me."

"Then put this on," he said, handing her a Kevlar vest.

She didn't argue with him.

"It'll be quicker to go in through the garage," she said. "The front door opens onto the deck that wraps around to the back stairs. It's why I usually come and go through the garage and use the stairs that lead to the kitchen. Let me show you where the remote control is."

"You don't have it in your car?"

"No. Sabra never remembers where hers is if she needs to get in, so I leave it here. And the remote for the other garage doesn't work with this one," she said, removing a brick halfway up the wall. "Otherwise she has to go all the way around to the back to enter through the front door. I never put my car in the garage anyway."

She handed him the remote, but instead of going in, he took out his phone and dialed a number.

"This is Sergeant Brad Hollister. I need backup," he said and gave the address. "Ten-four."

"We're waiting?"

He nodded. It wasn't five minutes before three patrol cars pulled into the drive. Brad assigned one of the patrolmen to stay with Kelsey, and he sent another one to the steps at the back of the apartment. With his gun ready, he raised the garage door, and she inched closer as he and the other patrolman climbed the stairs to the kitchen.

"Police! Come out with your hands where I can see them!"

When there was no response, Brad repeated his command and then whipped around the door and disappeared inside. She tensed, expecting gunfire any second. When he appeared in the doorway, air whooshed from her lungs.

"All clear. You can come up."

She grabbed her purse and computer bag—once she got upstairs, she was not coming back down. By the time she climbed to the top, the muscles in her legs had turned to wet noodles. "H-has the apartment been trashed?"

"No, it looks really neat. I don't see any signs of an intruder. Are you sure you didn't leave the door open?"

Kelsey shook her head. "I never even leave it unlocked."

She stepped inside and laughed out loud.

"What's so funny?" he asked.

"Someone has been here, but I don't think it was an intruder."

"What are you talking about?"

"My sister." Kelsey definitely had to get a place of her own. "She cleaned my apartment and must have swept the deck and didn't completely close the door. The wind probably blew it open." She was going to throttle Sabra. "I'm sorry to cause so much chaos."

"No worries," he said. "I'm just glad it wasn't an intruder. But look around while I call Sam about that bodyguard."

"Sure, but I don't think there's any need." Kelsey looked through the kitchen and her bedroom. Everything seemed normal. "Let me look in the office and then you can go."

A blue light emitted from the room as she rounded the corner, and she hesitated. "Brad? Can you come here a second?"

He hurried down the hall, his phone still in his hand. "What is it?"

"Did you check my office?"

"Yes. It was clear. Why?"

"My computer is on. I always turn it off when I leave, and it should still be off."

"Maybe your sister turned it on."

"Sabra would never touch my computer." Kelsey walked to her desk and sat down. With a few clicks, she started a program to scan her computer.

"Do you think someone hacked into it?"

"Impossible. A hacker couldn't get past my router. The only way I could be hacked is if I opened an email with a virus, and I haven't received any suspicious emails."

"Is that the only way?"

"If I downloaded a file from an unsafe URL. And I never do that, either. I never download or open anything I don't recognize."

Her computer dinged that the scan was complete, and Kelsey peered closely to see what the program had found. She didn't see any unusual activity, but she was too distracted right now to be sure. When Brad left, she would run it again.

"Everything is okay?" Brad asked.

"I think so. If I find anything later, I'll call you." She stood and walked to the door with him just as a man joined the officers standing in the drive.

"That must be the security detail Sam said would be arriving. King said he's the best that Rutherford Security has. I'll check him out."

She placed her hand on his arm. "Before you go, thank you and tell the officers that as well."

He nodded. "See you tomorrow?"

"You know where I'll be."

He nodded. "I'll come by the museum sometime tomorrow morning."

After Brad left, the man came up and introduced himself. "If you need anything, I'll either be patrolling the perimeter of the property or in the car," he said. "Here's my cell number."

Kelsey took the card he handed her. "Thank you."

She closed the door and walked back to her office, intending to run the scan once more. The monitor was black, and she wiggled the mouse.

An image of Lily appeared on the screen, one she'd never seen before. Someone had hacked into her computer and inserted Lily's photo as the desktop wallpaper. But why threaten Lily?

25

KELSEY SAT DOWN HARD in front of the computer. Her hand shook as she dialed Sabra's cell number. Two rings, three . . .

"Hello?" Sabra said, her voice low.

"Where are you? Is Lily all right?"

"We're at the movies. And of course she's all right. What's wrong?"

Kelsey's world righted briefly. But the threat wasn't over. "Someone hacked into my computer and uploaded a photo of Lily as the desktop wallpaper. Don't leave the theater until you get a call from the police. Got it?" She walked to the front door.

"You're scaring me."

"I meant to. We'll talk when you get home." She disconnected and dialed the number on the card. "Can you come inside?"

While she waited for the bodyguard, she dialed Brad's number, and when he answered, Kelsey said, "I think you'd better come back. He hacked my computer and threatened Lily."

"I'll be right there."

"Door's open, so come on in."

Once she explained the situation, the bodyguard immediately called the police to get an officer to go to the theater, where Sabra was waiting. Kelsey's hands shook as she moved the mouse to wake her computer. Whoever was after her had made a mistake when he hacked her computer. She would find this lowlife and turn the information over to Brad.

Kelsey opened the network monitoring software program she'd installed on her computer to analyze communication to and from her computer and barely noticed when Brad arrived.

"How did this guy get into your computer? You said it was impossible."

"I don't know." She chewed the inside of her cheek while she clicked on her email account and scanned for any unusual emails. Kelsey's breath stilled when she came to the security job she'd bid on Sunday night. She hadn't even hesitated to open the bid. She wanted to bang her head against the desk. Stupid mistake.

"Here's how he got in." Kelsey highlighted the email.

"What is it?"

"This is the only attachment I've opened recently. It's a bid for a security job. I'd heard this company was changing security specialists and queried them. When I opened the application, it must have launched a silent download that infected my computer. Let's see what we can find out about this baby."

Kelsey typed in a filter for ports, and when the command turned green, she hit apply. "I've set a program to search a log for communication between my computer and other computers about the time I bid on the job."

"Does everyone have that program?" Brad asked.

She shot him a lopsided grin. "No. But it comes in handy in my field of work."

Her screen filled with IP addresses, and she scrolled from the top, looking for a program with the company name from the email. She found it and took a screenshot. When she examined the screenshot, she noticed a strange file named a.exe extension and an open port. Immediately she knew he was listening to her computer. Kelsey clenched her jaw. He knew everything she was doing—when she logged on and what she searched for on the internet and when she logged off.

She dug deeper for where and when communication with the program occurred. The where was the Ben Hooks Library, and the when was Sunday night.

Kelsey turned to Brad. "This file, a.exe," she said, highlighting it, "is on my C drive, and I didn't put it there." She pointed to another column. "This IP address is the library on Poplar. He was using their Wi-Fi."

"English, if you don't mind," Brad said.

She tapped a line on her screen. "This is the program he installed on my computer. It had the capability to set Lily's photo as my desktop wallpaper. And he did it using the Wi-Fi at the Ben Hooks Library."

"You got all that information from that screen of letters and numbers?"

"Yep. And no telling what else he's tampered with. I'll be up all night checking. The thing is, he waited until after I checked the computer the first time tonight, and that means he's installed a program that lets him know when I'm online."

"Don't delete anything," Brad said. "I don't know a lot about computers, but can't we use this somehow?"

Kelsey studied the screen. "He probably doesn't know I

197

have any idea of how he put the photo on my computer. If I leave the program open, we may be able to catch him hacking in again and maybe he won't be using public Wi-Fi. Then I can trace his IP address and find his location."

Suddenly small footsteps clattered down her hall, and Kelsey turned just as Lily burst into the room.

"Why did that policeman come get us?" she asked and flung herself into Kelsey's arms.

She hadn't expected Lily to be so upset, and she had no cover story.

"He's a special agent," Brad said, lowering his voice to a whisper. "Because you're a special person."

The child's eyes grew round. "Really?"

"Yes," he said. "Why don't we go find your mommy?"

Thank you, Kelsey mouthed as he took Lily's hand. Who would have thought Brad would have a way with kids? She followed them out of the office to the living room, where Sabra was waiting with her husband.

"Your flight to Minnesota leaves at eleven tomorrow," Mason was telling Sabra. "That should give you enough time to pack. And my mother will be thrilled with your visit."

"That's wonderful," Kelsey said, giving Mason a nod of approval, but the look he shot her was anything but. Not that she blamed him. If she hadn't been playing with fire, none of this would be happening. *Hendrix and Rutherford would still be dead*. That she couldn't deny, but knowing Sabra and Lily were out of harm's way would take some of the pressure off.

"I'll call my brother in the morning, and he'll take you to the airport," Mason said.

"No," Sabra said. "We're staying here in Memphis, with Mom and Dad."

"What?" Kelsey cried. All three of them turned and stared at Sabra.

"My mother is expecting you," Mason said, his voice rising. "I would take you to the airport except I have a meeting with the mayor, and it can't be moved."

Same old Mason.

"You won't be up there for long," Kelsey said. She looked at Brad. "Will she?"

"She sure won't," Sabra said. "Because *she* isn't going. I talked to Dad, and he's beefing up security at the house. You have no way of knowing that this . . . this person won't follow us up to Minnesota. And there won't be any security there. Lily and I will be much safer at Dad's."

"You are getting on that airplane—"

"Daddy, why are you talking so loud?" Lily said, tears rimming her eyes.

"He's just tired and cranky, like you get." Kelsey pinned Mason with a hard stare. "Isn't that right?"

He ran his hand over his short red hair. "Come here, pumpkin. I'm sorry if I scared you, but I really want you to go see Grandma." He picked Lily up and set her on his knee.

"But I want to stay here with Pawpaw Sam."

Her brother-in-law pressed his lips together and looked first at Lily then Sabra. He turned to Brad. "Do you think they would be safe at Sam's house?"

"It does have a security fence all the way around it," Brad said, "and if he hires guards to patrol the area . . . well, like Sabra said, it actually might be better than Minnesota, where you won't have security personnel."

Mason kissed Lily on the forehead and hugged her to his chest before he pulled Sabra to his side. "Then maybe staying with your dad would be better."

Sometimes Kelsey forgot that Mason really cared for his family, but seeing him with Lily reminded her of his commitment to them. She sighed. If anything happened to Sabra or Lily because of her . . . Somehow she had to figure out who this killer was and put him behind bars.

26

MORNING CAME MUCH TOO EARLY FOR BRAD. He'd spent another hour after he left Kelsey trying to put the puzzle pieces together, and then he'd taken Tripod for a run on the dirt road behind his house. Having open spaces was one advantage to living on the edge of the city.

And now he was on his third cup of coffee from the Keurig someone had donated to the break room.

He doodled on his desk calendar. Why had someone broken into Kelsey's computer? The question had not ceased to run through his mind since last night. Did the killer think she'd written up an account of what happened last Thursday night and stored it on her computer?

If that was the case, it was an indication of how the hacker thought—or possibly it involved his line of work. He probably wrote reports routinely. Like a detective . . . or salesman . . . or executive. But what linked Hendrix's murder to Rutherford's? Other than Kelsey? He looked up when Lieutenant Raines stepped into his office. "Morning, sir."

David nodded. "Have you settled on a case?"

"Yes, sir. Probably two—or one and a half, since the second one may be an active murder."

"Rachel Sloan's box of bones?"

"It's an interesting case, and I'd like to explore it." He sipped his coffee. "Caldwell is doing the autopsy this morning, and we'll know if it's murder or not."

"Sloan okay with you exploring it?"

"Yes, sir. She invited me to sit in on the autopsy."

"Good. I like to see teamwork between Homicide and the Unit. You said two cases."

He hesitated, remembering the ribbing about having a romantic interest in Kelsey yesterday morning . . . Had it been just a day ago? "Paul Carter disappeared twenty-eight years ago, and after he left, numerous artifacts from the Pink Palace Museum were confirmed missing. There's been no trace of him since. I know it's not a murder case, but if I can track him down, it would bring the family closure and return the artifacts to the museum."

David rubbed his jaw. "I wouldn't spend too much time on it. Even if you found him, the statute of limitations on his crimes has run out. Do you have any leads?"

"No." He hated to admit the chances of finding Paul Carter were slim to none. "I thought I'd give it a week, and if nothing shows up, I'll choose another case."

"Good deal. If you need anything, let me know."

After David left, Brad checked his watch. Nine thirty. Kelsey should be at work. He dialed her number. "How are you?" he asked after she answered.

"Very tired, but I couldn't find any evidence he left any surprises on my computer other than Lily's picture."

"Good. I was going over your father's file, and I'd like to pick up that box of papers at the house on Snowden sometime today."

"We agreed on five thirty, right?"

"Just double-checking."

"You know, you might want to check out that old desk too," she said. "There may be some files from the museum in it."

"I'll look tonight. Do you plan on taking it?"

"Definitely. Thought I'd make arrangements to get someone to pick up the desk and deliver it to my apartment this weekend."

"I can borrow my dad's truck and help you. By the way, is your bodyguard with you?"

Her voice dropped. "You'll be happy to know he's lurking around somewhere just outside my door. You'll also be happy to know I decided not to attend the autopsy on the bones. There's too much to do around here."

Brad chuckled. "You'll get used to having him around."

"It just seems unnecessary to have a bodyguard here with so many other security guards in the building."

"The same security guards Walter Rutherford had," he said.

She had no response for him, and they talked for another minute. He disconnected without telling her that Rachel had texted that Dr. Caldwell was examining the bones midmorning if he wanted to be there. He'd been surprised when Rachel offered to let him work with her, and he looked forward to puzzling this mystery out. The first thing he wanted to know was why the bones had been delivered to the museum. Maybe when they discovered the identity of the body, it would make sense.

The West Tennessee Forensic Center was only a few blocks from the CJC, and he was there in ten minutes, just in time to catch Rachel. "Leaving already?" he asked.

She held up a paper bag. "Doc extracted a bullet from a

rib—L7, he says, and I'm taking it to ballistics to see if there's a match anywhere in the system."

"So it was murder," he said.

"Looks that way."

He looked past her to Dr. Caldwell. The medical examiner had the bones laid out on a flat table and was measuring what looked like a leg bone.

The doctor looked over his glasses at Brad. "Good morning, Sergeant. This shouldn't be nearly as bad as our last autopsy together."

Brad hoped not. The last time he was there, the doctor was autopsying a floater they'd dragged out of the Mississippi River. "Any other interesting finds?"

The doctor wiggled his hand as if he were holding a cigar. "Just getting started, my boy, just getting started."

Brad laughed. "Doc, most people don't even know who W. C. Fields is."

"All the more pity," he said with a shake of his head. "Grab a pair of those gloves and help me out here."

The lab must have been short staffed. He pulled on the latex gloves as the doctor spoke into his microphone, identifying Brad. Then he reached and picked up another bone.

"Can you tell if this is a male or female?"

Dr. Caldwell looked up. "Oh, definitely male. See the pelvis, the streamlined opening. And how thick the skull is here behind the ear. Can't tell the age yet, other than he's an adult, or how long he's been in the ground."

The medical examiner was good at reading Brad's mind.

The ME straightened up and pushed his glasses up on his nose. "Would you check the crate and see that all the bones are out? Detective Sloan was helping until we found the bullet. Just examine the plastic, and when you're done, fold and place it in the evidence box."

"Where's your assistant?"

"Called in sick, and there are five bodies waiting after this autopsy."

Brad took the plastic sheet from the crate and started at one end, rolling it as he went. "Nothing in it."

"Check the crate," Caldwell said without looking up.

He peered into the wooden crate, and something red in the bottom caught his eye. A ring, maybe? Using his pen, he nudged the stone, and it came loose from the crack that held it.

"Here's a ring," he said and examined it. *University of Pennsylvania 1971.* Dread filled his stomach, and he tried to dismiss it. But how many people in Memphis graduated from the University of Pennsylvania the same year as Paul Carter? He tried to read what was on the inside, but dirt and the tiny engraving made it impossible.

The ME laid the bone in his hands on the table. "Let me see."

Brad handed it to him, and Caldwell spoke into the mic again, describing the ring. When he finished, Brad said, "Does it have initials engraved on the inside?"

His muscles tensed as the ME used a magnifying glass to examine the inside of the ring. "Yes. J . . . Hold on a minute."

As in John.

Caldwell turned so he could catch the light. "JPC," he said. "Tell you anything?"

John Paul Carter. "Tells me I'm pretty sure I know who the victim is and that he's been in the ground for twenty-eight years." He took out his phone and dialed Rachel. "I think I know who our victim is here," he said. "Paul Carter, former director of the Pink Palace Museum."

"What?"

"I found a ring that could possibly belong to him." He explained about the initials. "I believe his dental record will confirm it."

"Do you have the name of his dentist?"

"Not yet. I thought I'd give Mrs. Allen a call."

"I have a couple of things for you too," she said. "I just talked with Reggie. Hendrix was a CPA and worked with Rutherford on different projects, and he handled their taxes, so it's a link we need to explore."

Could be a coincidence, but Brad and every cop he knew didn't believe in coincidence. "You said two things. What was the other?"

"That bullet? It matched the ones that came from Hendrix's and Rutherford's bodies, as well as the one I dug out of the tree yesterday. And they were all fired by a gun that was used in the 1954 House of Representatives shooting. Last place it was known to be was—"

"The Pink Palace Museum," he said. He'd seen it on the list Tomlinson had faxed over. The ring and now the bullet. The ring was positive proof the bones belonged to John Paul Carter, and the bullet connected the murder to the museum. "Why don't we release the information to the news outlets that the two bullets from Hendrix and Rutherford match the 1954 shooting?" he said. "That might stir up someone."

"I like that idea. Do we want to release the information on Carter's death once we get confirmation?"

"Let's hold off on that, at least until I can tell Kelsey." He closed his eyes. She expected him to find her father alive, not dead. How was he going to tell her she'd actually been handling his body?

27

Brad couldn't tell Kelsey he thought the skeleton was her father's remains until he knew for certain. There was no identification in the box with the ring. Evidently, his killer removed those items but forgot the ring.

He had returned to his office to review Carter's file, but it held no answers. Foul play evidently had not been on Sergeant Warren's radar. When he had proof that the remains were Carter's, Brad would contact Warren and see if the new information jarred his memory. Brad dialed Cynthia Allen's number from his contacts. When she answered, he asked for the name of her ex-husband's dentist.

The line was silent, then she cleared her throat. "Are you telling me Paul is dead? That you've found remains that you think . . ."

"I'm not sure, ma'am. Yes, we have found remains, but I would prefer you not relay that information to anyone until we're certain one way or the other. Especially not to Kelsey."

"Don't worry, I won't. But yes, he did see a dentist here in Memphis. Dr. Gilbert."

"Is he still practicing?" Brad opened a browser and typed in the dentist's name and waited. His computer was slow.

"I, uh, I don't know. He wasn't my dentist, so I haven't kept up with him. He was right next to the library on South Highland. I believe the library is closed, and he's probably not there any longer. I'm sorry I can't be of more help."

His search yielded a list of dentists in the Memphis area and two with a last name of Gilbert. "Do you know what his first name was?"

"I don't remember . . ."

"How about Franklin? Or Clayton?"

"Clayton. I believe that was it."

"Thanks. It looks as though he may still be practicing." Brad glanced at the address. "But he's on Poplar now."

"I'd like to be there when you tell Kelsey," Cynthia said. "She already feels terrible about Sabra and Lily having to leave their home. I'm not sure how she'll react when she learns her father is dead."

He remembered her reaction when he told her about finding the file. "That would be a good idea."

Brad had been so focused on Kelsey and the remains that he forgot about her sister and niece. "Did Sabra and Lily get settled in without any problems?"

"Yes. They're out by the pool with a couple of security people." There was a hesitation on the line again. "Brad, you keep my daughter safe, you hear?"

"Yes, ma'am. But she's a hard one to rein in."

"I know. So I'm depending on you to watch after her."

He thought about Kelsey dangling from the roof of the building on Front Street. Nothing like more pressure. "I'll do my best."

He said good-bye to Cynthia and then dialed the number

for the dentist. The blurb on the website said they were open Monday through Friday, eight to five. It would be easier to get the information he wanted in person, possibly using his badge—it went a lot further than saying over the phone that he was a sergeant with the MPD.

Twenty minutes later, he found the dentist's office and parked in the only space left. The man must be good. When he approached the reception window, the receptionist's eyes widened and focused on the gun on his belt. "M-may I help you?"

He held out his badge. "I'm Sergeant Hollister with the Memphis Police Department. Is there any way I can speak with Dr. Gilbert?"

"He's with a patient right now. Can you wait until he's finished?"

"Yes, ma'am." Brad found an empty seat in the crowded room beside a young mother with a boy who looked to be Lily's age. He smiled at the towheaded child when he peeked around his mother's arm. Then he noticed the abundance of small chairs. A pediatric dentist. His hopes crashed, and he debated whether he should even wait. Just as he was about to leave, a nurse opened the door and called his name.

"Dr. Gilbert said to bring you to his office and he'll be with you momentarily," she said.

"Yes, ma'am." He followed her to the dentist's office, and she closed the door behind her when she left. Guess the gun was bad for business. He perused the diplomas on the wall, quickly realizing this was not the dentist he was looking for. The door opened, and Brad turned as a man his age entered the office. He held out his hand. "Sorry to have bothered you, Dr. Gilbert, but I was looking for a much older man."

"Probably my father, but may I ask why?"

"I have remains that I believe belong to a patient of Dr. Clayton Gilbert—Paul Carter."

"Yes, Clayton Gilbert is my father, but he's retired. However—"

"Then he's still living?" Hope rose in Brad's chest.

"Yes. And all his records are stored at his house." Gilbert grinned. "He's an armchair detective now and actually dreamed of the day someone would need them."

Brad couldn't believe his luck. "Do you think he could see me this afternoon?"

"Let me give him a call."

A few minutes later, Brad left the dentist's office with an address in Germantown and a retired dentist anxious to see him.

Dr. Clayton Gilbert met him at his front door, his faded blue eyes dancing. "Come in," he said. "As soon as we hung up, I searched for Paul Carter's records, and they're on the kitchen table."

He followed the older man down a hallway lined with framed photos. One, a sunset over water, caught his eye. Somehow the photographer had caught a sailboat in the setting sun. "Did you take these photos?" he asked.

"Yes. After I retired, I discovered I had a little talent for photography."

Little? These photos were professional quality. Then he realized he'd fallen behind the dentist, who moved faster than a lot of detectives he knew. In fact, as agile and young-looking as Gilbert was, Brad wondered why he had retired.

X-rays attached to a metal clip and dental charts were spread out on the island workstation in a kitchen that would be a chef's dream. Gleaming cookware hung from the ceiling over an island that held a prep sink. His mother would love this kitchen. "Your wife must love to cook," he said.

A shadow crossed the older man's face. "She did."

A tender subject. Brad turned his attention to the X-rays. "In the skull we have, there's a gold crown on the bottom right jaw. Is that consistent with your files?"

Gilbert held the clip to the light and pointed to the third X-ray from the top. "See this one? That's a gold crown." He set it on the table and picked up a larger panorama X-ray. "And here it is again. There should be several large fillings in the bottom teeth, as well."

Sadness tempered Brad's satisfaction of knowing the identity of the victim. It was hard enough giving bad news to families he didn't know. In spite of her seeming indifference to her dad, his news would shake Kelsey. "Do you have a folder to put these in?"

He didn't need Dr. Gilbert's help to deliver the X-rays to the medical examiner, but one glance at Dr. Gilbert's wistful eyes, and he said, "Do you have time to come with me to the West Tennessee Forensic Center and show these to Dr. Caldwell? I'll be glad to bring you back home."

"You bet. Other than playing a little golf and tinkering around with my camera, I don't do that much. Not since my wife died. She was the only reason I retired. Edith wanted to travel, and I was always too busy with the practice." He sighed. "At least we had two years."

In the car Brad said, "Have you thought about going back to your practice?"

Gilbert fastened his seat belt. "No, but I am thinking about doing mission work. There are people right here in Memphis who need dental work and can't afford it."

Brad knew a few of them. "If you ever have time, I help out at a youth center. There are kids there who have never been to the dentist. And it'd be great if you could teach a photography class. We're always looking for something to get the kids involved in."

"Let me think about it."

Brad didn't want to give him too long to think—inertia would set in. "How about going with me this Saturday?"

"Let me check on something first." Gilbert took out his phone and scrolled through it. "I can do it," he said. "I couldn't remember when my granddaughter's birthday was, but it's next weekend. This will give me something to look forward to."

Rachel was with the medical examiner when they arrived, and after Brad made the introductions, he said, "I thought it'd be to our advantage for Dr. Gilbert to match the teeth to the X-rays."

"Good thinking," Dr. Caldwell said.

When the dentist finished his examination, he nodded. "The X-rays definitely match these teeth, and in my professional opinion, they belong to my patient, Paul Carter."

Brad hadn't realized he'd been holding his breath until he exhaled. "Now the hard part begins—who killed him and why."

"Yeah," Rachel echoed. "And how does a twenty-eight-year-old murder relate to the two murders last week?"

He picked up the ring on the table. "I have another question for you. Who sent the bones to the museum and why? Obviously, the sender knew the remains were Paul Carter's. Why not just come forward with them?"

"If I might add my two cents," Caldwell said, "it sounds like two people are involved and one turned on the other."

"Or," Brad said, "the sender, whether the killer or an accomplice, wanted the family to have closure but didn't want to be implicated."

"A killer with a conscience? That would be a twist," Rachel said. "But why now?"

Why indeed? "Until we know, I suggest we keep the identity of the bones under wraps," Brad said. "In fact, I suggest we don't reveal any information on the bones. See who that shakes up."

28

KELSEY SCANNED THE SHEET listing the artifacts stolen over the past ten years. Forty-eight pieces of varying value and composition. She looked at the two men across from her in the director's office. "You're saying there was no inventory of the artifacts after my father left until the date on this first line? Ten years ago?"

Robert Tomlinson glanced at Jackson King, then shifted his gaze back to her and nodded. "Of course, that was before my time as director here. We have conducted inventories every year that I've been in charge."

"Why didn't you do something about the thefts once you knew they were happening?" she asked.

"We quietly conducted inquiries." A red blotch crept into Tomlinson's face, and he fingered the knot on his tie. "If the thefts became public knowledge, it would affect donations."

"The stamp taken Saturday night was worth twenty thousand," Kelsey said. "Would you have reported it if Rutherford hadn't been killed?"

"Of course. It's the most valuable piece taken," Tomlinson said. "As far as the other articles that have been taken, I attributed them to employee theft—someone saw something and took it home. We held in-service training focusing on the thefts to encourage employees to keep a watch for anyone taking the artifacts. And the number of pieces missing went down for the last two years."

"But you never involved the police?" Kelsey asked.

"No." The director nodded toward Jackson. "When we hired Rutherford Security, I advised them to report any thefts to MPD, but—"

"Mr. Rutherford didn't want to," Jackson said, "thinking it would tip our hand that we knew the thefts were occurring. He hoped the thief would get overconfident."

"But that didn't happen," Kelsey said. Her phone vibrated and she checked it. Brad? "Excuse me a minute, gentlemen."

She stepped outside in the hallway and answered. "Hello?"

"Can you spare me an hour?"

"I'm in a meeting with Jackson King and the director right now."

"Give me a second."

She heard him tell someone that she was with King and Tomlinson, and then it sounded as though he were arguing about something.

"I need to talk with them as well," he said when he returned to her, "but you don't have to be there."

"We're in the middle of a meeting, and I can't very well leave. Does it concern me?"

He hesitated, and she knew it did.

"I'll be there in fifteen," he said.

After she disconnected, she returned to the men. "Brad is joining us. He has news of some sort."

"Sergeant Hollister?" Tomlinson said. "Does it have anything to do with this case?"

"He didn't say, but he definitely wants to discuss something with you," she said. Different reasons for Brad wanting to see her whipped through her mind—reasons that included the museum. Maybe they'd found the shooter. Or some of the artifacts that had been stolen?

"Then let's try to finish our meeting before they get here," Tomlinson said. "Tell us what you've learned about the camera feed."

Kelsey refocused her mind on the security details they'd been discussing. "Not much more than I already suspected. His normal mode of operation is to insert a recorded film that loops until he removes it, but evidently it malfunctioned Saturday night, resulting in the blank screen. Then yesterday, he inserted video into all the outside cameras. And all the IP addresses trace back to the Ben Hooks Library."

"Could the killer work there?" Tomlinson asked.

"No," Jackson replied. "Well, he could, but according to my IT, he's more than likely just using their Wi-Fi. Do you have anything else to add?"

"No. I'm still comparing camera feed against the incidents of theft, and as soon as I have my results, I'll bring them to you." Kelsey stretched her shoulder muscles. "We've been here for over an hour. I think I'll run to the café and grab a peach tea. Can I get you gentlemen anything?"

After they declined, she walked to the café. Had Brad discovered something about her father? But why would he want to talk to the other two? Another thought disturbed her. Perhaps she should have told them she had asked Brad to find her father. She was almost surprised that Tomlinson had not mentioned her father in all of this. He'd been at the museum then—she'd looked at his employment records, along with all the others. Surely Tomlinson noticed the similarities in the thefts. It was almost as if her father had returned and somehow found a way to steal the current items.

Brad and Rachel Sloan were seated in Tomlinson's office when she returned with her tea. She had not been expecting the detective. "That was fast," she said, returning to her seat. "You two must have been close."

"We were."

She was puzzled by Brad's terse words. "What's going on?" she asked and took her former seat.

"Yes, why did you want to see us?" Tomlinson asked, and Jackson nodded in agreement.

Brad took out his notepad as Rachel stood. Evidently she was doing the talking, but something about them both was off-kilter.

"I need any files you have on the P .38 automatic that was used in the 1954 assassination attempt in the House of Representatives. My information indicates it was stolen by Paul Carter," she said, sending Kelsey an apologetic nod.

"That's your turf," Jackson said, looking at Tomlinson.

The director shifted in his chair. "The, uh, gun in question was donated by one of the men who was wounded back in 1954. Those files are archived."

"Can you pull them?" Rachel asked.

"I suppose, if it's important."

Kelsey sat, stunned. Why were they asking about items her father stole? Did they actually think he was the killer? She leaned forward. "Why is this gun important?"

"That's what I want to know," Jackson said.

Rachel and Brad exchanged glances, then he said, "The bullets taken from Hendrix's and Rutherford's bodies as well as a slug Detective Sloan retrieved after yesterday's shooting all match the gun used in the 1954 shooting."

Blood drained from Kelsey's face. "Are you saying my father is the murderer?"

Jackson turned to her. "You're Paul Carter's daughter?"

"Yes." She should have told him before now. "And if that makes any difference about my job, well—"

"No, I'm just surprised."

But she saw the doubt in his eyes. "Mr. Rutherford didn't tell you?"

"No." Jackson turned to Tomlinson. "Did he tell you?"

"Didn't say a word," he said. "But now that I know and thinking about her résumé, it's not surprising."

Kelsey didn't know if he was complimenting her or not.

The director turned to her. "But if I'm right that the detectives here are suggesting your father may be behind all of this, will that affect your performance?"

Would it? "No. I want to catch this murdering thief no matter who it is." But surely her own father wouldn't be trying to kill her? Unless he didn't know what she looked like. She turned to Brad. "Do you think my father has returned to Memphis and is he the person you're trying to catch?"

Brad looked as though he'd bit into a lemon, and Rachel . . . she just looked miserable. "Never mind," Kelsey said. "You don't have to answer that."

29

"Kelsey, I'm sorry, but we don't have enough information to make that call," Rachel said.

"But it is a possibility?"

Brad could barely stand to see the pain their questions were causing Kelsey. But she was holding up. Probably would hate him when she found out the truth. But he totally agreed with Rachel that they would get more information if no one knew Paul Carter was dead.

"I'd say the MO for the thefts is the same," Tomlinson said.

"And how would you know this?" Brad asked.

"I had already been working here a couple of years before Carter left. Started at the bottom and worked my way up. And I remember when we learned the gun was stolen." He nodded at the security director. "You were here as a summer intern, if I recall correctly."

"I was, and was questioned like everyone else." Jackson frowned. "Say, didn't Mark work here as well?"

"My brother?" Tomlinson shrugged. "I don't believe he'd started to work here yet."

Mark Tomlinson. Brad flipped through his notepad to

the names he'd jotted down when he went through Sergeant Warren's files on Carter and found Mark's name. It was in the list under people the sergeant had questioned after Carter's disappearance—right next to Robert Tomlinson. Interesting. "So there was no confirmation anything was missing until Carter left?"

Jackson and Tomlinson exchanged glances. "There were rumors floating around that pieces had disappeared, but he would have been the last person anyone suspected," Jackson said.

Kelsey's pencil hit the table with a slap and she stood. "Do you mind if I go to my office? I'm not contributing anything, and I have work to do."

"That's fine with me," Brad said and Rachel agreed. The other two might talk more freely with her out of the room, and he didn't want to see her hurting the way she was. "I'll come by your office before I leave."

Her look indicated he needn't bother. Once the door closed, he turned back to the two men. "Is there anyone currently working at the museum who was here when Carter disappeared?"

"My assistant, Helen Peterson . . . Julie Webb," Tomlinson said, then he turned to Jackson. "Whatever happened between you and Julie? You two were quite the hot item."

"What are you talking about?" Jackson snapped.

"Saw you one time up in the attic, putting away boxes of files. Or at least that's what you were supposed to be doing."

Jackson shook his head. "I have no idea what you're talking about."

In spite of his protest, Brad noted the relationship in his notes and added Webb's and Peterson's names. He didn't know why he hadn't thought to interview Helen Peterson. Fact was, he'd barely noticed her at all. The woman seemed to fade into the background. "How long has Ms. Peterson worked here?"

Tomlinson and Jackson exchanged glances. "I think this is the only place she's ever worked," Tomlinson said.

Interesting. "Can you think of anyone else?"

"I'll have to run a query and see how many employees we have with twenty-eight or more years." He scratched his jaw. "Couldn't be that many."

"I'd appreciate that," Brad said. "A couple more questions, and then we'll let you two get back to work. Do either of you know if the ammunition was kept with the stolen gun?"

"I don't know about then, but it wouldn't be now," the director said. "We keep any ammunition well away from the firearms we currently have. But Julie could answer that question, since she was working as an assistant to the collections manager back then."

"Well, I want to thank you two for answering our questions," Rachel said and smiled at the two men. "We may be back with more, so would you mind kicking that time around in your mind, see what shakes out?"

Tomlinson nodded, but Jackson folded his arms across his chest. "You've asked what we think. Now I want to ask what you think happened."

Brad sat back and let Rachel field the question. He thought she should have asked more questions, but she was a good detective. He'd just have to trust that she knew what she was doing.

"We don't have enough information to hazard a guess, because that's all it would be. What we do know is that the murders and the attack on Kelsey are connected because of the gun."

"Those bones that showed up here—are they connected to any of this?" Jackson asked.

Tomlinson almost choked on a sip of Perrier water. "Don't even breathe that possibility," the director said. "A glut of calls have hit the museum already over Rutherford's death. Don't add to it. And for all we know, that box may have been a prank and not even real bones."

"Is that true?" Jackson said, turning to Rachel. "That the bones are fake?"

"Unfortunately, they are real bones. Dr. Caldwell at the Forensic Center is doing an autopsy on them," Rachel answered for Brad. "But Mr. King, I'd like to ask how well you knew Troy Hendrix. In looking over Rutherford Security's financial records that your secretary provided, I noticed checks made out to him."

Brad stilled. This was the question he wanted answered.

"What are you talking about?"

"Rutherford Security, the company you are a partner in, was paying Hendrix for some type of service."

"I don't know what you're talking about, but give me a second." Jackson took out his phone and dialed a number. When someone answered, he said, "Was Troy Hendrix working for us?"

A minute later, he thanked them and hung up. "He's the accountant who handles our taxes and a few other things like the financial forms for a government contract dealing with a security job due the first of the month. It seems I have a lot to learn about the company."

"So you didn't know?"

"No. I've invested in a lot of the business but I'm not involved in the day-to-day operations. Rutherford handled that sort of thing in the past, and I don't know who will handle it now. Not me for sure, since I'm not a numbers person."

"What percentage of the business do you own?"

"Forty-nine percent. Rutherford's part went to his heirs, but I hope to buy them out."

Brad wrote *Rutherford's heirs* on his pad with a dash. *Check the security company's net worth.* Money was always a motive for murder. And even though the three murders appeared to be connected, they might not be, at least not for the same reason.

◆

Kelsey set the miniature bareback rider and brush she was using to clean it on the table and pulled off the latex gloves. She had immersed herself in cleaning the pieces of the miniature circus, hoping to put the question of whether her father could be the murderer from her mind.

But the fact that a bullet from a gun her father supposedly stole had been fired at her wouldn't go away. The same gun had been used on Mr. Rutherford and Hendrix. *Hendrix.* She pinched the bridge of her nose and closed her eyes, trying to bring up the image of the silhouette she'd seen through the window last Thursday night.

Suddenly light flashed in her mind, and for a scant second, a face appeared. Then it was gone. She tried to force the image back. But it was no use.

She stood and walked to the window. Raising it, she breathed in the scents of honeysuckle and rhododendron below the window. Somewhere a siren wailed and the whop-whop of a helicopter drew her gaze to the sky. A blue-and-white medical chopper was flying toward downtown.

There'd been a helicopter Thursday night, something she'd almost forgotten. Could that have been the flash of light? The office was a corner room . . . the strobe lights had almost illuminated her. Could they have swept by the other window, putting the man in full view? It had only been for a second, but long enough for his face to register somewhere in her brain.

Or her brain was playing tricks on her. She would wait and see if it happened again before she told anyone. She turned as someone knocked on her open door. Helen Peterson.

"May I come in?" she asked.

"Sure. I was taking a break from the circus."

Helen entered her office. Again, she was dressed conservatively, this time in white linen slacks and a pale blue jacket over her darker blouse. She pointed to the bareback rider. "I don't envy you, restoring all these small pieces."

"I'm actually enjoying it," Kelsey said and sat behind her desk. She'd marveled at the detail Clyde Parke had put into the figures he carved. The man had loved woodworking and had spent twenty-five years creating his masterpiece. Knowing that she was restoring something created in 1930 satisfied the part of her that loved being a conservator.

"What?" she asked at Helen's wide-eyed stare.

"Looks like a bunch of tedious work to me. I'm just surprised you're taking so much time with it when it's not your real job," she said. "Mind if I sit?"

Kelsey's body tensed. "Of course not, but what are you talking about?"

"Oh, don't worry, I won't tell anyone you're really working for Jackson."

Why would Helen know that? Surely that information wasn't in Kelsey's employee file at the museum. "So Mr. Tomlinson confides in you?"

She smiled. "Not really, but not much gets by me. You've spent way more time with Jackson than the conservator ever has, so there had to be a reason, and you just confirmed my suspicion."

Kelsey decided not to confirm nor deny her statement, but she would have to be more circumspect about meeting with Jackson. Hopefully, no one else had noticed. She picked up her brush and tapped it on the desk to knock out any dust. "How long have you worked here?"

"Since I was eighteen. Started out as a guide for the tours and worked my way up to the director's assistant. Robert is the third director I've worked directly with." She hooked a strand of dark hair behind her ear. "So, what do you do for fun?"

"Not much." The woman could change directions faster than Lily. "I read. And go to church on Sundays, entertain my niece . . ." Kelsey stopped. "And I climb rocks."

"Well, I'm having a party Saturday night, if you'd like to come."

Ms. Peterson must not be too observant if she didn't know Kelsey had a bodyguard and someone shooting at her. Wouldn't that ruin her party if he decided to attack? "Maybe. Can I let you know?"

"Sure. It's only Tuesday, and the party will be real casual." Helen tapped her fingers on the chair. "I saw the police here earlier. Have they learned anything about yesterday's shooter?"

Finally, the reason for her being there. "Not that I know of," she said. "Did you see anything?"

"Oh goodness, no. I had gone to lunch." She leaned forward. "Have you heard who the target was?"

"Maybe there wasn't a target, just some druggie firing a gun."

"Maybe." Helen looked doubtful. "And what about those bones that arrived yesterday. What do you know about them?"

"Nothing yet, except they aren't ancient."

"Well, I think it's odd that all of this is happening. Do you think these things are connected?"

"Why would they be connected?" Kelsey glanced toward the miniature horse waiting for her to finish.

"Oh, I'm sorry. I'm hindering you from your work." Helen stood. "But think about coming to my party."

"I will." *Not.* The woman was just plain nosey. Kelsey couldn't imagine spending a couple of hours being grilled by her at a party.

30

AFTER THEY LEFT THE DIRECTOR'S OFFICE, Rachel turned to Brad. "Scared you there for a minute, didn't I."

Brad laughed. "I thought you'd forgotten to ask Jackson King about Hendrix and then moved into who got Rutherford's share of the business."

"His answer makes what was complex even more so. What if the murders have nothing to do with the thefts?" Rachel said. "Hendrix was a CPA with ties to Rutherford, and worked a lot of accounts. He could have stumbled onto money laundering or some type of fraud and mentioned it to the wrong person."

"Or he could have discovered some type of discrepancy in the security firm's books," Brad said as they approached the hallway to the conservator's office.

"That's true. What are you going to tell Kelsey?"

He hooked his thumb in his belt. "I don't know yet. Certainly not telling her about her father here. Cynthia Allen wants to be present when I do." He snapped his fingers. "I haven't called her back."

Rachel checked her watch. "I'll be finished for the day by the time I stop by the Forensic Center to see if Dr. Caldwell has any new information."

After Rachel left, Brad dialed Cynthia Allen's number, half hoping she wouldn't answer. He hated delivering bad news over the phone. She answered on the second ring.

"Did you find Dr. Gilbert?"

"I did."

"What did you find out?"

He hesitated.

"The remains—it's Paul, isn't it?"

"Yes, ma'am."

"After you called earlier, I knew it had to be. I've never quite bought the idea that Paul stole those items and walked away from Kelsey."

"Do you know who was the first one to suggest the thief was your ex-husband?"

"It was so long ago, I'll have to think about that." She paused. "When do you plan to tell Kelsey?"

He thought a minute. "We're supposed to go to the house on Snowden at five thirty for her to pick out what she wants to keep from the shed. If you can be there . . ."

"I'll be there. Just promise me you won't tell her before then."

"I promise." He disconnected and snapped his phone back on his belt before tapping on Kelsey's door.

"It's open," she said.

He stepped inside and found her standing at the window, looking out. When she turned around, regret pinged his heart again. "Look," he said, "I'm sorry for what happened in there."

"Then why did you do it? It was like an ambush. Why did I have to be there?"

If only he hadn't promised her mother he'd wait. If he could tell her, she would understand that looking for a murderer sometimes required subterfuge.

"I . . . will you trust me on this until I can explain?" If there'd been another way to do it, he would have, but Rachel felt they needed to act before news of Carter's death leaked. They were in agreement that someone who worked at the museum twenty-eight years ago killed Paul Carter, and both men had been there at the time.

Once Carter's death was public, the murderer would be much more on guard and careful about what he said. And maybe not only the murderer. Anyone associated with the museum at the time of his death would be a person of interest and might not want the skeletons in their closet rattled by an investigation. At least today's session had netted them more information, along with two more people to talk to.

"When will you be able to explain?"

"Soon." He checked the clock on her wall. "Look, it's almost four thirty. Why don't I follow you home and then you can ride with me to the house on Snowden?"

"Because I'm not finished with my work. I'll just meet you there."

"What time are you clocking out?"

"Five."

"I'll wait. We'll let your bodyguard know he won't be needed on the way out." He looked around for a chair.

"Not in here—I wouldn't be able to concentrate with you here. Go look at the exhibits until five."

"Good idea." But he had a better one. When he stepped out of Kelsey's office, he nodded to the young man guarding her door and explained he wouldn't need to accompany Kelsey home. Then he turned left and walked to the collections director's office. Julie was working at her computer.

"Do you have a minute?" he asked.

"Of course. Take a seat and let me close this program out."

He sat in the chair she indicated. Julie Webb's personality was evident in the tastefully decorated room. Various American Indian pieces of pottery were on display as well as a model of a Depression-era farm truck. Eclectic taste.

"Now, what can I do for you?" She swiveled to face him. "But first, did you learn anything about the bones?"

"When I left the Forensic Center, Dr. Caldwell was still working on them."

"Peculiar thing, someone sending a crate of bones here."

"We discovered something even more peculiar today," he said. "A pistol stolen from the museum almost thirty years ago was used to kill Mr. Rutherford and another victim."

Her mouth dropped open. "You're joking, right?"

"No."

"That must be the gun used in the 1954 shooting at the House of Representatives." She shook her head. "But I thought Paul Carter stole that gun."

"It's on the list of artifacts missing after he disappeared."

"So you're saying that maybe he didn't steal it . . ." She frowned. "Because I know he's not back in town shooting people."

Julie's reaction surprised him. "Why do you think that's far-fetched?"

"I knew Paul Carter, and he would not come back to Memphis, not even to shoot people. He was a nice man, and the rumors almost killed him."

"What rumors?"

"Just days before he left, someone started a rumor that he was stealing artifacts."

"Why do you think he didn't fight the rumors?"

"He said you can't fight rumors, that people who knew

him wouldn't believe the lies." She sighed. "He just wasn't a fighter. He thought if he ignored them, they would go away."

"Do you know who started them?"

She shook her head, and then she pressed her lips in a thin line. "I do know Jackson King repeated them."

And was perhaps the reason she broke up with him. "Did you and Jackson ever date?"

"I suppose Robert Tomlinson brought that up." A red tinge filled her cheeks, and she glanced down at her clasped hands. Then she smoothed back a strand of chestnut hair and looked up. "One kiss with someone around here, and no one ever forgets it. Or allows me to."

"I take it you don't like Mr. King."

She flattened her hands on the desk and stood. "He's a boor and a gossip. Would you like a drink? I grabbed a pitcher of peach tea before they poured it out at the café."

"Sure." Kelsey had liked it the other day. Might make a good peace offering. He accepted the Solo cup and sipped the tea, and tried not to make a face. Must be a woman thing. He set the cup down as Julie returned to her desk. "How many of the people who were working here when Carter left are still here?"

She doodled on a scratch pad. "I was here, Robert Tomlinson, his brother Mark—he was working in shipping then and worked his way up to building manager—and there are a couple of guys who worked in maintenance that have been here forever . . . and Jackson, of course." She leaned back in her chair. "But wait, Jackson doesn't exactly work here now, and Robert didn't work straight through. He went to work for the city for a few years before returning here as director."

Brad added Mark Tomlinson's name as a definite. Why didn't his brother remember he worked here with Carter?

"You said Jackson King gossiped about the thefts. If you don't think Carter stole the artifacts, do you think Jackson could have?"

"Jackson?" She seemed to mull the idea over. "Only if he was certain he wouldn't get caught. A scandal like that would have gotten him cut off from his father's money. Conrad King was a stickler for honesty and propriety."

"You seem to know a lot about the Kings."

"We went to college together, and my father and Conrad King are friends. Excuse me," she said as her phone rang. After she answered, she put the call on hold. "Do you have more questions?"

"Not for now." He stood and picked up his Solo cup. "But I'll probably be back. Do you mind if I take Kelsey a cup of your tea?"

"No, please take some."

Brad paused outside her office. He was getting a very interesting picture of the employees at the time of Paul Carter's death. Then he walked to Kelsey's office and tapped on her door, hoping the tea would smooth things over.

◆

A knock at the door startled Kelsey, and she glanced at the clock. Was it already five? "It's open," she said and pulled her gloves off.

"Peace offering?" Brad said, holding out a red Solo cup when he came into the room. "Peach tea."

He must think she was a pushover. "It'll take more than peach tea to make up for what you did," she said.

"Not trying to do that. I just remembered that you like peach tea."

He remembered? Her double-crossing heart warmed. And

she was thirsty. Grudgingly, she accepted the cup. "Where'd you get it?"

"Julie rescued a pitcher from the café before they poured it out. Are you ready to go?"

Kelsey drained the cup and set it on the table. "Just a sec." She wrapped the spotted horse in a cloth and returned it to the box before grabbing her bag with her laptop in it. "I'm ready. And thank you for telling the bodyguard you are escorting me home. He said there would be someone else at the apartment and gave me his number to call when we started that way."

"Good. Why don't you leave your car in the parking lot and ride with me? We can pick it up on the way back?"

"Sure." She allowed him to open the car door for her, even though it made her feel a little ungrateful. Then she reminded herself of how he'd made her father look like a murderer. The silence in his car grew as they drove toward the house. Evidently he was going to let her stew. Finally she could stand it no longer. "What have you learned about the bones? Anything important?"

"Dr. Caldwell isn't through yet."

What kind of answer was that? She was willing to bet that the ME had given him *some* information. But if he didn't want to talk, so be it. She stared out the window as they drove across town, her thoughts turning to her father. No one, including Brad, would ever make her believe he had fired shots at her. Her father loved her. She was as sure of that as she was the stars would be out tonight.

She glanced at Brad. He was gripping the steering wheel like he was ready to fight it. Something wasn't adding up. When he turned into the drive, she blinked. "What's my mom doing here?"

"She's early," he said, his voice so low she almost didn't hear him.

"You knew she would be here?"

"Sort of."

"You don't *sort of* know something like that. Either she called you and said she'd be here or she didn't. But why?" Fear grabbed her stomach, twisting it.

"Maybe she decided not to sell the house."

"She would have called *me* if that were the case." Kelsey opened the car door, not waiting for him to come around. "Maybe she'll tell me something."

She hurried up the steps. "Mom, where are you?" she called. She walked through the open front door and came to a full stop. Memories bombarded her as she stared at the eggshell-blue walls.

"Kelsey," Mom said, coming from the kitchen.

"You never changed the color," she said softly. Even though she'd been only seven the last time she was inside the house, she remembered the blue walls and how peaceful they had made her feel. It was why her bedroom was painted this color.

"No. I guess I always wanted to keep it the way it was when we were a family here. Even though we didn't live here long."

"Don't sell it, Mom. I think I want to live here."

"It may be too late for that, sweetheart."

Kelsey glanced at her mom. Her eyes were red, and she wouldn't look her way. Why had she been crying? Kelsey's chest tightened, making it hard for her to breathe. She wanted to leave. Right. Now.

"Why are you here?" she whispered.

Her mom shot a quick glance at Brad, and Kelsey turned to him. "I don't know what's going on, but I don't like it."

"Neither do I," he said and took a deep breath. "I'm afraid

I have something to tell you—it's what I couldn't say at your office."

"I asked him not to until I could be with you."

"S-Sabra . . ." Kelsey couldn't get her sister's name out. "Is she—"

"No, it's not Sabra," her mom said.

"Then who is it—I know it's someone." Her blood pressure was going to blow the top of her head off if someone didn't tell her what was going on.

"It's your dad," Brad said.

"He is not the killer!"

"No," her mom said. "He's not. I'm afraid . . ." She swallowed hard, shook her head.

"He's dead, Kelsey. I'm sorry," Brad said. "The bones that were delivered yesterday were his remains."

His words sucked the air out of the room. *Dad, dead?*

Impossible. He was off somewhere, away from all the pressure. "No . . . no!" She looked up at Brad. "My father is not dead. He . . . he's in Argentina or Colombia. But he's not dead!"

Her mother wrapped her arms around Kelsey. "It's okay, baby."

Kelsey's arms hung limp in her mother's embrace. No, it was not okay. She closed her eyes against the image of his body in the plastic bag as her chest ached from the pain of knowing she'd held his bones in her hands.

31

Brad could handle a woman's tears better than he could Kelsey's stoicism. She had listened without a flicker of emotion as he described finding the ring and the dentist confirming that the teeth matched his dental records for Paul Carter. And now, she was encouraging her mother to return home.

"I'm fine. Really," Kelsey said. "Go home to Sam. It's not like I saw my . . . him just last week."

She couldn't say "my dad." It was the only tell that showed her distress. The look of helplessness Cynthia shot Brad deepened his own worry. "I'll make sure she gets home all right," he said.

With one last look at her daughter, Cynthia walked toward the front door, where she stopped and turned. "If you're serious about living here, I'll see what I can do."

"Perfect." Kelsey's smile was brittle.

Once Cynthia's car backed out of the drive, Kelsey said, "Do you mind? I'd like to walk through the house while you go to the shed and pick up the files you want."

"You sure?" He didn't want to leave her. She seemed so

calm on the outside, but tension radiated from her like a tightly wound coil. "I'd like to see the rest of the house."

The odd look she gave him said she knew what he was doing.

"I'm okay—I'm not going to fall apart."

He wasn't too sure about that, but he honored her wishes and went to the shed, grabbing the box of papers. Once he put them in his trunk, he hurried inside the house. She was standing where he'd left her.

"That was quick," she said.

"Just one box. I'd still like to see the house."

Kelsey nodded, and he trailed her as she walked from room to room, her tension increasing with each room. She stopped in a small corner room with windows facing a huge magnolia tree and walked to the window closest to the tree. "This is where my climbing probably started," she said.

He joined her and stared up at the top of the magnolia. "You climbed this when you were seven?"

"Actually I was five and half when I climbed it the first time. Dad said . . ." She took a shaky breath and blew it out. "It was easier to think my father was in some faraway place totally ignoring me than it is knowing he's dead." She lifted her chin. "I need to climb."

"Not that," he said, pointing at the tree, suddenly aware of how close they stood when her perfume enveloped him.

"No. There's a place I go to climb—the Rock Zone—but you don't have to go. You can take me back to the museum, and I'll get my car."

"No. You dismissed your bodyguard, so I'll take you." Heights were not his favorite thing to do, but he wasn't leaving her alone tonight. "Do you have your gear?"

"In my car." Her face fell. "And it doesn't make sense to go all the way to the museum for it. I can get a good workout on the bouldering area, and I can do that in these tennis shoes."

"Is there a beginner climb? You know, like the bunny slopes?" He had never climbed and had never planned to. He did work out, so maybe he wouldn't embarrass himself too much.

"Why don't you just watch? I'm the one who needs to work off some energy."

That worked for him.

◆

When Brad saw the first wall inside the Rock Zone, his gaze traveled up to an overhang. "That thing is straight up."

"That's the climbing wall, and it's probably fifty feet," she said and showed her pass, then stopped to buy a bottle of liquid chalk. "The bouldering wall isn't as high, probably only fifteen to twenty feet. And over there," she said, pointing across the room, "is another shorter climbing wall. Lily has mastered the first level on it."

"Why doesn't that surprise me? Are you sure she's not your kid?"

"I wish. What do you think?" she said, nodding her head toward the bouldering area.

"It's awfully tall."

"Not really. Lily loves it."

"Big surprise."

"Hey, Kelsey. Good to see you today! Just bouldering tonight?"

She turned and waved at a man coming down the wall. "Yeah, don't have my equipment," she called to him and then lowered her voice. "He's an instructor."

"The guy standing on the floor with the rope—what's he doing?"

"That's his belay partner. The partner and the rope are to stop his fall when it happens."

"Fall?" He looked up again.

"It is a dangerous sport, you know, but he rarely falls. Come on, the bouldering area is back here."

Brad looked over his shoulder as they walked away from the climbing wall. "What do you do when you come to that overhead ledge?"

"You go over it." She knelt and tightened the laces on her tennis shoes. When she stood, she said, "Sure you don't want to try bouldering?"

"Yes, I'm very sure." He hyperventilated just thinking about it. When they reached the bouldering area, he breathed easier. The walls were much shorter, with various colored objects spaced across them. A boy Lily's age was climbing on the wall nearest him and was trying to pull himself over a ledge. Where was the father? He should be waiting to catch him when he fell. "They just turn kids loose here?"

"His mother is right there," she said, pointing to a woman on the floor. "And she wouldn't catch him, just help him fall correctly. I'm going to stretch first."

He thought she meant stretching exercises, but instead she pulled herself up on the wall and climbed sideways across it, stretching her arms and legs. Once she reached the far side, she worked her way back to the middle and then began her ascent. There were overhangs at different levels, and Kelsey bypassed the lower ones and worked her way to the one in the middle. There she swung her leg over the ledge and pulled herself up.

He figured she'd come back down, but instead, she worked her way to a higher overhang, repeating the process until she stood at the top of the boulder. Then she worked her way down and started all over. After the sixth trip, he began to worry. She was visibly tired, and he feared she would make a mistake. At the highest overhang, her pull-up was much slower, and then suddenly she fell.

With his heart in his throat, he ran toward the wall as she hit the mat and rolled, then jumped up.

"I'm okay," she said, then bent over and braced her hands on her knees to catch her breath. "My . . . arms . . . gave out."

"Are you crazy? That's a fifteen-foot drop." He had to be an idiot to let her do this. "I should have stopped you when I saw you were getting tired."

"Excuse me?" She raised her hand. "I'm okay. Not the first time I've fallen." She pinned him with a hard stare. "And it won't be the last. And for the record—you don't tell me what to do."

"Somebody needs to." The words were out of his mouth before he thought. He stepped back. "Sorry, I shouldn't have said that, but you almost made me have a heart attack."

Her expression softened. "I'm sorry for that, but I'm not trying to kill myself. I'm an advanced level climber, so there's no need to worry."

Brad didn't care what level she was, falling was falling. "You're not invincible."

"I know how to fall as well as when to quit." She crooked her arm. "Ready to leave?"

His shoulders relaxed. "Definitely."

"Maybe the next time we come, you can try it," she said as they walked out the door. "Wear loose clothes, and we'll rent your shoes. I'll even show you how to fall."

"That's supposed to make me say yes? Although you did make it look easy that first time you went up." He scanned the area. The parking lot needed more lighting. Anyone could be lurking in the shadows. Because the lot had been so full, he'd had to park near the busy street, and he guided Kelsey toward it.

"Did you leave your trunk open?" she asked.

Across the parking lot a light shone from his trunk, and a dark figure moved.

"Hey!" Brad yelled.

The person looked toward him and took off running toward the street.

"Go back inside," he said.

"What?"

Brad turned to Kelsey. "Hurry—get inside the building."

Her eyes wide, she wheeled and ran.

When he looked around, the man was gone. Brad reached for his gun and remembered he'd left it locked in the console before they entered the gym. Kneeling, he grabbed the ankle gun he usually wore and crept between the parked cars, listening for sounds over the hum of traffic. Nothing but normal sounds. Cars coming and going—he had no way of telling if one of them was his guy.

Brad returned the gun to its holster and approached his car. The trunk had been jimmied open, and the files belonging to Paul Carter were gone. He checked inside the car and opened the console. The gun was still there, and he strapped it on. Whoever the thief was only wanted the box of papers. He took his phone out and dialed the dispatcher and requested a patrol car to take a report.

While he waited for the patrolman, Brad went back inside the gym.

"Did you catch him?"

"No. Not even sure it was a male—too far away. Could you tell?"

She shook her head. "I didn't see anyone. That's why I had trouble understanding why you wanted me to come back inside. What did they take?"

"Your dad's papers."

She frowned. "Why would they want—" Her eyes widened, and she covered her mouth with her hand. "No," she said, shaking her head. "Tell me the person trying to kill me wasn't here."

"I'm afraid he was. No one else would have any reason to take them."

"That means he was watching us at the house. But why did he wait until we were ready to leave to steal them?"

"Either he likes to press his luck, or the person I saw was someone who came along later, saw the jimmied trunk, and planned to help himself."

Either way, the killer knew their every move. He could up his game any time, and tonight showed Brad that he would be helpless to stop him.

32

"You don't have to help me into the car," Kelsey said. The light from the overhead streetlamp cast shadows in the car. "I'm not falling apart."

"Can't a guy just be nice?" Brad replied, leaning in to check her seat belt.

She made a face at him, and he grinned. Then he straightened and blocked the light, creating a silhouette of his body.

In an instant she was hanging eleven stories outside the window Thursday night. *The man in the room.* Brad moved and the streetlight almost blinded her. The killer's face flashed in her mind.

She screamed.

He jerked the car door open. "What's wrong?"

"I saw it again."

Brad knelt beside the open door. "Saw what?"

"The killer's face."

He took her hands, stilling them. She hadn't even known they were shaking.

"Take a deep breath. You're hyperventilating."

She leaned back against the seat and filled her lungs and

released the air. As she focused on her breathing, her body quit shaking. If only she could hold on to the memory of the face. "I saw him. The killer."

"Tonight?"

"No. Thursday night. Remember I told you I saw a flash of light in the room? I must have seen his face, because this is twice that I've had an image pop into my mind superimposed on the silhouette. But I only see it like a flash, and then it's gone."

"That's why the killer thinks you saw him." Brad rubbed his chin, an odd look on his face. "Have you ever been hypnotized?"

She stared at him. "No. Do you think hypnotherapy might help me see the face more clearly?"

"It's possible. I've seen it work before."

"Who would I see?" She would do just about anything to be able to identify the face. Ever since Brad revealed her father was dead, the desire to catch the murderer had grown from a tiny seed to a full-blown obsession. It had been all she thought about as she climbed and was the reason she hadn't realized the strength in her arms was gone.

"I have an idea, but let's talk more about it tomorrow." He stood. "Do you think you're okay now?"

She nodded. "Let's get my car so I can go home."

"How would you feel about leaving your car at the museum? We can call your bodyguard so he can drive to your apartment, and I can drop you off and pick you up in the morning."

Did she want to be without a car?

"Your bodyguard will have a car if you need one."

The question must have shown on her face. "Okay. Let me call him to go to the apartment."

"I'll wire the trunk shut."

While Brad took care of the trunk, she called the number her bodyguard had given her, and he assured her that he would be there and have the apartment secured by the time she arrived.

"Thank you," she said and was about to end the call. "Oh, check the top of the doors before you go in. I put tape across all the doors before I left so I would know if any of them had been opened. I even put a strip across the garage door at the bottom."

She hung up as Brad slid into the front seat.

"I heard that. Good idea," he said.

"Yeah. If anyone comes into my apartment, I want to know about it," she said. "He'll be there by the time we get home."

"Good deal."

Kelsey let her body sink against the seat, feeling each sore muscle and bruise caused by the fall. The Rock Zone had good mats, but still, she'd fallen fifteen feet and hit something solid. Practicing how to roll when she fell had paid off, though.

She should have known better than to climb another round after two mistakes. First, her foot had slipped on an easy foothold and then she'd misjudged a handhold. Sometimes she didn't understand why she pushed beyond her fatigue. Yeah, she did. It was the only way to build endurance, not because she thought she was invincible.

She glanced at Brad's profile, smiling at his square jaw. Stubborn jaw. But he was a good man. He'd stayed with her after delivering that awful news. Despite how badly she'd treated him earlier today.

Except, he hadn't trusted her with the truth. Did he think she couldn't keep a secret? No, that wasn't it, or he wouldn't have told her at all. "Do you think someone at the museum killed my father?" It was so hard to say those words.

"Strong possibility," he said. "There are at least five people working at the museum now who were there when your father was killed. Robert Tomlinson and his brother Mark, Jackson King, the—"

"Jackson worked at the museum twenty-eight years ago? He would have been a teenager then."

"Eighteen. He was a summer intern. Julie Webb worked there, as well, and remembered your dad." He frowned.

"What?"

"I just realized your stepdad was on the board of trustees at the museum twenty-eight years ago."

"Surely you don't think Sam . . ." She studied his face. He did. Well, Brad was wrong about that. Sam Allen would not hurt a soul. "Grant was collections manager at the time as well."

"Your uncle?"

"Yes. I don't know if Mom told you, but she met Sam and Grant in college and they became good friends. Dad was Sam's and Mom's professor, and the four of them worked on an archaeology dig in the Giza Pyramid Plateau in Egypt. That's where Sam met his first wife. Sam and Grant still do digs here in the States occasionally."

"Were your parents married when they were in Egypt?"

"They were. Mom stayed with the dig until she was pregnant with me and decided she didn't want to deliver a baby in the desert, so she came home. Dad didn't return to the States until I was a year old."

"Do you know when Sam and Grant returned?"

"About the same time as Mom, I think." She turned his question over in her mind. Funny, she'd never connected the dots between Sam and her mom. Or how it seemed as though Sam had always been in her life, especially after his first wife died. Even more than her own father. And then not long after her dad left town, her mom and Sam married.

She looked up. "You don't think Sam killed my dad, do you?"

◆

"Everyone is a suspect at this point," Brad said as he started the car and backed out of the space. Sam and Paul both loved Cynthia, but had Sam been in love with Cynthia in Egypt? Cynthia hadn't wanted to marry Sam because of Paul, even though they were divorced. Maybe Sam decided to get rid of his problem.

Not that he thought there'd been any impropriety on Cynthia's part, but it had happened before—a love triangle resolved with the death of one of the participants. But why would Sam kill Hendrix and Rutherford, and most of all, why would he try to kill Kelsey? He didn't like the answer that came to him.

Was Sam afraid Kelsey had seen his face? He stopped for a red light and glanced at Kelsey. She'd leaned her head back on the rest and had her eyes closed. But closing them didn't hide the tears seeping through her lashes.

"I'm sorry about your dad," he said as the light changed and he pressed the pedal.

"Me too."

They drove a few blocks before she spoke again.

"It's funny. All my life, I've been okay with him leaving. I mean, I hated that he stole the artifacts and left behind a ruined reputation. But I understood why he ran away. Because that's what I always wanted to do.

"I didn't let people get close to me in high school. I was afraid they either liked me because of Sam's money, or if they passed that test and I let them past the wall I'd built, I was afraid they'd find out my father was a thief." She sighed. "And now I'm full of guilt because I believed he stole the artifacts and ran away so he wouldn't have to face the consequences."

Brad turned into Sabra's drive and pulled around back to Kelsey's apartment. He didn't know what to say. Kelsey wasn't the only one dealing with guilt. All those years ago, he'd thought she was an arrogant rich kid and had judged her for it.

"You need a good night's sleep," he said.

"It probably won't be tonight." She sat up straighter. "Oh look, there's my bodyguard, and he's checking the tape on the garage door."

He followed her nod, recognizing a fellow police officer at Kelsey's garage door. Tim Corelli. With five kids to put through college, he was like more than a few MPD cops who picked up security jobs to supplement their income. "I didn't know he was moonlighting with Rutherford Security."

"You know him?"

"Tim? He's a uniformed officer." Brad lowered his window. "Wait up and I'll back you," he called.

Nodding, Corelli walked toward them. "I already have the remote. I'll get the door up." He turned and pointed the remote toward the garage door.

Brad didn't know if he saw the light flash first or heard the explosion that blew the door out, pitching the police officer to the ground.

With Kelsey's screams in his ears, he was halfway out of the car when the shock wave rocked him back. He jerked his phone out and dialed 911. "There's an explosion at . . ."

What's the address? He pulled it from his memory and shouted it into the phone. "There's an officer down."

Pocketing his cell, he ran to Corelli, but Kelsey beat him there. She knelt and felt his wrist.

"He's alive," she said. "But his pulse is too fast to count. And it looks like he might have hit his head."

Brad knelt on the other side. All he could think of was those five beautiful kids. "Come on, man, stay with us."

The officer's eyes blinked open. "What happened?" he whispered.

"Explosion. Can you cough?"

"What?"

"Can you cough? Your heart rate is high. I need you to cough!"

He gave a weak cough, and Brad said, "Harder."

"I hear a siren," Kelsey said.

They couldn't get there fast enough to suit Brad. Footsteps ran toward them, and he looked up. Sabra's husband.

"What happened? Was it the water heater?" Mason asked.

He thought it was an accident? "You have anything to cover him with?"

"I have blankets in the bedrooms," Mason said.

"Would you get one? It might keep him from going into shock." Brad tried to get Corelli to cough again. A minute later Mason handed him a duvet.

"It's the first thing I found," he said.

Brad took it from him, and Kelsey helped wrap it over the injured man. Minutes later firefighters and paramedics were pouring past Sabra's house to the garage apartment in the backyard.

"His heart rate is really fast," Brad said to one of the paramedics.

"We've got it from here."

Brad grasped Tim's hand. "You're going to make it."

His eyes widened. "Wait." He tried to sit up. "The tape—"

"You two take this up later," the paramedic said, moving between his patient and Brad.

"No! I have to tell him."

"What about the tape?" Brad asked.

"It was intact."

Brad barely noticed being hustled out of the way by another medic. Either it was a gas explosion or . . . He turned and sought Kelsey, his throat constricting when he couldn't find her. He scanned the area, finally spotting her at her sister's back door with a detective he recognized from the Bomb Unit, Lieutenant Robinson.

Brad took out his cell and called Rachel Sloan. When she answered, he said, "I need a place for Kelsey. I think someone just tried to kill her again with a bomb. Any chance we can put her in one of the safe houses we use for witnesses?"

"I'll check and see. Is she all right?" she asked. "What happened?"

"Not sure yet, but I believe someone planted a bomb in her garage. She's shaken, and one of our uniformed officers was injured. Tim Corelli. He was moonlighting as her bodyguard."

"I'll be right there. Is Corelli going to be okay?"

"I think so. And call Reggie—Kelsey may have seen Hendrix's murderer Thursday night. It was so brief, she only got a flash of his face. And let me know as soon as you can about that safe house," he said and hung up. He'd had no experience with the safe houses, only that they were used occasionally for witnesses in big cases.

His cell rang. "Hollister," he barked into it.

"Brad?"

Elle. *Wait. Is it Tuesday night?* "Sorry, I'm in the middle of something."

"Oh. I . . . I thought you might be home soon."

"I'm afraid not. Look, I'm sorry, but I'm dealing with an emergency."

"Oh, sure," she said. "I'll hang around a little longer, and if you don't come soon, I'll leave the dish I made on the stove. You can have it when you get home."

He hated the hurt in her voice but didn't know what to do about it. "Are we still on for dinner Saturday night?"

"You don't have to work?"

Brad couldn't guarantee it. "Shouldn't. I'll call you tomorrow." He pocketed the phone. As long as he was a detective, the job would come first sometimes. Not always, but there would be nights like tonight, and it would be interesting to see how Elle handled it.

He jogged over to the back door, where Kelsey was sitting on the steps with her head in her hands. He addressed Robinson, who was standing nearby. "You think it's a bomb?"

Robinson glanced toward the apartment. "Yep. Figure it was on the garage door opener and that's what took the brunt of the explosion. If he'd put a delay switch on it, it would've damaged more of the apartment. Of course that's me guessing. Won't know for sure until the investigation is complete. Cooley is bringing his bomb detection dog."

Brad didn't need the dog to tell him it was a bomb. The odor of ammonia was burning his nose. This changed everything, and Kelsey wasn't taking a step anywhere without him by her side.

The lieutenant jerked his head toward the stretcher the paramedics had brought in. "Who's the victim?"

"Tim Corelli. Patrol officer. Been a cop maybe seven years."

"Is he going to make it?" Kelsey asked from where she sat.

"I think so. Main thing will be to make sure there's no internal bleeding and get his heart rate back to normal. Are you okay?" Brad asked Kelsey. Seemed like he asked her that a lot.

She shrugged. "About as well as the next murder target. I called my parents, and they should be here any minute. Where'd Mason go?"

He had no idea where her brother-in-law was, but he'd seen a patrolman stretching tape across the drive. "I'll make sure they get past the crime scene tape." Brad turned to the detective. "The owner thinks it might be a gas explosion. Maybe a water heater."

"The water heater is in the garage," Kelsey said.

Robinson shook his head. "That would be quite a coincidence—an explosion just as someone remotely opens the garage door."

"Corelli said the tape Kelsey put at the bottom of the garage door was intact," Brad said. "But whoever placed the bomb inside could have seen it and taped it back."

The lieutenant rocked back on his heels. "Sounds like this explosion was up close and personal."

33

AN HOUR LATER Kelsey was still sitting on Sabra's back steps. She stared at the activity in the garage. Her spirits sagged. What if the bodyguard had not walked back toward them? He would have been killed. The thought almost made her throw up.

Why had she called her parents? She couldn't go home with them and put everyone in more danger. But where would she go? She jumped when someone touched her arm.

"Kelsey?" Brad said. "You were spacing out."

"Trying to figure out what I'm going to do," she said, standing to stretch her legs. Her mind kept looping over the same thing. Someone wanted to kill her, and they didn't care who they hurt in the process.

Overhead she heard the whop-whop-whop of a helicopter and looked up. "Police?" she said.

"No, that's a news chopper. Evidently, it's a slow night."

She could just see the headlines now. *Bomb Destroys Local Woman's Home.* "Does the media know who's involved?"

"Other than indicating it's a possible gas explosion, we're just saying 'No comment' when someone asks a question.

And that's what the investigators canvassing the neighborhood are telling your neighbors. No need to stir up fears that we have a mad bomber loose until we know more."

No, not a mad bomber, just someone who wanted her dead. She rubbed her face and then massaged her temples. "Do you think the same person who stole the papers planted the bomb?"

"Possibly," he said.

She looked toward the garage and blew out a breath. "I don't know where I'll stay now."

"You need to be in a safe house."

A safe house? "I thought that was just for witnesses. And I'm not a witness—I can't remember what the man looked like."

"You're a potential witness. I called Rachel, and she's checking on something for you."

At least it was better than bringing danger to her parents' doorstep.

"The bomb detection dog is here," Brad said.

She followed his gaze to a beautiful golden lab as it trotted ahead of his handler toward the garage, sniffing the air. Once inside, the dog immediately sat down by a piece of debris on the garage floor.

"He's found explosives," Robinson said.

A piece of her heart died when she heard the confirmation. Her knees buckled and she sank to the porch step. There was something so sinister about someone trying to kill her with a bomb.

Movement near the side of the house drew her attention. Mom and Sam. She wanted to go to them, but her body would not move. Her legs wouldn't hold her up if she stood. Brad walked to the uniformed police officer detaining them, and in a minute they came toward her.

Her mother sat next to her and put her arms around her. "Honey, I can't believe this is happening. Are you all right?"

Kelsey nodded. If she had to tell one more person she was fine, she would scream. "I shouldn't have called you."

"Nonsense," Sam said. "I wish I hadn't gotten you involved with Rutherford. None of this would be happening."

Had it only been a few days ago that she was playing the Phantom Hawk? It seemed a month. What she'd thought was such a good idea was possibly the worst idea she'd had in her life.

"Do you think the same person who shot at you did this?" Sam asked.

"I don't know."

"Mr. Allen," Brad said, "did your wife tell you about Paul—"

"Yes. This"—he swept his arm toward the garage—"terrible thing knocked it out my mind." He knelt beside Kelsey. "I'm so sorry, honey. How are you holding up?"

You don't think Sam killed my dad, do you? She wished she could put that question out of her mind and flinched when he put his arm around her. But Sam did sound genuinely concerned.

He shook his head. "What a stupid question. Of course you're not holding up. Why don't you come back to the house with your mother and me now? Any questions Brad or anyone else has, they can come there and ask."

"No!" Her face burned. "I'm not putting you in—"

"We want to put her in a safe house," Brad said.

Sam stood. "Judging by what happened here, I can protect her better than the police."

Brad rocked back on his heels. "How about Sabra and Lily? If Kelsey went home with you, it might put all of you in danger."

255

"He's right," Kelsey said as the back door opened and Mason stepped outside. "Where've you been?"

"Talking to Sabra, trying to keep her from coming over here. She wanted to make sure you're okay."

Standing, Kelsey whipped out her phone and walked away from the others. Should've already called her sister. What if this person went after them and used them as leverage? "Don't you dare come over here," she said when her sister answered.

"I won't. Mason made me promise not to. But I think you need to leave town. Go somewhere it's safe."

If there were such a place, Kelsey would. But whoever was trying to kill her seemed to know her every move. "I'm safer here with Brad. You have someone with you, right?"

A low laugh came over the phone. "Oh yeah. We can't even go to the bathroom without someone following us. If it's not the security people, it's Mom. We're going stir crazy."

Tension eased from her shoulders. "You do what they say." Her gaze followed Brad as he met Rachel at the corner of the house. "Look, I have to go. I'll check on you tomorrow. Give Lily my love."

"Where are you staying?"

"Brad's arranging a safe house."

"Good. Take care of yourself. You're the only sister I have, and I want to keep you." Sabra's voice cracked.

"I love you too," Kelsey said, smiling.

She glanced toward the garage again. Rachel was now talking to the lieutenant from the bomb squad. Kelsey couldn't remember his name. He pointed toward them, and Rachel nodded and walked her way.

"There you are," she said. "Are you up for answering

a few questions? Robinson said I could take your statement. He's going into your apartment with the dog and his handler."

"Is that dangerous?"

"Shouldn't be—he thinks if there was another bomb, the first one would have triggered it."

Rachel glanced at the others. "Who else was here?"

"Only me," Mason said. "And I hadn't been home twenty minutes."

"Did you notice anything suspicious?"

"No, I pulled into the garage that's on the front and went straight into the house. I didn't even look out toward Kelsey's place."

"No unusual noises?"

He shook his head, and she turned to Sam and her mom. "Can I get your names? And were you here?"

"I'm Cynthia Allen, Kelsey's mom, and this is my husband, Sam. We weren't here—had just finished dinner when Kelsey called."

Rachel switched her gaze to Sam.

"We really don't know anything," he said.

Her phone rang and she answered it. After a brief conversation, she disconnected and turned to Kelsey's parents.

"I believe that's all I need from you two," she said. "But I do need to speak to Kelsey and Sergeant Hollister privately, if you don't mind."

"But I do mind," Sam replied. "I'd like to take my daughter home. She's dead on her feet."

"Stop acting like I'm not here. I can speak for myself." Kelsey touched Sam's arm. "I am not putting my family in danger. You two go home and take care of Lily and Sabra."

Her mother raised her hand. "But Kelsey—"

"Please," she said. Somehow she had to make them leave. "Let the police handle it."

"Kelsey's right," Brad said. "And I promise you, I'll keep her safe."

Kelsey didn't think anyone could keep her safe.

Beside her, Sam studied Brad. "I believe you'll do your best. I just hope it's good enough," he said. "Come on, Cynthia. Let's let them do their job."

She hugged her mother. "I'll be okay."

A lump formed in her throat as they walked away. She wished she could believe that.

34

Brad pulled Rachel away from Kelsey and her parents. "What happened?"

"That was Reggie. They're not giving us a place. She's not a witness in a case yet," she said.

"You're kidding. What are we going to do?"

Rachel shook her head. "I can't take her to my apartment. I have a roommate."

"I am not leaving her unprotected." Brad bit his bottom lip. "How about my house? If you can stay there with us."

"It's a plan. One we'll have to sell to Kelsey."

Rachel didn't have to convince him of that.

Just as he approached Kelsey, the handler of the bomb dog came out of the garage. "It's all clear," he said. "No other bombs."

"Do you know what was used?" Brad asked.

"No way to tell for sure until it's analyzed. For my money, it's ammonia nitrate and fuel oil. The detonator was wired to the garage opener, and when Corelli pressed the button . . ." He spread his hands. "Is he going to be okay?"

"I heard over the scanner that he was stable," Rachel said.

"How does the rest of the house look?" Brad asked.

"Most of the damage is in the living area over the garage. Bedrooms are intact."

"Did you say my bedroom is okay? How about my clothes?" Kelsey asked. "Can I go upstairs and pick up a few items?"

Brad hadn't seen her walk over. "No. It's still a crime scene," he said.

"Oh." Her shoulders drooped. "At least my car wasn't parked in front of the garage door—that's where I usually park."

Kelsey swayed and Brad reached to steady her. She needed to be away from here. It wouldn't take much of a wind to knock her off her feet.

"Let's sit in my car," Brad said. "And decide what we do next."

She allowed him to lead her to his car, where he helped her get settled in the front seat. Then he motioned Rachel over. "Get in the back," he said. "That way we can talk."

When he slid in the driver's side, Kelsey had her head bent over with her fingertips pressed against her eyes. "I'm taking you to my house," he said.

"What?" She raised her head, and confusion flickered in her eyes. "I thought . . . you said something about a safe house."

"My house is safe."

"I don't think that you meant your house earlier."

He sighed. "I'm afraid that deal fell through. So, you're going to my house, and Rachel is going with us."

"No. I'll go to a hotel. Surely this . . . this monster wouldn't blow up a hotel just to kill me."

"Going to Brad's house is the safest thing you can do," Rachel said. "You'll have two cops guarding you."

"But—"

"No buts," Brad said. "It's your only option."

Kelsey braced an elbow on the console and chewed her thumbnail. He waited, fearing anything he said would make her dig her heels in. It would be much better if the idea appealed to her.

She took a breath. "Okay, I'll go to your house tonight. But we have to pick up my car. I'll need it to get to work in the morning."

"We'll talk about that after we get to my house," Brad said. No way was she going to the museum tomorrow, even if he had to hogtie her.

A crowd of reporters was hanging around the end of the drive, and he ignored the requests for comments, just waving as they drove past them. His cell phone rang, and he glanced at the number on his dashboard. *Andi.* His sister. He should have expected her call, but he hadn't seen her in the crowd of reporters. He pressed the answer button on the steering wheel and said, "No comment, and you're on my speaker phone, so be careful how you react."

"Bradley Hollister, I can't believe you're involved in this and you didn't give me a heads-up."

"I told you no comment."

"At least tell me if it was a bomb and give me the victim's name."

"No comment."

"Braaad . . ." Andi drew his name out in two syllables.

"Okay, I'll tell you we're investigating the possibility of a gas explosion."

"And not a bomb?"

"That's all I'm giving you."

"If it's not a bomb, why won't you let me interview the victim?"

261

"No comment." He chuckled when she emitted a growl over the phone.

"Thanks for the crumb you tossed me."

"You're welcome."

Brad disconnected and turned right at the next corner. His house was located as far east in Memphis as anyone could get and still be in the city limits. It took fifteen minutes longer than necessary with him making turns and taking streets he wouldn't normally take in case they had a tail, but when he turned onto his street, no car followed.

He pulled into the well-lit drive, and his lights caught Tripod waiting at the fence. At least if anyone came around, he would bark. Brad pressed the remote garage opener, shuddering as he imagined what would have happened if Kelsey had pulled up to her garage and pressed the remote.

They went in through the kitchen, and a wonderful aroma greeted them. The food Elle cooked. He'd totally forgotten about her.

"Rosemary chicken?" Kelsey set her laptop on the counter. "How?"

"Wow, you're a neat freak," Rachel said. "Are you sure you live here?"

They'd both spoken at the same time, and he answered Kelsey first. "Elle was here earlier."

Then he addressed Rachel's comment. "What is the big deal about putting things where they belong when you're finished with them?" That's all he did. And he had a cleaning person come in once a month. "Don't tell me you two are messy."

"I am," Rachel said. "Disorganized, at least."

He turned to Kelsey. "I saw your place last night—it was pretty neat."

"Not like this."

He opened the door that led into his backyard and let Tripod in. The dog danced on his three legs while he ruffled his fur. "Tripod, I want you to meet Rachel and Kelsey."

Kelsey dropped to her knees. "Aw, he's so pretty," she said, rubbing his golden coat. "What happened to his leg?"

"I don't know. He'd already lost it when I got him at the shelter."

"Well, he's a sweetheart." She stood and yawned, stretching her arms out. "I wish we'd stopped at Walmart for a change of clothes."

He groaned. Clothes had been the last thing on his mind, and he didn't even have toothbrushes. He turned to Rachel. "If Kelsey makes a list, do you mind picking up what she needs? I'll pay for it. And get anything you need."

"I'll give you a credit card and pay for yours as well," Kelsey said and stopped in front of the stove. She took the lid off the chicken. "Do you mind?" she asked. "I'm starved."

He picked up the note Elle had left. "There's potato salad in the fridge."

Looking at Rachel, he said, "Better put some sort of break-fast food on there—I only have cereal. But why don't you fix a plate and eat first."

"I'd rather wait until I get back," she said.

A few minutes later Kelsey was sitting at the island. "So Elle has a key to your place."

Her voice was subdued. She had to be exhausted. Probably why she was picking at her food after saying she was starved.

"I keep one inside the garage on a nail."

He fixed his own plate, then sat across from her. "You're not eating," he said. "Elle's a good cook."

"I'm sure she is."

263

He picked up a second chicken leg with his fingers just as the dog let loose with a frenzy of barks. He wiped his fingers on a napkin and pulled his gun just as the doorbell rang. Couldn't be Rachel. She just left. He eased to the window and looked out. He holstered his gun. "It's Elle."

He opened the door. Even at this late hour, she looked elegant in flowing pants and a white sweater. "I wasn't expecting to see you back here."

Smiling, she stepped inside and set her purse on the table by the door before handing him a grocery bag. "I noticed you didn't have any milk for your cereal in the morning, and I ran to the store . . ." Her smile faded as she glanced past him, and her face turned crimson. "Oh, I'm sorry. I didn't know you had company—"

"It's not what you think," he said as he put the milk in the refrigerator. "Elle Deveraux, Kelsey Allen. Her apartment was blown up tonight, and she needed a place to stay."

"Here?" Elle frowned. "Just the two of you?"

The question rankled. He pressed his lips together.

"No, not the two of us. Detective Sloan will be back in a bit," Kelsey said and stood. "I think I'll go to the bathroom and freshen up," she said. "If you'll tell me where it is."

"Down the hall on the right," Brad and Elle said in unison. When they were alone, he turned to her. "You thought—"

"I didn't know what to think. You didn't tell me you had a girlfriend Sunday."

"Because I don't." He had thought about kissing Kelsey. Brad shook the thought off. "She's part of the investigation."

"Your cold case investigation?"

"Yes."

Suddenly her face softened, and she moved into his space. "I'm so sorry. Seeing her here just threw me."

Her perfume tickled his nose. He could see how she might jump to conclusions. A smile pulled at his lips. She *had* cooked dinner for him. "Forget it. And thanks for dinner. It's very good. Would you like to join us?"

She glanced toward the hallway. "That would be—"

The doorbell rang, and Rachel called out, "It's me and I'm starved. Open the door before I drop something."

Shrugging an apology, he hurried to let her in and took several of the bags.

"Who would have thought I could get in and out of Walmart so fast? Oh," she said when she saw Elle.

Brad made the introductions and Rachel said, "Thanks for making dinner. It smells scrumptious."

"Uh, thank you," Elle said and picked up her purse. "I think I'll head home. I'm sure the three of you have a lot to discuss, and I have to get up early in the morning to catch a flight to LA."

"I'll walk out with you." He didn't think Kelsey's stalker had followed them, but he wanted to make sure Elle got away all right. "Thanks again for dinner," he said as he opened her car door. "Sorry it didn't turn out like you planned."

She stroked his cheek. "Me too. We'll try again Saturday night?"

"Let's touch base Friday night," he said, staring into her blue eyes. She still sent his heart racing, but . . .

Elle leaned over and kissed his cheek. "Until Friday."

He walked back to his front door, his mind tangled like fishing cord. Elle was ready to commit to their relationship, he felt it in his bones. So why wasn't he more excited?

35

Rachel was the only one in the kitchen when Kelsey returned.

"I put the clothing I bought on the sofa," Rachel said.

Kelsey nodded and helped put the groceries away. She didn't think she could have taken it if Elle and Brad had still been in the room. And that bothered her. She had no claims on Brad. But it certainly looked as though Elle did.

"So that was Elle," Rachel said. "She's not quite what I expected."

"Me either. She should be a movie star." Kelsey certainly couldn't blame Brad for being in love with someone that beautiful. For a second, she wondered what it would be like to be that beautiful and have someone like Brad love you. Not happening. She was and always would be that nerdy teenager. "You didn't meet her when they were engaged?"

"No. He never brought her to any of the get-togethers we had. I don't think she likes it that he's a policeman."

Elle Deveraux is not the wife for Brad. The thought almost made her drop the bananas. Maybe Elle was beautiful and cooked like a celebrity chef, but he loved being a cop. If she couldn't support him in a career he loved, she had no business going after him.

The door opened and Brad came inside. Was that lipstick on his cheek? Her heart sank. Didn't he see that Elle was all wrong for him?

"I'm still hungry," he said. "How about you two?"

"Sounds good," Rachel said and fixed her plate. "Come on, Kelsey, finish your plate."

She wasn't hungry, but she had to eat to keep up her strength. When Brad finished, he glanced at the wall clock, and she followed his gaze. Eleven thirty. Morning would come too soon.

"We probably need to make a plan," he said.

"Dessert first," Rachel said. She opened a package of lemon crisps and set it down in the middle of the table.

Kelsey took a cookie from the bag and munched on it. "Can we do this in the morning? I almost went to sleep eating."

"No, we won't have time in the morning," he said. "There's a meeting first thing tomorrow Rachel and I have to attend."

"I'm going in to the museum tomorrow," she said.

Brad sat up straight. "No, you're—"

"Don't say it," Kelsey fired back. "You two can't stay with me twenty-four hours a day. Think about it—the museum is the safest place for me—he won't try to kill me there."

"He already has! Or have you forgotten yesterday afternoon when he fired shots at you in the parking lot?" Brad's voice was angry.

"And he killed Rutherford at the museum," Rachel pointed out in her calm way.

"Rutherford didn't have a bodyguard, and I do."

"But a bodyguard doesn't have my training, or Rachel's."

She was so tired of playing this cat-and-mouse game and blew out an impatient breath. "Why don't we use me for bait, then. Spread it around that I saw the person who killed Hendrix. I can't live the rest of my life waiting for him to kill me."

Brad's eyes widened. "No way. Besides, that's why he's trying to kill you—he already believes you saw him."

"Then arrest me. You can control what I do, and I guess I'd be safe in jail."

"Don't tempt me," Brad said. "And I'm not trying to control you. Just the situation."

"It's the same thing," she retorted.

"Excuse me," Rachel said, waving a napkin between Brad and Kelsey.

They both turned and stared at her.

"Thank you," she said. "Let's look at this objectively. Kelsey might actually have a couple of good points." She pinned Brad with a hear-me-out look.

"I'm listening."

"One, you can't keep her here if she doesn't want to stay, and two, Rutherford was killed because he was alone in the vault. As long as she stays inside the museum with a bodyguard with her, he won't show his hand. Going to work really might be a good idea."

He rubbed his jaw with his thumb. He was at least thinking about it. Kelsey wished she hadn't said he was trying to control her—she could see the comment stung.

"Think about it," Kelsey said. "I'll go crazy sitting here alone, and what if he figures out I'm staying here? He's figured out everything else." She leaned forward. "I'm telling you, it's the best place for me to be if I'm not with you. If I'm there, I can check the personnel records to see which current employees worked at the museum twenty-eight years ago."

"I don't like it. Not one bit. But then, I don't like anything about this case." He studied her. "Okay. But I'll take you there before we leave. And you're right about him figuring out where you'll be. It is almost as though he has a direct pipeline."

That was what frightened her the most.

36

Kelsey woke before her alarm sounded with sunlight peeking through the blinds. She frowned. The sun shouldn't wake her. Unless it had started rising in the west. She rose up on her elbows. A black dresser. Tan walls and no curtains over the windows. This was not her bedroom.

Last night's events came crashing in on her. She was at Brad's. She collapsed back onto the bed and rolled on her side, cocooning herself in the blanket. Her dad, the bomb, her destroyed apartment . . . She was in a nightmare that would never end. *Do not fear, for I have redeemed you; I have called you by name; you are Mine!*

Kelsey stilled. The Bible verse she'd learned not long ago. She wanted to grab hold of it and cling to it. What was the rest of it? Something about God not taking a person out of trouble, but walking with them through it.

She threw back the covers and looked for a Bible in the room. Not finding one, she looked for her laptop and remembered leaving it in the kitchen, so she grabbed her phone. She didn't remember exactly where the verse came from anyway, so she typed the words she remembered into Google. Isaiah 43 came up, and she clicked on the link and read the next verses.

> When you pass through the waters, I will be with
>   you;
> And through the rivers, they will not overflow you.
> When you walk through the fire, you will not be
>   scorched,
> Nor will the flame burn you.
> For I am the LORD your God.

If only she could believe that.

People let you down; how did she know God wouldn't too? And when you depended on someone else, you gave them control of your life. Not something that was easy for her. Early on in life, Kelsey had learned she was the only person she could truly depend on. She wasn't even sure she'd know how to depend on God.

With a sigh, she read the passage on her phone again. Her sister would tell Kelsey to just trust God and ask him to help her. Kelsey turned over and faced the wall. Maybe if she counted sheep . . .

The aroma of fresh-brewed coffee drew her from sleep, and she jerked her eyes open. Seven thirty? Kelsey threw back the blanket and quickly dressed in the jeans and T-shirt Rachel had bought last night. Not normal dress for the museum, but these weren't normal times. She hesitated at the mirror, remembering how put together Elle had been last night. Kelsey shook her head. Glamorous was not her. Never would be.

Brad looked around as she entered the kitchen. He was dressed for work in his usual white short-sleeved shirt and navy pants, and the dishes they'd left in the sink were gone.

"Good morning," he said. "Coffee?"

"Please, and good morning to you too." Brad looked as though he hadn't slept, either. A Bible lay on the counter, and the sight encouraged her. Evidently, they'd had the same idea. While comforting, she hoped his search hadn't opened a box of night crawlers. "I meant to help Rachel do the dishes, but I overslept."

"Appreciate the thought, but Rachel didn't wash the dishes. I did."

"But you look so normal," she said, laughing, and accepted the cup of coffee he handed her. Their fingers touched, sparking a flurry of heartbeats. For a brief second their eyes connected, and time froze. He looked away first.

"I'll have you know growing up my mother thought boys should know how to cook and clean as well as girls, thank goodness. Otherwise, I would have starved after I moved out on my own."

"Wise woman." She sipped the coffee, noticing the clean cut of his jaw and how his lips quirked in the corner. *Come on, Kelsey, you don't have time for this.* She stared down at her cup. "You make great java. Did you stay up all night?"

"Not the whole night," he said, glancing at the Bible. "Reggie called around midnight and your car is clean. No bomb."

For a second, she'd been able to put last night's terrifying experience out of her head, but the news quickly brought home that she was not out of danger.

"Are you hungry? Rachel bought eggs and cereal, but that's about it. She had cereal before she left for downtown."

Not eating wasn't an option no matter how much her stomach protested. "Cereal is fine for me too. Exactly how much sleep did you get?"

Brad waved her off. "That doesn't matter. I've been thinking. Evidently you got a glimpse of the killer Thursday night, but for some reason you've buried it. I know a psychologist who is trained in hypnotherapy, and I'd like to see if I can get you in today."

Kelsey had had no dealings with hypnosis. "Do you think it will work? That this doctor will help me see his face?"

"I think it's worth a try. I can call now—I have the doctor's cell phone number."

She had nothing to lose. "Do it. I'm ready to try anything."

Kelsey caught herself holding her breath as Brad scrolled through his phone and made the call. *Breathe.* The doctor answered and she breathed again. Brad explained what he wanted, and then his lips quirked upward.

"Thanks, Doc." He disconnected. "One thirty. I'll pick you up."

She checked her watch. Almost eight. "How soon will you be ready to leave?"

"The question is, how soon will *you* be ready?"

"Fifteen minutes?"

"Might as well take thirty. If we wait until eight thirty, rush-hour traffic will thin out, and it won't take us any longer to get to the museum. And I called Jackson King to alert him that we need a bodyguard at the museum with you at all times."

Brad got her to the museum a little after nine and idled his car just outside the entrance. "I would stay with you, but there's a general meeting to discuss the bomb at your house, and I want to be there. If anyone asks, just say you can't discuss it. And stick with your bodyguard until I return."

She saluted him. "Aye, aye, sir."

He shook his head. "Sit tight until I get your door."

Once they were inside and he'd handed her over to the

security guard who'd been assigned to her for the day, he said, "I'll call you before I leave the CJC. The doctor's office isn't far, so it won't take long to get there."

Kelsey could get used to being looked after. She rounded the corner with the bodyguard trailing her and almost ran into Mark Tomlinson. "Oh, excuse me."

He eyed her silently. "Are you okay? I heard something on the news last night about an explosion in your neighborhood."

She stiffened. He knew where she lived? She'd only listed a post office box when she filled out her employee paperwork. "Yes. It was my apartment, but the police have asked me not to talk about it."

"I had no idea it was you, just that the explosion was in Central Gardens. Sorry for your loss."

He didn't sound very sorry. "Well, I'm fine. Just didn't get a lot of sleep last night. But I planned to find you later this morning to ask a couple of questions. Do you have a minute?"

His mouth tightened, and he glanced toward the security guard leaning against the wall. "Only a minute. I'm on my way to check a nonfunctioning light switch. What do you want to know?"

She shifted the bag with her laptop in it to her other hand. "I need to access certain personnel files on my computer. Is there a code I need?"

He shrugged. "You'll have to ask Helen Peterson. I don't deal with computers other than what I have to for the job. Don't like them, don't like to use them."

Then that would let him out as far as hacking into her computer. "You were working here when my father was director. Do you—"

"Who's your father?"

She'd forgotten that only his brother and Jackson knew who her father was. "Paul Carter."

For the first time since she'd met him, Mark Tomlinson's permanent scowl changed, replaced by surprise.

"That was your father?"

"Yes. Do you remember him?"

Mark nodded. "He was a decent man."

"Thank you." Kelsey hadn't expected the sudden change in his manner.

Mark looked at her oddly. "Seems like I remember a little girl with him sometimes. Was that you?"

He remembered her? "I came to visit at the museum sometimes. Are you familiar with the people who were employed then and who are still here now?"

"That's something you'd have to ask my brother. Anything else?"

She'd hoped to bypass asking the director.

Kelsey glanced at the key ring hanging from his belt. Only one. She'd been puzzling over how the thief got into the vault, but if he had access to Mark's key . . . "I assume every office has a different key. Does that key on your belt fit all the locks?"

"Of course. You don't see fifty keys on my belt, do you?"

"Are you the only one with access to the master key?"

"As director, my brother has a duplicate, and Mr. Rutherford had one."

"Do you know where Mr. Rutherford's key is?"

"Probably either in his personal effects or Jackson King has possession of it. And since you're working with King, you can ask him that question yourself. Now if you will excuse me, I have work to do."

Like she didn't. That was what his tone indicated. "One

275

more thing. How hard would it be for someone to get your key to make a copy of it?"

"Only over my dead body. I take this job very seriously, and it's never out of my sight. Whoever is stealing the artifacts did not get into the storage room because I was careless. So unless someone can take a photo of it hanging on my belt and make duplicates, it would be impossible," he said.

"Actually, the possibility of someone doing just that is quite real." She'd researched the software.

"You're kidding! So now I have to carry it in my pocket?"

"It's a scary world out there. How about your brother. Do you know where he keeps his key?"

"Locked in the vault. If he needs it, and he can't find me, he has to get the registrar to let him into the vault, and the registrar is the only person who has the combination to the vault, other than me, since Rutherford died."

Two sets accounted for, and unless someone had photographed one of the master keys and made duplicates, she only had to locate Rutherford's key. She would ask Jackson about it. "How about the code that's used for each room? Is there a master list?"

"No."

"But what if someone quit their job without passing on their code?"

He sighed. "I can reset any keypad to the default login."

She ignored his impatience. It was the first time she'd actually been able to stop him long enough to ask questions. "So there's a sequence of numbers that resets the keypad?"

"Yes, Ms. Allen."

"Is it written down anywhere?"

"Yes. In my office. And no one gets into my office unless I'm there."

Since he was edging away, she said, "Thank you for your time." She started to walk toward her office and turned back. "Wait. Can I ask you one more question?"

He about-faced, annoyance stamped on his features. She was beginning to believe the man really didn't like her. He crossed his arms and waited for her.

"Do you have any idea who the thief might be or how he gets into the rooms where the artifacts are stored?"

Mark's right eye twitched. "If I did, I would have already told the police."

The building manager had an idea, all right, but he wasn't sharing it. She palmed her hand up. "Sorry to have bothered you. I'm done with the questions."

"I hope so."

The bodyguard trailed her as she walked to her office. After she unlocked the door, she keyed in the code before opening it. On a hunch, she looked over her shoulder and scanned the ceiling and found what she was looking for. A camera was positioned just below the ceiling to track activities in the hallway.

"Looking for something, Ms. Allen?" the bodyguard asked.

"Not really." She couldn't keep thinking of him as "the bodyguard." "What's your name?"

"Phillip McFall."

"Okay, Phillip, come on in and make yourself at home."

She took her laptop from the bag and booted it up. Thinking with someone hovering around might prove difficult. She squared her shoulders and stared at the screen. It had already been proven the thief could tap into the camera. It would be no problem for him to turn it and capture an employee keying in the code on the keypads. He could probably even take a photo of Mark Tomlinson's key hanging on his belt.

37

A TRAFFIC SNARL HAD DELAYED BRAD, and the meeting in Homicide was ten minutes into the briefing when he slipped in and took a seat in the back row.

"Glad you could join us, Brad," Reggie said. "Lieutenant Robinson just finished giving his report that confirms the explosion was caused by a bomb, and it looks like it was homemade and relatively small. Powerful enough to have killed anyone standing close enough."

As Tim Corelli almost found out. "Was C-4 used?"

"No. Ammonium nitrate and fuel oil."

Probably the easiest bomb to make if you didn't get your head blown off. Plus, the materials weren't that hard to obtain. "How about the neighbors? Did any of them notice anything unusual late yesterday afternoon or early evening?"

"Neighbors on either side worked until six yesterday," Reggie said. "And the ones across the street didn't see anything unusual."

After a few more questions, Reggie handed out assignments and dismissed the detectives.

"Do you have a minute?" Brad asked. Too many things

had happened too quickly, and he needed fresh eyes on Paul Carter's case. "You too, Rachel, since these cases are tied together. Do you have time to sit down in my office and bat ideas around?"

Reggie checked his watch. "I can give you thirty minutes, then I have a meeting with the director."

"I'm good for an hour," Rachel said.

Brad found another chair and brought it to his office for Reggie, and then he erased the whiteboard on the wall. Warren's folder with the investigation reports was on his desk. "I thought if we laid it out, we could tie some of these threads together."

"Where does it all begin?" Reggie asked.

Brad wrote *Paul Carter* on one side of the board at the top. "With him. And the attempts on Kelsey's life are tied to her father's murder, if for no other reason than the same weapon was used. We have zilch on Paul Carter's murder, though."

"I believe the same person is responsible for everything," Rachel said. "I believe whoever was stealing from the museum murdered Carter, but I don't believe he did it alone."

"Why?" Reggie asked.

"The bones. The murderer would never send the bones to the museum."

Brad wrote *The murderer had a partner* under Carter's name. "But why did he dig up the bones in the first place and why now? It's been twenty-eight years since the murder."

"And why send them to the museum?" Rachel said.

They all three fell silent.

"Maybe Carter's death was an accident," Reggie said.

"Okay . . . let's follow that thread. What if Carter discovered the thefts and threatened to expose the thief?" Brad said slowly.

"Maybe they scuffled," Rachel said, "and the gun he'd stolen was handy and the murderer shot him or they were fighting over the gun and it went off. Then he has to get rid of the body."

"And he panics and calls someone," Brad said, writing.

Reggie nodded. "His brother, a close friend . . ."

"And they bury the body," Rachel said. "And fuel the rumors that Carter was stealing artifacts."

"But the only way that will work is if someone knows the artifacts are missing from the museum. So an audit is requested." Brad walked to his desk and looked through the file. He'd seen something about an audit in one of Warren's reports. When he didn't find anything, he scratched his head. Wait. It hadn't been in a report. "When I talked to the detective who investigated Carter's disappearance, he wasn't sure who on the board had asked for an audit. I need to check with him again to see if he has recalled the name."

"So, we're looking at someone who worked at the museum as the murderer," Rachel said.

"Or has connections to the museum," Brad said. "But why shoot Hendrix and Rutherford with a gun that ties back to Carter?" He walked back to the whiteboard and wrote the two men's names, then to the side, wrote *Walther P .38* and drew a connecting line.

"Maybe it's the only gun he has, and he probably had no idea Carter's remains would show up." Reggie scanned through the reports. "Was ammunition for the gun stolen as well?"

"No, but it fires nine millimeter cartridges—no problem to get. And I bet the killer never even considered that a ballistic test had been conducted on the bullets from the 1954 shooting at the Capitol building and were on file. He may have even thought using a gun that old would confuse us."

Brad wrote information about the gun on the board. "I still don't understand why the bones were shipped to the museum. Could we brainstorm that before Reggie has to leave?"

"I've been thinking about that," Rachel said. "And how I would feel if a member of my family murdered someone, even if it was accidental. Would I turn them in?"

She shifted her gaze first to Reggie, then to him. "You have brothers, Reggie, and Brad, you have a sister. What would you do?"

Brad tried to envision a scenario like what Rachel described. Could he turn Andi in? Even though the question was rhetorical, his chest tightened. He glanced at Reggie, who was tapping his fingers on the table. He and his four brothers were tight. Could either of them turn in a sibling for murder? One thing he knew for sure, if Brad hid a crime like that, it would eat at him like a cancer.

"If we, as police officers sworn to uphold the law, struggle with this hypothetical question, what would an ordinary citizen do?" Rachel leaned back in her chair. "Gentlemen, we possibly have a real situation where this happened. What do you think would be the first requirement the killer's accomplice would have?"

"It better never happen again," Brad said. He nodded his head. "And when it did—"

"The accomplice freaked out," Reggie finished.

"But he still can't turn the killer in," she said. "Even though he's trying to kill Kelsey."

"Maybe he thought if Carter's body surfaced, it would scare the killer enough that he would back off," Reggie said as he stood. "Time for me to go, but I think you're on the right track. Keep working at this, and look at who had connections to the museum twenty-eight years ago."

After the lieutenant left, Rachel said, "Reggie may be right. If we release the information that Carter was murdered and his remains have surfaced, the killer might back away from Kelsey."

"Or he might go after his accomplice," he said.

"That's a possibility I think we need to risk. Why don't you call your sister and give her the story? She always makes us look good in the press."

He smiled. That would really earn him brownie points with Andi, and he could use the lift he'd get from making one person happy. He made the call. "Busy?"

"You know I'm always busy," Andi said. "Are you calling to tell me what caused the explosion last night?"

"No, that information isn't being released yet. But I am giving you a press release. Skeletal remains discovered in a crate from the Coon Creek Science Center have been identified as those of Paul Carter, one-time director of the Pink Palace Museum, who was accused of stealing artifacts from the museum. You can lead in with 'Twenty-eight-year-old disappearance solved.'"

"Where are the bones now?" she asked. "And where can I get more information on this Paul Carter?"

"His remains are at the Forensic Center on Poplar. And you can probably find all you need in the *Commercial Appeal*'s archives. One more thing—Paul Carter is Kelsey Allen's dad."

"Oh wow. Have you told her yet?"

"Yes, but I need to let her know it's going to hit the news."

"I owe you one, big brother. This will be my lead story at six. When are you coming for dinner at Mom and Dad's?"

"Soon." He hung up and said, "It'll be on the nightly news, and I need to let Kelsey know. But first I want to finish these notes."

Brad listed the known people who were at the museum when Carter was murdered. Jackson King, Julie Webb, Helen Peterson, Mark and Robert Tomlinson. "Can you think of anyone else?"

Rachel shook her head. "I'm not familiar with the people at the museum. I thought Kelsey was going to check that out today."

"She is." He remembered two more names and wrote them on the board. Sam and Grant Allen. Then he speed-dialed Kelsey's number. His stomach clenched. Why was the call going to her voice mail? "She's not answering."

"She has a bodyguard with her, right?"

He nodded.

"Then give it a minute and call her back. I just thought about something else we haven't considered. Carter's killer could be a woman."

38

KELSEY REREAD THE ARTICLE about the app that could make a key from a photo and shook her head at how easy it was. All she had to do was take a photo of a key with her phone, and the app would find the code that she could print out. Any locksmith could then make a copy.

Just when she'd limited their possible suspects to three people—Mark Tomlinson, Robert Tomlinson, and Jackson King if he had Rutherford's key—another possibility opened up. Not that any of the three seemed the type to steal artifacts for a personal collection, especially Mark. On the other hand, she didn't really know them. Was it possible she was judging Mark by his grouchy personality?

But maybe that grouchiness was because he thought his brother was the thief. Which would make Robert Tomlinson the thief/murderer. Which seemed far-fetched. But was it far-fetched because she liked the director better than his brother? And the same question could be asked about Jackson.

She would not make a good detective—she let her emotions color her thoughts. Her time would be better spent checking to see if a camera could be trained on the doors of the artifact storage rooms. She quickly signed in to the site and found the hallway camera for the storage area. With a couple of clicks she was able to reposition the angle of the camera and zoomed in on the keypad. A minute later someone knocked at her open door, and Jackson King stuck his head inside the room.

"I see your bodyguard made it," he said, nodding to Phillip. "How are you faring after last night?"

"I'm here, and I think that's all I'll say."

"Take it easy today." He glanced toward her computer. "I just received a phone call from the security room. Are you playing with the cameras?"

She'd forgotten they were being closely monitored now. "Oops. I should have called you before I started fooling around with them. But I'm glad to see someone caught it so quickly. Oh, by the way, do you have Mr. Rutherford's master key for the building and offices?"

"Yes. It's always in my pocket. Why?"

"I'm just trying to figure out how the thief gets into the storage rooms."

He sat in a chair beside her desk where he could see her monitor. "What are you looking for there?"

"Just checking to see how hard it would be to use the camera to get the code for the keypads."

"And?"

"See for yourself." She pointed to her computer screen, where the camera feed was playing. "I've aimed the camera straight at the keypad, but I can't judge if a person standing in front of the door to enter the code would block the view."

"You keep watching, and I'll go enter the code."

A minute later he appeared on camera at the door leading into the storage area, and when he entered the code, she plainly viewed what numbers he put in.

"Could you see what I keyed in?" he asked when he returned.

"Afraid so." She chewed the end of her thumbnail.

"You're good," Jackson said.

Kelsey shrugged. "It's not hard when you know what you're looking for."

"But not everyone would know that." He glanced at Phillip. "You want to take a break?"

The security guard checked with Kelsey, and she nodded. "Get yourself some coffee."

When they were alone, Jackson said, "I like the way you work, and I've been thinking . . . would you be interested in joining Rutherford Security as a junior partner?"

"What? Partner?" She shook her head. That came out of nowhere. "I don't have the money to buy in."

"You wouldn't need money." He sat in the chair. "Let me be honest with you. Walter Rutherford was a wonderful person, but he didn't want to change with the times, and we've been losing clients. We . . . I need someone like you, someone with fresh ideas and who knows computers, because I'm not that good and I certainly don't have your expertise."

"Do you own Rutherford Security now?"

"Not yet, but I will as soon as I can buy out Walter's heirs."

She rocked back in her chair. A junior partner in an established firm? She wouldn't have to scramble to get clients because no one knew who she was. As a partner, she'd still be her own boss . . . She took a breath. "Let me think about it. I totally wasn't expecting this."

"I don't expect an answer right now." He stood. "Don't overdo it today."

"I won't. Do you know how that security guard who got hurt last night is?"

"He's going to be all right. Scheduled to be released later today. Are you sure you're okay? You look tired."

She rolled her shoulders. "I won't lie—this whole thing has been rough."

"I'm sorry all of this is happening to you. Did you go home with Sam and your mother last night?"

"No." Kelsey was tempted to tell Jackson where she was staying, but Brad had told her not to tell anyone.

He looked as though he wanted to ask more. "I guess I'd better let you get back to work."

"I wanted to ask you about that. Am I still working undercover?"

"I think right now that's the best approach. Other employees might confide in you more readily if they think you're one of them."

"Won't they wonder about the security guard?"

"By now everyone knows someone fired shots at you Monday. They just don't know why, but they know how security conscious Tomlinson is, so I think you're fine. If anyone should confide in you, let me know."

"I was surprised yesterday when Helen Peterson knew I'm working undercover. More or less said she'd guessed I was working with you, but I wonder if someone told her."

"Robert could have. He totally depends on her, but you don't have to worry about Helen. She's very discreet. It probably would be a good idea, though, for people to see you working in your capacity as conservator."

Kelsey nodded. "Good to know that about Helen, and I'll get to work on the circus within the hour."

She didn't mind working as the conservator at all. Restoring the miniature pieces was almost as good as a tranquilizer, and put her mind in order. Something she needed if she was going to consider the job offer Jackson had just made. "When do you want an answer about the job?"

His face lit up. "Glad to see you're thinking about the offer. But take your time. I'm going over the accounts with the heirs' attorney next week—I think we have about a hundred accounts right now."

"That many?" she said.

"Oh yes. The ones you're familiar with are the museum account and the accounting office you broke into, as well as your stepfather's building. I think our most interesting client is my dad's scrap iron place. You'll have to see the crusher in action. It reduces a car to a cube."

Only a man could get excited about a car crusher. "I noticed when I was poking around that the museum's personnel files have been uploaded into the networked files," Kelsey said. "Do you know how far back they go?"

"No, but you can ask Robert."

"I don't need to bother him. I'll just log in and see what I can find before I start work on the circus."

"Then I better let you get to work. I'll send McFall in."

"Before you go, I hope it's okay that I have a doctor's appointment at 1:30, but it could run over."

"Are you ill?"

Kelsey hesitated. She didn't want to explain she was seeing a hypnotherapist, not even to Jackson. "It's nothing serious, just something I need to get checked out."

He studied her a second, then nodded. "Of course, take as much time as you need."

As Phillip slipped inside the room, Kelsey logged in to the system and accessed the personnel database. While she waited for it to load, she picked up her phone. Brad had called. Why hadn't she heard it ring? She checked and somehow had turned the ringer off. He was probably frantic, and she quickly dialed him back.

"Where were you?"

She held the phone away from her ear. "You don't have to shout. My phone got turned on silent." For a minute she thought he'd hung up, and looked at her phone. Nope, still connected. He was probably counting to ten. "I didn't know," she said.

"I was just about ready to come with my siren blasting."

"But I'm okay, and Phillip is here in the office with me. Do you want his cell number?"

"Yes."

She requested it from the young man and relayed it to Brad. "And I'll try not to turn the ringer off again. What did you want?"

"The story about your dad has been released to the press, and I didn't want it to catch you off guard."

"Thank you. I knew it would have to be sooner or later."

"We hope it may deter whoever is after you."

She didn't know how her father's death being made public would accomplish that, but she was all for the killer forgetting about her. "Was that all?"

"No. Have you discovered anything about the employees who were working at the museum when he disappeared?"

"I was doing that now. You want to hang on while I look around in the files? Or do you want me to call you back?"

"Why don't I just drop by there in an hour? Then we can go to lunch before your appointment."

She'd pushed the appointment to the corner of her mind. Kelsey checked her watch. It was only ten. "Make it closer to noon. I need to put in some time on the circus or people will start wondering about my job."

"See you then."

He'd really sounded anxious when he answered, and she said, "Thanks for worrying about me."

"You're welcome," he said gruffly.

Smiling, she hung up. Brad was different from the other men she'd dated. Dated? Where did that come from? They were not dating. It was all about the case, and as soon as he caught the man after her, they would go their separate ways. With a start, Kelsey realized she enjoyed being around Brad and would miss him. Except he had Elle. The thought unsettled her as she turned to the computer screen.

Where to start? She opened a program that allowed her to search for employees with twenty-eight years of service. The query returned three employees. Julie Webb and Mark Tomlinson and Helen Peterson. Why wasn't the director on the list? She distinctly remembered him saying he'd been at the museum when her father was there.

Maybe he left for a period of time. She needed to rephrase her query. This time she entered the year her father was director. The query brought back twenty-one names. They must have been running the museum on a shoestring budget.

She scanned the list, looking for names she recognized. Julie's and Mark's names were there as well as Robert Tomlinson's. Jackson King. Helen Peterson, and her step-uncle, Grant Allen.

Kelsey hit print and rocked back in her chair. She couldn't imagine any of these people being a killer. They had to be on the wrong track or it had to be one of the names she hadn't recognized.

39

AFTER BRAD TALKED WITH KELSEY, he made another copy of Carter's file and drove out to pay another visit to Sergeant Warren. The retired cop was wearing his ball cap, and his packed bags sat on the bed. "Leaving?" he asked.

"Yep. Doctor discharged me to go home, providing I stay off of ladders."

"Probably a good idea. Thought I'd check and see if you remembered anything else."

"I've been thinking, pulling things together, and it was Conrad King who requested the audit. Seems there were rumors that items were missing about the time Carter took off. The audit was going on while I investigated. Didn't get a list of all the articles until after I closed the case."

"Did anyone strike you as suspicious?"

Warren shook his head. "From the get-go, everyone was talking about the missing artifacts, and I can see now that it influenced my investigation. What can you tell me about Carter? Any idea where he is?"

Brad hesitated. "I'm afraid someone murdered him twenty-eight years ago."

"No way." The retired sergeant leaned back in his chair and removed his cap. "Do you know how it happened?"

"He was shot with a pistol stolen from the museum." Brad hated telling him, because now the retired sergeant would spend the rest of his day, maybe the rest of his life, going over the case, looking for what he missed.

"I didn't see that coming," Warren said. "That puts a whole new spin on everything."

"I brought a copy of the file. Thought maybe if you went over it with this new development in mind, something might come to you."

Warren took the folder Brad held out. "How do you think it went down?"

"I've been brainstorming with Reggie Lane and Rachel Sloan, both in Homicide, and we figure two people are involved, maybe one covering up for the other."

"That would certainly make it easier to spread the rumors about Carter. I'll work on remembering who pushed that the most."

Brad checked the clock on the wall. Almost noon. "Do you have a ride?"

"My neighbor said he'd come after me. I'll use the time until he gets here to go over the file."

"Call me if you come up with anything."

"Believe me, I will."

◆

For once, the tedious work of restoring artifacts didn't take Kelsey's mind away from her problems. She put down the lion and picked up the lion tamer and used a small brush to get dust out of the crevices while her bodyguard looked on.

If it wasn't the upcoming psychologist appointment looping through her mind, it was the names of the people who had worked at the museum when her father was murdered. Immediately, she dismissed Julie's name. She just couldn't see her killing anyone unless she was psychotic, and Kelsey had seen no evidence of that.

She didn't want to believe it was any of them. Perhaps there was someone they were overlooking, like someone in maintenance or a groundskeeper. She felt a presence and turned. Julie. Her face warmed, and she silently chided herself. No way could the collections manager tell that Kelsey had just wondered if she was psychotic.

"I didn't know you had someone with you," Julie said.

"This is Phillip McFall. Mr. Tomlinson assigned him to me," she said.

"Because of the shooting, I guess." Julie glanced at the miniature pieces on the table. "I see you're making a little progress, but your face is flushed. You really ought to wear one of those," she said, pointing to a box of disposable masks on the worktable. "It'll keep the dust from causing allergies."

Kelsey put down the brush. "You're probably right, but it's so hard to breathe with one of those things over my nose." When Julie made no move to leave or carry on a conversation, Kelsey said, "Did you need something?"

"No, I just ran into Mark and he said you were inquiring about employees from twenty-eight years ago. Any particular reason?"

Kelsey wrestled with whether or not to tell Julie about her father being dead. If it was going to be on the evening news, did it matter if she told her now? "The bones that were delivered here . . ."

"Yes? Have you found out something about them?"

Kelsey nodded. "They are the remains of my father, Paul Carter."

Color drained from Julie's face. "You're Paul's daughter?" She covered her lips with her fingers. "Wait, Paul Carter is . . . dead? How did he die?"

"He was shot."

"But . . ." She shook her head. "I thought he . . ." She glanced at the chair. "I'm having a little trouble comprehending this. Do you mind if I sit down?"

Kelsey hadn't expected the news to throw Julie. "How well did you know my dad?"

"We were friends, and I greatly respected him." She sat in the chair and stared at Kelsey's face. "You must look like your mother."

Goose bumps rose on her arm from the intense study. "I do. Do you know anyone who might have wished him dead?"

"I can't believe he's dead. Are you certain the bones were his?"

"Yes."

"I don't understand." Julie frowned. "Why were they sent to the museum? And who sent them?"

"I believe that's the question the police are asking."

The collections manager twisted a ring on her right hand. "Yes, the police would be involved, wouldn't they?"

"You were here when my father disappeared, and you knew the people working at the museum. Does anyone stand out as a thief or killer?"

"Oh my." She took a deep breath and stood. "I'll have to think about that. I'd hate to accuse anyone."

"Please do think about it. I'm sure Brad or Rachel will be interviewing you soon."

Alarm flashed in Julie's eyes. "Yes, I suppose they will. If you will excuse me, I need to process this."

She hurried from the room. That had been interesting, but as Kelsey reviewed their conversation, not really informative. She was still deep in thought about it when Brad tapped on her door. She looked up, and his grin sent her own lips curving up.

"I like the smile. You were looking mighty serious before," he said. "You keeping a good watch on her?" he asked Phillip.

"Yes, sir. But so far she hasn't gone anywhere."

"I'll take over for a couple of hours."

Once they were alone, Brad said, "Did you get a list of the employees?"

"Yes." She handed him the sheets she'd printed. "One sheet is current employees who have twenty-eight years of service, so it doesn't give names like Robert Tomlinson or Jackson, who worked here off and on. The other is a list of all the employees from twenty-eight years ago."

"Good job. Saved me a bunch of time." He raised his eyebrows. "Ready to get something to eat?"

"I'm really not hungry."

"You need to eat. You're not nervous, are you?"

"Wouldn't you be?" She'd never liked going to the doctor, and one poking around in her mind was especially scary.

"I suppose I would. How about a barbecue?"

"Too heavy. Why not just grab something at the café and eat here in my office?"

"That'll work. Be right back."

When he returned with ham sandwiches and peach tea, she told him about her morning and the junior partnership offer from Jackson.

"I don't blame him for trying to make you a part of his company. You might even think about becoming a cop."

She shook her head. "Too dangerous."

He had his sandwich halfway to his mouth and set it on the small plate. "You're kidding."

"No. What you do day in and day out is extremely dangerous. You might as well put a bull's-eye on your back."

"And you don't think dangling from a winch above the street or climbing up a straight wall is dangerous?"

"The way you say it makes it sound dangerous. It's not something I do every day. Besides, it's different when I'm in the middle of it, and you keep forgetting that I'm an experienced rock-climber."

"I can't wait for the psychologist to get ahold of you."

She could. "What's his name, anyway?"

"Her name—Dr. Andrea Bowling."

Some of her tension about the appointment eased. "She's not going to make me crow like a rooster, is she?"

He laughed out loud. "It's nothing like that. I've seen her work with a patient before. You will be fully aware of everything, just very relaxed."

Kelsey blew out a shaky breath. "Okay. That sounds doable."

After they finished their sandwiches, he gathered the wrappers and plates and disposed of them. "You ready?"

"As I'll ever be," she muttered. The sidelong glance from him prompted her to speak louder. "Yes, I'm ready."

The psychologist's office was on Union, not far from the Methodist Hospital. At least if she went off the deep end, the hospital was nearby. At promptly one thirty, they were ushered into a spacious room with a desk and recliner as well as a sofa and were told the doctor would be in shortly.

"I don't have to lie on the sofa, do I?" Kelsey said. Every comedy skit she'd ever seen involving a psychologist had the doctor talking to the patient stretched out on a sofa.

"No." The reply came from the other side of the room near the door. "Not unless you want to. Hello, Sergeant Hollister," the doctor said in a well-modulated voice, and then extended her hand to Kelsey. "I'm Dr. Bowling."

Kelsey didn't know what she'd expected, but not this rotund woman with dancing blue eyes behind oversized glasses. She shook hands with the doctor. "And I'm Kelsey Allen."

"Would you like to sit down?" Dr. Bowling motioned toward the recliner and sofa. "I'd like to explain what will happen and answer any questions before we start."

Kelsey chose the recliner, and the doctor sat in the straight-back chair.

"Before we begin, do you have any questions?"

"Why don't you explain first, and if I still have questions, I can ask then."

"Fair enough. Have you ever been hypnotized before?"

"No."

Dr. Bowling nodded as she made notes. "First of all, I want you to understand that you will not be asleep and you will remember everything we talk about. You are not under my control or any kind of spell. Now, tell me why you want to be hypnotized."

She glanced at Brad.

"Yes, Sergeant Hollister told me what you wanted, but I'd like to hear it from you."

"I keep seeing flashes of white that I think is someone's face, but the image doesn't stay around long enough for me to recognize who the person is." She explained the circumstances and when she thought she saw the face. "I thought maybe hypnosis would allow me to hold on to the image."

"I can't guarantee that will happen, but shall we try?"

Kelsey ran her fingers over the smooth leather of the chair. "What do you want me to do?"

"Sit back in the chair, and if you'd like, lift your feet so you'll be more comfortable—like you're going to watch a movie."

Once she was comfortable, Dr. Bowling spoke in soothing tones, asking her to relax each part of her body, starting with her feet and ending with her face. "Let your eyelids relax. They're growing heavy now. You're at the top of a staircase in a nice quiet room. Take the first step down and feel yourself relax. With each step you will feel yourself growing calmer and calmer."

Kelsey's breathing became even and slow as her tension slipped away.

"You're at the bottom of the stairs. How do you feel?"

"Good. Calm."

"Good. Let's go back to Thursday night. What are you doing?"

"I'm standing on top of a building." She breathed in. "I smell barbecue. And feel a cool breeze on my face."

"Okay. Let's move forward fifteen minutes. What are you doing now?"

"I'm in a harness, climbing out a window." The memory was vivid. "Now I'm coming up the side of the building." Kelsey shifted in the chair. "I'm uncomfortable. I need to stop the winch. Oh no. There's a helicopter with strobe lights to my right. I'm worried the pilot might see me."

"Go ahead and stop the winch."

"There, that's better, and the helicopter is gone. There's a light on in this office. It wasn't on when I came down. I see someone."

"Can you see their face?"

"No, the light is shining against them. Just their outline."

"Is it a man or a woman?"

"I can't tell. Looks like a large person. Maybe a man. He's bent over, doing something to the lamp. I hear the helicopter again and there's a flash of light! I see his face! He's coming to the window and he has a gun. I've got to get out of here." She struggled to move. "Can't breathe . . ."

"Kelsey, listen to me. You are safe. He is not here. You are safe. Breathe very slowly."

She took a deep breath.

"Now take another one. Remember that you are safe. Can you still see the face?"

"White. I see something white," she gasped and struggled to breathe.

"Take another deep breath. You are perfectly safe here. Do you see those steps you came down?"

She sucked in air and nodded.

"You're going back up those same steps. Count them as we go up, and when we get to the top, you will rejoin us. One, two . . ."

Kelsey slowly came out of the altered state of consciousness and took another deep breath. "I thought hypnosis was supposed to relax you."

Dr. Bowling gave a soft laugh. "Most people I hypnotize aren't being shot at or going up the side of a building. Do you remember the helicopter?"

She nodded.

"How about the man and the lamp?"

Kelsey chewed on her thumbnail. Today was the first time she remembered him bending over the lamp. She closed her eyes and tried to pull out the image she'd seen. "Yes, but I still can't see his face."

40

BRAD SQUEEZED KELSEY'S HAND. He'd hoped Dr. Bowling would get more from her memory. "But at least we know we're dealing with a man. And you remembered the helicopter."

"I remembered the helicopter yesterday, but I never thought to tell you," Kelsey said.

"But don't you think this helped you?" He believed it had. He turned to the doctor. "Do you think another session might help her to see the man's face?"

"Wait," Kelsey said. "I'm not sure I can do this again."

Dr. Bowling pushed her glasses up on her nose. "I think she should give it a couple of days. Sometimes in cases like this, there's a delayed response. The image could suddenly become clear any time." She looked at her calendar. "This is Wednesday. If you haven't remembered by Monday, would you be willing to try this again?"

He glanced at Kelsey, doubtful she would go through it again, but she surprised him and was nodding her head.

"You don't think it would help to do it earlier, say Friday?"

Brad asked. Every day she didn't remember the man's face was a day the shooter could be standing right beside her.

The doctor tapped her pen on the desk. "Tell you what, let's do it Saturday if she hasn't had the desired results."

"Thank you, Dr. Bowling," Kelsey said.

When they walked out into the bright sunlight, she checked her watch. "We have a little time, so why don't we drive over to the house on Snowden and see what's in the desk there. Dad may have kept museum papers in it."

"Sounds like a winner to me," Brad said. He'd planned to go after he dropped Kelsey off at the museum, anyway. As they drove across town, he kept an eye on traffic behind him and took the long way around to the house. If anyone was following them, he couldn't see it.

When they pulled into the drive, he was struck once again with the uniqueness of the home. He walked around to open her door, surprised that she'd waited for him this time. Not a breeze stirred the May heat that felt more like the middle of June.

He scanned the area for a place the killer could watch them unobserved. Somehow he'd seen Brad load the box into the trunk of his car. There were several cars parked up and down the street that he hadn't noticed yesterday. A couple of them had tinted windows too dark to see inside. And two blocks down was a convenience store where his car could be observed by anyone.

"Trying to figure out how he knew you took something from the house?" Kelsey asked.

"Yeah. Did you ask your mom if the people were going to buy the house?" he asked as they walked behind the house.

"Too much has happened, and I never thought of it again. I'll give her a call tonight."

"Have you talked to her today?"

"Twice. She still wants me to come home."

He stopped and turned her to face him. "I'm a cop and I can protect you better than anyone."

She raised her head, fear showing in her green eyes. He wanted to make this nightmare go away. He wanted to take her in his arms and tell her everything was going to be all right. But they both knew that until the man was caught, she wasn't safe, not even with him.

With a lift of her chin, her eyes narrowed and a hard glint darkened her eyes. "This won't last forever. He will make a mistake. And we'll catch him."

I'll catch him, Brad wanted to say, and if he had his way about it, Kelsey would be on her way to Alaska until this was over. "Let's look in the shed."

The double doors stood ajar.

"Didn't you lock this?" Kelsey asked.

"I did. I bet the files he took didn't have what he was looking for. He must have come back."

Brad opened the doors and groaned. The desk drawers were pulled open, and papers were scattered everywhere. "Looks like whoever took the box in my trunk didn't find what they wanted."

"So he came back here. What do you suppose he's looking for?"

"Something that would incriminate him."

She cocked her head. "But why wait this long?"

Brad had no definite answer. "How many people knew that your dad's papers were stored here?"

Kelsey shrugged. "No one, except Mom. I didn't know, and Sam even seemed surprised at dinner the other night."

He thought back. Sam had been surprised, but that didn't

mean anything. "Do you suppose he said something to some-one?"

"Tomlinson said he'd talked to Sam. Do you think . . ."

"I don't know what I think. But I'll have a talk with the director when I drop you off." He glanced at the mess. "At least we know what's in the desk and on the floor isn't worth going through. Shall we look through some of the other boxes?"

Kelsey stopped at the desk and stared at it. "I just remembered that Dad showed me a hidden recess one time . . . He wrote me notes and hid them in a secret compartment." She touched one of the panels on the desk, but it was solid. The smile she gave him was apologetic. "I thought that might slide back and reveal the hiding place. Even if we find it, there might not be anything in it anyway."

She pressed another panel and it slid back, exposing a cubbyhole. "Oh! This is it. He put my notes right here on the shelf."

Brad knelt beside her and used his phone to shine a light in the recess. "There's something white stuck behind the shelf."

He stuck his hand past the recess and shifted the paper with his fingers. "It's bigger than the hole and feels like a folder. Check and see if there's another larger recess."

Kelsey pressed the other panels to no avail. "Dad must have put whatever this is on the rolltop and it slid down in the space."

They pulled the desk out, and Brad examined the back. Nothing short of destroying the desk would get the paper out. When he straightened up, Kelsey was working in the cubbyhole.

"There's a tiny bit of space between the front and back panels," she said. "I think I can move the folder and pull the papers out."

"Go for it."

He shined his flashlight on the cubbyhole again. She inched the folder to where she could slide her fingers inside it. "I think I've got one of the sheets."

If they were lucky, they would be stapled together. Sweat was dripping off his face. "You want me to fan you?"

"No, just hold the light where I can see what I'm doing."

Once she separated the papers from the folder, she trapped the top of the papers between two fingers and twisted. "It's rolling up."

"How are you doing that?"

"It comes from rock-climbing and manipulating the cracks. There. Got it." She drew the rolled-up papers out. "No more snide remarks about my rock-climbing. Okay?"

"Yes, ma'am. What is it?"

She unrolled the papers. "Looks like some sort of list."

He looked over her shoulder, and the first thing he saw was the shrunken head that had been listed in Sergeant Warren's report. Below it were some of the other missing artifacts he'd seen listed. "This is what our thief was looking for. Your father must have been trying to discover who the thief was. What's on the second page?"

She flipped the sheet. "I think you're right. It looks like he was compiling a list of suspects." She looked closer. "Well, maybe not suspects. Looks more like a list of all the employees."

He scanned the list. Mark and Robert Tomlinson, Jackson King . . . Beside him, Kelsey gasped.

"Sam and Grant's names are there."

There were three other names he didn't recognize. He scanned the rest of the writing to see if Paul Carter had an idea who had taken the artifacts, but if he did, it wasn't written on this paper.

"So he knew someone was stealing artifacts," Kelsey said.

"And anyone who worked there could have taken them. Probably wasn't as much security then as now. I just wish he'd been more specific."

The file didn't add anything to the information he had. The only thing it did was to confirm people he already suspected. Except Helen Peterson's and Julie Webb's names weren't on the list, even though Brad hadn't completely ruled them out. "I don't think your dad was hiding this. It's too general. It just got stuck there."

A text dinged on his phone. Rachel wanting to know if he had time to brainstorm with her and Reggie.

"Are you going back to the museum?"

"I had planned to and work on the security angle." She checked her watch. "But it's after three now."

"Want to come to the CJC with me and discuss the case?"

"You think I can help?"

"I think we need fresh eyes." And it would keep her with him and out of trouble.

"So, actually I'd be working on finding out who stole the artifacts. Let me call Jackson and let him know I'm tracking down leads."

41

At the CJC, Kelsey opened her computer bag and handed Brad the papers they'd found in her father's desk. While he made copies, she powered up her laptop. She hadn't recognized a few of the names and wanted to run a check on them once he returned her copy of the list.

Kelsey scanned the whiteboard. Must be what they'd brainstormed earlier. Her father's name and the other two victims were written at the top. She swallowed hard. Would her name be up there next? She shook the thought away. Not if she could help it.

Below the victims' names were those people who had been employed at the museum when her father was director and were still employed or connected some way. Sam's and Grant's names were up there. Brad handed her a copy of what they'd found, then handed one to Rachel before he added three more names to the board, people she didn't know. Last, he added Julie's and Helen's names.

Reggie came into the room as she said, "I don't think Sam's and Grant's names should be there."

All three of the detectives turned to look at her.

"Why?"

She knew her stepfather and uncle like she knew herself, and neither of the men would kill her father . . . or try to kill her. But these detectives would need more than her gut reaction. "My dad may have been jealous of Sam. Maybe he thought Sam stole his wife. I don't know—I've never discussed that with my mom. But I know their character, and they wouldn't be involved in anything like this."

"I'm sorry, but we never truly know anyone," Rachel said. "In this business I've discovered the blackest hearts in the nicest people."

Kelsey refused to believe the two men could have anything to do with her dad's murder or attempting to kill her. She eyed the names on the board she didn't recognize. If only it could be one of those people, because the suggestion that someone she personally knew had killed her father and wanted to kill her . . . it was unimaginable.

Her gaze dropped to the next item on the whiteboard, and seeing the question in black and white sent another chill through her. "Why do you think my father's remains were sent to the museum?" she asked, her voice cracking.

Rachel's face softened. "I know this must be hard for you."

"Hard doesn't even touch what I feel," she said. She would never forget the pull that crate had on her on Monday. It was like her spirit knew. "Do you think it's possible the killer had an attack of conscience? Or were they being cruel and taunting me?"

"I can tell you it wasn't because of the murderer's conscience," Brad said. "If it was, he wouldn't be trying to kill you now."

"We think the killer has an accomplice, and maybe after they found out Rutherford was murdered in the vault and the stamp had been stolen, the accomplice either became angry or scared. If we can discover who that person is, I believe we can break all the cases." Reggie leaned back in the chair. "But right now it's like a puzzle with no answers."

Brad turned to Rachel. "Do we have the analysis of fibers or particles found in the plastic wrapping?"

"Partial." Rachel pulled a folder from the stack in front of her. "The soil found in the plastic and in the crate was consistent with this area. Speaking of puzzling, there were traces of petroleum in the analysis. And, there were a couple of carpet threads caught on the bottom of the crate, which would help if we find the vehicle that transported the crate."

While they talked, Kelsey glanced at the paper and entered the first name on the list plus *obit* into a search engine. Wait. Did Rachel say something about petroleum? Why would there be traces of petroleum on the plastic? She tuned back in to their conversation.

"Did the lab indicate the source of the petroleum?" Reggie asked.

Rachel scanned the document. "They're still running tests, but my bet would be motor oil."

Brad listed what they'd learned from the analysis. "What type of places would have motor oil? Other than a service station?"

"Auto repair shop," Rachel said.

"Junkyard," Reggie added.

"You should see the crusher in action. It can reduce a car to a cube." "How about a scrap metal place where cars are crushed?"

Brad paused. "What made you say that?"

"Jackson King told me just today about his dad's scrap

iron company. We're looking for a burial site from twenty-eight years ago, and that one might fit the bill."

"You may be right." He put *scrap iron businesses* on the board.

"Let's each of us take a person on the board and interview them," Rachel said. "I'll take Robert Tomlinson and his brother."

Reggie said, "How about the people who worked at the museum twenty-eight years ago but aren't there now?"

Kelsey checked her computer. She had hits for her search, and she clicked on the first one, a funeral home in Memphis. "The first person is deceased," she said, reading the page.

"What?" Brad said. "How do you know?"

"I looked him up." She read the name. "And the obituary says he was a former employee of the museum."

"Check the others," Reggie said.

The others weren't as easy to find, but after several tries, she located an obituary for the second one and reported it. Then she looked for a Facebook page for a Junior Coleman and found four hits. The first two were kids, the third one lived in Michigan, and when she clicked on the *About* link for the last one, she found the Pink Palace Museum listed under *Former employment*. Her eyes widened when she saw his present workplace. "Found him, and he's working at the Coon Creek Science Center."

"You're kidding." Brad looked over her shoulder. "I feel a road trip coming on. Check and see what their hours are. And get their number."

She entered the question into the search engine and two clicks later had the answer. "Ten to four."

"How about tomorrow morning?" Rachel said. "The place will be closed today before we get out of Memphis."

"Maybe I can get the director's phone number from Julie, and he could provide an address for the man," Kelsey said. She scrolled through her contacts and called her. A few minutes later, she relayed the number to Brad and he made the call.

"The man in question is out of town today," he said when he disconnected. "But he'll be there by nine in the morning—they have a camp scheduled at noon."

Kelsey's cell rang. It was Sabra, and she quickly answered, fearing the worst. "Is everything all right?"

Her sister's laughter quickly eased the knot in Kelsey's stomach.

"We're fine. Dad thinks you need some R & R. He's cooking out tonight and wants you to come by for supper. And bring Brad too."

"Let me check with him." He might have a date with Elle. She turned to him. "Cookout tonight with my parents?"

"Sure."

Too bad, Elle. Kelsey questioned Rachel with her eyes, but the sergeant shook her head.

"I have a dinner date, but I'll catch up with you two at Brad's house by nine."

"We'll be there," Kelsey said to Sabra. "Can I stop and get anything?"

"No, just bring yourselves. Lily is so looking forward to seeing you. She's been worried."

Lily was too young to have that kind of pressure. "You tell my niece that I'm like a cat and always land on my feet."

42

THIS TIME WHEN BRAD approached the Allen house, a guard operated the gate. Sam Allen had taken the security of his daughter and granddaughter very seriously. Perhaps it would have been a safer place for Kelsey as well. "Would you rather be here with your family instead of at my house?"

"It's not a matter of preference," Kelsey said. "My presence here would be too dangerous for everyone. If this madman did attack, one of them might get hurt in the crossfire. I still shudder when I consider Sabra and Lily could have opened that garage door if they'd been home last night instead of here."

He admired the way Kelsey soldiered on. She'd been through a lot the past few days, and yet her thoughts were for someone else. There was a lot of courage in the woman sitting next to him, and he glanced at her. Today her short hair framed her face instead of the spikey look from Saturday, and he liked the way it made her green eyes look even bigger.

"In the morning I'll take you to work before I go to the science center," he said as the gate swung open. "That is, if you're comfortable working there without us around."

"I'll be fine. I plan to look through the personnel records again, and go a little deeper than just names. Who knows, maybe someone listed 'bomb making' in their résumé."

Brad laughed. "That would be awesome." He pulled to the circle drive and parked. "I hope you don't mind, but I'm going to ask Sam and your mom a few questions."

"I don't like it, but I understand. You don't seriously believe Sam has anything to do with this, do you?"

It was hard to know how to answer her. Almost ten years as a homicide detective had taught him that people weren't always what they seemed. "I hope he's not, but he and Grant are on that list your dad made."

"I thought we decided that was just a list of employees."

"Kelsey, they worked there at the time of his death. I can't ignore that."

The front door opened, and Lily shot down the porch. "Aunt Kelsey! You're here!"

Kelsey didn't wait for Brad to open the door but scrambled out and caught Lily in her arms. "You're not supposed to run out the door like that," she said.

"But you didn't get out. I was afraid you would leave."

He climbed out of the car. Seeing the two together and the love they shared kindled a desire for a family of his own. Kelsey swung Lily around and caught him watching them. Their gazes lingered, then Lily patted her cheek and Kelsey shifted her attention to the girl.

When Elle laid down her demand that it was her or his job, he hadn't given much thought about the family his choice would cost him. He was too busy nursing the wounds she had inflicted. But what if he'd chosen her over the job? His life might look a lot different, and he might even have that family he'd always wanted.

It's not too late. Elle was back in his life, and he'd thought once that she was everything he'd looked for in a life mate.

Just then, Kelsey turned and smiled at him. Now he wasn't so sure.

Lily wiggled out of Kelsey's arms and ran to him. "Come on, Mr. Brad," she said, pulling on his hand. "Pawpaw Sam has our burgers ready."

"Yes, ma'am."

Over Lily's head, Kelsey's dancing eyes met his again. With a start, he realized he had a problem. It wasn't Elle he saw himself taking in his arms and kissing. It was Kelsey. *Not good, Hollister. Not good.* This was getting complicated, and he couldn't let anything cloud his mind right now.

He climbed the steps and once again was struck by the contrast of hominess and wealth. He found that same contrast in Sam and his brother Grant. Saturday night they'd looked as though they'd belonged to the Memphis elite, but tonight they were dressed in sports shirts and khaki shorts. If he ran into either man in a hardware store, he would never guess they had taken a small parts store their father left them and turned it into a franchise with stores all over the United States.

Judging by the laughter around the pool as everyone chowed down on Sam's burgers, the two preferred being regular guys. He watched as Grant limped toward a table. He'd noticed the limp Saturday night and had meant to ask Kelsey about it.

Brad swung back and forth on interviewing the men here in Sam's home. Probably be a breach of etiquette, but if the opportunity presented itself, he'd grab it.

"Burgers are good, aren't they," Kelsey said as she sat in the patio chair beside him.

"Best I've had in a long time." He glanced up to see why

she sounded so upbeat. Her smile stretched almost from ear to ear. "What's going on?"

"I asked Mom about the house, and she'd been meaning to tell me the people backed out."

"That's wonderful."

"I know. I've been worried about where I'd live after this was over. I'll miss seeing Lily every day, but—"

"Aunt Kelsey, Mr. Brad, watch me!"

His gaze followed Kelsey's to the pool, where Lily was on the diving board. "Does she know how to swim?"

"Since she was three."

The girl hit the water in a cannonball. "She's fearless. I don't think I could swim when I was six," he said.

"She's been around Kelsey too much," Grant Allen said as he set his half-full glass on the table. "Mind if I join you two?"

"After that comment, yes." Kelsey's warm grin said otherwise.

He sat in the wrought-iron chair and propped his left foot in another before he felt his shirt pocket. "Don't think I'll ever quit wanting a smoke after dinner." He reached for the toothpick on his empty plate and stuck it in his mouth. "So, Paul's remains have been found," he said and immediately winced. "Oh my goodness. There I go sticking my mouth in my foot again. Sorry, Kels."

She shrugged. "That's okay. Like I told someone earlier today, it's all surreal."

"What do you know so far, Brad?"

He shook his head. "I'm sorry, I missed that."

Kelsey laughed. "I bet he's still focused on the mouth in the foot picture." She turned to Brad. "Grant always gets his metaphors backwards."

"I do not, just that one," he retorted and repeated his question.

Brad mentally sorted through what he could tell him, glad for the opportunity to perhaps get information. "Actually, I'm hoping you can fill in some of the missing parts. Does anyone stand out in your mind from that time who might have wanted him dead?"

The older man stared off in the distance. "Before Paul was offered the director's position, I was collections manager and had applied for the job. But they chose Paul, brought him back from Egypt to take it. Always liked him, though, and we talked a lot. I told Sam he ought not go after Cynthia even though they'd been divorced for three years. You see," he said, turning to Brad, "Paul thought she'd eventually go back to him. Not that my brother ever listens to me. But he certainly wouldn't do Paul harm."

"How long had you known him?" Brad asked, noticing how Kelsey hung on to every word he said.

"Met him when Sam and I signed up for a dig in Egypt. He and Cynthia were already married then."

"So you all have known each other awhile."

"Yep, since early college days. Paul was Sam's archaeology professor. Cynthia's too. And I met him on the dig. Sam was heartbroken when she chose Paul over him."

The picture Brad was getting didn't reflect badly on Sam, but it did show a reason for wanting Paul out of the way. Grant shifted his leg and rubbed it. "What happened to your leg?" he asked.

"I can tell you that," Kelsey said. "He broke it saving Sam's life."

"Aw, girl, it wasn't anything like that."

"That's not the way I hear Sam tell it." She turned to Brad.

"They were caving and fell off a ledge. Sam wasn't hurt, but he'd fallen farther than Grant and couldn't get out."

The older man chuckled. "He sure didn't have your rock-climbing skills."

"Anyway, Grant had broken his leg in the fall, but he was closer to the top and was able to climb out, broken leg and all."

"And the leg didn't heal properly," Grant finished for her. "I just remembered something about Jackson King."

Kelsey held her finger up. "Let me finish. Sam didn't want him trying to crawl out with a broken leg, but Grant did. He got out and dragged himself half a mile before he found help. By the time the rescue team got to Sam, hypothermia had set in. He would have died if Grant had waited like Sam insisted."

"Wasn't that big a deal. If I hadn't gotten out in the sun, I would've died too." He folded his arms across his chest. "About Jackson. Seems to me, he had sticky fingers."

Brad sat up straighter. "What do you mean?"

"The way I remember it, Paul caught Jackson helping himself to a package of typing paper and some pens. I thought Paul ought to get rid of the boy, but as usual, he gave him another chance. Who's to say King didn't graduate to some of the artifacts?"

He had a point, but Jackson had only been eighteen and possibly didn't think of it as stealing even though it was. Still, Brad had a hard time thinking Jackson King could be involved with the killing. "How about Robert Tomlinson? What do you remember about him? Or his brother?"

"Knew Mark better than Robert. And he was just as negative then as he was the last time I saw him. Maybe because he always had so much responsibility on his shoulders. He put his brother through college, you know."

Maybe he'd stolen a few of the artifacts to help out. Except Brad couldn't find a trace of any of the artifacts being sold.

Grant slid his foot to the ground and stood. "You might want to look at Julie Webb too. Seems like her brother got into some serious trouble about that time. I remember her asking me where she could borrow a significant amount of money." Then he nodded. "See you around."

"That was certainly interesting," Kelsey said after he was out of earshot.

"Yeah. I need to check with Rachel and see if she's the one who interviewed him." He'd like to compare notes. Call him suspicious, but it seemed odd that Grant pointed the finger at everyone but himself.

Lily bounded up. "Did you see me? Did I make a big splash?"

"You did," Kelsey said. "And I can't believe how tall you're getting."

The girl stood taller and pulled on her swimsuit. "I know. That's why I have to have a new suit. Mom says it's too little. Can you go with us tomorrow?"

Brad smiled as Kelsey made a face. "I have to work tomorrow."

Lily frowned. "Then come play Go Fish with me. You too, Mr. Brad. Mom's playing."

"He doesn't want to play a card game, but I'll come," Kelsey said. When her niece ran to get the cards, she said, "You can thank me later."

"I'll thank you now. What time do you want to leave?"

"Give me about forty-five minutes. I miss being with Sabra and Lily."

His cell rang. It was Lieutenant Robinson from the Bomb Unit, and he answered it.

"Thought I'd let you know the apartment has been re-leased. Ms. Allen is free to do whatever she wants with it."

He thanked the lieutenant and decided to wait until they left to tell Kelsey, since she seemed to be enjoying her time with Lily. He wandered around the patio area to a rose garden his mother would love and bent to sniff a red and white rose.

"That's a double delight," Cynthia said from behind him. "Do you like roses?"

He turned around. "I do, but my mom likes them even better."

"When this terrible time is finished, I'll invite her over for tea. Do you have any idea . . . ?"

"I hope soon." He'd love to be able to say they'd have this madman caught tomorrow.

"Do you know when Paul's, uh, remains will be released? I want to plan a simple memorial service."

"No, ma'am, but I can find out tomorrow."

He followed her gaze to where Kelsey was playing cards with Lily.

"This has been really hard on my daughters," Cynthia said. "Especially Kelsey. She worries about someone else get-ting hurt."

"Yes, I was thinking that earlier. But I've learned one thing about her in this investigation—she's resilient."

"Oh yes. I'm sure you've also learned she's Little Miss Independence. She thinks there's nothing she can't do."

"Yeah, I've noticed she doesn't like help."

"That's stating it mildly. I'll never forget when Sam bought a computer for the house. Kelsey was ten. She got the how-to manual that came with it, and by the time she was twelve she was creating her own programs."

"So Sam is good with computers too?"

"Not as good as Kelsey or even Grant."

Brad tucked that bit of information away to discuss with Rachel. He tilted his head. "Have you thought of anything more that might help with the investigation since we talked the other night?"

She shook her head. "Sam would be a better person to talk to. And Grant, but I saw you talking to him. They both have had many more dealings with the museum than I have. Grant, especially. I don't know if he told you, but he applied for the directorship at the same time as Paul, but Paul was more qualified, and older."

"He did. How badly did Grant want the job?"

Brad held her questioning gaze.

"Not bad enough to kill Paul, I can assure you. The museum was absolutely not the right job for him."

Still, at the time it could have been a blow to Grant. "How about Sam? How did he and Paul get along?"

The question brought pain to her face. "My husband did not have anything to do with Paul's death."

"I hope you know I don't enjoy asking these questions," Brad said, gentling his voice.

"I know that, and before you ask, Sam and I were only friends before my divorce and his wife's death."

Brad didn't doubt that one second on her part. But he wasn't too sure about Sam's.

43

Kelsey stared at Brad as the gate closed behind them. "You mean we can go right now and pick up my clothes?"

He laughed. "Yes, ma'am. Lieutenant Robinson said you're free to do whatever."

"Oh, wow. I hope they don't smell like smoke." She could also assess her furniture to see how much of it she could move to the house on Snowden. Her mind whirled with plans. Abruptly she sank back into the seat and groaned. What was she doing? She couldn't move. She couldn't do anything until this madman was caught.

"What's wrong?"

"I want my life back!" She pressed her fingers to her temples. "I'm ready for this to be over."

"We'll catch him, Kelsey. I promise you. He's getting cocky, and he'll make a mistake. The announcement about your father being found will shake him up, and he's bound to feel us closing in."

"We have a list of people my dad thought could be stealing. Why can't we hack into their computers and see if there's anything incriminating in them?"

"Maybe because it's illegal? And we don't know that it was

a list of suspects. Besides, I'd have to have a court order to do what you're suggesting, and I don't have enough evidence against any of the people on the list to get one."

Brad's way was so slow. "What's wrong with fighting any way you have to? Even Jesus said to be cunning as a snake and guileless as a dove," she said as they stopped at a traffic light.

"Kelsey . . ."

When she looked around, frustration was stamped in his face.

"Don't quote Scripture at me, especially something taken out of context. I want this guy as bad as you do, but if I do what you're suggesting, any evidence I found would be thrown out, and he could go scot-free."

Her cheeks burned from the truth of his words. "The light changed," she mumbled. When had she slipped past bending the rules to outright breaking them?

With a sigh, he gunned the motor. She was still mulling that thought over when Brad pulled into Sabra's drive. He parked and came around and opened her door.

"Ready to go up?" he asked and held out his hand for her to take.

"Yeah. Look, about what I said. I know you can't break the law . . . I just feel so helpless."

"So do I. But we'll catch him with plain old investigative work. Knocking on doors, talking to people, following leads. It works, maybe not as fast as you'd like, but when we catch him, the evidence will stick."

The intensity in his voice raised goose bumps on her arm. She took his hand, feeling his strength. The world needed more men like Brad Hollister. Impulsively, she kissed him on the cheek. "Thanks."

He touched his face. "What was that for?"

Kelsey ducked her head. "For keeping me on the straight and narrow."

He lifted her chin until she was gazing into his hazel eyes.

"You're a strong woman with a good moral compass. You would have come back to it, just like you did."

He thought she was strong? And noble? Joy bubbled up from deep within her, and she straightened her shoulders. "I hope so."

"Trust me, you would've. Shall we go up the back stairs?"

She stared at the garage. "Is the apartment safe?"

"Yeah. It wasn't a huge bomb, and it won't take a lot of money to repair the damages. Could've been a lot worse."

He didn't have to tell her that. Inside the apartment, she avoided the front area. "What's stinging my nose and eyes?" she said.

"Burned electrical wires."

"Have they been able to tell what kind of bomb it was?"

"It was a homemade bomb," he said. "And, unfortunately, the materials are easy to get. Our suspect has already demonstrated he has the intelligence to make one."

Kelsey hurried to her bedroom. The sooner they got out of there, the better she would feel. She grabbed her makeup and several sets of clothes that could be easily washed and worn. As they backed out of the drive, she said, "At least I can use my bedroom suite in the house."

"When you get ready to move, I'll help you."

"You mean you're going to hang around when you don't have to?"

"Yeah, you've kind of grown on me." He winked as he wheeled out of the drive.

Pleased, she leaned back in the seat. Once her life did return to normal, it'd be interesting to see where Brad fit into it.

44

Thursday morning, Brad woke early and dressed, strapping the ankle holster to his leg, then checked his watch. Just enough time to give Tripod a little exercise, so he took a Frisbee from the closet.

Tripod's tail thumped the ground when he stepped out into the humid air. "Don't look at me like that," he said. "I can't go running this morning. Too hot and I'm already dressed."

The dog sat on his haunches and whined. Brad laughed and tossed the disc. With a bark, Tripod was after it.

"He's pretty special," Kelsey said from the patio.

He hadn't heard her come out. Whoa. This morning she was wearing dressy jeans and a soft green sweater the color of her eyes. Her short hair was still wet and more pixyish like yesterday than spiked, but she still looked saucy. He found his tongue. "Yeah, he is special. You're up early."

"I thought I'd make breakfast."

"Pretty and you cook too? Better be careful. I might propose."

"You better wait until you taste it," she said, laughing. "It won't be anything like Elle's."

For a second he imagined what it would be like to be married and have someone to share things with and no more lonely meals. Tripod nudged him and dropped the Frisbee at his feet. A good thing too—it hadn't been Elle he imagined being married to. He grabbed the Frisbee and tossed it for Tripod to run after again. "Let me get washed up."

◆

"Thanks for breakfast, even if it did make us late," he said when he turned off Central into the museum drive. It was after nine and he'd hoped to be on the way to McNairy County by this time, especially since thunderheads were forming. "And for the record, the proposal still holds."

"Yeah, right. Can't believe you'd marry someone just for their cooking."

"You haven't tasted mine. It's how I stay so skinny."

"You're not skinny, you're lean. You know—lean, mean, fighting machine."

He shot her a quick glance. He didn't know when or how, but they had turned some sort of corner. Other than Andi, he rarely joked with a woman. For a second, he thought about asking if she wanted to drive to Coon Creek with them. No. Kelsey would be too distracting, and he needed to keep his mind on the case right now.

"I expect we'll be back in three hours," he said when he parked his car at the back of the museum. "Try not to get into any trouble while I'm gone."

"Moi?" Kelsey raised her eyebrows.

"Yes, you."

"Just because you and Rachel are going to be out of town doesn't mean I'll do something crazy."

324

If only he could be sure of that. "What are your plans this morning?"

She patted her computer bag. "First I want to check my computer and see if he's hacked in again."

"You still have the program running?"

"Yeah, and I didn't see any evidence of him hacking in again yesterday morning, but I was too tired to check last night."

He nodded. "Okay, that shouldn't take three hours. What's next?"

She turned and pinned him with a hard stare. "Really? You want a minute by minute accounting of my time?"

Heat shot up his neck, burning even the tips of his ears. "If I know what you're doing, I can focus on interviewing the man at Coon Creek."

Her eyes softened, blending with the jade-green sweater.

"Like I said before, I thought I'd check the employee records and see if anyone lists computer skills on their résumé. You should be back by then. If you're not, I'll work on the circus."

"That sounds safe enough. Just keep your bodyguard with you at all times. And we'll be texting back and forth." He came around and opened her door, offering his hand. The smile she gave him tripped his heart.

He was in trouble. And he'd broken a major rule. Somehow, some way, Kelsey Allen had become more than the target of a murderer, and that was not good. At least until he caught the killer.

"Are you all right?" Kelsey asked.

"Um, yeah." Her full lips, red like ripe strawberries, drew his attention. He suddenly wanted to kiss them. Not really suddenly—he'd been thinking about kissing her all morning now.

"Well, you look worried. I'll be fine while you're gone."

He snapped his attention back. What was he thinking? He was charged with protecting Kelsey, not kissing her. "When this is over, would you go out with me? You know, like a real date?"

"What?" Pink flooded her face.

Brad could not believe he'd just said that, but it was as though he had no control over his mouth. And now he'd embarrassed her. "I-I'm sorry, I don't know what I—"

"Yes," she said.

"Yes?" His heart dipped. "But you seemed—"

"You surprised me, that's all."

He couldn't stop the silly grin that spread over his face. "Okay."

Then he remembered Elle, and his excitement cooled. What was wrong with him? Men who strung women along always disgusted him. But which woman was he stringing along?

After Brad left her with the bodyguard, he walked back to his car, and by the time he met Rachel, reality had set in again. Not only did he have to make a decision about Elle, but thinking of Kelsey as the desirable woman she was could get them both killed. *Kinda late to have those thoughts, buddy boy.* He had to get his mind back in the game.

"You want to ride with me?" Rachel asked.

"That makes no sense," he said. "Your car is parked in the garage and mine is ready to go."

She stared him down. "Who stole your toys this morning?"

"Just get in." He sighed. "Sorry. I don't look forward to driving to Coon Creek . . . and I guess this case is getting to me."

She slid into the passenger's side and fastened her seat belt. "He's bound to make a mistake."

Brad pulled away from the curb and headed in the direction of the interstate. "He hasn't so far. I hope this isn't a wild goose chase we're going on today."

"Junior Coleman is the only one on Paul Carter's list we have left to interview. I checked him out this morning and he's clean—not even a traffic ticket in the past ten years. Transferred to the job at Coon Creek two years ago. As far as I can tell, Facebook is the only social media he does—no Twitter or Pinterest or Instagram page. My gut says he's not the one, but I hope he can provide insight on the other people on the list."

Brad hoped so too.

45

"YOU SEEM HAPPIER TODAY, MS. ALLEN," her bodyguard said. "I like that tune you're humming. What is it?"

Kelsey realized she'd been humming the song running through her head, and she ducked her head. "Just a song I heard a few years ago."

"Well, it's nice to see you more relaxed," he said.

"Why, thank you, Phillip." She keyed in the code. "I'm sorry you're stuck with such a boring person."

"The more boring the better," he said with a laugh.

She liked the young man guarding her and realized she knew nothing about him. Looking at him, she'd guess he was about thirty. "Are you married?" Kelsey automatically glanced at his ring finger. That would have been an easy answer if she'd only looked.

"Yes, ma'am. We have a little one on the way."

Her heart melted. "Oh, that's wonderful!"

Would she ever have a little one on the way? At thirty-five, she didn't have a lot of time left. But no need dwelling on something she had no control over. So why did she think of Brad? She shook the thought off and focused on Phillip. "Your first?"

"Yes, ma'am. And before you ask, we don't know if it's a boy or girl. My wife wanted to wait and find out when the baby's born."

"Some women prefer it that way." Not her. She would want to know as early as possible so that she could decorate her baby's room and buy clothes. Brad would make a good father—she'd seen him with Lily. Kelsey brought herself up short again. Reality check, girl. There was a little thing about having a husband before she could think about a baby, and even if she and Brad dated, who was to say what their future held. There was always Elle to consider, and *she* had history with him.

"I better get to work," she said. "Make yourself comfortable on the sofa there."

Kelsey booted up her computer. If she didn't find out who this killer was, she wouldn't have a future. Once the computer was up and running, she ran the application she'd installed after he hacked into her system. It wasn't designed to stop an attack but to secretly track the program he'd loaded onto her computer when she'd opened his email, logging every time he accessed the program, all the while tracking his activity.

Her heart paused. He'd logged in three hours ago. She clamped her fist tight. This time she would track the fox back to his lair with the IP address the new program captured. The last time, he'd erased all signs that he'd been in her computer other than the photo of Lily. This time the program made it appear to him that he'd erased his tracks again, but had in fact captured every keystroke he made.

With a few clicks, she was at his router, and the program was requesting a password. Kelsey switched over to a Linux drive and used a brute force application to crack the password.

Suddenly her screen went black and she dropped her head. Busted. She rebooted. But there was no need to try and get in again. The hacker was smarter than she'd given him credit for. He had his system rigged to shut down if brute force was attempted.

This guy was top notch. Could it be Jackson? Her gut said it was someone who could keep tabs on her at the museum. She shook her head. It was hard to believe the head of security was trying to kill her. Besides, he didn't know that much about computers—it was why he wanted to hire her.

Kelsey had noticed Julie was fairly competent when it came to computers.

She logged into the museum's system and then into the employee files to see if any of the employees listed computer skills on their profiles. First she looked through the ones in the folder she'd created. No luck. Then she ran a query for computer skills and received ten hits.

One by one she reviewed their files. When the ninth one popped up on her screen, she blinked. Oh wow! This guy had all types of certifications, three in computer networking alone. Thunder rumbled as she reached for her phone and called Brad.

"Find something?" he asked when he answered.

"Yeah. Mark Tomlinson says he doesn't know anything about computers other than what he has to know for the job. But his résumé says otherwise."

"Really. We're about half an hour away from the science center. Shouldn't take long to interview our guy and an hour to return. Stay away from Mark until I can get back."

"Aye, aye, sir."

"I'm serious, Kelsey."

"Me too. I promise, I'll stay right here in my office with Phillip and work on the circus. And it sounds like we're in for a storm, so you be careful driving."

Was it possible it was Mark? The guy was a grouch, but a murderer? Her heart sank. What if the real killer had put that in Mark's personnel file? As she pocketed her phone, the door opened.

"Good morning," Jackson said when he entered the room, then nodded to Phillip. "Take a break, would you?"

"I'm fine," Phillip said.

Jackson lifted his eyebrows. "I'd like to discuss something in private with Ms. Allen. And when we finish, I thought we might get a cup of coffee in the café."

"Yes, sir."

After Phillip left, Kelsey waited.

"Hold on a sec. Before I forget, let me get something." He opened the door and rolled an oversized utility cart into the room. "I'm taking the employee records back to storage. My men have gone through each and every one. If you're finished with the ones you have, I'll add them to these."

"I don't have any—all my searches have been online," she said.

"Oh, I thought you had several boxes of files. Sorry, I'll get this out of your way in a minute." He sat in the chair beside her desk. "So, have you given any more thought to becoming a partner?"

"Not really. I've had way too much else on my mind."

"I figured as much but thought it wouldn't hurt to ask, and encourage you to consider my offer. I really believe you'd bring a lot to the company."

His words brought a glow to her heart. For a second she

could see her name on their door. "Thank you. Are you going to keep the name Rutherford Security?"

"I have mixed feelings about that. Our reputation is built on the Rutherford name, but I wouldn't mind seeing our names in the title."

If she took his offer, neither would she. Kelsey looked him over. "I don't believe I've ever seen you so dressed up, not since the fundraiser."

He buttoned his suit coat. "I'm leaving for a meeting with the mayor as soon as I deliver these files."

She tilted her head, looking up at him. "Before you go, did you know Mark was a computer expert?"

"Mark? Sure. He's a gamer. I've heard Robert complain about all the time he spends on it."

"You're kidding. He told me he knew next to nothing about computers."

"He must have just been pulling your leg," Jackson said, shaking his head. "He cut his teeth on the DOS program." He glanced at his phone. "My ringer is off and I have three calls." He dialed a number. "What do you need?" His eyes widened. "What? How could that have happened?"

"What's going on?" she demanded.

He looked at her and shook his head. "I'll be right there." He pocketed his phone and turned to her, his face pale. "Someone has taken your niece."

Her stomach dropped to her knees. *No! This can't be happening.* "How?"

"They were at the mall. She was standing by her mother one minute and gone the next."

"Where was their bodyguard?"

"He became ill after they stopped in the food court for coffee and doughnuts." He stood. "I'll take you there in my car."

She grabbed her cell phone and her breath caught. Why hadn't Sabra called if someone took Lily? Kelsey would have been the first person she would have reached out to. And those supposed calls Jackson had received . . .

Kelsey jerked her head toward him. He hadn't moved and there was barely room between him and the crate for her to pass. He turned and their gazes collided.

Time stopped. She was no longer in her office but hanging outside the building adjacent to the Allen Auto Parts building, staring through a window at a man. A man with silver hair. *The flash of white.* Then like the snap of a finger, she was back at the museum, and the man from Thursday night stood between her and the door. She tried to scream, but her vocal cords were frozen.

Kelsey sprang into action, barreling into him. But he didn't go down. Something pricked her neck, like a bee sting. She raised her hand to rub her neck, but the room swirled and the phone tumbled out of her hand.

Jackson moved beside her, and suddenly she was spiraling down a tunnel into darkness.

46

IMAGES SWEPT THROUGH KELSEY'S MIND like a slide show. A little girl and a man. It wasn't Lily, though. Then her dad was flipping pancakes and smiling into the camera . . . He blew her a kiss. *I love you, Kelseygirl.*

Gradually the images faded, and she was swimming underwater. The surface was so close. With a strong kick, she pushed through and broke through the top, and she took a shuddering breath. Kelsey was lying on something hard. A wooden floor, maybe? But where?

Sitting up was impossible—her hands were confined behind her back. She blinked and opened her eyes, but she may as well have kept them closed, for all the good it did. If she could put her hand in front of her face, she wouldn't be able to see it.

"You really should have stayed away from my computer. Did you think I wouldn't know?" He gave a hollow laugh. "You should have stuck to the museum's employee files."

She recognized Jackson's disembodied voice from somewhere behind her. How could she not have known?

"You didn't get any phone calls." She sounded weak, and if her heart pumped any harder, it would come through her chest. "And Lily hasn't been kidnapped."

"I wanted to get you out of the building, but you didn't cooperate, did you? But it still worked out."

If only her head would clear. She pulled against whatever bound her hands, but there was no give. *Keep him talking.* "You can't get away with this. Brad will know you did it."

"I'll get away with it." His voice was so certain. "And then life can go back to normal."

His life, maybe. He muttered something, but she couldn't catch the words. "Where are we?"

"Somewhere you'll never escape from."

As her eyes became accustomed to the dark, a pinpoint of light drew her attention. A boarded window, maybe? Her eyes drooped and she shook her head, trying to keep herself awake. They had to be somewhere inside the museum, probably in the attic, where odds and ends were stored and well away from any traffic. From the muted sounds of Jackson's voice, the room was soundproofed . . . or full. At least a bit of air-conditioning flowed into the room. She wouldn't die of heatstroke.

"Why did you kill my father?"

"I didn't. No more talking."

"Wait! If you didn't kill him, what's this all about?"

A burst of light and then the closing of a door answered her.

Her eyelids grew heavier and Kelsey fought to stay awake, but it was no use. Whatever Jackson had injected into her neck was stronger than she was.

◆

Brad pulled up to the stop sign. If his memory was right, they turned left and then immediately right into the drive for the center.

"Do you even know where you are?" Rachel asked.

"I think so."

"I told you to use the GPS."

"I don't think it'll work here." He checked his phone. "No signal. Wait—there's the sign." Relieved, he followed the arrows and pulled in front of a long building.

"This is the Coon Creek Science Center?" Rachel asked as she climbed out of the car.

Brad scanned the area that included two plank buildings set among the woods. Scattered around were picnic tables that he remembered sitting at as a kid and washing the mud away from the fossils he'd found. Didn't look a bit different. "It's a working site," he said and approached the main building.

Inside, a man in shorts walked toward them. Brad introduced himself and showed his badge. "This is Detective Sloan and we're looking for Junior Coleman."

"He's down at the site. I'm Luther McCoy. Is he in trouble?"

"I hope not. It has to do with his time at the Pink Palace Museum."

"I've known Junior a long time. He grew up around here."

"Do you know if he's good with a computer?" Rachel asked.

"Junior? Uh, no," McCoy said, laughing. "I have to put his time in every week. Come on, and I'll take you to the creek where's he's working—he's getting ready for the kids who will arrive at noon."

After a short hike, they found Junior at the creek, wearing cutoff overalls and knee-deep in mud with a shovel in his hands. When they approached, he pushed the ball cap he was wearing to the back of his head.

"Howdy," he said. "Something I can help you with?"

Again, they introduced themselves, and Brad said, "We're investigating the murder of Paul Carter and—"

"I knowed it!" he crowed, climbing out of the creek bed. "Told my wife all those years ago that Mr. Paul never ran off with those things. He was a good man. What can I do to help you?"

Brad took a step back as the giant of a man crossed the grass toward them. "How long did you work at the museum?"

"Seems like all my life." He scratched his head. "Went to work there in maintenance when I was eighteen, and I'm forty-eight now."

Thirty years. "Do you remember Mark Tomlinson?"

"He was my boss the last few years. Another fine man. Took over his family when his dad died and put half his brothers through college, including the spoiled one."

"Spoiled one?" Rachel said.

"The museum director. Can't abide that man. He's the reason I transferred here to the science center. That, plus my wife wanted to move back home."

"There were several of you working at the museum when Paul Carter went missing and who are still connected to it." Brad rattled off the list of names. "Can you tell me anything about any of them?"

"Julie was a cute little thing back then. Still is, or was, two years ago. She and Jackson had a thing years ago. I think he's seeing that Helen Peterson now, though. They try to keep it quiet, but like most folks, they don't see janitors as real people."

Julie and Jackson and then Helen and Jackson. Huh. Brad never would have guessed. "Of the people I've mentioned, who would have the best computer skills?"

"I remember Jackson was always talking about knowing the latest thing about them. And Julie."

"How about Mark?"

"Mark?" The man looked down at his muddy boots. "Can't say I've ever heard that about him."

Brad's cell phone rang, and he pulled it from his belt. He couldn't see the screen because of the sun glare. "Hello?"

"Reggie . . . you . . . to . . . here."

Sounded like Reggie, and he was upset. "You're breaking up. Let me call you back."

"You'll be lucky to get service here at the creek," McCoy said. "It's better at the office, but still not good."

They hiked back to the office, with Brad attempting to call Reggie back every few steps. Finally the call connected. "What's going on?"

"An hour ago, Kelsey's sister tried to call her, and when she didn't get an answer, Sabra called me. I'm on my way to the Pink Palace now."

Blood thundered in his ears. *Kelsey.* "We'll be there in an hour, but call me if you hear from her."

He turned to Rachel. "No one has heard from Kelsey for the past hour." He sprinted for the car.

"I'll drive," Rachel said when she caught him.

Brad gladly gave her his keys. He'd probably get them killed. Besides, he needed the time to think. Fifty minutes later, they swung onto Highway 385 at Eads, just outside of Memphis.

"Where to?"

"Let's start at Kelsey's last known location. The Pink Palace." His phone rang. *Reggie.* "Did you find her?"

"No. Jackson King says Mark Tomlinson knocked him out and kidnapped her."

47

BRAD PACED THE DIRECTOR'S OFFICE. When they had arrived twenty minutes ago, the visitors' parking lot was empty, but police cars and an ambulance were sitting at the back entrance. And now a paramedic was examining Jackson King's head.

"What do you mean, the cameras are down? How long?" Brad fisted his hands and scanned the four people in the museum director's office. Not that he expected Phillip or the paramedic to know. But King or Tomlinson should. He'd kept quiet until now, letting Rachel ask the questions.

"My brother can't be involved in this," the director said.

"Well, he is," Jackson snapped. "He must have turned the cameras off when he came to work this morning."

The paramedic handed Jackson an ice pack and instructed him to keep it on the back of his head. Then he packed his supplies into his medical bag. "If the headache gets worse, go to the ER."

Brad moved to let the medic out the door.

"I don't have time to go to the ER," Jackson muttered as the door closed. He held the ice pack to his head.

Tomlinson scrubbed his face. "I can't believe this is happening. This isn't like Mark."

"You can't believe it's happening. How do you think I feel?" King said. "One minute Kelsey and I were leaving her office to get coffee, and then Mark rushed in, knocked me out, and when I came to, she was gone."

"Where's his car?" Rachel asked.

Phillip spoke up. "I checked, and it's gone. Mr. Tomlinson gave a description of it to the police an hour ago."

So, by now the DMV should have Mark Tomlinson's license plate number to go with the description. Brad pinned the young man with his glare. "Why weren't you with Kelsey?"

"Because I sent him out," Jackson said. "I wanted to discuss something in private with Kelsey."

"What was that?"

The security director rubbed the back of his neck. "I wanted to discuss the partnership I've offered Kelsey with Rutherford Security. She accepted, and we were going down to the coffee shop to celebrate when Mark busted in."

Kelsey had told him about the offer, so he could see Jackson sending the bodyguard out to discuss it, but the timing was horrible. His gaze collided with Rachel's. Stepping back and letting her run the show was the hardest thing he'd done in a while, but it wasn't his case. Neither was it a cold case. He hoped it wouldn't be a homicide.

"Let's go over this once more," Rachel said to Jackson. "You two were in her office when Mark Tomlinson came in."

"Yes. Like I said, she'd just agreed to become a partner in the firm."

Brad eyed Jackson. He appeared to be telling the truth, and he certainly didn't hit himself over the head. He turned as the door opened and Reggie joined them. "Any news?"

Reggie shook his head. "No. No one saw Mark leave with or without Kelsey."

Brad turned to Tomlinson. "I'd like to see Mark's office."

"Crime scene techs are going over it now," Rachel said. "And Kelsey's office."

Again a gentle reminder that this wasn't his case. He eyed Tomlinson. "How about you? Where were you when all this was going on?"

"Excuse me?" Tomlinson's eyes widened. "You don't think—"

"We don't think anything right now," Rachel said. "I'm sure Sergeant Hollister was just trying to get a picture of what everyone was doing this morning. So why don't you give us a summary."

The museum director cleared his throat. "Phone records will show that I've been on the telephone quite a bit this morning. Went down and spoke with Julie and returned a crate of files to the archives. And then this awful thing happened."

Brad looked over the notes he'd taken. He exchanged looks with Rachel. "Has the museum been searched?"

"Yes. The Rutherford people assisted."

"Can we search again?" Brad asked.

Rachel snapped her notebook shut. "Brad, there's no reason to believe she's here. I need you to assist in interviewing people."

He cocked his jaw. "But no one saw Mark take her out."

"He probably used one of the rolling bins," Tomlinson said. "There are any number of them around this place. I used one myself when I returned files to the archives. Someone's always moving large items from one place to another."

Brad wanted to do more than interview people. What

if Mark had her stashed somewhere in the building until night, when no one would be around. "I'm going to search the building again."

"And I'm going to interview the other employees," Rachel said. "I'd hoped you would help me with that."

"Reggie can help, and I'll join you as soon as I take a look around."

"I'll go with you," Jackson said, slipping his blazer on.

Brad eyed him. He'd feel better having Jackson where he could see him. Plus, he probably knew the building better than anyone other than Mark Tomlinson. "Let's start at the top."

"The top floor is used to store everything except artifacts, and it's pretty big and cluttered."

Might be a perfect place to hide someone. "Why don't we start on the east side and work our way to the other end."

It didn't take Brad long to realize searching the attic with its maze-like pathways through the stored items would prove difficult. "Are there any parts of the attic sealed off into rooms?"

"There are a couple of rooms, but it's all like this, practically wall-to-wall junk."

He surveyed the wing they were in. He just didn't see Mark hiding Kelsey there. Maybe Rachel was right, that his time would be better spent interviewing the other employees. "Let's take a look at the west end before we quit."

48

THE NEXT TIME KELSEY WOKE, the fog in her mind had cleared. She had to get free before Jackson returned. But the darkness overwhelmed her, and she had no idea how much time had elapsed. Her arms ached from being behind her. If she could get her hands in front of her, it would make it easier to get the restraints off. Grunting, Kelsey tried wiggling her arms past her hips, but her hands were bound too tightly.

"Even if you get loose, you can't get out of here."

She whipped her head toward the new voice. "Mark? Where are you?"

"In the corner."

"Do you know what's going on?" The tiny pinprick of light caught her eye again, and she blinked to see if it went away. Still there.

"Yeah. He's going to kill you and pin it on me."

That was why Jackson was so certain he'd get away with it. "You don't know anything about computers, do you?"

"I can turn one on and fill out the forms I need to and that's about it. Whenever Walter tried to explain something about how the internet security worked, it went over my head."

Jackson was actually very smart. He'd created a computer-savvy persona, and with Mark dead, no one could prove it wasn't correct. Jackson would find a way to convince people that Mark had hidden his talent.

Not if Kelsey could help it. She struggled to get her hands past her hips, pulling on her arms until she thought they'd come out of their sockets. But either her arms had to grow or she had to turn into a contortionist. Or stand up. She ran her thumb along the restraint. Smooth, so not rope. Plastic, maybe?

"What are you doing?"

"I'm trying to get my hands in front of me so I can untie them."

"Won't do any good. I heard him lock the door—even if you had your hands free, you couldn't get out of this room."

"We can yell."

"The police have probably cleared everyone out, and if they haven't, we're still on the west side, where no one ever goes. There's no one to hear us."

Thanks, Negative Nancy. "If we can get our hands free, we can climb out the window."

"And do what? We're in the very top of the Pink Palace. It's at least forty feet, straight down to the ground. I'm not jumping and I can't climb down."

"I can." She yanked on the restraints, and pain shot up her arms. "Do you know what we're tied with?"

"He used a zip tie."

A zip tie? She'd seen a video on how to break restraints using zip ties, but the person had been standing. Just like in rock-climbing, there was always more than one path up the wall. Kelsey rolled over on her stomach. If she could get on her knees, she could get to her feet. But even with years of exercise and rock-climbing, she couldn't do it without the use of her hands.

And the darkness. It would drive her mad. With every muscle tensing like a wound spring, Kelsey forced herself to breathe deeply. Panic would only make things worse. Where was that light she'd seen? She turned her head, seeking the tiny pinprick again, and her whole being leaped when she found it.

"We have to get out of here," she said, her voice startling her in the quiet. Staying in this room was not an option. If there was a pinprick of light, there was a window. "Or at least get our hands free," she said. "That way we can attack him when he comes back."

"I've tried, but the zip tie doesn't give. And just so you know, he has a gun."

She hadn't even considered a gun. "When do you think he'll come back?"

"Maybe a couple of hours. Can't tell how much time has passed. I figure right now he's dealing with the police looking for us."

Then they had a little time. "Do you believe in God, Mark?"

"Been praying."

A dart pricked her heart. Kelsey should have been. She sought the tiny light again. Maybe if she had depended on God for guidance, she wouldn't be in this mess to start with. But someone had to catch the bad guys, and that's all she'd wanted to do.

"How does God help you in a situation like this?"

"He gives us strength," Mark said slowly. "And he brings us ideas."

Like how to overcome a gun? Maybe it wouldn't hurt to ask.

Lord, show me how to get out of this.

Seconds ticked away. Kelsey didn't know what she'd expected, but not silence.

49

DEFEAT. NOT SOMETHING KELSEY WAS ACCUSTOMED TO. Her arms and hands ached from trying to get them over her hips. And her wrists burned and were bound to be raw from straining against the ties. Why she couldn't get to her feet puzzled her—it was like she had no strength in her legs. The injection. Whatever was in it had affected her muscles. Maybe if she rested a minute. Mark had been quiet. Evidently he'd accepted his fate.

"I know why he wants me dead. I saw him in Hendrix's office the night he killed him," Kelsey said. "But what made Jackson choose you to take the fall?"

"Making it appear that I killed you and then took my own life will solve all of his problems."

"But you're not telling me how or why," she said.

Silence.

She should be trying to get her hands free again, but the question hung in the darkness between them. The question he wouldn't answer.

A deep sigh came from the corner. "Look," Mark said. "I'm really sorry about something."

She waited, her mind conjuring wild possibilities, like he'd set the bomb or stole the papers from Brad's car.

"I sent your father's remains to the museum. Should've done it twenty-eight years ago."

Her breath caught in her chest. "You killed my father?"

"No. I found Jackson and my brother standing over your father's body. I found out later he'd caught them stealing artifacts. Robert was all to pieces, said it was an accident, but Jackson was as cold as an ice cube. I wanted to go to the police, but I couldn't. Our mother had just had a bad heart attack. Robert in prison . . . it would have killed her. I wasn't willing to risk it. And turning Robert in wouldn't have brought your father back."

A thousand questions bombarded her. "What made you bring his remains to the museum now?"

Once again silence filled the dark room.

"I'm dying of cancer. And your family needed closure." Then he sighed deeply. "And Robert had promised me there would be no more killing. I didn't know about Hendrix until later, but I knew Saturday night either he or Jackson killed Walter Rutherford, and something inside me snapped. I left the party and drove to King Scrap Iron where we had buried your father . . . I'm so sorry."

She imagined him driving through the graveyard of cars, searching for the grave.

"It was so long ago. How did you find it?"

"I've seen that grave every night for twenty-eight years in my dreams. I knew where it was . . ." He sucked in another breath. "I had put a stake where we buried him. A marker of sorts, because every grave ought to have something that says, 'I was here' . . ."

But he still couldn't turn his brother in.

"Jackson figured out I was the one who removed the body from where it was buried. Told me he'd kill Robert if I told what I knew."

"Do you know who else is involved?"

"Helen. She'll do anything Jackson wants her to do. He's the ringleader," Mark said. "Robert told me years ago Jackson sold the artifacts to a fence who in turn sold them to people for their private collections."

"But Jackson was only eighteen! How did he get connected with a fence at that age?"

"Believe me, he was plenty smart for eighteen," Mark said. "I'm pretty sure now he and Robert are still taking artifacts from the museum and selling them to private collections. I figure one of them was stealing the stamp, and Rutherford caught them."

"Why was Hendrix killed?"

"I don't know, but when I confronted Robert, he indicated Hendrix was part of the fence. I figure he and Jackson got crossed."

Kelsey turned and sought the tiny light. In the blackness, it kept her oriented. "Thank you for bringing my father's bones home," she said. "And . . . I'm sorry you have cancer."

If they didn't get out of this room, Jackson would get away with murder again. If only she could get to her feet or get her hands in front of her. She played the video she'd seen in her mind. The person had been standing and brought the force of his hands against his stomach, and that had broken the ties.

Why couldn't she do the same thing only with her hands behind her? She still had to be on her feet. Getting on her knees was out. Rising from a sitting position had always been simple, but she'd never realized how much she depended on her hands. Had to be more than one way to accomplish this. Kelsey scooted forward until she reached the door, and then wiggled around until her back was against it. Using her legs, she pushed her body up the door until she was standing. *Victory!*

Now how did that video go? The instructor had leaned forward and brought his hands down hard and the ties had magically separated. Here went nothing. Kelsey leaned forward and whacked her wrists against the top of her hips.

Her shoulders sagged. Not enough momentum to break the locking bar. *Wait.* She'd forgotten he said to make sure the locking tab was between her two hands. She felt where the zip tie was fastened.

It was over her left wrist, and it had to be in the middle. Kelsey twisted the zip tie until it was where she wanted it. Once more, she bent forward, and this time she raised her arms as high as she could and rammed them hard against her hips, pulling against the plastic cords at the same time.

Her hands flew apart. *Yes!*

"Did you get loose?"

"Yeah. I'll help you in a minute." She rubbed her hands to get the circulation going. "Where are you?" she asked him. "Talk so I can find you."

"I'm in the corner."

"You're going to have to do better than that." She felt the air in front of her. "How long do you believe we have?"

"He won't do anything until after everyone leaves. Like I said, pretty sure he's busy right now with the police."

Kelsey dropped to her knees. Too much danger in falling over something if she tried to walk. But Mark was closer. "If people are looking for us, why don't they search the attic?"

"I'm sure Jackson has convinced them I'm holding you hostage somewhere else."

The scent of his aftershave tickled her nose. "Old Spice," she said.

"What?"

"You're wearing Old Spice. Like my dad." She reached out, touching his shoulder. "Got you. Can you stand?"

"If you can help me up."

Mark was a big man, and when he leaned into her, she stumbled. "This won't work. Use the wall to brace against and I'll help you."

He scooted around and, just like she had, used his legs to push himself up.

"Ow!"

She'd heard the bump just as he cried out. "Sorry. Come closer to me so I can feel where the lock is on your tie."

"Can you find my hands?"

She ran her hand down his arm to his wrists. Just like hers, they were off center, and she adjusted them to the middle. "What you're going to do is bend over and raise your arms as high as you can and then bring them down hard against your hips. That should break the lock."

He raised his arms and she moved back and heard the snap when the lock broke. "Now we have to figure out how to get out of here."

"I'm telling you, it's no use. We'll break our necks if we jump—even if we found the window and got it open."

"Stop it! Being negative will only defeat us. Maybe we can get the door open," Kelsey said. "Do you have your keys?"

She heard a low gasp.

"He forgot about the master key when he took my car keys . . ." For the first time, hope sounded in Mark's voice.

But Kelsey's thoughts went in the opposite direction. Jackson thought of everything, even moving Mark's car to send the police away from the museum. How could they hope to overcome him?

"Ow!" Mark cried again. "Watch the eave, it's angled. Point me toward the door."

Easily said, but she couldn't remember which way to turn. "Better crawl so we don't bang into something else," she said and dropped to her knees. "I'll go to my right, you go to the left."

She kept her bearings by keeping one hand on the wall as she crawled. Her fingers touched a hinge. "Here it is. Bring your key."

"Where are you?"

"Feel your way along the wall back to me. Do you think there might be a light switch in here?" she asked.

"Should be."

His voice was getting closer. As Kelsey stood, she ran her hand up the side of the door, and then moved to the wall, feeling for a light switch. Nothing on this side. Smoothing her hands across the wood, she felt for the doorframe. Just beyond it, her fingers touched a switch and she flipped it.

Nothing.

She ran her hand back to the doorknob and twisted it. Wouldn't budge.

"What's going on?" Mark asked, his voice shaky but near her.

"Door's locked. Can't get it open. Are you all right?"

"About as all right as I'll ever be."

"See if your master key will work on the lock."

She heard keys clinking together and then scratching. He'd found the door lock.

"This one doesn't fit. Let me try the others." More scratching, then a soft moan from Mark. "They don't work."

She dropped her head. What was she going to do now? She rubbed the side of her face. Time was getting short. "Do you think the window you were talking about is where that tiny light is?" she asked.

"You've seen it too? I thought I was imagining it."

Kelsey crawled her way to the wall and the pinpoint of light. "It's not boarded with plywood but planks," she said. The light came through a knothole. "Do you think we can get them off?"

"Let me see."

She tried to remember if there was a drainage pipe on the west side of the building. It didn't matter. If she could get out the window, she could get to the drainage pipe she'd used Saturday. She heard him crawling, smelled his aftershave when he stopped beside her.

"Whoever built this used one-by-eights, and there doesn't seem to be any middle studs. Probably twelve-foot boards."

He actually sounded excited. "What does that mean?"

"It means we may be able to break through. Hold on—the board where the light shines is splintered."

She felt him move back, and suddenly he thudded against the wall. "Are you okay?"

"Yeah. I'm too close to the wall. I need to find the middle."

"I'll crawl from one side to the other." She crawled to the wall and turned around, counting each time she put her right knee down. She bumped her head on twelve, and then backtracked to six. "Should be right here."

"Let me try it there. I'm going to step back a little more, so don't let me run over you."

She scooted toward the far wall, and he crashed against the boards, succeeding in letting in more light.

"They make it look so easy on TV," he said, panting. "One more time."

353

"Wait," she said, feeling the wall. "The splintered board seems looser."

"Let me take my belt off. I'll press above it and you see if you can wedge the buckle in to give us finger holds."

She took the belt he pressed into her hands and then waited while he strained against the top board. The crack grew wider, letting more light in. Finally she shoved the buckle between the two boards. "There. Now what?"

"We need a bigger wedge."

"How about my shoe? It's a wedge." She slipped off her sandal and slid the toe end into the gap.

"Move over, I'm going to pound it down."

In the dim light that had filtered in, she watched as he used his fist to beat her shoe deeper in the crack.

"Okay. You pull on the board on your side of the shoe, and I'll push on this side. On the count of three."

On three she pulled with all her might, and the board popped loose, tumbling her back. "We did it!" she cried.

Whoever had built the room had left a narrow walkway between the wall and the window.

"All we need is enough space for you to get through," he said.

"You're not coming with me?"

"I can't climb down a wall, but you can. So go get help."

50

"WHAT'S ON THIS SIDE?" Brad asked, climbing the stairs to the west side of the Pink Palace.

"Years and years of junk," Jackson said, his voice sharp. "There's no place for him to hide Kelsey up here."

"I still want to take a look-see, but you can go back downstairs if you want."

"No, I'll stay. I just don't think they're up here."

The skin on the back of Brad's neck prickled. He couldn't put his finger on why it was so important to check out the attic, but the more Jackson downplayed the possibility that Mark had hidden Kelsey there, the more determined he was to look.

Brad made the turn at the top of the stairs and stepped into the attic. Jackson had not been kidding about the junk. The place was a mess with boxes and chairs. Halfway down, it appeared there were two rooms. To his right were a couple of dress forms and what looked like steel rods. Like the other side, a layer of dust covered it all. In the dim light, he glanced at the floor and froze. Was the dust on the floor disturbed? He unsnapped his holster.

Suddenly, in the stillness of the room, a man's voice yelled for help.

Brad pulled his Glock. "Who's there?"

He caught movement in the corner of his eye. Jackson held a .45 with a silencer on it. With lightning reflexes, Brad moved, but Jackson clipped his right shoulder with the butt of the gun. Pain ripped down Brad's arm and he dropped his weapon. Jackson came at him again, and Brad lunged for the automatic in his hand. They struggled for the weapon, and it went off.

The shot rocked Brad's head.

51

SOMEONE WAS ON THE OTHER SIDE OF THE DOOR. Maybe it was Brad! A gunshot rang out.

"Hey! We're in here," Mark cried.

"Don't do that! It might be Jackson."

What if he had shot Brad? Kelsey crawled back through the opening into the room. "We don't know who's out there."

"It might be the police."

"I don't think so." She'd like to think Brad had found her, but if he had, why wasn't he knocking the door down? She pictured him lying on the floor, bleeding.

She had to move fast.

"I think I can reach the rest of the attic on the other side of the wall, and from there I can go down the stairs."

The deep creases in his face smoothed out. "Good thinking." She locked eyes with Mark. Regret reflected in his.

"I'll only hinder you, but if I stay, maybe I can slow him down. Go and don't worry about me," he said.

She held his gaze a second longer. "Thanks," she said.

"God go with you," he said.

The sound of the lock turning in the door froze them both.

Maybe it was Brad! No, he'd be calling her name. Evidently, Mark thought the same thing.

"Go," he urged. "Now!"

Kelsey turned from him and squeezed through the opening in the planks. Someone in the past had laid a wide board across the rafters just out from the wall, but she had to watch where she walked. She glanced up and saw another network of rafters high above them.

Behind her voices shouted. Brad? No. Jackson. Screaming at Mark, and then she heard more popping.

Her heart sank. He'd killed Mark. She just knew it. And maybe Brad. No. She wouldn't believe that. Kelsey focused on moving forward. She had to put as much distance between her and Jackson as she could and reach the main floor of the attic. Why hadn't the wall ended? She'd thought access to the rest of the attic would be closer.

Hopefully Jackson would think she had climbed out the window to the roof.

52

A STORM RAGED IN BRAD'S HEAD, thunder pounding his skull. The pain meant he was alive. The last thing he remembered was fighting Jackson for his gun.

Kelsey! He'd heard her voice. No, not her voice. A man's. *We're in here.* Kelsey had to be with him. But how long ago had that been? Why wasn't anyone coming to check on the shooting? He fumbled on the floor for his Glock. Gone. Cell phone too.

Brad pulled the small automatic pistol from his ankle holster and then struggled to stand. His head reeled, and he touched where the bullet had grazed him, bringing away wet fingers. Half an inch more and he'd be dead. Jackson must have thought he'd killed him.

He had to find Kelsey. He scanned the dim room, spying an open door. Inside, he found Mark Tomlinson on the floor, bleeding from a chest wound. He knelt beside the man, feeling for a pulse. Weak. His eyes flew open.

"Jackson," he whispered. "After Kelsey."

He glanced toward the hole in the wall. The window was open. "Did Kelsey go out on the roof?"

"No . . ." Mark took a shuddering breath. "Looking for the stairs . . ." He coughed. "Find her . . ."

With pain beating a tattoo against his head, Brad climbed through the opening. The window gave off light, and he scanned the area to the left. Was that movement? He squeezed his eyes closed and opened them again. Everything still spun, but he could make out Jackson's silhouette in the light of another window ahead.

53

No! Kelsey wanted to beat her hands against the wall that stopped her forward progress. She was boxed in. No way to the main attic.

She glanced behind her. Couldn't see Jackson, but she knew he was there. The open window hadn't fooled him. Light filtered in from the dormer windows in the attic. It was barely enough to see the plank beneath her feet and to avoid the boxes that were stacked against the wall. The wall that stood between her and freedom. She knelt between two stacks of boxes marked *Fragile*, and her fingers brushed something rough. Burlap bags. She stood and leaned her head against the framing.

There was no way out. Retracing her path would take her straight to Jackson. Was it time to stand and fight? But how, against a gun? Her heart caught in her throat. There had to be something she could do. *God, I can use a little help here.*

She looked down at the boxes again. Fragile. Glass? Kelsey looked up at the roof, where another network of rafters criss-crossed the building, and a plan formed in her mind. Could she risk it? She had no choice. It was her only hope to come out of this alive. As quietly as she could, she opened a box. Glass beakers. Perfect.

A board creaked. She glanced over her shoulder. Someone moved. Not someone. Jackson. Light from the second window they'd passed outlined his body, and then he disappeared only to reappear seconds later. He must be checking to see if she was hiding inside the windows. Only two more windows to go.

She had to act now.

Kelsey grabbed two of the burlap bags and used one to wrap five of the beakers in so they wouldn't clink together and then placed them all in the other bag and tied it to her arm.

Grabbing an overhead brace, she pulled herself up and hooked her leg over a rafter. She climbed higher, taking care to not bump the burlap sack, then walked the rafters toward the last window she'd passed and stopped. This is where she'd wait.

Kelsey looked down. The distance to the floor looked like a fifteen-foot drop. She'd fallen from higher.

She heard him panting before she saw him. Opening the sack, she got ready.

"King!" Brad's voice sounded hollow from the other end of the room.

Below her, Jackson turned and fired.

Kelsey hurled the beakers on either side of Jackson. When they crashed on the floor, he turned, jerking his head first one way, then another. He took a step her way. She waited until he was just past her.

Kelsey dropped from the ceiling, feet first. She landed on his shoulders, knocking him forward as they hit the floor. She rolled away from him as the gun he held skittered across the floor.

He crawled toward it.

Couldn't let him get it. She jumped on his back and went for his eyes.

Screaming, he tossed her off like she weighed nothing. Just as he grabbed for the gun, Brad kicked it away.

"Jackson King. You are under arrest."

54

HE HAD A CONCUSSION. Brad leaned against a stud and fought the blackness that threatened to close in again. He had Jackson King, but he didn't know if he could make it down the stairs with him. And he couldn't let Jackson know how blurred his vision was.

"Have you found my Glock?" he asked, his voice sounding shaky in his own ears. He'd taken Jackson's revolver away from him and stuck it in his belt since the silencer made it too long to go in his holster.

"Got it." Kelsey came close to him and gasped. "Brad, your head is bleeding!"

"Just hold that gun on him." He shook his head, trying to clear it. It was so dark, he could barely make out Jackson's form.

"Brad! He has a gun!"

"Looks like we're at a standoff," Jackson said and lifted his hand. "You really should have checked to make sure I didn't have another pistol."

Brad groaned when he saw the weapon. Stupid mistake, but maybe he could bluff him. "Hardly. Someone will come looking for us soon."

"You won't last that long."

"Give me your cell phone."

"Nope. You'll have to shoot me to get it, and I don't believe you'll risk me shooting her first. Just let me walk out of here and everyone will make it out alive."

"No!" Kelsey's voice was fierce. "You're going to pay for what you've done."

"Your boyfriend here needs a doctor. What are you going to do if he passes out?"

"You have to go downstairs"—Brad paused to get his breath—"and find Rachel and Reggie."

"Brad . . . ?" Kelsey said.

"We can't force him to move or get his cell phone without killing him. I'm not leaving you with him." He forced his eyes to stay open. "So our only chance is for you to go for help."

She stuck the Glock in her waistband. "I'll be back as soon as I can."

Brad nodded and felt her questioning gaze on him. "I'll be fine."

He would force himself to stay conscious until she was well away from the attic. Brad jumped a few minutes later when the faint clatter of something hitting the floor echoed in the attic.

"You better go see about her."

He hesitated.

"I'm okay!" Kelsey yelled.

Thank goodness. He had to do something to stay alert. "Why did you kill Paul Carter?"

"I didn't."

If only everything would quit spinning. "I don't suppose you killed Hendrix or Rutherford, either."

"Come on, you'll never stay on your feet long enough to take me in. Let me walk out of here."

"No." Pain shot through his head, making him wince. Suddenly, Jackson lunged toward him. Brad fired, and the shot went wide as Jackson barreled into him.

He caught Jackson in a bear hug, pulling the man down with him. They rolled on the attic floor. Cold steel pressed against Brad's chest. He wrenched away as Jackson fired. The bullet pierced his chest, burning like a hot iron.

Adrenaline pulsed though Brad's body. Had to stop him. He grabbed at Jackson as he pushed away. But Jackson kicked free and bolted in the same direction Kelsey had gone.

55

When Kelsey couldn't quickly find the gun she'd dropped, she abandoned the search and climbed through the opening. *Hurry.* A groan stopped her. "Mark?"

"Did you get him?" he whispered.

"Yes. I'm going for help."

"Hurry."

"I will." She dashed out of the room down the stairs and soon burst out into the second floor. Voices rose from the first floor.

"Help! Someone help!" Making as much noise as she could, she dashed across the balcony. *Rachel!* On the bottom floor, the detective looked up as Kelsey waved frantically.

"Brad's in the attic holding a pistol on Jackson," she yelled. "I'm going back."

Kelsey sprinted back to the stairs and took them two at a time.

She was almost to the top when a shot rang out. Her heart leaped into her throat when she heard footsteps coming near. No time to find the gun she'd dropped. Should she wait for Rachel? What if he got away? He could take the other stairs.

She scanned the room, searching for something to defend herself with. She spotted a steel rod on the floor, and she grabbed it and sprinted to the side of the door.

Kelsey pressed her back to the wall, waiting.

There was a thud, then Jackson swore.

He was inside the room.

Footsteps pounded up the stairs. Maybe Rachel . . .

Jackson burst through the doorway. He stared toward the stairs and wheeled just as she brought the rod down on his head.

He staggered, and his eyes widened as he saw her. He pointed the automatic at her.

The gunshot roared in her ears.

Jackson stepped toward her, but then his hand fell to his side as he crumpled to the floor.

Blood stained Brad's white shirt as he staggered in the doorway.

"Kelsey," he whispered. He dropped his pistol and sagged against the door.

56

FELLOW POLICE OFFICERS, family, friends—Kelsey knew only a handful of the people who filled the surgery waiting room. Her mom sat talking to Brad's mother across the room. His sister, Andi, paced the floor while his dad talked to Rachel.

What if he died? Kelsey closed her eyes and prayed for God to spare Brad.

"He's going to make it." Sabra squeezed her hand.

Tears sprang to her eyes, and Kelsey clamped her jaw shut to keep her chin from quivering. She needed to speak to Mrs. Hollister and took a fortifying breath before she walked to her chair and knelt. "I'm so sorry this happened."

Barbara Hollister patted Kelsey's hand. "This wasn't your fault. My son was doing what God called him to do. And I'm thankful you weren't hurt."

Now Kelsey knew where Brad's compassion came from. "Thank you."

Why hadn't they heard anything about Brad yet? He'd been in surgery for two hours.

The door opened and Kelsey's heart dropped. Elle. She

was coming her way. Probably to ream her out for Brad getting shot. Well, she couldn't say anything Kelsey hadn't thought.

No matter what anyone said, she couldn't stop thinking that because of her, Brad lay unconscious on an operating table, fighting for his life. She averted her eyes, hoping Elle would choose somewhere else to sit.

She stopped to talk with the Hollisters, then looked around and made eye contact with Kelsey. She flinched at the deep concern in Elle's face.

She approached Kelsey. "I just heard on TV it was Brad who was shot. He was working a cold case; how did this happen?"

"He saved my life, so blame me, not him."

She sat in the chair beside Kelsey and buried her face in her hands. "I don't blame anyone, but this is exactly what I feared would happen. Maybe now he'll decide to do something else."

"Don't count on it."

Elle stiffened. "You think he'll want to keep being a detective?"

"He's a decent and honorable man who wants to keep people like you and me safe. That's not going to change because of what happened today."

Elle's eyes widened. "You're in love with him," she said.

Kelsey held her gaze. "How I feel is immaterial and doesn't change the truth in what I said."

A doctor dressed in scrubs entered the room and walked to Barbara and Bob Hollister, and Kelsey leaned forward, trying to hear what he said. When she caught only a word or two, she stood and moved closer.

". . . made it through the surgery," he was saying. "But he

lost a lot of blood. We're moving him straight to ICU until he stabilizes."

"Thank you, Doctor. When can we see him?" Mrs. Hollister asked.

"Soon," he replied.

He was going to be all right. Kelsey blinked back the tears that burned her eyes. She could breathe again.

57

A WEEK LATER, Brad sat in a chair and stared out the hospital window, wanting to go home. Two more days, the doctor had said. At least he had a window. Meant he wasn't in ICU any longer. Everyone said he'd been lucky. Jackson King's bullet had nicked a lung, collapsing it, but had missed his heart. The first bullet had missed his brain. Personally, he didn't think luck had anything to do with it.

"Come in," he said to the soft knock, hoping it was Kelsey. She hadn't been to see him, and he didn't know why. Elle had told him she'd called once when he was sleeping.

Elle peeked her head around the door. "You're sitting up," she said.

"Yep." He smiled through his disappointment. Elle had been there every day, hovering, ready to get whatever he needed. So far they'd tiptoed around the shooting and how it related to his job.

"Did the doctor say when you could go home?"

"Maybe day after tomorrow. And the first thing I'm doing is stopping on Poplar and getting me some Corky's barbecue."

"If you'll let me know, I'll drive you home and we'll make that stop."

He shook his head. "No need. Will has already volunteered. The doc said I could go back to work in a month."

Color drained from her face. "I see." She took a breath and reached for his hand. "That's good, if you think you'll be well enough in a month."

Her smile was brittle and her voice too tight. "I will be. Elle—"

"Brad." She shook her head. "I'm sorry, you go ahead."

"No, what were you going to say?"

She swallowed. "I can't do it. Kelsey said I had to stand by you if you decided to return to work, but I can't. I'm sorry. She was right, though. You deserve someone who can support you in what you love to do. And I've tried. Thought I could do it. But when you said just now you were going back to work . . ." She blinked back tears. "I'm sorry."

He squeezed her hand. "I'm sorry too. You're a wonderful person, Elle, but I'm not going to quit being a cop."

"I know. And you need to find someone who can cheer you on." She kissed his cheek. "I think it's time for me to go."

After she left, he tried to busy himself with the exercises the physical therapist had given him, but his heart wasn't in it. Why hadn't Kelsey been to see him? When lunch came, he picked at the baked chicken and salad. Maybe he should call her. Except he didn't have his cell phone with her number in it.

The door opened and his nurse came in. "Ready to go down for a chest X-ray?"

"Sure." Anything to get away from this room and his thoughts.

Someone was standing at the window when the nurse

wheeled him back from X-ray. It was difficult to see the person against the light.

"You're back," Kelsey said, turning around with a white sack in her hands.

"Kelsey! You came." He inhaled. "And you brought barbecue? How did you know?"

"I got a phone call from Elle, and she said that's what you wanted."

"What else did she say?"

Kelsey hesitated. "That's not important."

He stood and walked to her, taking her hand. "I think it is important. Did she tell you I'm going back to work in a month?"

She nodded. "I think that's wonderful."

"Do you really?" Brad looked into her green eyes that held excitement for him, and he stroked her cheek. "You know we've never had a proper kiss."

Her eyes widened, and her lips parted slightly. "I know," she whispered.

"I think we need to fix that," he said, lowering his lips to hers. He slipped his hands behind her back and drew her close. Her lips tasted like strawberries, and then he kissed her deeper. She returned his kiss, surprising him with her passion.

They broke apart, and he stroked her cheek again. "I don't want to take this too fast, seeing that we haven't had a first date yet, but what do you think about Christmas weddings?"

A smile stretched across her face. "Is this a proposal?"

"Not exactly, just something to be thinking about."

"Then I'll tell you right now. Christmas is my favorite time of year."

Patricia Bradley is a published short story writer and co-founder of Aiming for Healthy Families, Inc. Her manuscript for *Shadows of the Past* was a finalist for the 2012 Genesis Award, winner of a 2012 Daphne du Maurier Award (first place, Inspirational), and winner of a 2012 Touched by Love Award (first place, Contemporary). When she's not writing or speaking, she can be found making beautiful clay pots and jewelry. She is a member of American Christian Fiction Writers and Romance Writers of America and makes her home in Corinth, Mississippi.

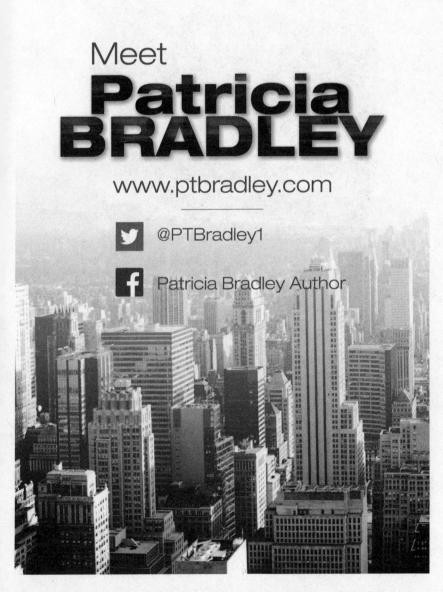

Meet
**Patricia
BRADLEY**

www.ptbradley.com

@PTBradley1

Patricia Bradley Author

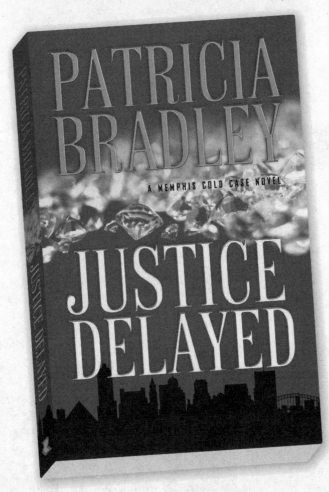

Also by Patricia Bradley ...

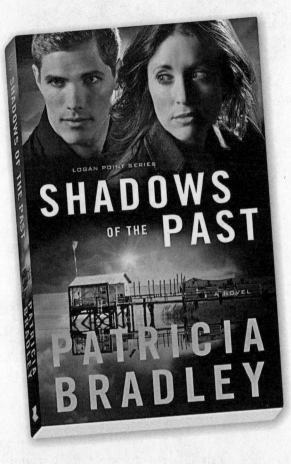

After twenty years, psychology professor and part-time profiler Taylor Martin has a lead on her missing father's whereabouts— but someone doesn't want her to find him.

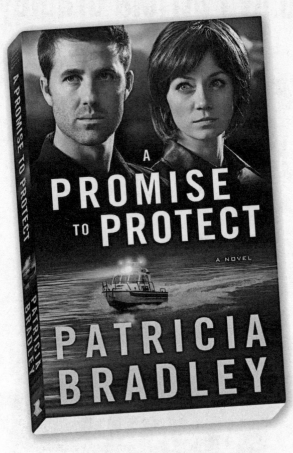

In a steamy small town of secrets, danger, and broken promises, a woman reaches out to a former love to save her brother's life—can she prevent her own secret from being revealed?

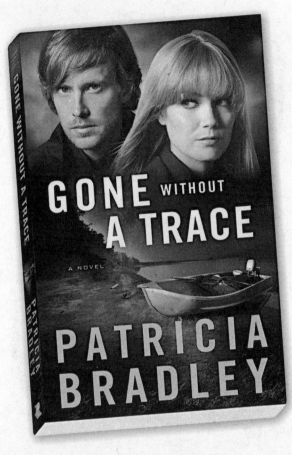

When a high-profile case strikes homicide detective Livy Reynolds as eerily similar to her own cousin's disappearance, she must work with the distractingly handsome Alex Jennings to solve the mystery.

Revell
a division of Baker Publishing Group
www.RevellBooks.com

SILENCE IN THE DARK

PATRICIA BRADLEY

SILENCE
IN THE DARK

A NOVEL

PATRICIA
BRADLEY

After Bailey Adams sees something she
shouldn't, trouble follows her home—
leaving her running for her life.

Revell
a division of Baker Publishing Group
www.RevellBooks.com